Keira stared through Roshannon's eyes down two arms' lengths of flashing steel past a flickering, wrapped sword point and into the face of the gold- and green-eyed man from the marketplace.

The shock of the meshing ruined Roshannon's timing. Cursing, he sidestepped Tanta's sword a bare second too late, and the edge of the blade stung his forearm. Muttering under his breath, he regained himself. Keira shared the pain and burrowed deeper, riding him, tasting his thrill and his exuberant agility as he lunged now sideways, now back, then circled the intent silver-haired man who reminded her so much of Hippolla. Tears that would have burned her eyes stung his eyes instead, blurring his vision.

Roshannon cursed again, blinking, catching himself, compensating, strengthening his guard. His eyes were her eyes, his sight her sight, and his sweat stung the corners of her eyes and clung to the upper rim of his lip until her tongue licked it away . . .

WHEEL OF DREAMS

Salinda Tyson

A Del Rey® Book
BALLANTINE BOOKS • NEW YORK

A Del Rey® Book
Published by Ballantine Books
Copyright © 1996 by Salinda Tyson

http://www.randomhouse.com

Library of Congress Catalog Card Number: 95-96186

ISBN 0-345-39430-5

Manufactured in the United States of America

First Edition: August 1996

10 9 8 7 6 5 4 3 2 1

In memory of my mother and father.
And to Marta and the fiction circles.

❀ 1 ❀

Keira Danio hurried into the kitchen, flexing fingers that were stiff and swollen from milking and cheese making.

A coach had bogged down in the muddy road that bordered her father's fields. In the nook by the hearth, the coachman was already trading tales with the manservant, Rahn, who had braved the downpour to offer hospitality to the driver and his passengers. A traveling coach always meant news, or at least rumors, so it was a welcome treat.

The stranger's oddly silken, southland voice distracted Keira from the headache tightening its grip on her skull. She leaned against the wall, closing her eyes a moment. But the images that ambushed her, waking or sleeping, immediately formed behind her eyelids.

Blood pounded in her ears, steady as a rhythm of hoofbeats. She gritted her teeth, willing the specters away. The visions of bare feet swinging at the gallows, of the wheel, of Terrak's face bending over her, his arm raised to strike her, of armies and severed heads, began fading. From the great room came the sound of men cursing the weather and scraping their muddy boots on the hearthstones.

She opened her eyes. Deva walked into the kitchen, glanced at her thoughtfully, and offered her a bowl of hot cider.

"You've still got the winter melancholy, mistress," the old servant said, frowning. "Drink up before you take anything out."

Keira held both hands around the bowl to keep her fingers from shaking. She drank slowly as Deva walked into the great room, wondering if the old servant could see beneath her sorrow, to the strange dreams that had haunted her since her mother died. Sometimes she imagined the dream pictures congealing in the air and

1

marking her forehead like a brand. She gripped the cider bowl tighter, intent on banishing the troublesome images.

Deva tapped her shoulder as she returned to the kitchen. "Five of them," she whispered. "With wet clothes and fouled tempers. A squire, his son, a liege soldier home from the wars."

"A soldier? Is an army coming this way?"

"No, no more soldiers, no army coming this way. There's a factor, a bell maker who makes cannon now." She poked the fire higher and swung a soup kettle closer on its iron hook. Instead of speaking, she made the hand sign for a priest.

A spy for the Sanctum? The two women exchanged looks as they checked the larder and prepared food.

Keira's heart thudded as she entered the great room. She lowered her eyes and stood at attention.

"Father," she said.

He did not turn his head. "The daughter of the house herself will serve you."

Keira raised her head in acknowledgment and curiosity. Ten candles and five strangers gave the long trestle table a certain dignity. The room had not looked so stately since midwinter, when she and Deva had served the priest and her father the ritual meal after her mother's funeral. Listening to the men's voices and accents, Keira went to the cabinet where rakka, wine, and tea were stored. Her stomach rumbled with hunger and she felt apprehensive. Lately even the simplest tasks haunted her—while making cheese this morning she had seen, in the foam and sliding surface of the creamy milk, shapes that recalled dreams and made her brood.

If her father caught her dawdling and daydreaming he would beat her again. She needed to study his face and listen to his voice to guess his state of mind. Predicting which way his thoughts might twist or how he might pounce on her was impossible. Her mother's death had made him increasingly unpredictable—he had threatened to sell her to a wine merchant even before she refused Terrak. Offering what remained of their pinched spring stores to travelers would likely put him in a foul mood, because he would have to petition the Sanctum for recompense later. Yet tonight he seemed in a good mood. It must be the Sanctum priest—all houses had to offer priests a bed and food, and who would dare be stingy to a Sanctum representative?

She focused on the simple rituals of serving wine and tea. But the patterns of light and shadow sliding over the curved bottom of a tea bowl suddenly formed the seeming shape of a severed head. The bowl slid in her fingers. Grinding her teeth, she set it carefully before the priest. Glancing at the tea bowl again, she saw it was just a simple, lacquered bowl after all. Her heart pounded. Would the priest smell the dreams on her, see the strange fantasies reflected in her eyes?

She ducked her head, struggling to collect her thoughts, suddenly glad of the head covering. Its stiff sides flared out around her face and neck, cutting her peripheral view but blocking her face, if she turned aside, from the priest's bright, inquiring eyes and her father's sharp glance. The strangers could see her eyes only if she faced them with chin raised.

Men were strange creatures to her, frightening yet entertaining, and always to be contemplated from a distance. The priest and the richly dressed, red-faced squire wore the beards of married men, and the squire's ruddy-complected son had red-gold down sprouting on his square chin and upper lip. The boy would soon be of an age to be taken to the temple, where the priests would shave his face and pronounce him marriageable. Keira's father would shave his beard and mustache after the season of mourning, and when his face was bare again, likely court the widow Arren.

Keira's mouth tightened at that thought. She forced herself to attend to tea bowls and wineglasses. Keeping her eyes properly lowered, she concentrated on the strangers' hands and gestures, peripheral flashes of profile, and choices of words. They spoke of war against the northern Blasphemers or the infidels across the sea. Only on market days could Keira hear news and rumors. She strained her ears to catch every crumb from this feast of voices speaking of faraway places.

"My wife and daughter," the squire said, "will ruin me with their demands for the finest spidersilk." He leaned back in his chair. "The witches might win the war not on the battlefield, but in the marketplace, their weaving guilds in Cartheon have such strong monopolies."

Cartheon. Keira repeated the name thrice in her mind, like a talisman, the name of the great northern city the priests never ceased to rail at. But this priest, she saw with disappointment, made a sour face and changed the subject.

The factor, whose faceful of wiry black stubble reminded Keira of a boar's, grumbled about the laziness of his apprentices. Gulping his wine in one draught, he set down his bowl with a clatter. Wine trickled down his chin and he wiped it with his shirtsleeve.

The soldier, she saw with a little shock, was one of the seafolk from farther north along the coast. She cast careful, rationed looks his way as she moved about the table. His long hair and beardless skin made him somewhat resemble a woman. It was impossible to tell his age. The left side of his face was unblemished, but on the right side, a fading scar ran down his jaw. A curved, sheathed sword hung over the back of his chair, and the squire's son eyed the man's marked face and weapon with open curiosity.

Even in the bright light of the candles, no stubble showed on his chin or above his lips. The market storytellers claimed the seafolk men never grew beards, no matter how old, nor looked aged. She got a sudden inexplicable itch to run her finger across the soldier's chin, to feel whether he had any beard or not.

Moving around the table in an excited haze, she tried to keep one eye and one ear on her father. She poured wine and offered the men the last of their store of dried plums, soaked in mint tea to make them soft and fragrant.

The squire leaned over the table, displaying sleeves richly worked in gold and silver thread. "Does your daughter embroider fine?" he asked.

Her father sighed. "I am afraid that is not one of her skills."

A knot formed in Keira's stomach as she eyed the squire's fantastically embroidered sleeve. Gold and silver work caught the candlelight and shimmered like fire on the man's robe. Only a rich man with many servants, one who might buy his way into the ka'innen class, could afford to let his daughters spend their days doing such work. She seldom had time to embroider, and when she did it was a mess. Clumsy with a thimble, she always pricked her fingers. The patterns of the stitches tried her patience, acquired strange shapes, and pulled her into daydreams. She would much rather go to the horse market or listen to gossip and tales at the fair. Her mother had embroidered; but after she had been buried, Keira's father had thrown all her needlework into the fire.

Keira stared, spellbound, at the embroidered sleeve, seeing shapes form there.

The man she had just served murmured, "Thank you." She started. It was the soldier, the mercenary.

His voice was softer than she had expected, and he looked directly into her face. She stared a moment at his black eyes and his skin that was a color between honey and copper, and stepped backward in confusion. Caught off guard by the attention to herself, she lowered her eyes.

Her father waved his glass in the air with weary anger. She moved to serve the priest, the final stranger.

"Daughter," the priest said, for priests called all women *daughter*.

Keira bowed to him.

Her mother had hated priests and never trusted them, and Keira did not like the way this one eyed her. Surely he would smell her dreams or see their reflections floating on the surface of his wine.

But she served deftly, noting that her father was only half-drunk, and then she withdrew to the doorway. Her hands shook. Her mouth watered at the scent of the mint-soaked plums; she had eaten nothing all day, just a few ladles of milk from the bucket.

The six men raised their goblets in unison and carefully tilted the fragile glasses over the edge of the table until a single red drop from each spilled onto the floor.

"God's part is given," the priest said.

Keira backed toward the kitchen. The six new drops soaked into the floorboards would stain the wood the color of old blood. Deva would sprinkle salt over them to keep them unfading, a testimony to the proper faith of the house. Keira thought how stingy and solemn men were when they offered wine to god: one careful drop.

"To the fertility of the house," the squire said. He nodded to his son.

"To the fertility of the daughter of the house," the squire's son said. He blushed slightly.

The men raised their glasses and drank.

"You are kind and proper, gentlemen," her father said. "But I think the fertility of my daughter may not be great."

Keira backed inside the kitchen, to the spot where she could hear everything and see her father's back. He was in one of his moods. "Do you presume to know god's will, brother?" she heard the priest ask.

Her father coughed. "No man may know his will. A man may suspect a pattern, though. My wife died two months ago. My daughter is the only live child she bore."

There was a general murmur of sympathy.

"Consider the malign influence of witchcraft," the priest said. "It is very strong in this area."

Her father downed his wine. "Less strong than it was. Three were hung at Clawton Crossroads, last Sunday night."

The priest made a sign of blessing. The squire's son shifted in his seat and sipped his wine.

A sick taste rose in Keira's throat as she remembered the hanging, and the dream of three hanged bodies that had haunted her after her mother's death. But the glasses needed refilling. She circled the table, pouring wine, then resumed her post by the kitchen door. The men downed the wine with increased appetite, spilling not a drop this time.

Her father twisted in his chair, frowning at her and tapping his neck. She felt a tendril of hair that had strayed from beneath her wimple. The sign from him sent her back to the kitchen, where she tucked the escaped hair under the cloth.

Deva, breaking the limed seal on a crock of pickled meat, muttered to herself about the shortness of their stores. Keira thought they were both contemplating a diet of oat gruel until the hunters could go out and the kitchen garden was bearing again. Deva poured rakka into the small kettle, grabbed a handful of dried herbs from the wall, and crumbled them into the liquor, making a brewet to pour over the meat.

Keira leaned against the kitchen wall, feeling warm and safe for a moment.

"How old is the daughter?" she heard the priest ask.

"Eighteen," her father said. "And yet unwed."

"The younger wed the better." The priest clicked his tongue. "Otherwise their heads go soft or wild. Are there no men in these parts of proper age?"

"The war has taken them," her father said slowly.

One more drink would spill the story of Terrak and the whipping, Keira thought.

She took bread out to them, then a platter of pickled meats, dried apples, and sweet-thorn fruit. She slipped past her father back to the safety of the doorway, noting on her way that the priest ate and partook of wine as if he thought more of his bodily health than of his soul.

The squire glanced about. "Those hangings would look so much finer with embroidered edges," he said. "You should see my youngest daughter's needlework."

Keira watched her father's eyebrow rise. He called for rakka, and she set out the shallow wooden bowls.

The factor, heated by the wine and food, tried to coax the soldier into betting on whether northern soldiers would march south.

The soldier laughed. "Let them stay beyond the borderlands. I have no taste to fight again, just yet."

"Ever fought the witches? Ever seen one, dead or alive?" the factor demanded.

"No, nor have any desire to," the soldier said. He covered his wineglass when she came to fill it.

Keira stood by the doorway, repeating to herself with relish the names of foreign cities: Lian Calla free port, capital of the seacoast and island federation; Bala Koth, far to the east; and I'Brin, north beyond Cartheon in the Ice Kingdoms. She soaked up the heady scent of wine, rakka, and abundant food, sneaked a plum and bit of pie to nibble on, and was unseen until more food or drink was needed. She was only a pair of hands; she was invisible.

The squire continued babbling about his youngest daughter, not married a year and already with a swollen belly, and his eldest daughter, who had borne two sons and also did fantastic embroidery. His every gesture showed off the finely worked borders of his sleeves. He held up his purse, the coins inside clinking softly, to display the wheel worked on it in gleaming, tiny, rainbow-hued cross-stitch.

Keira's father whispered to the priest, his fingers steepled. Keira strained to hear what the soldier and the factor said of northern armies, while keeping a wary eye on her father. He caught her eye and tapped the priest's goblet impatiently.

As she moved to fill it her hands slipped on the heavy carafe. A red wave of wine sloshed onto the table beside the priest.

Her father turned his bloodshot eyes on her. Her stomach knotted as she sopped up the wine with a cloth. She was no longer invisible, no longer safe.

"Forgive me, Father, for my clumsiness."

"A pretty speech, daughter. It does my heart good to hear it. Now that you ask my forgiveness, why not ask it for your willfulness and disobedience? That would do my soul, and yours, even more good." His voice boomed in the room.

Keira's cheeks burned. She finished blotting the wine. She noticed every vein in her hands suddenly, and the line of dirt under her thumbnail.

"What willfulness and disobedience is this, daughter?" the priest asked. He held his glass to be filled.

"Something my father punished me for." The wine gurgled as she filled the priest's glass. Her hand was sticky and unsteady.

"Something," her father mocked. "Something indeed. I chose a husband for my daughter, who said she would rather die than marry him."

"Blasphemy," the priest hissed. The company grew still.

"I whipped her well. Since that man was not good enough for her, I warned her I might sell her to a complete stranger. Perhaps one of you is interested."

The priest looked at Keira and narrowed his eyes. "I am already wed, brother, but perhaps these others are not."

Last time, drunken over a ko game, her father had offered her to a wine merchant, who protested in the end that he already had a wife, could not afford to keep another, and slapped her father's back and laughed at them both. But Keira's mother had been alive then, and she knew her father would never sell her while her mother lived.

Keira stood with her back against the door frame, clutching the wine carafe in both hands. She shook her head slowly, her chin raised defiantly. The strangers regarded her as they would livestock at the fair. She stood straighter. Very well: the better the livestock looked, the higher the price it fetched.

"Father," she said. "Father, do you jest?" Her voice rang in the room. The undulating candle flames and the faces of the strangers blurred before her.

"It shames a house when a maid your age is still unwed," the priest said. "For the good of your own soul, your father offers you." He spoke in the kindly tone used on children who were slow at lessons. "I will bless the union."

She bit her lip, almost laughing. No one was looking at her

now. The five strangers regarded their rings and toyed with their goblets. With his thumbnail the squire's son traced the grain of the table. At last the squire raised his head, and said in her direction, "If you do not agree to this, we will not agree to it."

"Do you truly wish to be rid of your daughter, man?" his son asked. The boy's pale face reddened to the ears.

Keira felt calmer. She considered the faces of the strangers, wondering if they were good men, or cruel men, like her father or unlike. Or did it matter? Go north if I die, her mother had said to her: north to the great city. And Keira wondered which one of them was traveling farthest north.

Widows with neither wealth nor kin sold themselves into service to keep from starving, especially in cruel spring, the pinch-gut season before the land yielded its new bounty. At fairs, poor families sold their daughters into service to the highest bidder, to pay their rent to the hold master, or dissolve their debt to the Sanctum. Her father had the right to sell her and protest would only make him more adamant. Besides, if he got a good price for her, he would approach the Sanctum treasurer and buy the fields that their neighbor Terrak had coveted. If her father wed the widow Arren, he would get two sons and two daughters to help work his larger freehold. Keira disliked the pious widow, who was quick to suspect witchcraft in her neighbors.

"After I die," her mother had said, "you know he will marry the widow. And I fear for you, that she will accuse you of witchcraft, of taking the souls of all my stillborn children. You know what she is."

Keira drew a careful breath, not wanting any of them, especially her father, to think she willingly agreed to be sold.

"Your will be done, ka." She bowed her head. "But no reasonable man would take me undowered, father. I agree to be offered if the mare I bought at Kerlew Fair is offered with me."

The factor leaned forward and rubbed his chin, looking her over as if she were a brood mare. A better bargain, to get horse and wife in one stroke.

Her father gave her a look that would have portended a beating. "Agreed," he said slowly. "My daughter judges horses well, I wish you all to remember." He gestured her away. "Go. I'll see you wed at dawn."

* * *

Deva paled at the news. "He's mad. He's playing one of his games."

"No, he's drunk. But he has the right." It was a game, Keira thought, but one she had a chance to win. She felt suddenly calm. *Perhaps I'm mad myself.* Her mind flew from stranger to stranger. Not the factor; she remembered his leer and his cruel mouth. Not the squire's son: if he married her, he would likely treat her as a servant so his sisters had more time for their blasted embroidery. The boy was barely older than she; he would not have the estate to support a wife in a separate house unless his father was a rich man indeed. Thinking last of the soldier, the scar-faced man, she felt a strange hollowness. She wondered how long the bargaining would last.

The two women went upstairs and set to work sorting her possessions, until Deva left to answer her father's call.

Once alone, Keira rummaged in the bottom of her clothes chest and pulled out a flat, wooden box. Inside lay a necklace, a string of pearls and gold and silver beads, secret wealth her mother had given her.

"For impossible circumstances, for bribery if it will save your life," her mother had said, before she died in the fever. "If I die, go north, north to where the sea eats away at the edge of the world. And never speak of your dreams to any man, especially a priest."

How far north did the soldier live? Lian Calla, he had said, where the people raised the blackflower tea her mother had loved.

Keira ran the pearls through her fingers. She latched her door from the inside and opened the seams of her old, gray spidersilk cloak. Into the open seams she laid the unclasped necklace, and began to sew with furious haste.

"Deva?" Keira called as she heard footsteps.

"Mistress?"

Keira opened the door a crack. "How is it going?"

"Your father showed them your mare in the barn. 'She's ready for breeding as the girl is, I warrant,' that factor says when he claps eyes on the mare. Mistress, your father's a hard man, harder since your mother died, but he told truth about you. 'She chose the mare and bargained very shrewdly for it,' your father says. 'The knack of keen bargaining is a fine quality in a wife, even if she cannot embroider.' That squire near choked. Even the priest snickered, Rahn told me." Deva chuckled to herself.

"Who is bidding?"

"The factor and the squire's son." Deva lowered her voice. "Your father told them you were real healthy, that the pox left only that scar in the middle of your forehead and some on your arms. He said you brew good ale, and that's truth. Then the factor says, 'But she's clumsy enough to spill good wine.' Your father asked four silver tors, opening price. The priest tells him, 'Keep her, brother, if the price doesn't rise to your liking.' He said he had no money to buy women for the temple, but preferred younger ones, whose ways aren't so set.

"That squire frets about your not embroidering fine, but he egged his boy to lay down money when your father said your son would get the land. The factor, he's a bad one, says, 'But she's taller than a woman has a right to be, and has no tits to speak of. How much does she eat?' " Deva snorted. "That factor grumbles and curses, but there's no bottom to his purse."

Keira twisted her hands in her skirt. "What of the soldier, the beardless man?"

Deva shrugged. "He just watches everything. I don't think he took three sips of rakka all night. Oh, he asked how your mother died."

Keira's father called from below, and Deva hastened down the hallway. Keira paced to the window, pushed the shutters open a hand span, and staring out, traced a spiral with her fingertip on the wood.

"Lian Calla," she said, just trying the name on her tongue. "Lian Calla. How far north is Lian Calla?"

The soldier glanced at the piles of silver coins stacked before the squire's son and the factor, and turned the rakka bowl in his fingers. Talking and joking, the two had laid their money down like men at a cattle auction.

His memory of the girl irritated him more than their matter-of-fact bidding. She had moved around the table like a faceless woman; from the side the head covering had hidden her face totally. From the front, the cloth tucked under her chin hid her neck. She was dressed as stiffly as a doll, with not a hair showing, except, just once, that stray reddish curl that had sparked her father to shoo her from the room.

Something in her eyes reminded him of a young sentry with shot nerves who had stood too long on watch.

The sharp odor of rakka dragged his attention back to the stifling room. He sipped from the shallow bowl, holding the liquor in his mouth a long moment before he swallowed.

The factor looked pleased when the squire, speaking for his son, stopped bidding. "If she does not embroider well," he muttered to his son, "I cannot see paying more than this." One by one, he dropped his coins back into his purse.

The factor downed more rakka and looked about smugly, wiping his mouth with the back of his hand.

The soldier frowned, still tasting rakka on his lips. He fished his purse out of a cloak pocket. Damn, Nikka, he told himself, you must be crazy.

Against the factor's fifteen pieces of silver, he laid four sea pearls knotted on a string, a liege payment, rarer than gold. Even the priest exclaimed.

The girl's father stared at him, transfixed a moment, and smiled.

The factor grinned sourly, then dropped his coins by twos back into his deep purse.

Her room grayed with dawn. She sat numbly on a chair. She had hardly slept and her fingers were sore with needle pricks.

Deva knocked and Keira opened the door. Deva had been unable to tell her the results of the bidding last night. The priest stood beside the servant.

"Come, daughter," he said.

She followed, hating him for intruding on her last moments with Deva.

In the great hall the company waited in a semicircle, straight and solemn in the half light, as if they were awaiting an execution. Her father stood a few paces to the side. The priest grasped her hand and led her to the center of the arc of strangers.

The soldier stepped forward, and a hot stab of excitement surged through her. The burned-down candles threw light across his features, picking out the silver slash that marred his face; he looked stern. Her fingers had turned to ice and they stung. How far north is Lian Calla? she thought, trying to fill her head with nothing but that thought. And how much farther north is Cartheon?

The priest performed a quick ceremony. Within minutes, she was transferred from her father's keeping to the keeping of a total stranger. "You may give the woman the four kisses," the priest said.

The soldier bent to kiss her forehead, stooped to kiss her breasts, then knelt before her, placed his hands about her waist, and pressed his mouth to her belly.

Her father handed the priest two rings, the wooden one they had taken from her mother's dead hand before they buried her, and the silver band from his own finger. The priest intoned a blessing, held their left hands together, slipped the silver ring on the soldier's hand and the wooden ring onto hers. Her father, as sita or Sanctum-appointed notary of the area, had written out two copies of the wedding contract. Keira watched the soldier write "Nikkael Roshannon" in a large, bold hand. He handed her the quill. Her father gave her a warning glance and she scrawled a ragged mark, afraid to write her name in front of the priest.

The priest directed all present to sign or make their marks as witnesses. He tore the first contract in half, gave one half to her and the other to Roshannon. After the priest blessed it, he gave the second copy to her husband entire, should he wish to repudiate her.

Keira embraced Deva in the kitchen.

"He gave the master four pearls for you," her mother's faithful old servant whispered. She fussed with Keira's head covering, tweaking the folds into place. "May he treat you as Rahn has treated me. Not all men are devils, and the seacoast folk are not so priest-ridden. I wish you well, mistress."

Keira nodded. "I wish you well, Deva." She hugged the older woman again, resting her face against the servant's shoulder. They drew apart, suddenly awkward. Keira brushed a hand over the smooth, old benches, touched the butter churn for luck, glanced at the hearth and the bunches of dried herbs hanging from the rafters, then turned her back on it all and walked out into the kitchen garden with Deva.

Geese had invaded the walled garden and congregated by the

bee houses, hissing to themselves. Keira stooped by habit for a pebble to toss at them, but Deva cracked a willow wand in the air and drove them off.

The coachman soothed his four team horses and checked their harness. Rahn handed Keira's small trunk up to the squire's son, who had settled in the seat by the coachman. Nodding curtly to her, her father led up the mare. Rahn tied the mare on behind the coach with a long lead, while Keira's father clasped hands with the priest and the soldier.

Keira whispered to the mare to calm her, and twined her fingers in the silky black mane. Stroking the mare's neck, she glanced around the hold. The stout, red gate before the entrance to her father's freehold stuck out proudly, the only bit of color in the landscape. Her eye swept over the shapes of the stables and dairy, the herders' calving sheds clustered behind the house, and the sweet-thorn orchard and the little hill where her stillborn brothers and sisters and her mother were buried. The fields behind her father's house abutted Terrak's land, and east beyond his holding was the Kerlew road. She had never been farther from home than Kerlew Fair. She pressed her face against the mare's warm neck and took a last look at the broad, iron-bound double red doors of her father's house, the doors that were flung wide open for only two reasons: to welcome in a bride or let out a coffin carried high on the shoulders of men.

She glanced up at the shuttered window of her room a moment, whispered a final endearment to the mare, and gazed northward, where the sky was clearing and everything was unknown. She noticed the soldier looking at her and lowered her eyes.

"Well, girl." Her father jerked his chin toward the coach.

The soldier handed her into the coach and climbed in beside her. The priest scrambled in just opposite Keira at the window, the space in the coach so narrow that his knees bumped hers. The squire settled opposite Roshannon, while the factor got in and latched the door.

Soon her father's grain fields rolled past, and the timber bridge over the creek where the village women gathered to wash clothes on the rocks, and the road to Clawton Market—all the world she knew.

Every jolt and lurch through potholes made the factor curse. He stretched, bumping his knees against the squire's.

"Even a swayback nag," he said, "wouldn't break the buttocks so much as this contraption."

Keira bit her lip to keep from laughing. If we were milk and cream on the way to market, she thought, we'd be churned to butter in no time.

The factor poked his head out the window, peering at the fields and vineyards and well-kept temple estates. "At the rate we lurch along, my apprentices and journeymen will have robbed me blind by the time I return." He began discussing cannon and weapon making, the casting of iron and bronze. Roshannon questioned him with what Keira thought must be a soldier's professional interest.

The squire peered out the window while the priest lectured Keira.

The strands of his lecture, about the duties of wives and the shortcomings of women, grated against her, while the details the factor was spewing forth distracted her. "Spiritual busybodies," Rahn had once called the stern, new-order priests before Deva told him to hush if he valued his head. "Their true interest is how much gold and how much food they can scare out of a body. And how much hatred they can stir up against folk they want the army to march on." Keira inhaled the scent of the rain-freshened countryside and began to daydream as the coach jolted and lurched.

At Clawton Crossroads the priest leaned out for better sight of the hanged witches.

"You attended the hanging, Mistress Roshannon?" he demanded.

Roshannon elbowed Keira in the ribs, and she nodded.

The coachman slowed the horses to a walk, on the priest's request.

After the windy dawn, the corpses swung slightly. Two children who had been tossing stones at the bodies fled as the coach halted. A huge raven perched on the crossbeam of the gibbet, screaming and spreading its wings.

The priest drew his head back in. "One of the souls remains to mock us."

Keira pinched her nostrils against the smell. She stared transfixed at the three pairs of dead feet stirring in the breeze. It was exactly the dream image that had come to her weeks before, soon after her mother died. The two women were barefoot, but the man's left leg still wore a rumpled stocking and a tattered shoe. Old Giles, he who spoke to animals and had helped her train the mare. And Mistress Treya, who had helped at her mother's last childbed. The other woman was a stranger from another village. Keira pressed her fist against her mouth, and bit her tongue to keep her nausea back.

"The wages of blasphemy," the priest recited.

Keira felt the soldier's shoulder stiffen against hers. Her eyes glazed over with memory. The three had stood at the gallows with the ropes around their necks. "I have done no blasphemy. You are the blasphemers," the stranger woman said clearly before the priests gagged her and shoved all three off the narrow scaffold.

The bodies twitched for over a quarter hour, while everyone assembled watched. It was not an easy way to die, nor did the priests mean it to be. No bags of mercy stones were given the condemned to grant them a quicker death. No one had dared hang on their legs to ensure their necks broke swiftly.

Keira blinked, trying to banish the knowledge that her dreams had shown her what would happen.

The priest leaned forward to study her. "Their bodies are left here to teach a lesson," he said. "But their souls are damned forever, lost to the Wheel."

Horrified, Keira wondered if the priest could somehow perceive the dreams behind her eyes, smell the essence of them leaking through her skin like sweat. She nodded nervously, clasped her hands in her lap, and daydreamed of strangling him.

The horses snorted, growing restless at the smell of death. The coachman cracked his whip.

Traveling north and west all day, the coach reached unfamiliar landscape by afternoon. Keira grew excited, glancing out the window at rolling hills and clustered villages.

Last year she had gone to Kerlew with Rahn and Deva, to the annual fair that drew horse traders and artisans from the entire southlands.

She savored that memory as the coach jolted and the priest lectured. Kerlew Fair swarmed with rumors, the smell of exotic food, and the taste of freedom. Her father had conceded that she, a sita's daughter, should have a riding horse, and entrusted money to Rahn. The two servants rode with her in the wagon to the fair, flanking her everywhere she went and acting as her intermediaries when she bid for the mare.

On the return trip, Rahn pointed out an ancient, eroded stone and knelt to brush the weeds away from it. It was like one of the old stones she had found as a child, with a cross and wheel usually hacked across the original image. Round as an egg and warm with the sun, it was an oddly comforting shape, Keira thought. A faint tracery of the original carving showed curves and faces. Blasphemer's stones, the priests called them, and encouraged people to break them and set them into walls.

Around a tiny campfire at night, Deva and Rahn told stories the priest would have disapproved of. Rahn commented that he would beat neither a woman nor a horse, and when Keira asked him why, said he would not like to be kicked back someday by either, and besides, a beating never made any creature work harder. The servants treated her like a daughter, and taught her to set snares on common land, fish, and tell direction from the stars. Keira asked about Cartheon.

"It's two weeks north and west of here on a good horse," Rahn said, but would say no more.

The fair gossips said Cartheon perched magically on the edge of the world, built on both sea and rock.

Keira prodded Rahn for more information, but he shook his head and rubbed his chin. He and Deva had come from farther north as a dowry gift with her mother. They claimed to have seen the sea, and Keira had always craved their stories.

Two weeks north and west on a good horse. The thought turned in her mind.

To Keira's relief, the priest got out that afternoon in a village surrounding a temple estate, while the rest of the company climbed out in a river town where urchins ran alongside, touching the coach's sides and begging for coins. The coachman cursed and tossed them a bronze piece. Six boys in tattered clothes leaped for it, cracking their heads and snapping at each other like a pack of dogs. One scrambled away with the prize and the others chased him across the village common.

At twilight the coach stopped in a free-chartered town called Blackhall. Roshannon paid for a room at the inn and the stabling of Keira's mare, and they ate a meal in the smoky common room before going upstairs. There were few travelers; not until high summer and the time of fairs would the roads be busy, even if the war continued. A maid brought up bread, a decanter of wine, and glasses, and lit two miserly candle stubs.

"You'll have the bed to yourselves this time of year," she said. She left, clattering down the stairs.

Roshannon hung his cloak on a peg and paced, stretching his long legs. He set his small soldier's pack against the wall next to her chest of belongings, hung his sword on a peg by the bed, and poured himself a glass of wine. Watching her, he spilled a careful, ritual drop, then sniffed the wine. She hung her cloak on a wall peg near his sword.

"Would you taste the wine, wife?"

"I have never tasted wine," she lied. "It is forbidden."

"It is not forbidden if I bid you do it." He seemed amused and held the glass out to her, so that she could just smell a tart, fruity aroma. "It is good."

"If you bid me taste, husband." She sipped carefully. The pale greenish yellow liquid went straight to her stomach, where it radiated like the sun. She reminded herself to be wary and handed his glass back.

He lolled at the window, looking at the stars. "What kind of man was he—the one your father wished you to marry?"

"A man I had no wish to marry."

He closed the shutters and turned to face her. "You had no wish to marry me or anyone else. You wanted to escape your father."

Her cheeks burned. "Did you want to wed me? Or did you like the thought of acquiring my mare?"

He grinned in a way she could not entirely hate. "A good mare is a good mare." He touched her arm. "You truly preferred death to marrying this man your father chose?"

"Yes."

"What do you know of death?"

Vivid pictures of the hanged bodies at the crossroads, and her mother, and the recurring nightmares poured through her mind. "Surely not as much as you, husband, who have been to war."

He poured himself more wine. Amazingly, he did not chide her for not serving him, but leaned against the stone hearth and turned the glass in his fingers. "What do you think of me, wife?"

He waited for her to answer, for her to step into the snare, no doubt for his amusement, so he could rebuff her. She suspected she had married a man much more subtle and dangerous than her father.

"I did not think that men valued women's opinions," she said. "Having known you only one day it is hardly wise to judge you, husband."

He bowed and laughed. "Cautious and discreet. Your father described only your faults, so I must discover your virtues."

"There is no virtue to be discovered in any woman, according to the priests."

"The priests know some things but not others." He frowned at her a moment. "Take that thing off."

"What?" She started.

"The head covering."

Hesitantly, she touched its folds. He took a step toward her. She tugged aside the neckcloth and pulled the wimple and veil from her head. Clutching the head covering in one hand, she let it drop to the floor as he moved closer. Her hair spread across her shoulders.

She felt naked, indecent, totally revealed to him. No more could she lower her face and depend on the wimple to hide her expression and let her be invisible.

"Look at me, wife."

She did, remembering that her father only looked her in the eyes before he beat her. But she could not look away from the soldier's eyes. He sees *me,* she thought frantically, he sees into my self, as no one else has ever done.

He touched her shoulder and slowly curled his fingers into her hair.

The room seemed to narrow and shrink, until only the circle where they stood facing each other was real to Keira. Perhaps it was the effect of the wine. She blinked, suddenly longing for the familiarity of her own room, her own hard, narrow bed, the voices of her own servants. She wondered if he would beat her.

The stranger who was her husband touched her face. His fingers traced the line of her jaw and neck. She stepped back, twisted, and stooped to blow out the candles. His hand came down on her shoulder.

"Let them burn, wife. I would like to see what I have acquired."

She lay very still in the bed while shards of dreams and notions of flight sifted through her head. Gray light showed through the crack between the shutters, though it was not yet dawn. She edged her thigh away from his and turned to look at him. He smelled of wine now, and he had not before. She wrinkled her nose. If she stayed as his wife, how many clannish relatives had he to spy on her? How long before her belly would swell? She remembered her mother's labors, the smell of sweat and blood. If she did not go now, would another chance come?

Her fingers curled into fists; gathering her resolve, she slid soundlessly from the bed, padded across the floor, and opened his pack. Inside were a strange wooden tube, an extra linen shirt, breeches, and a jerkin, soft and worn with age. Shivering, she put on the clothes, tucking her hair inside the shirt. The legs of the breeches fit but the waist bagged, so she tied her sash tight about it. She drew on her own soft-soled boots, tucked the breeches in, and paced quietly about the room, enjoying how freely her legs moved. Putting on her cloak, she smoothed her hands over the seams and their burden of treasure. She considered the sword hung on the wall, but knew nothing of its use. She bumped into his overturned boots, picked them up to move them out of the way, and felt something hard and cold inside. With her fingertips she puzzled out the shape, a sheathed knife strapped inside either boot. *What manner of man are you, husband?* She drew the long, narrow dagger. Hesitating only a moment, she cut the left sheath free of the boot and tucked it inside her breeches' waistband, resheathing the dagger. She snatched his hat and her skirt from the wall peg and glided to the door, praying the floorboards would not squeak.

He stirred, muttering in his sleep. She froze, waited. Twisting off the wooden ring, she crossed the room and put it on the floor beside the chamber pot. Carefully, she pried a gold bead and one pearl from her cloak lining and stuffed them in his pack. The bed creaked as he stirred. She glided to the door, grabbed the half loaf of bread from the table, and left.

Stuffing the bread inside her cloak, she crept down the stairs that led past the kitchen. Tiny noises sounded in the darkness around her. A jewel-eyed cat curled on a kitchen table leaped softly down and brushed her legs. She caught her balance against a table and knocked her shin.

Sausages, ripening cheeses, and ropes of braided garlic and sourgrass hung from long hooks in the rafters. She took a sausage and sourgrass for tea and went outside.

In the barn the stable boy snored heartily in the loft. No doubt he would be beaten, but she hardened her heart and saddled her horse. Removing her ear tag, she tossed it in the bottom of the left saddlebag. While the mare nuzzled her hands and whickered softly, Keira stuffed her saddlebags full of grain.

She swung up at the mounting block. Two weeks north and west on a good horse. The foredawn air tasted cold and intoxicating. The waning old moon hung high in the western sky. Her breath and the mare's rose in plumes. Signaling with her knees, she guided the gray over the soft turf of the stable yard. Farther down the road she pressed the mare into a canter. She gulped the air like wine, checked the stars, took the highway north to Cartheon, and rode.

❀ 2 ❀

Roshannon's eyelids fluttered as he rolled over. His mouth was as dry as the infidel lands and his head ached. His eyes opened; squinting, he recognized the inn room, filled with the gray, ghost light of dawn. He curled his toes among the covers and reached over to her side. His hand closed on emptiness.

He propped himself up on his elbows. "Keira?"

He pushed the covers aside and slid out of bed. The icy floorboards stung his bare feet. The skin around his skull had shrunk tight as wet leather. In the stable yard a cock crowed, and he winced at the sound. He knew now what was wrong: he could not remember a single dream.

"Keira?" He licked his lips and spat a sour taste from his mouth. What he needed was a skinful of water. He looked around the room. Shadowy mounds of clothes lay heaped on the bare floorboards—his clothes, her clothes, and his boots.

He frowned at her side of the bed. Usually the smallest noise woke him. But he had not slept so soundly since the last woman he had taken to his bed or since the last time he had drunk wine. He glared at the empty bottle on the table and groaned; his whole body ached as he stretched.

Shivering, he yanked on his breeches and snatched up his rumpled shirt. Her boots, her skirt, and his hat were gone. His sword and cloak still hung on the wall pegs and her chest of belongings stood against the wall.

He rubbed his eyes and on sudden impulse went to his pack to dig out his comfortable old shirt. The pack was closed in a different way. Cursing, he flung it open. His favorite old shirt, a pair of old breeches, and his worn, quilted leather jerkin were gone.

His fingers struck something cold and hard in the bottom. He pulled out a carved gold bead, whistled softly, and dumped the pack. A sea pearl struck the floorboards, rolled, and lay gathering the light to itself. Picking up the pearl and gold bead, he spotted the wooden ring beside the chamber pot. A sharp whiff of stale urine assailed his nostrils and cleared his head. He scooped up the wooden band and slipped it onto the little finger of his right hand. He crossed the room and elbowed the shutter open. The pearl glimmered blue-silver in the pale light and the delicate script of the ancient steward lords of Cartheon stood out plainly on the gold bead. The bead must have come south before the Carthe lords severed trade agreements with the Sanctum generations ago.

"By the Wheel," he said.

Much more to thee than met the eye, wife. Already the sea pearl shone with greater luster, warming in his palm. *So you buy yourself back from me and pay me for my own clothes with this? Woman, we will have a long talk when I catch up with you.*

Stooping, he picked up a long dark hair that gleamed with a reddish cast. A sudden memory of the rich, thick waves of her hair against his skin caught him unawares.

Pacing, he glanced around the room. By candlelight and with her in it, the room had been a fitting wedding chamber. Now its emptiness mocked his spirit.

He had knelt before her and taken off her boots. She laughed in spite of herself when he tickled her feet, and he laughed with her, glad to see her tension ease somewhat.

Unclothed and silent, narrow-hipped and long-legged, with her arms crossed over herself, she had watched him, the single candle flame reflected in her eyes.

Never been kissed? he thought. Never lain down in the sweet grass beneath a blooming apple tree? Never even been touched by another man? A strangely rousing thought, that, he had to admit with the still-analytical side of his brain. Only by her own choice would a seacoast girl be virgin when she wed. To hold out against the body denied life; denying life was the southlanders' chief accomplishment.

He had wanted to tell her it was only one of the chief pleasures of life she was facing here, but he suspected she would never believe his words. He kissed her neck, her throat, and ran a finger down her spine, feeling the welted scars of the whip marks across her back. She put her hands on his chest, stepping backward to stare at him, more in wonder than in fear, it seemed. Her fingertips curled against his skin. Suddenly she stroked a finger across his side, then snatched her hand away as if fire had burned her.

But her embarrassment both touched and thrilled him. She blushed magnificently, her face and neck reddening down to her breasts. Aye, her blushes warmed the blood. And a certain wild tangle of emotions shimmered in the air around her, like a rare spice that he could almost smell in her hair and taste on the surface of her skin.

Much later he watched over her as she slept curled in the sheets, and wondered what he had done, buying a woman. Mouthful by mouthful he had drunk down the bottle of yellow wine and studied her scarred back by the light of the guttering candle. The lashes had been laid on with a heavy hand.

By the Wheel, what had made her run?

He pulled on his boots. His fingers touched the reassuring knife hilt in the right boot, and found the left boot empty.

He cursed again. She had dressed in his old clothes, taken the knife, and fled. No woman had ever run away from his bed before—certainly he had given this woman no reason to do so. He snatched his cloak.

Was it a game they played? Had the father feigned the peevish, drunken farce of selling his daughter to a stranger, only to have the stranger wake to an empty place in the bed beside him? He laughed sourly. No, that shy girl was no trickster; she had never been with a man before.

Kneeling over his pack, he rearranged its contents, fingering the blowgun. He tossed the clothes she had left into the chest and shoved it under the bed. Thoughtfully, he tucked the gold bead and pearl into a pouch hung inside his cloak, and fastened his sword.

Downstairs the common room stood empty. An ill-laid fire was smoking in the hearth.

"God's thousand names, but what have you done with my tinderbox?" the landlady's voice roared from the kitchen.

Roshannon crossed the big, low-ceilinged room on his way to the stable, where he did not expect to find the mare.

The maid who had fetched wine and candles last night scuttled from the kitchen with an armload of firewood. "My lord." She bobbed her head at him, keeping the top twigs in place with her chin.

Roshannon went outside. In the stable yard the landlord and the stable boy stood glowering at each other over the horse trough. A fat, spotted milk snake, of the kind that farmers kept to hunt vermin in their barns, lay coiled round the boy's neck and shoulders and nosed into his hair.

"I didn't steal the mare or tell a thief about it, master," the boy said. A red welt showed on his left cheek.

"You lie and I'll sell you at Kerlew come harvest." The landlord's breath plumed on the frosty air and his eyes glittered in his broad face.

Roshannon cleared his throat.

The landlord turned, smiling nervously when he saw who it was. He appraised Roshannon and the sword at his side, and bowed, a calculated, flattering bow low enough to satisfy the touchiest overlord. "Ka. My lord, good morning to you."

Roshannon nodded. The boy edged backward a few steps, shifting the serpent across his shoulders.

"Lord, the mare you stabled last night is missing." The landlord coughed and wrung his hands.

"I haven't passed it to thieves," the stable boy said, shivering.

"I know," Roshannon said. "I believe my wife rode back to her father's house. The mare was her dower portion. Her father will send her to Lian Calla, with an escort this time to keep her from bolting."

The innkeeper peered at him with interest and relief. "You say there's no theft, only your wife riding away home?"

Roshannon nodded.

The man looked amused, perhaps at the inability of foreigners to control their wives.

"If you don't mention this matter," Roshannon said, "I won't say it happened at your inn."

The landlord nodded and snorted in the boy's direction. "Ka, my humble apologies. If this one wasn't so worthless, it'd never've happened."

Roshannon glanced from boy to man. "If you fed him better, man, his ears might be that much sharper," he said.

The red-faced landlord turned without another word and stomped into the inn. The boy retreated into the warmth of the barn.

Roshannon knew Keira would not ride back to her father's

house. He splashed water from the horse trough across his face
and paced across the stable yard. Chickens and goats scattered.
The fowl had scratched and pecked among a set of hoofprints, almost obliterating the tracks that led onto the road. But clean prints
showed in the soft turf by the highway. She had urged the mare
into a trot here, he thought as he bent to consider the tracks. Not
broken into a gallop until she was far enough away not to rouse
the sleepers in the inn. Dew collecting in the prints had softened
them. Three or four hours before daybreak she had ridden north.
He paced along the road.

A fragrant sweet-thorn hedge bordered the highway, and tiny
black birds flitted from its twisted branches as he approached.
Something among the thorns glinted, long reddish hairs tangled in
the hedge. Reaching among the long black barbs, he scraped the
back of his right hand, but retrieved the hair and wound it about
his wrist.

He sucked the blood from the scrape and strode back across the
stable yard.

Perhaps he had been too fierce with her, too insistent with
someone so innocent. Perhaps he should have pinched out the
candle, crawled into bed, and turned his back on her. She would
have found that easy enough to bear, unless she had planned to
run from the first. Yet he would swear she had wanted him to buy
her. He remembered her as she had stood backed against the door
frame when her father had offered her, like a soldier ready for
execution. He closed his eyes. The light hurt his head.

He yanked open the inn door. The sweet scent of burning
cherry wood filled the common room, and the other guests drank
spiced tea quietly, minding their own business, yet observing him
from the corners of their eyes as he took a seat. He was the only
seacoast man in the place, and although his journey from the
southern port of Ke Leithe had inured him to that aloneness, he
felt uneasy. A maid promptly fetched him a steaming bowl of tea
and a slab of black bread.

The clatter of crockery and scraps of a hearty argument drifted
from the kitchen. "A whole, fine, Lian Calla sausage gone," the
landlady screeched. Her husband's rumbling voice could be
heard calming her. A minute later both landlord and lady stalked
into the common room's doorway. The landlady glared at
Roshannon, who stared coolly back at her. The landlord's mouth

tightened as he watched Roshannon. Finally he yanked his wife back into the kitchen, telling her to keep her mouth shut.

Roshannon bent over his tea bowl, inhaling the fragrant spice. He almost laughed as he sipped the steaming brew, picturing Keira helping herself to provisions in the kitchen on her way out. How far and how fast would one desperate woman in his old clothes travel? That fine mare would tempt thieves.

At least I did not buy a boring woman, he thought.

Roshannon rode outside with the coachman, watching the rich southern plains give way to gentle rolling hills fringed with the remains of great forests. The coach rolled past broad vineyards and Sanctum estates. Four or five more days northwestward and the dense forests and terraced fields that clung along the seacoast would be visible. Five or six days on horseback, riding hard, would bring him to Lian Calla again. A rush of images filled his head, of sleek ships rounding the islands off Lian Calla free port and gliding into harbor. He was suddenly homesick for the great bathhouses and the philosophers that lounged in the shade of the porticoes, tempting passersby to play at ko and the meanings of life. He longed to play ko again with his cousin Ni'An, and to see his mother's dark eyes assess him from her high seat on the clan council that ruled Lian Calla. He thought of his mother, her hair loose, wading into the waters of the harbor at the blessing of the port.

What had possessed him to buy that girl? There had been something about her he still did not understand, and his head was in no shape for hard questions today. He could imagine Ni'An roaring at this story. He groaned and narrowed his eyes at the morning as the coach lurched through holes. Yet, strangely enough, no experience with other women matched what he remembered of the night with her. The longer the coach jolted, the more his head cleared.

The first time their eyes had met as she was pouring wine at her father's table, he sensed a mystery. She looked down immediately, yet the sense of encounter remained, a tantalizing puzzle.

And once, in the bed, he had imagined his own flesh and spirit fraying and weaving into hers, twisting inside out until he fancied he was seeing himself through her eyes, as if they had traded awarenesses.

That happened *before* I finished the wine, he reminded himself. He ran his fingers through his hair and caught the coachman eyeing him warily.

Roshannon cursed again, thinking how deceptive the light, fruity, yellow-green stuff had been. It had been a long time since he had drunk wine.

He craved a bath, to ease the pain in his head and body, but no public bathhouses stood along the highway. Southerners considered public bathing a vain, sinful practice. After the Schism, they had destroyed the baths, carted off the stonework to build temples, and done their best to forget the custom of bathing. Seacoast men who served as Sanctum mercenaries often joked about the stench and body hair of Sanctum men, especially the married ones, rumored to harbor generations of lice and fleas in their drooping mustaches and beards.

At Black Cross, the next free-chartered town, he quit the coach and bought a dun stallion with the last of his silver. The horse trader had not noticed a boy pass.

"What of a gray mare, with black stockings, a black mane and tail?" Roshannon asked.

The man rubbed his chin. "Aye, that fine gray. That I remember, just after dawn." He eyed Roshannon's sword and held the stallion as the other man swung into the saddle.

"Did he say where he was going?"

"Not a word. Just touched his hat and took the north road."

She had traveled fast. Roshannon thought of what he would do when he caught up with her.

Mist as white as milk curled about the hills rising from the plains, and as the sun rose, the haze faded against the brightening sky. The earth smelled fragrant and full of promise.

Daybreak raised Keira's spirits. She rocked in the saddle, half-dizzy with the notion of freedom. The mare tossed her head and sidestepped sharply, as if to question her. Keira leaned forward and loosened the rein.

No more beatings, she thought. I will die before that.

The countryside fell away behind her, a patchwork of planted and fallow fields, the cluster of temple estates, holdings, and villages, the few free-chartered towns, and the ribbons of highway and streams. She halted by a willow-choked creek to fill her water bags and let the mare drink. Under the shelter of the trees, she prized a silver bead from her cloak lining, for she needed to buy provisions as soon as possible. Gold would draw too much attention and be too difficult for a small market money changer to give honest coins for.

At noon she came upon a market crossing where those lucky enough to have extra stores were selling their goods at exorbitant prices to travelers.

The rich, sweet smells of fresh horse manure and food mingled in the air. Folk spoke with a strange, rapid cadence here, and appraised her with interest. Keira steeled herself, kept her voice gruff and low, and bargained for salted meats, dried fruits, and grain for the mare.

Leading the mare through the gathering knot of people, she studied the women. They averted their faces quickly beneath the head coverings, and their lowered eyes took in only bits and pieces of the world, crumbs of experience and sensation. She prodded herself to hold her head high, to square her shoulders. Adjusting her stride and manner to mimic men, she fastened her cloak to hang high on the left and sweep low on the right, as Roshannon had done.

She peered critically into a booth at braided strings of dried plums, figs, and tart, brown wedges of apples.

A withered merchant eyed her. In meter, he chanted the merits of his wares. "The best in all the land from Bala Koth to the great sea," he boasted.

Keira snorted and rubbed her nose as she had seen her father do. "Withered as old crone flesh," she said. "Probably taste of the dust you raised getting them here in your donkey cart."

"A tor a string." He spat and rubbed his hands, eyed her horse and cloak.

"A third tor, clearly." She turned away.

The old man coughed. "A half tor."

She turned slowly back toward him, concealing a grin. About a string a day, she figured, and selected ten. She dropped the silver bead into his broad, callused palm.

He hefted the silver to feel whether it was hollow or air-pocked, and extracted a scale from a pouch. She caught him trying to cheat on the weight and kept sharp watch while he counted out bronze tors and half tors.

Every minute she feared a hand would descend onto her shoulder and spin her about. A booming voice would announce to all that she was a woman in man's clothing, a runaway wife due to be returned for a reward.

No hand descended. She bought dried meat, stowed her purchases in the saddlebags, and went on her way.

She touched her hat brim to acknowledge the occasional travelers that hailed her. The merchants complained that the priests were greedy for tithes, and said that farther north, army supply trains had stripped their choicest wares and impressed their servants into the army.

In late afternoon, Keira squinted at a way marker with equal measures of apprehension and exultation, eighty miles from the only world she had ever known. Although pocked with mud holes and often diminished to a rutted cart track, the road wound on, carrying her forward in a rhythmic dream.

The countryside became wild and desolate. In one place, sheep grazed within a Sanctum's tumbled walls. People clearing stones from the walled, hillside fields stopped their labor to stare briefly at her. She gladly chose overgrown paths, so long as they ran north and west.

She glanced over her shoulder all day. No one she saw had yet resolved into the shape of her husband pursuing her. Her fears were stupid, she told herself. Why should he pursue her? He would curse her, consider his honor offended, pocket the gold bead and pearl she had left, curse her again, then forget her. Or would he?

Her mother could answer that question, if only her mother were here. For her mother had always had the clear sight that saw patterns and gatherings of possibility and figured the likeliest outcomes. She wondered idly what her mother would have thought of Roshannon.

Near twilight she found a small cave and an eroded god stone near a stream. No Sanctum mason had chiseled the austere cross and wheel over the ancient figures. The worn side contained a fruiting tree with a crescent moon floating over it. Carved clearly into the less eroded side of the stone, a man and woman lay locked in embrace.

Keira turned away, remembering his touch.

She knelt over the stream, studying her reflection: pale skin, arched eyebrows, and dark hair with a red gleam. Sea-gray eyes, he had said. She tried to cast the memory of him aside. She evened up the earlier job she had done cutting her hair when she stopped in the middle of the morning. She had cut it more to banish the memory of his touching her hair, but also to aid her disguise. His knife sliced like a razor and the hilt fit easily in her hand. Rocking back on her heels, she dropped additional hanks of hair into the stream.

She weighed the dagger in her hand. Its fine workmanship unnerved her.

She rubbed her thumb along the pattern of engraved beasts, vines, and trees that encircled the ivory hilt, ran her index finger along the unknown inscription carved in the blade. Fumbling in the dark, she had taken something of unexpected beauty. She sheathed it brusquely, telling herself she was being a fool.

She scooped handfuls of sour cress from the stream and watched a water snake, its pattern of green and blue scale as rich as enamelware, slide fluidly downstream. If she trailed her hand in the water long enough, minnows re-formed in groups and darted unconcerned through the arched vaults of her fingers. Keira stood up. Her reflection swirled and broke and re-formed, a tall, straight boy's likeness. She dropped a pebble into the center of the image and turned on her heel.

While she gathered fallen wood and boughs from the woods encircling the meadow to make a bed, the mare rolled in the meadow grass. Keira rubbed her down and tethered her. In the cave mouth, Keira heaped the fragrant boughs into a pallet. She devoured a quarter of the spicy, pilfered sausage, licked the sweet grease from her fingers, and finished the bread.

Her legs and buttocks ached from the dawn-to-dusk ride. She massaged the inside of her thighs, her eyes closed. As part of her punishment for refusing to marry Terrak, her father had forbidden her to ride for the past two weeks, because he knew that exercising the mare was one of her chief pleasures. She had never been so sore from riding before. Munching the raw, tart, mustard-flavored cress, Keira pulled her boots off. She propped herself against a smooth rock that had soaked up sun all day, stretched out her legs, and eased her shoulders back.

A sudden memory of Roshannon came to her, of his shadowed, graceful body with its wide shoulders and narrow waist.

The candlelight had revealed the pale, silvered lines of old scars across his ribs, and a crosshatch of scars on his forearms, each a trace of death faced and turned away, the marks of men fighting with sword and dagger. Strangely, the scars reminded her of the strokes made to practice writing.

He had unfastened her dress and slid it down over her shoulders. He traced the lines of the scars on her back. When he turned her about to face him, she stared into eyes so black she could not make out the pupils. The priests said the seacoast people were devoid of true souls, though they possessed full powers of reasoning, which made them valuable mercenaries in the Sanctum's wars.

He had offered her more wine from his glass. The floor and the walls settled dreamily as the tart liquor slid down her throat.

He stood a little behind her, his fingers curled in her hair. He kissed the nape of her neck, his touch making her feel drunken and disoriented. She feared he was working magic. The line he drew between her breasts and across her belly seemed to lay open her flesh. Her body quickened where his fingers rested.

He would have great power over her, she saw.

When she stared into his black eyes, she feared he could see the reflections of her dreams in her eyes. She did not think she could hide anything from him. He smiled at her, his smile a scythe come to reap her soul.

Their shadows arched up the wall and across the ceiling while the candles flickered. They came together like beasts, wrestling and joined into a greater beast, until she lost track of her own body.

His voice, like his touch, pulled at her in alarming ways. Wife, he called her, and thou, he said to her. Men used the honorific among each other, when old friends met after long separation, or between brothers. No man she had ever known had said *thou* to a woman except in mockery. Maybe his people followed different customs, or he had acquired strange habits in the foreign wars. Curious man; he had even asked her what time of the moon she bled.

Keira shifted position against the rock. She closed her eyes and rolled her shoulders against the stone. The pepper-and-mustard taste of the cress lingered in her mouth. She drew her cloak around her, unsheathed the knife, and stared at the ornate hilt.

In the dying light, she peered intently at its scene of a hunting cat stalking a deer, with wolves, rabbits, wild swine, and hawks living among the forest in a strange peace.

An artisan had rendered each minute hoof, paw, and antler exquisitely—surely someone who had taken great pride and joy in his craft. Labor is prayer in the service of god, said the Sanctum priests. But they insisted that work result in plain, somber, unornamented objects. To what kind of god would the man who carved this make offering?

Did the witches do such work in praise of their northern gods?

Two cold thoughts struck her. One: Roshannon might have killed a witch lord, or any lord, and taken the knife. What soldier would be able to resist such a prize? She pictured him stripping a body, searching for booty. Two: The dagger was a lordly thing so rich that even the merchant who had bid for her would not dare carry its like until he had bought himself a lord's earring. And though she preferred to think Roshannon was just a soldier who had grabbed battlefield trophies, her sudden misgivings told her he could be the knife's true owner, a ka'innen lord himself, with clear right to land and a house earring. He had not told the priest, her father, or her anything about himself. The ka'innen were the overlords who held sway over vast tracts of the countryside, who raised their own armies and ruled the city-states, and caused most of the world's troubles due to their greed and arrogance and intrigues. Few of their kind had ever ventured near Kerlew, but relayed their whims and demands through their vassal lords, who also served as their tax collectors.

Keira remembered Deva's words. "He gave the master four pearls for you."

An acid taste filled her mouth. She turned the fine dagger over again in her hands, trying to recall if Roshannon's ear had been pierced. She had not noticed, and cursed herself. When a Sanctum lord bought something, it remained his, the lordly honor bound up in its possession. Keira had watched a lord ride down an escaped slave woman on the track between her father's and Terrak's fields during harvest two years ago. The woman had been among the wandering gleaners Keira's father let into his field. Keira had offered the sweated but jovial gleaners water, and asked where they hailed from, when the sound of hoofbeats came up the track. Two riders on fine bays approached—an overlord and his young son.

The gleaners prostrated themselves among the stubble of the field. The one who drank last let the ladle drop into Keira's bucket and fell to her knees, forehead to the ground. As a free-holder's daughter, Keira stood by the bucket, her head merely bowed. Lordly goings-on interested her, but usually meant bad fortune for someone.

"Whose fields are these?" the lord demanded, dismounting and handing the reins to the boy who rode beside him.

"Ka. My father's, sita Evin Danio," Keira said. As she bowed, she noticed an empty sack slung over the boy's saddle bow.

"I would examine the gleaners in your father's field."

"Ka," Keira said, lowering her head another degree.

The lord went from prostrate woman to prostrate woman, jerking each one's head up by the hair and peering into each face. He had started farthest from Keira, who noticed as he progressed along the line that the gleaner who had drunk last was clenching and unclenching her fists.

He came to this woman, pulled her head up. She leaped up, jerked aside, and raced down the track. The lord leaped into his saddle and rode her down. As he came even with her he drew his sword. It flashed once. The woman's head flew into a patch of un-harvested barley, her body toppled like a broken doll.

A few minutes later, the lord rode back, the body slung across his saddle bow, the head held fastidiously by its long dark hair away from his boots. Blood spattered his saddle, leggings, and horse.

The boy, who looked about ten, handed him the bag. The lord cleaned his sword on it, dropped the head inside, and tied it to his saddle horn.

"I have sullied your father's barley and offer recompense," he said. Blood flecked his face and gloves. He dropped three silver tors into Keira's hand, nodded to her, and rode away.

Keira's fingers uncurled as she remembered the scene. The knife slid in her hand and its bright, sharp blade sliced her thumb. Sucking the blood, she stared into the gathering dark.

She turned the dagger in her hands again. If Roshannon was ka'innen, he would follow her and find her.

Roshannon propped himself against a tree stump, his legs stretched out before him. He was tired and sore—and several times he had spotted scouts and army supply trains gathering provisions. At last he stopped for the night, reconnoitering his campsite out of habit, shooting a hare with the blowgun and spitting it over a tiny fire pit. He felt angry and half-disgusted with himself for chasing after her like some besotted stripling.

Damn her, he had encountered a dozen branching highways and market trails today. Catching her seemed less and less possible, unless he knew which way she had gone. No one he asked had seen a gray mare, and folk increasingly looked as likely to rob him or curse him as speak to him.

Waves of heat shimmered above his tiny campfire. His eyes slid half-closed as he touched the strand of hair twisted about his wrist and turned the wooden ring on his little finger. Grease gleamed on the body of the roasting hare. The smell of cooking meat made his mouth water.

He stroked the wooden ring and the strand of hair, thinking about another way to search for her. His mind slid into the strange place beyond all his senses, the place from which he could read the emotions of those around him and an enemy's position or intent—and possibly touch this woman he had bought.

He had found the place while a boy. He had always been a lucky child, and he had a gift he learned others did not share, not even his cousin Ni'An. On the islands, clan hunters tracked beasts by droppings, by prints, by claw marks and tiny broken branches that marked their passage. He learned these signs, but found that he could track by other means, too.

Once during a deer hunt he had become separated from the others. He chased a hawk that suddenly disappeared. But as he pushed through the undergrowth, rising panic filled him. His heart drummed in his ears. He ran blindly, no longer sure what terrified him, until his breath caught in his throat and his ribs ached. At last he stumbled into a thicket and came face-to-face with a winded doe, great with young. Staring into the beast's wide eyes, he understood. The terror was the doe's. As the wail of the hunting horns crept back into his consciousness, he tasted her sharp, animal fear.

The doe wheeled and leaped into the undergrowth. He staggered toward the huntsmen's horns, called out and sent them sweeping away in the wrong direction. The eerie, shared fear still filled him, and when Ni'An found him, he fumbled for speech like a madman.

"You've seen the old man of the woods," the hunters joked among themselves. Roshannon only knew that he could not let them kill that doe, sensing that it would be a sort of death for himself as well. Afterward, though he had no great love for the sport, he learned to separate himself from any beast he hunted, building a wall between himself and the other creature at the final moment, so he could kill quickly and cleanly.

It had been worse with the first man he killed.

He shuddered, recalling it. But the odd sense had let him kill before he would have been killed. He learned to trust it. As a soldier, his "luck" helped him avoid ambush and mishap so well that the men he commanded called him Lucky Nikka. But he was unsure whether the sense could be used in other, gentler ways.

Closing his eyes, he imagined her: the pockmark in the middle of her forehead like a Bala Kothi rank mark; her quietness; her quality of utter aloneness. He waited.

Just as he was ready to abandon the idea, an abrupt surge of pain and desperation washed over him, heavy as waves rushing in. His left thumb throbbed and stung and he tasted blood in his mouth. His eyes burned, as if filled with unshed tears. He blinked, examining his left hand for a possible insect bite. His lips tasted faintly of blood, but when he brushed his fingertips across them, nothing was there.

Something popped. But it was only a resinous twig that cracked, a drop of grease from the spitted hare that sizzled in the flames. He rubbed his hands together, feeling foolish.

Damn the girl, by the thousand unspoken names of the Wheel.

❀ 3 ❀

She stepped backward. Her palm brushed the wood of the door frame behind her. Her father lunged at her, his hands hooked like claws. She staggered through the doorway. The motion knocked her head covering askew. Frantic, she batted it aside.

He grabbed her wrist, her hair, and yanked her around to face him. The sour smell of rakka washed over her.

"Bitch." His face pressed close to hers. His fingers twisted in her hair. "You disobey me, do you? You refuse Terrak?"

A hank of hair ripped loose. Her scalp burned. He slammed her against the wall and shoved her chin back with his free hand. "You dare disobey?"

"I will not marry him." She steadied herself and waited for another blow. She tasted blood on her tongue.

"Why must you look like her?" he whispered. "Why?"

Her father's broad face narrowed; his chin lengthened. The bloodshot eyes became pale and rheumy. She watched the priest's thin lips move and heard the dull thud of her head striking wood. The impact jarred her teeth.

"Why, women have no souls," the priest said. He leered in her face. His blunt fingers, clad in icy, silver holy rings, traced the lines of her face and neck. Her skin crawled.

The mocking face twisted. The gray stubble on the long jaw and upper lip disappeared. The hair grew long and dark, and a ragged scar shone along the right jawline. It was Roshannon, but the black eyes stared coldly, the mouth twisted. Like talons, the long fingers dug into her shoulders.

Keira screamed.

Drenched in cold sweat, she sat bolt upright, staring into the darkness. The sharp, fresh smell of broken tree boughs rose around her, and crickets hummed in chorus. The mare snorted.

Beyond the rock overhang, stars winked in the sky. The waning old moon rode high in the east.

She twisted on her makeshift bed. Damp tendrils of hair stuck to her neck and forehead.

Keira got up and splashed water on her face at the stream. Cross-legged on her pallet again, she stared at the trees as they reached shadow hands over the grass.

She drew her cloak tighter about her and lay down, breathing in the calming smell of the saddle as she pressed her cheek against it. She touched the sheathed dagger tucked under the saddle skirts and closed her eyes.

The sound of sheep bleating startled her awake. She propped herself up and frowned at the meadow and the fringe of trees showing through the cave mouth. Two lambs and a black-faced ewe were cropping the grass, though no shepherd was visible. The god stone rose like an ivory egg from the tall grass by the stream. She crawled from her pallet and pulled on her pants and boots, trying to make no noise. Her legs and buttocks ached and her teeth chattered.

The mare snorted. Keira tucked the sheathed dagger through her waistband, crept to the end of the rock, and peered around it.

The mare was backing away from a ram that advanced with head held high. A half-dozen ewes grazed placidly in the meadow, the most distant ones hard to see against the mist that obscured the bordering trees.

Keira dearly wanted to laugh at the confrontation between the ram and the mare, who was prancing backward with flattened ears. But she stepped away from the rock shelter as she pulled on the hat, scanning the meadow for a shepherd. She spotted no one, lifted the saddle, and set it atop the god stone.

The mare nuzzled her shoulders as Keira stooped to drink and fill the water bags. "Want to run, girl?" Keira said as she saddled the mare. She mounted stiffly, gritting her teeth at the ache in her buttocks.

Sunlight poured through the trees and caught on spiderwebs strung in the grass. At the woods she turned to look back at the rock shelter. She wished for spice tea, steaming hot so she could warm her hands on the bowl and sip slowly. Leaning from the saddle she plucked a sweet-thorn twig, stripped off the bark and red-tipped barbs, and popped it into her mouth, chewing vigorously to clean her teeth. The fresh, pungent taste filled her mouth. She threw the twig into the woods and jiggled the reins.

"West today," she whispered into the mare's neck.

On the plains about one hundred miles from the westernmost edge of the Blue Forest lay the great moving city that was the largest wing of the southern army. The army had been swept into being from the rich farmlands and vineyards of Ke Leithe northward, drawing recruits and camp followers from the wheatlands and hard-pressed freehold towns until it had swollen into a small nation unto itself. Distrust or hatred of the northerners, desire to see other lands, and a greed for loot glued it together; and the priests' railing against the heresies and witchcraft and riches of the northerners whipped it on. It was a great besom, raking men and resources to itself, leaving the land through which it marched scoured clean of any surpluses to see its folk through the last pinching weeks of spring.

As with all cities, it had clearly marked capitols—red banners on tall poles marked its captains' tents. A great white banner with a black wheel stitched on it flew from a pole before the archpriest's tent, marking the army's spiritual heart.

Just after dawn all was quiet about the archpriest's command post, his entourage deferring to his preference to begin the day with meditation.

But a bustle erupted about the tent of a Bala Kothi captain and a foot messenger raced to the white tent.

The messenger gave his news to the old manservant who waited, silent and attentive, outside. The camp cooks had begun to prepare breakfast, and the old man sniffed appreciatively and licked his lips at the smells.

He ducked inside the tent and stood listening at the curtain that walled off his master's meditation retreat. The archpriest was chanting prayers in a low, steady monotone. The old man slid a finger to the slit that allowed him to see inside before entering silently.

The archpriest was a tall, lean man, marked by the path of holiness and asceticism, and young for the office he held. But he held it because he was a zealot, a ruthless, merciless man guided by visions; so said the camp tongues that wagged. The youngest of the eight archpriests, he had been chosen by his much older brother priests to lead the army—because he was the only one spry enough to sit on a horse without falling off, the most irreverent camp followers whispered. Clad in a priest's red cloak, with his hair loose down his back, he knelt before a low altar, above which hung the simple black-figured banner.

The old man coughed to announce his presence, although he knew the news would be welcome enough to divert his master from any momentary anger at having his contemplation interrupted.

The archpriest turned, touching his fingertips to his forehead in obeisance to the Wheel. "Well?"

"Ka." The old servant bowed. "Harda's men brought in a witch."

"A witch?" Archpriest Lyrian Sena's eyes narrowed as he rose.

"Captured last night at the edge of the Blue Forest, being held in Harda's tent."

The archpriest considered a moment, buckled on his sword, and strode from his tent, calling to the grooms for his horse.

They had brought him other reputed witches, brought him news of executions for witchcraft; he had run after those rumors and tales like a dog going after a piece of easy meat, trying to find a true witch as the old books described them—one whose spirit floated free of the body. The supposed witches disappointed him. They were babbling peasants, poor freeholders, or hysterical women without a trace of the hellfire in them. He saw no final visions in their eyes, only the dumb blankness with which they faced their deaths. And the three hanged at Clawton Crossroads had been crawling with maggots by the time he arrived to inspect them.

This prisoner had better be a true witch, holding hellfire like a cup, or General Harda himself would get twenty lashes across his broad Bala Kothi back.

Sena's seven brother archpriests had told him to take care, digging and stirring in matters long at rest between north and south. He thought of them fondly but somewhat disdainfully as seven old, holy men, well meaning and devout but too feeble to confront the dark powers of witchery.

His mentor Ogan, the second eldest of the archpriests, had cautioned him, "Fighting witchery is like fighting an enemy whose face you will never see. Its spirit, its strange power, runs in the veins of both north and south. The Schism only called a truce between our two peoples, divided the land, turned us away from its power, let them embrace it. Your ambition will break that truce and change the world that we have known for generations. Think long about your course, for it is not the easy road."

"The easy road is not the one I travel," he had told the old man.

It had been Ogan who told him the priests' secret, the sacrament of the wine and rakka, that the priests controlled the vineyards and the production of wine and rakka, monopolizing its trade and guaranteeing its use as part of the sacrament—because the rakka, drunk regularly, blocked the tendency toward dreams and witchery. He now rarely consumed his ration of wine, waiting for a mysterious blossoming of himself, hoping that his own increased awareness would let him spot witchery in others.

Lyrian was excited as he reached Harda's tent. He dismounted and flung the reins to a boy.

He always hoped.

Inside the tent, the captured northlander stood between two of Harda's sergeants. It must cost him to remain standing so defiantly straight between his enemies, the archpriest reflected. A gash on the man's forehead was bleeding, a blood-soaked rag bound his left forearm, and someone had broken his nose, so a thin, red trickle had dribbled across his mouth, which he kept resolutely shut. Blood matted the left side of his silver hair, but his yellow wolf eyes looked straight at the archpriest.

Harda touched his forehead. The archpriest nodded, acknowledging the half-breed general. Harda's sergeants prodded the witch into a sitting position and settled on either side of him.

"Ka, you may go now," the archpriest told Harda.

Harda shook his head. "This prisoner is too interesting to me." He stroked his fingers over his stiff black beard that glittered with interwoven gold threads. With an almost absent gesture he sent away the woman who had been lingering in the corner of the tent, his whore that camp rumor said was a former temple woman. She dipped her head and left, turning once to look back at the witch.

The archpriest sat cross-legged, meeting the captured man's yellow beast eyes with a calm that was mostly careful façade.

Perhaps the knowledge that his life would end soon gave the

prisoner a strange peace and made him sit straighter, Lyrian thought.

He leaned closer. Being so near the captive man was like being pushed too close to fire. The man burned like a candle. An almost painful warmth bathed Lyrian. He imagined his skin withering and drying, charring in the blast of the mystery that they held between them. Hellfire, the archpriest thought, this thing the true witches carry, that I can feel, almost smell. He thrust his hands into his sash, afraid the others would see them shaking.

The captured man watched the archpriest's eyes. Something like fear and curiosity combined crossed his face.

"His name?" the priest asked.

"He would not give it to us," Harda said.

"We'll see what he will not tell us soon enough." The archpriest gestured to one sergeant. "Lay a fire."

They staked the witch out on the ground behind the captains' tents and began a long session of soft questions and threats, while a few picked soldiers leisurely heated knives and rods in the fire.

The archpriest sat beside the witch, coaxing and cajoling, talking theology as to a boyhood friend. The spirit is holy, the body dross, he said. Both are holy, the witch insisted. How can you say that flesh is holy? the archpriest asked.

A red-hot knife blade laid across the prisoner's bare chest made him no more tractable.

Lyrian wrinkled his nose at the smell of the man's scorched flesh. He opened his robe, baring his own chest, and the sergeant obliged by laying a hot knife to his bare skin. The archpriest ground his teeth together, becoming one with the wave of pain, until he achieved the peculiar ecstatic clarity he sought above all things, the separation of flesh and spirit. The archpriest touched the soldier's hand, and the man removed the knife without meeting his eyes.

Lyrian looked down at his enemy. "You see how fair I am; what is done to you is also done to me." A lie, of course. Only the very beginning of the torture was shared. Lyrian smiled as the prisoner's eyes widened. When they thought him mad, their fear increased.

He paced back and forth, sucking in his breath as a draft of cool air hit the new burns across his chest. He gestured the sergeant to continue with the witch. As the prisoner stopped screaming, the priest motioned the soldiers away and knelt by the witch, watching the yellow eyes.

"We both bear pain well, friend. But I feel the other in you," he whispered. "You know that. Tell me the name of the demon who possesses you, and how it uses your eyes and your body, and I may yet save your soul. For how can your soul be your own, when another feeds on it? I feel things these others cannot, for we are alike, you and I, brothers under the skin. I feel the fire of the other burning in you, as it burns in me."

The witch smiled, his yellow eyes wary, his lips wet with blood where he had bitten them.

"Why do you torment your brother?" he asked hoarsely, so low Lyrian was sure no one else heard. The witch spit in the archpriest's eye.

Later, Harda's soldiers pressed heated rods to the soles of the witch's feet. Their master did not share this treatment, for fear the sergeants, who lamentably lacked artistry in their craft, would do him irreparable damage. But torture him as they might, the witch said nothing and seemed to escape them. At last the yellow eyes stared unseeing, and the wondrous heat the archpriest had felt began ebbing from the northlander's lean body. The archpriest suddenly feared the man was already dead, his essence gone to join the demon spirit that had possessed him and sustained him, leaving a fleshly husk behind as a mockery. But a faint breath still issued from the captured man's nostrils.

Frustrated, Lyrian ordered the man cut loose, bundled in blankets, and carried to a tent near his own. Next morning he woke from another dream of witches—witch eyes, yellow wolf eyes, green summer eyes, like jewels, mocking, holding their secrets and closing at last in death—and stared at the pale roof and walls of the tent. A light wind drummed the taut woolen cloth, making a haunting sound like whispers too faint to understand.

He rushed to check the prisoner. It was a chilly morning, the sun not yet risen, the pale blue sky already filled with pink-tinged clouds. The soldiers who had guarded the witch were stamping their feet, chaffing their hands and staring at the sky. One knelt before the bundled figure of the witch, holding a burnished bronze mirror to the pale lips.

As Lyrian approached, he felt them all stiffen with fear or apprehension, these lesser men who did not share the strange, vital link he had felt with the witch, these lesser creatures who were not visited by visions of the future and other matters beyond their ken.

Impatiently, the archpriest knelt beside the soldier, wondering if the man had borrowed the mirror from one of the camp followers.

No breath clouded the smooth, polished bronze. The soldier wiped the mirror on his tunic, ready to test again. A crumb of journey bread clung to the corner of his mouth, and his face was dark with stubble.

Lyrian shook his head as he pulled up the witch's eyelids and stared into the dead yellow eyes. He touched the man's cheek, his fingers feeling for a pulse in the warmth of the neck. But the man's skin was so cool that he himself flinched at the contact.

The soldier with the mirror rocked back on his heels, his face full of horror and puzzlement. "Ka, the tricky bastard just died on us." He made a hasty obeisance in Lyrian's direction.

"How did this happen?" the archpriest asked.

"I don't understand it." The man looked ashamed and afraid.

Yet he fears not me, but the mystery of the witch's death, Lyrian thought, deciding suddenly that he would not have the soldier punished. The marvel of the witch's oddly easeful death would remain with the troops and make them hate the northerners even more. Such hatred was always useful. *Witches do not even die as we do,* the men would whisper among themselves.

"What happened, my son?" he asked.

The soldier stared blankly at the witch's body and eyed his companions to see if they were far enough away not to overhear his words.

"Ka, this man was alive, because I sat here with a lantern and in the light saw his eyes move. And he watched me as I paced back and forth. His eyes were moving when the sky lightened and I talked to him. He made no answer, but his eyes moved. He was alive. Besides, we did not beat him badly and the wound in his arm was bound up." His voice grew softer still. "No normal man would die like that."

Lyrian nodded, staring at the dead man's tranquil face. "They are not men like us. Remember that." A thought occurred to him. "Did you touch him?"

"He was cool, like he was last night, but not as cold as now. I kept the fire going all night."

Lyrian waved the soldiers away. "See you find me another witch or you will taste my anger. And next time do not fail to call me if there are changes you do not understand."

He knelt by the body, staring a long moment into the dead yellow eyes. His fingers curled—he wanted to slap the dead man's face, but didn't dare show such frayed control before troops.

The next one will not escape me so easily, he promised himself. He would send to the Sanctum fatherhouse for one of the more subtle examiners who probed the brotherhood for heresy.

"Take the body," he told a young captain. "Give it to the foot soldiers and camp followers."

An hour later the witch's body still lay in a little meadow beyond the captains' tents, untouched. The archpriest mounted and rode around the camp's perimeter, watching and waiting. Had the witch's mysterious death made even the soldiers' whores afraid to touch his silver hair, his strange, womanly face?

The archpriest visited Harda, who received the news with maddeningly unruffled calm. The Bala Kothi looked Lyrian in the eye and said in that slow, low voice, "Ka, my soldiers brought thee a witch and he died in thy hands."

"Where did you find him?"

"Outside the Blue Forest, on the plains where his clan was catching horses."

The archpriest glanced at his general, taking in the gold threads braided into the little beard as sharp as a pig snout, the rings gleaming on the broad powerful fingers, so many that the man's hands seemed armored, the jade plugs distending his earlobes, and the red sword belt that rode high over his belly. Behind Harda, his woman lay on a camp couch, only the tip of her nose and the curve of her mouth visible under the head covering. The archpriest had pointedly refused to accept food or drink from the hands of this woman, who was unclean. But he accepted a small bowl of watered, spiced rakka from Harda's manservant and sipped slowly, annoyed that the general showed no tendency to send his whore away.

"Ka," said Harda, "you had a look on your face when you entered my tent yesterday—the look of a man coming to meet his beloved, though I know you have forsworn the entrapments of the flesh. But now you have the look of a man in mourning."

"I hope your scouts can soon bring me another witch, to banish this look on my face."

My disappointment amuses him, Lyrian thought as he rode away from the general's tent.

But Harda would not dare fail to produce another witch. Troops would again sweep to the edges of the Blue Forest, where witchfolk lived alone in homesteads in the woods, unprotected by the walls and ships of Cartheon. In the gentle inland valleys, protected by encircling forests, crops came earlier, the orchards were already bearing fruit, and it was easier for an army to live off the land. And easier, perhaps, to catch witches, he had told his generals. His spies had told him witches had continued living in small, tight-knit communities in the woods and outlying areas, practicing their arts as healers, hunters, and archers, but trading and sharing their mysteries and crafts with their neighbors.

That made all those dwelling near the Blue Forest possible heretics, Sena thought, rubbing his chin. By the rule of the new order, the property of heretics was forfeit to the Sanctum. Of course, declaring all those living at the fringes of the forest heretic would likely turn the entire region into rebels, unless the lords were persuaded—by bribes or threat of annihilation—to betray their own people and administer over suitably devout southern freeholders who would be rewarded the confiscated lands. He had very little to pay his soldiers and faced the constant annoyance of their looting rousing the local populace against the army.

In the meadow below the captains' tents he was pleased to see the witch's stripped body had become a plaything. Someone had chopped off the head, with its peaceful dead smile, and mounted it on a pole. A soldier's whore in blood-spattered skirts hacked off the bright silver hair, laughing and passing handfuls to her sisters.

❀ 4. ❀

Keira woke abruptly, jerking upright in the saddle and drawing in the reins. She heard voices, tangled snatches of words blending into the wind.

For a moment panic froze her to the spot. She felt sick and angry with herself; she had ridden since dawn and fallen asleep in the saddle. She scanned the dusty bushes along the highway and the track beaten smooth with hoofprints. The sound of horses and the jingle of harness came to her clearly on the air. She rode back along the trail and dismounted, leading the mare into the woods on the highway's north side. She went far enough into the woods until she was sure no one could spot her or the mare, then climbed up into a leafed-out tree.

From high in its branches she could see around the bend: a knot of people blocked the road. The wind tossed snatches of their voices her way. Soldiers in dusty leather armor studded with glinting steel bosses paced across the highway, haranguing travelers. A drumroll sounded.

Keira thanked the luck that had woken her just in time, muttered a prayer, and climbed higher.

Archers with strung bows over their shoulders prowled the crowd. People protested as soldiers grabbed a chicken here, a goat there, or dragged bolts of dog woolens from wagons. The merchants she had met were right: the army would plunder whoever crossed its path.

Keira considered the range of the longbows and hoped her mare would not whinny at the smell of other beasts. Sweat trickled down her ribs as she willed her very breathing and the beating of her heart stilled.

Two wealthy landowners among the throng started arguing with the soldiers. They gestured indignantly, and Keira imagined

them protesting that they were on pilgrimage to the holy city
Kum, and so exempt from the army's demands. The bigger one
raised a whip to the soldier who approached his horse. The other
sita drew a purse, held it aloft, then tossed it at the soldier's feet.
The archer scooped up the purse, tucked it in his boot, and motioned the two riders on.

Keira thought of the treasure sewn up in her cloak seams. The
money in her purse was not enough to bribe the soldiers if they
caught her.

She had started climbing down, intending to skirt the army,
when a new figure entered the dumb show. A man wearing a
bloodred cloak strode up, and where he passed along the line, folk
knelt and lowered their heads. Soldiers bowed to him and touched
their foreheads. Keira's stomach tightened. Her initial wave of
panic had passed as she watched the scene before her, but a sudden strange fever surged through her. Her attention riveted on the
red-cloaked man.

The tall, thin newcomer wore a sword whose jeweled hilt
sparkled. Sunlight caught on his lavishly embroidered sash and
the gold wheel brooch at his shoulder.

Keira gasped and steadied herself in the tree. Even at this distance, she knew this man was a presence. His spirit burned,
steady and hot as a candle flame. An archpriest, come to make
war against the witches.

The soldiers made obeisance to him as he drew his cloak
around him. He held out what looked like a letter, lifted what
must be a signet ring from around his neck, and passed it to a
mounted man. The messenger saluted and trotted down the road
while the archpriest turned on his heel. The red-cloaked man's
precise movements and the weight of dismissal in his gestures
fascinated Keira.

Intrigued, she watched his progress. Wherever the red figure
passed, people knelt like grain bowed down by wind. The emotions of soldiers and villagers both—anger, resentment, and awe
mixed with reverence—lapped at her in her hiding place. Keira
imagined them begging him to pray for their crops, their children,
or their land. The heat of the archpriest's presence compelled her
attention. Her eyes fastened on him; he turned and stared straight
at her and the tree that hid her.

Spellbound, she stared through the tree leaves at him. For a moment she was blind and deaf to everything in the world but the flickering allure of the Red Man. She hugged the tree's thick trunk, praying for invisibility. Then the moment passed. The Red Man moved off among the soldiers. She frowned, her head beginning to ache.

Women lining the roadside wailed and keened over stock the soldiers had snatched to feed the army. The soldiers mocked them. On the other side of the highway, men setting up an entrenched encampment dug ditches to the cadence of the drum. A local black-robed magistrate, urged on by the crowd, directed the soldiers to camp in the resting, fallow fields and spare the newly sown ones. Soldiers waved him aside. A vast wagon train formed a rough circle on the flanks of the hill that rose above the road. Men shouted and chanted as they pitched low, black tents. The square towers of an ancient hold rose on the hilltop above them. Mounted men patrolled the zone between camp and highway, driving back locals and soldiers who tried to question each other and exchange news.

Not a half mile down the highway from Keira's tree, cavalrymen drove a single file of women and girls, who had probably been impressed from nearby villages to stuff and sew quilted body armor. Their words drifted up to her as they trooped by.

"Wait until the witches come, and get half-souled brats on you," one soldier told the women. "They will give you reason to moan."

A sudden wind whipped through Keira's tree, swirling bits of bark into the air, tossing branches, and cutting off her view. When the wind died down, the Red Man was nowhere to be seen.

She climbed down and went cautiously on her way.

She skirted the army for two days, fascinated and frightened, yet hoping for another glimpse of the Red Man. The army's position was easily read by marking the vultures that circled overhead like a retinue, waiting patiently for the remains of butchered cattle or the bodies of dead soldiers set out on hasty burial platforms.

On the second day, as she was searching out a campsite, Keira heard a moan, a muffled curse. Then a woman's voice, methodically consigning to the seven rings of hellfire each spoke of the Wheel and every soldier in the Sanctum army.

Particularly one Harrid Yellow Hair.

The rhythm of curses and gasps had a nagging familiarity. Keira crawled nearer and peeked through a bush.

The curser was a girl with her back to a tree, her faded black skirts looped up around her bulging pregnant belly, her head covering folded back across her shoulders.

She stopped cursing and drew a ragged breath, her eyes closed. Sweat shone on her skin, and damp strands of hair clung to her forehead. A cloak lay on the ground beside her and a belt with a sheathed dagger, likely for cutting the cord, hung over her left shoulder.

Keira adjusted her hat and stepped into the clearing. The girl stared.

"By the bloody Wheel, who are you?" She squinted as if the light hurt her eyes, too dazed or too far gone in pain to be afraid.

"A traveler," Keira drew the dagger, gesturing the girl to silence. "When will you drop your brat?"

"Soon, I hope." The girl's eyes focused on Roshannon's dagger. Her mouth moved methodically as she chewed something.

Keira watched the girl's face, feeling the ornate dagger and her high-handed words working, convincing the girl to see her as a lord who might end her miserable life on a whim if she did not cooperate. It suited Keira's goal, yet impersonating an overlord sickened her. If she were caught at it she had no doubt she would be killed. She hoped all the soldiers were proper Sanctum men who disdained birthing as women's business and avoided it.

"Were there no women to attend you in the camp?" Keira asked.

The girl laughed. "They wouldn't, 'cause he told them not to. My soldier cast me off weeks ago, tired of my belly. I ought to strangle his brat, eh?" The girl shifted whatever she was chewing to the other side of her mouth. Her words blurred like the speech of a lack-wit or someone who had drunk too much rakka. She closed her mouth and assessed Keira from hat brim to boot toes.

She giggled suddenly. "Ka, are you going to attend me?" She grinned. "Attended by a young lord, what an honor. You need one to warm your bed?"

"Warming someone's bed brought you to this pass. Are you so ready to warm another?" Keira forced disdain into her voice, hoping a soldier might chide a camp follower so.

She slid Roshannon's dagger to the girl's throat and clapped a hand across her mouth. "Shut your mouth, woman, and answer my questions." She took the girl's dagger and tucked it in her sash.

The girl's eyes widened in real fear. A moment later she gritted her teeth as contractions wracked her body.

About fifteen, Keira thought. Pockmarks pitted the skin of her cheeks and jaw. Spittle, colored green by the plug of whatever she was chewing, trickled from the corner of her mouth as she grimaced. Something to ease the pain, Keira wondered, as the smell of sour sweat made her wrinkle her nose. She sniffed again, for whatever the girl was chewing had a strangely familiar scent. The girl wore no ear tag or ornaments, only a curious hank of braided silver hair on a thong about her neck.

The girl groaned. "He took up with another when my belly got too big. Wait until her time comes—I'll chase her out of camp to have her brat alone." She stiffened with pain and another string of greenish saliva oozed from her mouth.

Keira looked down. Blood was trickling down the whore's bare legs.

The girl shifted her body heavily, eyeing Keira's dagger. "Ka, help me. Don't leave me alone. This one's my first."

"Tell me about the army."

The girl smiled slowly. "A trade for a trade. I'm a whore, I want something, too—more candlewood leaves."

Keira picked leaves from a nearby bush, never leaving the girl out of her sight. In between hearing curses heaped on many Sanctum soldiers, she got the story of the girl Otella's life—a hard winter and a harder spring, then bad harvests in the lands west of Kerlew, had ravaged her family's freehold farm, leaving her parents, brothers, and sisters near starvation. Her father had not even the meager dowry to sell her to the temple. So when the soldiers came through, she tagged along with the rabble of cooks, merchants, and camp followers who doubled the army's size.

After giving the girl another wad of candlewood leaves, it was easy to keep her talking about where the Sanctum army had been and where it was headed. The leaves seemed to quicken the tongue as rakka sometimes could. Keira made a mental note to gather candlewood for her saddlebags.

Otella began to push, and clutched the curious hank of braided silver hair hung about her neck.

"What is that?" Keira asked.

"My lucky piece." Otella gasped. "Witch hair. I got one of the best pieces. The other girls got hanks with spots of blood, but I got a nice clean piece from right behind the ear. I elbowed in and sliced it off with my dirk."

"Witch hair?" Keira reached toward the thing, her fingers moving almost by their own will.

The girl's fingers closed on it. "It's my lucky piece, from the witch Harda-ka brought to the archpriest. The men say the archpriest made the witch die just like that—poof, and his blood froze and his eyes were staring glassy. Before they put his head on a pike, we girls got some of his hair."

"Witches," Keira said, hoping she sounded contemptuous, though her heart was pounding. "How did you know it was a witch?"

"The yellow eyes, the white hair. But even without that the archpriest knew."

"How do you think he knew?"

The girl bit her lip and shrugged. She looked dazed but genuinely interested in the problem, and a bit flattered that a young lord with such a fine dagger would ask her opinion.

"Archpriest's a strange one. The girl who waits on Harda's woman told me stories." She glanced around. "When he gets prisoners and tortures them, see, he sometimes has his captains torture him at the same time. Pain sets him off, see. Just between you and me, I don't think he's ever been with a woman. And I wouldn't want to be the woman sent to his tent, neither." Her mouth twisted. "I saw the witch's body, the burns across his chest and feet, the blistered skin. They say the Red Man has the very same marks on his own body."

"The humiliation of the flesh strengthens the spirit," Keira said slowly.

"What a bunch of rot," the girl said between her teeth, and her waters broke.

Keira built a lean-to against the tree to shelter the girl. Waiting for Otella's baby to be born, she slipped into a half trance of memories about her mother's last childbed and the small square bedroom where her parents slept, which had become a woman's realm.

The smell of the candlewood leaves reminded her of a drink Deva had given her mother. Her mother downed it quickly, then immediately washed the bowl.

Mistress Treya and Mistress Rennet had arrived after Keira served her father's supper. Her mother paced, arm in arm with Deva. The tightened line of her mouth showed the rhythm of contractions, of pain and work. Her mother cried out, stooped over her great belly.

Mistress Treya nodded to Keira.

Keira began the undoing. She unlatched the window shutters. The sweet smell of cut hay flowed into the room, mingling with the tea steam. The sun had set; one star burned on the western horizon. It had been a scorching summer day.

She threw off her head covering and unbraided her hair. She undid every fastening of her dress, opened every chest, every drawer, every door of every cupboard, searched the room for knots to untie, and pushed the shutters open wider to ease her mother's labor. She held the door ajar and thrust a stone between it and the frame so no breeze would slam it shut and cause a locking of the womb. She undid the other women's hair, removed their head coverings, and loosened their clothes.

Hours later, Keira fetched tea and candles, careful not to look toward the downstairs room where her father waited to hear the news. A priest was chanting in the room, a constant, eerie, droning sound. Earlier he had checked to see that no woman had given her mother a potion to ease pain, so she would bear the pain a woman in labor was meant to bear.

The old women said childbirthing tea should always be bitter, but they gossiped while they sipped the bitter brew, safe from the disapproval of the priest. Safe to catch up on gossip. Safe to speculate about who would marry whom and who would prove a good husband or a nasty one, who would beat a wife or not. And if they heard the priest's robes brushing up the stairs, they would use the silent sign language to guard their privacy. Keira fanned her mother with a woven straw fan. Beneath the loose open robe, her mother's brown skin glistened with sweat. She held out her arm for her mother to clench, wishing she could share some of the pain.

Ah, the women whispered with each breath her mother drew.

Ah, they chorused each time she cried in pain, as if they were all breathing in the pain and letting it out of her body, as if all their bodies and spirits drew breath together and cried out together. The room was awash in smells of sweat and hot candle drippings, sweet hay and night air. At last Deva helped her mother to the birthing stool. The two older women, who between them had borne twenty children, stooped and offered their arms for clenching and support.

No men came near the birthing room, only the priest at the last, to trace wheels on the infant's feet whether it was dead or alive.

Keira pushed the hair back from her mother's sweated face.

"All day again," Mistress Treya said.

There was no crowning, no head appearing, only tiny, bloody feet. "With the wheel already on them," Mistress Rennet whispered.

Old Mistress Treya hushed her with a frown. She cradled the still child in her hands, bent, and blew in its nose and mouth as if she were crooning a song or cooling tea.

Mistress Rennet made a sign and grabbed the child's foot to draw a wheel on it. "The death is willed. Do not contradict the Will, sister. The body is without a soul, else it would live."

At last old Mistress Treya gave up. "The poor little one."

Exhausted and half-conscious, Keira's mother lay crumpled in bed. Keira sponged her forehead and body, while Deva and Mistress Treya stanched the bleeding.

"I will tell the priest the child is dead." Mistress Rennet moved the stone from before the door and closed it on her way out. Quickly, the women in the room had refastened their dresses, plaited their hair, retied knots, closed up chests and cupboards, so the woman in the bed would heal rapidly.

A year later Mistress Rennet had accused Mistress Treya of deviltry, of trying to call back the souls of stillborn children, and Keira, her own mother dead, had dreamt and later witnessed the hanging. As sita of the district, her father searched the clothes of those condemned, hunting for weights they might have concealed to help their dying. Had he searched Mistress Treya's skirts hastily, as if willing to grant her a final mercy?

Keira shook her head, hoping the memory of her mother would not bring bad luck to Otella and her child. But after pacing and moaning, cursing Harrid Yellow Hair until the stars came out, Otella produced a boy child.

Keira cleaned off the baby, cut the cord with Roshannon's dagger, and tied it off with a pliant candlewood stem Otella produced. Otella reached for the baby, cradling him and holding his feet still as Keira traced two careful wheels on the tiny, crinkled soles.

Otella grinned as she put the baby to her breast. "You are a strange man."

Keira grinned back at her and built a fire to keep beasts away. She watched over Otella until the girl and baby slept and the night was half through. After carefully building up the fire with long-burning ironwood, she slipped away, unwilling to stay longer so close to the army and the Red Man.

Near sunset Keira sat in the dimmest corner of an inn, facing the door and thinking of Otella, whom she had given a string of dried apples and sausage and left in the brush shelter with her baby boy. The bowl of steaming spice tea cradled in her hands somewhat improved her view of the world. Dust sifted out of her hair and tickled her neck. She wiped her sweated neck, pushed hair from her eyes, and devoured the bread, pickled vegetables, and salted meat the maidservant brought.

By the hearth, three quarrelsome neighbors hunched over a table, playing ko. Each accused the other of cheating. They were all cheating, and so full of rakka they would never find it out. Keira kept her eyes on her tea bowl. The clipped rhythm of their speech washed over her. Her eyes slid half-closed as she leaned against the rough timber wall.

A hand touched her shoulder. "Boy, come judge which is cheating," a low voice said.

Keira's eyes were slits. "I'm too tired to be a fit judge of anything." She retreated upstairs. The maid lit the way with a nub of candle, which she left in a tiny cell with a shuttered window. Keira sank down on the narrow bed. The mattress gave off a pleasant scent of pod down, mint, and fleabane. She eased off her boots, tucked the dagger under the lumpy pillow, and lay back with her arms folded under her head.

She floated above forested hills. Her body turned to sun belly first, then buttocks. The treetops touched her bare skin, gentle as feathers. Beneath the green canopy of the trees, Roshannon leaned against a giant beech whose twin trunks had grown into one tree. His face looked tired and grim. He held the strange tube she had seen in his pack. He drew the knife from his boot and tucked it in his sash, his thumb stroking its curved hilt.

Sudden fears assailed her, that if he spied her in the dream, he would somehow find her in reality. But she could not halt her body floating closer to his.

Another figure appeared, a Sanctum bowman in body armor stalking him, an arrow nocked. Moving from tree to tree, the archer tightened the circle about his intended prey.

She floated closer. The woods thickened, the earth snagged her dream body and pulled her down.

She stood in the forest glade. The tree trunks were black as bars against the light-dappled leaves. The archer crouched behind the shelter of a tree. Roshannon tossed a pebble. It struck the tree bark a hand's width from the lean man's shoulder. The bowman jerked in his direction. His shape, blue-black in the filtered light, flitted behind another tree. Roshannon edged around the tree, fitting a dart into the tube.

The archer advanced, his arrow ready. An arrow hissed from his bow, thudded into the beech tree sheltering Roshannon.

A savage joy surged through her as she imagined him dead, unable to follow her, unable to catch her. But Roshannon lifted the strange tube to his lips and huffed. The steel barb shot from the tube struck the archer in his unarmored throat as he turned. He clawed at his neck.

The man's sudden fear poured through the woods, the terror of the hunter realizing he is the hunted. A last ray of light caught on the curve of bent bow and bowstring as the lean man nocked his arrow and edged from behind the tree to fire.

Roshannon sprang forward and threw the knife. The archer staggered, the knife in his throat. His arrow hissed into the treetops. He sank to his knees and toppled sideways.

Roshannon crouched over the archer's body. The man's dead blue eyes stared blindly into the treetops, into her eyes, as she crept closer to peer over her husband's shoulder.

He pressed the dead man's eyes shut with his gloved fingers. He plucked a bloody metal dart from the fallen man's neck, wiped it clean in the leaves, and put it in his belt pouch. He pulled the dagger out and cleaned it before resheathing it in his boot. He hefted the curious wooden tube in his hand and stood up.

He took the bow and quiver of arrows, and found the archer's horse, a young bay gelding, near his own. He searched the saddle-bags, which held food and a carved leather rakka flask, and took the horse as a remount.

And so he saw her as she stood naked in the green twilight woods. His black eyes stared at her dream body. She crossed her arms over herself.

"Thou, woman," the dead man mocked. Roshannon caught her hand and pulled her to him. "Who are you, woman?" he demanded. But before she could answer, he was suddenly strangling her while the dead man laughed.

Keira sat bolt upright in the bed, staring into the darkness. Cursing softly, she told herself she was only frightened because she had dreamt of him. Would he be dead if the archer shot him in my dream? she wondered. Lying back down, she fell asleep again with difficulty. She woke before dawn, washed her face and hands in the horse trough, and mounted up. Her hands on the reins shook as she remembered her dreams.

She rode until the mare was winded, then cursed herself for a fool and drew the reins. She closed her eyes a moment, opened them, and stared at the countryside. It is just the highway I am seeing, she told herself, the ditches overgrown with mullein and wildflowers, a scraggly fringe of trees and fields bordering it. A bee drank from a wildflower, bent the stalk double under its fat, hairy body, then buzzed away, leaving the flower stem vibrating. Her heartbeat quickened and she felt suddenly afraid. The sky was so intensely blue it hurt her eyes. A veil seemed to drop from her eyes; she saw with the sharpness of a dream.

She blinked, feeling slightly dizzy and nauseated.

She shifted in the saddle, recalling the curious tube she had seen in Roshannon's pack, and in her dream. She felt its smooth polished wood against her fingertips, the balance of it in her hands, a ghost of sensation. She ground her teeth, wanting to scream.

She shut her eyes tight. A wash of images, faces, trees and shadows, passed behind her eyelids. It was not pain, but a constant thing that rode with her now. Something in her was changing. Not like the twitch of pain or the dull, draining ache that came when she bled. She groped in her mind for what it could be. She felt as she did when she woke with her dream eyes full, unable to focus on what was really in the room.

She bit her lip, imagining his hands on her skin, doing all the things he had done to her. No profit, no good will come of thinking about him, she reproved herself, and flicked the reins. Her skin flushed as she remembered Otella, whom she had left nursing a red, wrinkled boy child with a fine set of lungs. She wondered if she herself would bleed again when the moon was full. "My body feels different when I am carrying," her mother had once confided. "My hearing is sharper and my fancies strong and wild."

Keira flicked the reins and leaned into the mare's neck.

Either I am going mad or he has got me with child, she thought.

Sharp-eyed ravens and vultures circled the field death had visited, skimming closer on their black wings, and at last settling among the feast of dead men and horses left in a grassland near the Blue Forest.

As Xian Tanta regained consciousness, he first imagined he was dreaming in a hard bed beneath a mountain of covers, struggling to wake. He was sprawled on his back, imprisoned by cold, dead weights atop him.

Tanta soon suspected he was in the strange territory on the other side of life. The air reeked. The death smell filled his nostrils but his stomach did not revolt. Was this a ghost's awareness? Or had he been buried in the earth in southern style?

He shifted, clawing at the heavy darkness above. Weight slid across his shoulders and legs, and he realized dead bodies were pressing him down.

Panicked, he flailed his way through the tangle of corpses, the sick-sweet stench gagging him. He screamed, a hoarse, strangled sound, then shut his mouth as he realized where he was. Unseen, unheard, hidden beneath his dead companions, he had escaped death the first time, on the battlefield where they had all been killed.

He collapsed in the nest of dead men, letting the earth reclaim him for a while. He listened, trying not to inhale. No footfalls, no voices, no rhythm of hooves, which he should be able to sense through the ground.

The wind moaned across the hill, and there was a vague sound that he had to think a moment to identify, wings flapping and being folded, small sounds of birds or other creatures, no sounds of men. And a low, droning buzz.

He waited, his nostrils pinched closed. Memories came back to him: a last conversation with the stowaway Polla in the wagon train, the ambush, the enemy plentiful as stalks of grain in a field; the terrible song of steel on steel, the cries of men; his brother Connal's gurgling scream as a blade cut through his throat; then the thunder splitting Xian's own head, the steel biting his side, the roaring of the earth pulling him to his knees, claiming him, enfolding him.

He had scolded Hipolla to flee into the woods when they spotted the Sanctum force and, when she refused to flee, ordered her to stay with the other women because the Sanctum soldiers surely would not kill the women, too, but take them captive if they killed the men.

The clan had ventured into the rich pastures that fringed the Blue Forest to catch wild ponies, feeling safe because they had long traded with the nearby villages. They had gone lightly armed, twenty men, with the women and children traveling in three wagons. The clan had not realized they were being hunted until the hunters were on them: a group of villagers had hailed them as they were crossing grassland. As some of the clansmen rode closer, men on tall southern horses, in the long, drab capes the villagers wore, threw the disguises aside at the last moment to reveal Sanctum armor beneath. A troop of men followed. Sanctum men had never come this far northeast; Tanta knew they must have sheltered in the village until the clan rode close enough to attack. The villagers had betrayed them.

The wagons were our death warrant, Tanta realized, for they moved slowly, drawn by draft horses. But the pony archers rode between the wagons of women and children and the Sanctum men. They had frantically whipped the wagons toward the sheltering woods a few miles away, urging some of the women and children onto the half-tamed ponies caught from the herds. The archers held off the Sanctum men with their meager store of game-hunting arrows, killing perhaps a dozen of them. But their enemy was better armed and trapped them before they reached the woods. Some eighty soldiers shot the archers' ponies out from under them. From behind the shelter of their ponies' bodies, the archers made their last stand as rain began to fall. They had fired their enemies' arrows back at the soldiers when they could, but at last, their arrows gone, took out their dirks and short swords as the Sanctum men overran them.

A raucous croak sounded, dragging his consciousness back to the business of life. Wings beat the air. A creature hissed and growled.

He struggled, turning to face that sound, and discovered the source of the humming sound. Thousands of flies swarmed over the nest of bodies, forming a living, eerie black skin. He dragged himself clear of the heap of dead bodies, blinking until his eyes adjusted to the light. Three paces away, a raven perched on a dead man's chest, facing off a lean gray hunting cat.

The raven settled its wings and cocked its head.

The dead man's arm looked familiar. Its leather armband, carved with a pattern of interlacing trees, made Tanta choke. Connal's armband.

The raven pecked at the dead man's eyes.

Tanta roared. The hunting cat leaped; the raven flapped away. A cloud of disturbed flies buzzed into the air. He blacked out.

He regained consciousness with the heat of a warm, steady breath on his face. The young hunting cat that he had barely started training stared at him with intent green eyes.

"Cat." He held a hand out, wondering if it remembered him, or had feasted on the dead. Hunting cats would usually not do that. The young beast licked a line of sweat in the crease of his palm, then settled nearby, tucking its front paws beneath its body, blinking inscrutably at him.

Tanta propped himself on a shaky elbow, scanning the battlefield. Here and there armor and weapons glinted among the fallen bodies of men and ponies. Many corpses had been trampled into the mud, which had dried now around them like weird pyre wrappings. How long had he lain on the battlefield? Even with a fierce sun, that churning mud would have taken hours to dry. He pulled himself into a sitting position, feeling for the dagger sheathed at his side. His sword belt and sheath were gone. His right side was a festering wound. He pulled the slashed material of his tunic away, trying to see how bad the damage was. Flesh came off with the blood-stiffened material. He retched. Gingerly, with his fingertips, he felt the heat spreading from the wound, which had begun to bleed again.

I am a dead man, he thought.

He staggered upright, squinting at the sun halfway down the western sky. A wave of dizziness and nausea brought him back to his knees.

He crawled back to his brother Connal's body, where he put two stones over the eyes and folded the stiffened hands over the chest.

He crawled among the fallen, scaring away crows. Vultures who had come to feast paid him no mind. The enemy had left some weapons and gear, but burned the three wagons, and left the bodies for the carrion eaters. But he felt uneasy that he could not find the bodies of Amer and Mett, the horse trainers. They had either survived or been captured.

He ran his fingers through his hair, feeling a sticky clotted mess on the back of his head. He said a veda to distract himself from his thunderous headache, and probed his head wound with cautious fingertips, deciding to wait until he could wash the dried blood free of his hair.

He dragged a sword from beneath a dead man's body. He found a bow, some scattered arrows and a quiver, taking from the dead what they would no longer need. He found a stoppered leather water bottle and a rakka bottle. He sniffed the rakka, poured a good dose over the wound in his side, dribbled some over his head wound, stoppered the bottle, and slung it over his shoulder.

Grimacing as the rakka stung his wounds, he moved among the fallen, staggering to the charred wagons, searching for a sign of Connal's daughter Hipolla. She was not among the dead. He cursed savagely at the crows and ravens perched on the corpses, cursed himself that he had not fallen among his house comrades, cursed himself for his softheartedness in letting Polla stay with them once he had discovered her.

If they were overwhelmed, he had warned her, the Sanctum soldiers would spare no fighters, but might spare the women in the wagon train. He had insisted she wear women's clothes in exchange for persuading Connal not to send her home once they found she had sneaked along with them. By the Wheel, he hoped she had escaped.

For a moment, he wished he were dead. *Fool, you soon will be.*

He did not want to die in the open meadow among the others. He crawled downslope toward the cool green shadows of the wood.

❀ 5 ❀

The beat of a wooden clapper rang on the air: clackety, clack, clack. Keira reined the mare into a field to wait while the leper passed. The mounted outcast approached swiftly, anonymous beneath the folds of a voluminous black cloak sewn with white patches. Below the conical scarlet hat the face was a veiled enigma.

"Benediction to you, ka," a man's voice said from behind the veil. He kept downwind, so as not to spread the breath of contagion.

It was unlucky to be stingy with a leper; someone must have given him the horse he rode. Keira tossed a bronze tor into the man's upraised hand and waited until the figure had diminished into the distance before she resumed riding.

The smooth, rolling horizons of the south gave way to a pattern of hills and fringes of woods. Terraced fields alternated with patches of forest on the steep hillsides. In the forenoon, Keira passed a family driving a pack of longhaired wool dogs. At the sound of hoofbeats the dogs stood shoulder to shoulder across the road and growled. The mare snorted. Their master grabbed the animals' spiked collars and hushed them. Keira stared at the dogs' amber eyes and stiff shoulder ruffs. They protected folk from wild hunting cats, Rahn had told her, filled the stew pots when famine struck, and perhaps, Keira thought, frightened off soldiers who claimed goods as tax. Each spring, the beasts' thick winter undercoats were combed out, and the wool traded south. Temple buyers bought the dog wool to be woven into priests' robes.

The steep hills looked barely fruitful enough to support scavenger dogs and their drovers. Bare, dark woods shadowed the fields, as if waiting for a chance to encroach on the tilled land.

The family trudged along in silence. The man, an outholder who wore no earring, picked his way over the rutted track, tapping the hard ground with an iron-shod stick. As Keira passed, the woman glanced up, only her eyes showing beneath the curve of her head cover. A rough scarf concealed her lower face. She wore no boots, and filthy leg rags extended up under her skirts. She carried a red-faced infant slung before her, nursing it as she walked.

The man's stick rang on the stony ground; Keira recalled tales the innkeeper had recounted of folk pulled from their horses, robbed, and killed.

She wished man, woman, and child easy deaths and better reincarnations on the Wheel. She pressed her heels into the mare's flank and rode on slowly, not wanting to tempt the dogs to pursue them and snap at the mare's heels.

The pale green of the sprouting fields shone against the rain-soaked black of the woods. The air tasted sharp as mint and smelled of wet earth and leaves, a scent of awakening and renewal. But the sun slid behind the clouds and by noon rain pelted down, flooding the rutted track and making rivulets through the terraced fields.

During a lull in the storm she reached a temple nestled in a sweet-thorn grove. A thin, silent priest, who bowed and called her *ka*, led the mare to water and grain. In the courtyard portico, a temple woman gave Keira the ritual bowl of tea and slab of waybread. Keira stretched out on a bench inside the portico while rain hissed from the tiled, low-swept eaves and spattered on the bright mosaic floor of the courtyard.

The black-clad temple woman clattered away on raised wooden sandals. Across the rim of her tea bowl, Keira studied the courtyard and the image of the Wheel, which symbolized the will of god manifest in the world, worked into its mosaic floor. A small, rain-dappled, sunken pool formed the wheel's hub. From this hub radiated eight spokes, bound by the mosaic wheel rim. Figures of men clung to the spokes and sought footholds on the rim itself as they struggled toward the center. Outside the rim of the wheel were vines and animals, birds and fish, and a woman swimming and grabbing eternally for the edge of the wheel. The man above her lifted a bowl that glowed as he breathed his own soul into it and quickened the dust of the woman's soul.

Woman must be wed, the priests said, so her husband could

bear her poor half soul joined into his greater one, as her flesh was joined to his, to the center of the Wheel.

Keira tapped her foot restlessly against the flagstones of the portico, in time with the steady beat of the rain.

Without a husband, her soul would never attain the center of the Wheel. Perhaps it would strike sparks on the iron-shod rim and bounce into the realm beyond. She savored the strange taste of that thought as she sipped tea. What could the realm beyond be, the void itself from which all creation had poured into form and being?

Her fingers clenched on the tea bowl. She and Roshannon, wrestling on the bed of that inn room, had become one flesh. All her dreams afterward suggested that his soul had trapped hers. Carefully she set the tea bowl down, afraid of spilling the fragrant brew. The flesh become one, the spirit become one. It was, after all, as the priests said, the holy object of marriage.

She recalled that moment when, staring into his eyes, she had felt nothing stood between his skin and hers, her mind and his.

She moved her hand over her belly. Both she and Roshannon had only half a soul, according to the priests, but they might be right about this business of men carrying women's souls. She felt bound to the spirit of this man, a beast tied to a pole.

Her eyes stung as she stared at the magnificent temple wheel.

To a southern temple, only the black circle pierced by eight spokes, with a cold, square pool at the center, would be correct. A southern priest would stare at this luxury and sputter, "Blasphemy!"

Her father had threatened to give her to a temple as often as he had threatened to sell her. Yet life here might not be bad. The priests who daily used such a wheel to worship could not live poorly. But temples were notoriously nosy about women who presented themselves at the gate with no kin to speak for them or offer the customary dowry to the Sanctum treasurer. No easy escape for me, Keira thought. She tucked the waybread in her sash. She had lost her appetite. She had farther to go—north to where the sea ate away at the edge of the world, north to where the witches lived, north to the great city built on sea and rock.

She leaned back against the wall, gathering her resolve. From an inner room drifted the sound of interrogation. A priest's voice flowed into a low, steady thread. The other voice made a raucous counterpoint. It dipped and rose, edged with hysteria. Suddenly a man shouted. Something thudded and scraped. Through an arched doorway leaped a man clad only in a black skirt. His head moved back and forth, birdlike; his hands shaped a parody of a priestly invocation. He argued with a creature in the air.

Suddenly he noticed her. "Greetings." He cocked his head.

Keira set down her tea bowl and rose slowly.

Wooden sandals clacked. Two priests dashed through the doorway. They pinioned the man's arms and apologized.

"Ka, the demon in him is very strong and clever," the old priest said. "We cannot outwit it or persuade it out of his body by either philosophical debate or punishment."

The man hardly resisted them. Old, pale whip scars lay across his back. The priests addressed the demon inside his body, coaxing it out for further metaphysical debate. The possessed man smiled and laughed at the priests. He rolled his eyes.

"Boy," he whispered. Keira stiffened. "Boy," he said, "the demon is inside them, not me. But you see that, don't you?"

Keira shook her head and made a warding sign as the priests hurried the man away. The rain had slackened to a drizzle. She left her empty tea bowl on the edge of the courtyard pool, called for the mare, and went on her way. The eyes and voice of the demon-possessed man haunted her.

At twilight, Keira slid from the saddle, exhausted and mud spattered. She tied the mare in a sweet-thorn thicket, rested, and waited until moonrise to reconnoiter.

The smoke of many cook fires permeated the drizzly air. Her mouth watered as she moved cautiously through the thicket. She crept closer and closer to the source until she heard camp sounds and snatches of song, and smelled horses. She stopped downwind of the horse pickets and lay belly down, watching the encampment. Beyond the woods, tents stood in peaked, straggly rows, wet with rain and gleaming ghostly in the light of the rising moon. Closest to her, near the edge of the woods, packhorses stood in makeshift corrals, their backs to the wind, their heads down, breath pluming about their muzzles, their horsey smell comforting. She wondered if the Red Man was in this encampment, and shuddered, feeling irresistibly curious about him. She was just ready to start back to the mare when her senses pricked in a way she had learned not to ignore. Praying the moonlight had not caught on her face and given her away to those she sensed coming toward her, she lowered her head. Voices and footsteps moved along the line of horses.

"Damn the witches," one voice said. "They got our best horses. The cowards will not stand and fight, just steal horses; and the folk here have only nags and ponies."

"You think they'll come tonight?" a younger-sounding voice asked.

The other laughed bitterly. "Not even a fool would want these horses."

"Were any witches taken prisoner?"

"No more. But the archpriest wants some."

"Are the witches close?"

As the two men strode into a patch of moonlight, one silhouette shape looked about, as if a witch might be behind him or curling out of the smoke of a cooking fire. "Don't know. God help us, they could be." His voice was low and wary. "Harda tells us nothing, just march here, camp there." He gestured toward the tents.

"But the witches?" one voice asked.

"They hide in the woods and play games with us. They can make themselves invisible, but sometimes you know they're around."

"How?"

"Have you ever thought someone is behind you, turned quick, and seen nothing, yet known some bastard is there?"

"Aye."

"That's the witchy feeling."

When the voices and footsteps traveled around the far side of the corral, Keira crept back to the sweet-thorn thicket, cursing her luck that she had not run into a witch encampment. Such lax sentries must only mean that the Sanctum camp felt reasonably secure, or figured not even the witches would raid during rain. She rode on, putting as much distance as possible between herself and the camp.

Near dawn she stopped to catnap propped against a tree with the mare's lead rein tied to her wrist. Riding even at night and only catnapping during the day seemed to help keep away dreams.

From a wooded knoll at dawn she surveyed the blue-green hills

that closed in on the land, so different from the level stretch where
the army had camped. Wave upon wave of forest rolled away
against the horizon, all tinged blue by the effect of distance and
the peculiar hue of the trees. Witches live in the northern parts of
the Blue Forest and beyond, Rahn had said. She considered riding
straight into the trees, but the forest stretched east, not west, not
toward the city.

The trail she rode tunneled through thick woods, pierced only
at intervals by the sun. Tall trees grew close together, forming a
wall of blue twilight a short distance off the road. Scolding jays
and songbirds made flashes of color against the dark trees.

The land was changing. The forest thickened until the farms
and fields of men seemed paltry and petty compared to its solemn
wildness. She passed a ruined freehold, the lintel of the once
proud red gate crowned with mushrooms, the stone walls of the
house and outbuildings swallowed by creepers with shiny leaves.
She dismounted and walked the mare past the abandoned home-
stead. Insects whined around her face; she slipped on the rutted
track and scratched herself on catbrier.

It was near dusk when the track emerged from the woods
above a settled valley.

The smoke of cook fires rose from the houses clustered outside
the hold. Her heart pounded as she approached the outlying fields.
On the eastern horizon she could see dust clouds, marking the
passage of yet more troops.

Men were working the fields, and boys with slings patrolled
the sown plots to keep crows from snatching seed before it was
covered.

Wheel ruts scarred the edges of the fields, showing the army
had passed through. People who raised their heads to consider her
looked indifferent at best. No one riding through their countryside
meant any good to them, she thought. The temple taxed heavily,
the army even heavier. If two armies clashed here, bodies and
bones would enrich the soil, and children would starve.

She turned her face west into the warmth of the sun and dug
her heels into the mare's flanks.

The thick walls of the hold, or fortified inner city, overshadowed its village. Inside the large south gate, where she heard
the name of the place was A'Hrappa, a crowd had gathered in the
marketplace by the temple steps. The tightly packed booths and

mob of people blocked Keira's way. Tall, narrow houses of two and three stories hemmed in the market area. Annoyed and feeling caged, she reined aside. Rising in the stirrups for a better view, she glimpsed a woman, in the shapeless gray robes that Sanctum novices wore, being led onto the temple steps. Having no appetite for a spectacle, she searched for an opening in the throng and the buildings. She rode into a passageway that curved away from the market. The mare's shod hooves rang on the cobblestones, and urchins scrabbled out of the way. An alehouse pole protruding into the alleyway at rider's-head level almost poked Keira's eye out. She ducked, cursed, and slid from the saddle to walk the mare. The tunnel-like street stank of urine and offal; it twisted left and right and emerged in another corner of the market. She cursed again.

She wanted to be out of this town and on her way. To see over the heads of the crowd, she mounted.

Onlookers were pelting the woman standing on the temple steps with garbage. A man in a butcher's apron flung a bowl of what smelled like sour ale at her. A widow in a peaked black head covering pried up a cow pie with a crooked stick and prepared to launch it.

The bound woman twisted sideways, unable to protect her face with her hands. She turned her shoulder to the crowd, presenting less of a target. Something in the woman's posture made Keira stop.

"What has she done?" Keira asked.

"She's a witch," the widow said. "They ought to burn her or hang her."

Keira edged the mare closer to the temple steps. The woman stood tall and straight. Pale brown hair, free of any head covering, and nothing like the whore Otella's lucky hank of silver witch hair, fell loose on this woman's shoulders. But it was the custom to take a woman's head covering before she was executed. Other than this, there was nothing extraordinary about her appearance.

The burly man who held her on a rope yelled for order. He raised his hands for silence.

"Sell her and give the proceeds to the temple," a man behind Keira bellowed.

Keira guided the mare deeper into the crowd, forcing the

widow with the cow pie to sidestep and drop her missile, which
the mare trod underfoot.

"Silence," the burly man roared.

"Sell her and give the proceeds to the army," a man at the edge
of the crowd said. He was a prosperous-looking merchant with a
jade plug gleaming in his earlobe. He stood beneath the striped
awning of a leather trader's booth.

"This is a genuine witch," the man on the steps said. He twisted
the rope that bound the woman's wrists, forcing her closer to him.
"Captured and left in our keeping by the army."

The merchant hooted. "Why should we believe you that she is
really a witch?"

Fascinated, Keira watched the woman on the steps. The thin,
gray-clad figure stood proudly, and as far from her keeper as the
rope allowed. She stared over the heads of the jeering crowd, into
the darkening sky. Keira's breath caught in her throat. All her
dreams and fears of her father washed through her mind. She
urged the mare forward.

"A silver tor," the butcher yelled. "Surely a witch will not be
an easy maidservant. She'll have to be broken."

"Less if she is to be broken," the merchant said. "But is she a
real witch? Where is her white hair?" A man next to him clapped
him on the shoulder and praised his levelheadedness.

Keira stared at the woman, who looked to be her own age. Her
heart pounded. The crowd laughed and jeered, offering bids and
insults.

"One gold tor," someone yelled. "For a witch whore."

Two of the men in the crowd laughed and joked at that, pounding each other's shoulders. The smell of rakka drifted by Keira's
nose.

The widow had darted in next to the mare's shoulder. In either
hand she hefted jagged cobblestones. "Soul sucker," she cried,
her chin jutting forward as she cursed the supposed witch.

"You boy, on that fine horse with your mouth agape, what do
you say?" The burly man jabbed a finger in Keira's direction.

She started. The woman beside the mare sneered up at her. The
faces of the crowd surged around her, pale blurs. "Five silver
tors," she said, in a voice that sounded strange to her own ears.

The merchant with the jade earplugs scoffed and grinned. "A
pretty price for a useless toy."

The widow sucked in her breath. She dropped the cobblestones, her fingers forming the sign against evil as she slipped away. The crowd parted to let Keira through. The butcher in his bloodstained apron elbowed his way to the temple steps.

"What use will you put the witch to, boy?" he asked.

"Good use," Keira said.

The man snickered. "Are you old enough to know what good use is, ka?" He wiped his hands through the fresh blood on his apron. "She'll keep your bed hot, not just warm, if half the tales are true."

Keira let the mare prance in a tight half circle before the steps, clearing off the butcher and other leering idlers.

She drew rein and dropped silver into the temple man's hand. He counted it out while the reputed witch stared straight ahead. Her hair and robe reeked of sour ale.

"Be careful of her. She's tricky," the man said, tossing Keira the end of rope.

The bound woman stared up at Keira. Her eyes were green as the heart of summer. High cheekbones emphasized the otherness of those eyes. Her skin was copper hued, her shoulders broad, her face a mask. A magnificent earring, a wheel of jade and a wheel of amber joined by a silver clasp, hung at her left earlobe, half-hidden by her straight hair.

The temple treasurer wet his lips, seeing Keira eye the bauble. "Worth more than you paid for her, ka," he whispered. "But she says it's cursed. I wouldn't touch it if I were you."

Keira nodded, twisting the rope around in her hand. She headed toward the western gate. The witch woman jogged beside the mare, keeping the pace easily enough. At least the temple men had not taken her boots. A stocky woman spectator raised a rotten potato to throw, but dropped it when Keira's eyes met hers.

A thin, bearded man ran to stare at the witch. "A ka's boy with a prize," he jeered. He edged closer, pursing his mouth to spit in the woman's face.

Keira kneed the mare forward, her face hot. The man raised his hands and twisted aside as the mare's approach forced him against a wall. He slunk along the wall and disappeared down an alley. Keira cursed, feeling a surge of hatred for the staring people, the carts that blocked the narrow passages. The very stones of the house walls seemed to breathe hindrance.

She stared at the sun sinking in the west and kneed the mare down another mazelike street. A half-dozen rabble-rousers surged through the alley, shouting hoarsely. Hoisted on their shoulders rode a baker who was kicking frantically, his short-weight loaves tied about his neck.

Near the western gate Keira found a stable whose owner offered to sell her a cow-hocked old gelding, a sickle-hocked mare, and sundry other nags. She bargained in haste for the last beast he showed her, a rangy black highland pony with good shoulders and quarters.

She helped the witch woman into the saddle, made fast a leading rein, and rode out of the hold.

After twilight she stopped in a wood and helped the woman dismount. The woman let her bound hands hang before her. Her shoulders drooped, but her strange green eyes blazed.

"Well, boy," the witch said. "If you have your way with me, I promise you'll have no pleasure in it."

Fascinated, Keira watched the steady green eyes. She gnawed her lip. Perhaps the possessed man's demon had jumped into her; perhaps she was mad. What in a witch's nature made the Sanctum priests hate them so? What about this woman had enraged the A'Hrappan widow so much she was ready to throw cobbles?

The green-eyed woman drew another breath. "I will curse you so that you will never have a son by any woman, I will curse you—"

"Spare your curses. I do not think they would affect me."

"Do you think yourself proof against witches?"

Keira shook her head. "No. It is just against that particular curse I feel proof."

The green eyes narrowed. "Why is that?"

"Because I am not a man. Or even a boy." Keira watched the green eyes. An uneasy vision of the witch woman somehow knocking her down, finding the dagger, killing her, and stealing her clothes slid through her mind. Warily, she edged closer, opening her jerkin and travel-stained linen shirt.

The other stared at the band wrapped about Keira's breasts and backed away. Keira watched the green eyes. Suddenly they both grinned.

"This is a strange day," the other said.

"Aye, it is. Are you really a witch?"

"Do you doubt me? Why did you buy me?"

"To set you free. So you can show me the way to Cartheon."
Keira fastened her shirt.

The other girl shook her head in amazement.

"If you are truly a witch, you know the way to Cartheon, don't
you?" Keira asked.

"Why should a southlander go to the great city?" The witch's
eyes narrowed. The earring gleamed against her cheek.

"To be free," Keira said simply. She gestured at the earring,
feeling uneasy, sure that it was a house sign and that the witch
might be ka'innen. "Is that cursed?"

"Perhaps," the girl said. "It's the badge of Tanta clan. I'd rather
die than give it up." She studied Keira. "What makes you think
you can get to Cartheon?"

"I can try."

"I might stand a better chance by myself," the witch said.

"You have little choice. You were lucky not to be hanged or
burned, but only bought by me. In those clothes, everyone would
know you'd escaped from a temple and stone you or turn you in
for a reward."

The witch frowned. "Surely no southlander heads for Cartheon
without dire reason. What are you running from?"

"Will you come with me of your own will or not?"

The witch grinned. "Unbind my hands and I will be a more
useful companion."

"Not until we are farther along."

"You come from far with speech like that," the green-eyed
witch said. "How far?"

"Near Kerlew." Keira studied the woman's profile. The two
had halted in the woods by a tiny stream, in a place the witch
judged safe for the night. Keira helped her dismount, because of
her bound hands; the woman lapsed into a sullen silence, standing
with her wrists pressed close together to avoid the chafing of the
rope. Keira shrugged, wondering which the woman resented
more: having her hands bound or having to be helped down from
the pony.

Digging in her saddlebags, Keira chose one of the rags she had
cut her skirt into, balled it up, wet it at the stream, and began rubbing down the mare. Keeping an eye on the witch, she reflected

that if she was indeed pregnant she would never use the rest of the rags as she had originally planned. She hummed to herself as she worked, scratching between the mare's ears. The woman watched her. Keira balled up another rag and threw it to the witch.

The woman snorted but managed to pick up the rag, then rub down the pony with awkward vigor.

Keira finished first and slipped the bridle to let the mare roll in the grass before she tethered her for the night. "How far is Cartheon from here?" she asked.

"Six or seven days' unhindered journey. But to get there we must dodge the army. And the borderlanders may trouble us."

"From the last rise above the hold I could see the Blue Forest stretching across the land. Why not travel through it?"

The woman shook her head. She finished rubbing down the pony and slapped its flank. It trotted off to the end of its tether and whickered.

"This part is full of spies and trouble," she said. "Listen, I'll make a pact with you. I am honor bound to help you since you helped me, so I will take you within sight of the towers of Cartheon. Then I must leave you and go search for my kin. It's safer to enter the forest from the north, because the southern end is full of reivers and soldiers." She held out her bound hands. "You must trust me sometime. Will you undo these?"

Keira untied the bonds, not wishing to reveal the dagger.

Rope burns darkened the woman's brown wrists. She massaged the abraded skin gently with her fingertips and flexed her hands. "Where did you get the clothes?" she demanded.

Keira straightened. "My—husband." She wondered why she had so much difficulty pronouncing the words, then felt foolish for having told the witch woman anything.

"Your husband?" The other woman was scraping a clear patch on the ground with her boot toe.

Keira nodded. "I took his clothes six nights ago and fled."

The witch sat back on her heels, an elbow balanced on her knee. "So this husband was a disagreeable lout? I have heard that southern men are. So you stole his clothes and ran away from him?" Grinning, she appraised Keira with something approaching respect.

"Not exactly from him." Keira took a deep breath as she

thought of his touch, his shadowed face, and the dreams, the connection between them.

"From what, then?" The woman scratched signs in the bare ground with a stick.

"Other things. After my mother died, my father beat me. He wanted me to marry a man I hated. And my dreams . . ."

The woman looked up sharply. "What do you know of dreams?"

Keira met the green eyes, shrugged, but kept her mouth shut. She had probably already said too much. She had no reason to trust this woman.

At last the witch rose, frowning at the pattern of lines she had scratched in the black earth. She glanced sharply at Keira. "I must thank you for saving me from my enemies. My father was a witch lord, and he and his men were ambushed at the edge of the Blue Forest. I think my whole clan died there. I am Hipolla Tanta, of Tanta clan."

"Hipolla?" Keira said, testing the strange name on her tongue. "I am Keira Danio." She hesitated before the green eyes that measured everything. "I don't know whether I saved you. Because you don't have white hair, some of those folk thought the man was just trying to pass you off as a witch to get a higher price."

"But they would have enslaved me and I would have had to escape myself."

"Yes." Keira stared at Hipolla's thick, dark hair, thinking of the lucky piece worn around the whore Otella's neck. "If you are really a witch why don't you have white hair?"

"Some do not. My father's hair didn't turn white until he was much older than I am now."

"Hmm," Keira said.

But Hipolla crouched over her sketch, tapping the stick amid the jumble of lines. "We should head for the Hand, the sea that cuts inland above Lian Calla—" She slurred the names together, Keira noted. "—and cross the headlands above it, right into Lyssa, Cartheon's port."

The Hand, Lyssa, Cartheon. Keira rocked on her boot heels as she bent over the lines drawn in the dirt.

Hipolla touched her hand. "Do you trust me, Keira Danio?"

Keira glanced at the rope burns on Hipolla's wrists. She looked up. "Do you trust me, Hipolla Tanta?"

They nodded to each other as dusk settled among the trees.

"We must keep constant watch and build no fires," Hipolla said. She leaned against a tree trunk and Keira eased down beside her. They munched dried fruit and passed the water skin. In the glade, the mare and pony grazed on new grass. Double measures of grain for them both, for a long ride tomorrow, Keira thought. The small sounds of the horses, the crickets, and the forest wove a net around them.

"With a bow I could hunt," Hipolla said in a dreamy tone, "and fill our bellies with game."

Keira stared at her. "You hunt with a bow?"

"And use a sword, though not well. I sneaked along with some horse archers. My uncle didn't tell my father when he spotted me. He let me stay, but made me ride with the wagons, wearing women's clothes. A huge body of soldiers surprised them one morning. Our men were overrun. I don't think anyone escaped. Southern soldiers captured me and some other women from the healer's camp and baggage train, brought me to that temple, and put me in these robes. They refused to ransom me. And, in faith, maybe none of my kin are still alive to have bought me back." Her voice was low, her shoulders hunched in the shroudlike robe.

"What happened to the other women?"

"One killed herself, after soldiers raped her. The others, I don't know. We were separated."

"Did they touch you?"

Hipolla shook her head, her lips pressed into a tight line.

"Could you not have used magic to escape them?" Keira asked. She decided to trust Hipolla as far as she was able, but she would not reveal the dagger to her. Not yet.

Hipolla smiled sadly. "What do the priests say of us? Magic?" She sounded disdainful. "Magic cannot turn the blade of a sword—only another sword and skill in the hand that wields it can do that. There is no easy magic, only true dreams and the sight."

Keira shifted her shoulders against the tree trunk, wondering what Hipolla meant. The cool, almost mocking sadness in her words goaded Keira's curiosity.

Hipolla flicked a stem of dried apple into the trees. She lapsed into silence but offered to keep first watch.

Keira nodded agreement; she made sure an edge of her cloak

was caught under Hipolla's thigh so any movement would wake her. She closed her eyes, but with no intention of sleeping, stretched and rolled her shoulders. The magnificent temple wheel turned before her inner eye, and all the sounds of the forest sharpened in the growing darkness. Beside her, Hipolla chafed her arms inside her robe.

"That will not keep you warm." Keira opened her cloak and took off the jerkin. Hipolla whispered thanks as she accepted it.

Keira propped her head on the saddle and curled up beneath her cloak. She closed her eyes but was unable to sleep. Every time Hipolla turned or shifted, Keira was aware of it. Sounds ran through her like threads; she was wary of Hipolla, excited, and fearful of her own recurring dreams.

When Hipolla roused her, after what seemed like no time at all, Keira took her turn sitting propped against the tree, her cloak drawn about her and her arms wrapped about her knees, staring into the shadowed woods. The light of the rising moon changed the world into black silhouettes and silvery mist. Keira's speculations about the witch woman kept her awake until she woke Hipolla for the last watch.

A hand on her shoulder roused her at dawn. Keira stared up into green eyes, startled but glad she could remember no dreams. She must have fallen asleep at last, completely exhausted. She wriggled her feet inside her boots, reassured by the weighty feel of the sheathed dagger in her left boot.

Hipolla yawned and stretched luxuriously. Her face had lost its guarded, withdrawn look.

She sniffed. "I must find something to wear besides this robe. It reeks."

Keira grinned, wrinkling her nose in agreement at the tang of horse sweat and leather that permeated her own clothes.

❀ 6 ❀

"One hundred towers surround the city," Hipolla said.

One hundred towers. Keira rolled her eyes, tempted to dismiss Hipolla as a liar. A city with so many towers would have unimaginable riches. Keira's hands tightened on the reins. She savored the idea of such a city, like the taste of wine on her wedding night. But could the wealth from spidersilk and the red-sailed trading ships build a city with a hundred towers?

Bit by bit Hipolla doled out information or tantalizing rumors about Cartheon. It reminded Keira of market haggling—as little by little, a stubborn merchant could be persuaded to reveal more than he intended about his goods.

"The traders' city and the warehouses stretch ten miles along the shore," Hipolla added.

You set out bait as if I were a fish, thought Keira, who never missed a word she said.

"Yesterday you said you have never been there," Keira said.

"That does not make me a liar."

Keira grinned. Such lies would take great thought to concoct— they simply might be true. She wanted to trust Hipolla because she had no one else to trust, but she wanted to know what witchery was, too, without nagging Hipolla to talk about it.

The thought of a hundred towers made her dizzy. What had the servant Rahn said of Cartheon? Had he not told her its four great rings of walls nested one inside the other?

One by one Keira used all the names the priests had laid on Cartheon: City of the Damned, the City of Blasphemers. Seeing this irked Hipolla, she asked why the priests called the city such names.

"Because there is mold in their brains," Hipolla snapped. "And if you believe what they say, why do you want to go there?"

They were riding neck and neck, Keira holding the mare to the pony's slower pace. She dug her heels in the mare's side. She had an irresistible urge to race.

"You ask me so many questions," Hipolla said. "Aren't you going to answer mine?"

"I am curious," Keira said. "To see if what the priests say is true or not." She hesitated. "My mother told me to go there."

Hipolla gave her a sharp look. "Why would a southern woman give her daughter such advice?"

"She came from farther north herself. She spoke of the sea." Leaning forward in the saddle, Keira loosened the reins. The mare lengthened her stride, but Hipolla held the pace. Keira felt uneasy, unsure whether she could tell Hipolla that her mother's advice had been because of the dreams.

"Do you have family or clan in the north?" Hipolla asked.

Keira shook her head.

Hipolla smiled, incredulous. "What will you do, if and when you reach the city?"

"Find out what witchery is and what the city is like, and if you or the priests are liars."

"Hah. We have far to go yet, and how much longer do you think people will believe you are a lad? I am surprised no one saw through those clothes. You know, I thought there was something strange about you when first I saw you."

Keira grinned. "You only want to credit yourself with more vision than other folk." But the idea that Hipolla had noted something odd about her unsettled her. "Maybe folk cannot see what they cannot imagine."

"You should lend me your cloak, to cover this gown and make me less suspicious looking."

Keira shook her head. Once the cloak with its weighted seams settled around Hipolla's shoulders, she would realize it was full of secret wealth. "No man in these parts would show such care for a servant or a slave."

"Are you just being mean?" Hipolla asked.

Keira snorted. "Simply practical, and truthful." A hundred towers. She laughed softly to herself.

Hipolla glanced at her.

"Keep your head bowed, so," Keira told Hipolla, who rode a

little behind her, as a proper servant would. "You still do not ride quite like a slave or a woman."

"Nor do you ride exactly like a man," Hipolla said. "And you may miss something we should see."

Keira sparked at those words but took Hipolla's advice, squaring her shoulders and sitting as tall as possible in the saddle. "Now," she said to the witch woman, "draw your scarf like a veil across your face, so, and you can look where you will with no one knowing." She reined in close enough to tweak Hipolla's makeshift head covering into place.

She took a sisterly pleasure in the small action. The sound of their horses' hooves clopping along the dusty trail together comforted her.

They rode through carefully tended fields and orchards, past stone-walled holds so small they were hardly worthy of the name, by freehold farms with peeling, red-painted gates, and outcasts' huts. Wooden watchtowers loomed in the fringe of woods above the villages, and increasingly, they spotted men or boys perched in them, scanning the countryside for raiders.

Keira hailed a peasant. "Have you seen any soldiers?"

The man looked at Hipolla, then dropped his glance. "Some passed that way." He indicated the horizon, north and west, with a sweep of his hand. "We saw their dust cloud this morning when we came to work the fields." He drew his cloak about him in the chill and spat, eyeing the mare and the highland pony as if calculating their value and their riders' status.

Keira edged the mare forward when he stared anew at Hipolla. He stepped backward and lowered his eyes.

"Let the Wheel turn well for you, ka," he said, and bowed.

As Keira looked down at his lowered head, a curious sensation washed over her. Roshannon had bowed his head before her when he wed her, and kissed her belly. The memory tugged at her. She nodded curtly to the landsman and gestured Hipolla to move on.

Clearly the laborers working the windy, terraced fields expected no good of passing strangers. Men and boys were sowing a late crop on the high terraces, casting seed on narrow strips of stony soil hoarded behind fieldstone walls. A woman, sighting riders, grabbed her girl child and scuttled up a terraced hillside toward a knot of men, her long, hampering skirts held up to let her run. The woman was a cipher, a creature without a face. Is that how I looked, Keira wondered? Is that how I moved before I stole my husband's clothes?

"Do you think the men will attack us?" she asked.

"They can see we're not soldiers," Hipolla said. "We should be safe enough."

"Without obvious weapons we must look like easy targets."

"A day farther north, I know the land," Hipolla said. "We can make the borderlands; sympathy for the Sanctum runs thin there. But your speech will be a problem. Beyond the forest, near the Hand, you will be in more trouble than I am here, if you roll your arrrrhs."

Keira laughed at the imitation. She flicked the reins and called over her shoulder, "Then I must talk flat and fast as you do and turn my words up just before I stop talking?" She aped Hipolla's accent, ending with a final rising tone.

Hipolla smiled. "You are quick. But practice."

Keira had always longed for a sister, and enjoyed her growing sense of camaraderie with the northern woman. I have no magic, Hipolla had said. But everything about Hipolla whispered magic and mystery: the catlike grace, the quick tongue, the quality of otherness that shimmered in the air about her—the magic of a girl who had grown up among another people, in another kind of world. She rode as if she were an extension of the horse, guiding the hill pony with almost invisible signals of hand and knee. No woman or man Keira knew had moved in this way.

Hipolla grinned at her own latest attempt to roll her rs as Keira did. The green eyes flashed.

Keira did a double trill and laughed.

Images of sea and islands floated through Roshannon's head while he traveled the alien landscape, avoiding scouts and detachments of the Sanctum army. Thus he tricked himself for the better part of a day into not thinking of *her*.

The faithful pair of hawks circled overhead, a bowshot ahead of him, ever alert for the small game that he flushed as he rode along. He longed to share the birds' view of the landscape. The army left clear signs of its passage—streams of refugees and stragglers pulling rickety carts of belongings; fields and highways marked with the passage of hundreds of horses, foot soldiers, and wagons; and a wariness in the faces of the people whose land they had crossed.

The southern army culled recruits and supplies from the land and moved eastward and north, toward Kum and the heart of the Blue Forest.

But Keira Danio's trail had become impossible to divine.

Only after he had rubbed down the horses, hobbled them, and eaten did he let himself wonder if the trail she left was the sort anyone but a madman would follow. It was a trail delicate as a thread of spiderweb blown across his face.

And just as substantial.

He sat propped against a tree trunk, considering what to do, while he fed twigs into a tiny fire. The silver and wooden rings on his hand gleamed in the light. He cursed and pushed the wooden band back down his finger. It was always slipping; if he was not careful, he would lose it.

The landscape seemed to seethe with meanings and mysteries he could not decipher. He felt enmeshed in a wide net of uncertain nature. Remembering how surely his lucky sense had led him to his would-be ambusher, he wondered why the sense did not help him stalk that troublesome girl.

Riding west would bring him soon to Lian Calla, but he doubted she would head there, knowing it was his home. In strange business, best to trust the instincts. She had headed straight north in the beginning, so he continued north.

Each night she plagued his dreams, and he woke in the mornings with his hands clenched as if he had truly been strangling her in his sleep.

In one dream, while he regarded himself in a mirror, his own image became a perfect reflection of her, down to the pockmark in the middle of her forehead and the wary expression in her eyes. One dream contained nothing but a hot, formless redness that failed to resolve into anything decipherable. But the keen, surreal violence of his last, most vivid dream had startled him awake just before dawn. In it, he was strangling Keira, his hands closing on her throat, his thumbs crushing into the warm flesh over her windpipe.

He had never dreamed of strangling a woman, even when angry, and the dreams frustrated and puzzled him, like a stranger's dreams foisted on him. And the strangeness began with that girl.

He snorted, reflecting bitterly that when and if he found her, he might *want* to strangle her.

"Which way tomorrow, Nikka?" he asked himself aloud.

Roshannon shook his head and settled back against the tree trunk, stretching and yawning. Another dream of Keira still haunted him. In it, she had stood watching him, naked beside him in the woods where he had killed the archer who ambushed him. When he spoke her name, her feet left the ground and she floated skyward. He had woken amused at the glorious image of her floating naked just above the treetops.

Frowning, he stared into the woods, half expecting to see her. He had never felt such a connection with any woman before. Nor had he experienced such wild dreams since the fevers when his lucky sight awakened.

He banked the fire, the last one he would permit himself, and wrapped himself in his cloak.

He loosed his second self, letting it float free, above the fleshly man who stretched his hands toward the warmth of the red embers. Concentrating his will, he soared through the canopy of the forest, into the twilight sky. Summoning an image of her, he went stalking. Again, he could not touch her. Exhausted, he reknitted flesh and spirit.

The red embers winked in the darkness. Woman, he promised himself, I will find you.

He woke with another dream of Keira in a gown with a tall, ornately embroidered collar. She was laughing at him.

Beyond her rose a city with myriad towers, a place built on the edge of the sea and up to the bottom of the sky. It could only be the witch city, with its quarters forming the shape of a great spiderweb.

She laughed again and the city of illusion crumbled. Beyond her now stood Lian Calla's clan towers, the harbor's smooth waters gleaming like polished steel in the background. But a strange banner flew from the tower, a black pennant with a stark white wheel on it. Keira disappeared and he found himself suddenly in Lian Calla, wandering through the tea plantations toward the sea. At the edge of a field he came upon two men who had hitched a team of horses to a god stone. One man cracked a whip. The team strained; the whip snapped again. The god stone ripped from the earth, leaving a gaping raw hole. Men hewed at the stone with chisel and hammer, hatred in their eyes.

He shouted at them. They laughed at him. He smelled smoke. Below the tea plantations, workers' cottages and fields blazed.

He stumbled through the fields, his dream body weak-kneed and slow as an old man's.

His heart pounded with the memory of the dream vision. He cursed softly to himself, scanned the clearing, and whistled for the dun stallion. The horse snorted, approaching through the trees; the remount gelding whickered. Roshannon stood up, stretching to get the stiffness out of his back and thighs. He absently stroked the stallion's neck.

He faced north, then west toward Lian Calla, then brusquely turned to stare directly northward where the witch city lay. One set of instincts dragged all his senses after that woman on her fine mare, wherever she might be. The other pulled him toward Lian Calla.

In the days before he had become a mercenary, bands of traveling musicians had played in his mother's house. He recalled their dark faces, their eyes full of secrets, their hands coaxing impossible music from their stringed instruments. Now he felt like one of their instruments, with an eerie range of emotions being plucked from him unwilling.

Turning in a slow circle, he slammed his fist into his palm. The dun stallion's head jerked up at the crack of flesh on flesh. Roshannon hefted the saddle onto his shoulder and approached the horse, soothing it. He slid the saddle on, fumbling with the straps, cursing the contrary leather and the clumsiness of his hands.

"I wish that I were you," he told the horse. "With nothing on my mind but whatever horses think."

The stallion's ears pricked up; it rolled its great dark eyes at him.

Roshannon laughed. He stroked the horse's neck, tightened the girth strap, and fished the dead bowman's rakka bottle from the saddlebags.

He pulled the stopper and wrinkled his nose at the reek of the liquor. He licked his lips, knowing well enough how it would affect him. Yet if he did not dream he would not dream of her.

He traced his thumb over the patterns carved in the leather, cursed again, slid the stopper firmly back into the bottle, and tucked the leather flask into the remount's saddlebags. *Keep your head clear, Nikka, and all your dreams remembered.*

"Do we head north today?" he asked the dun stallion. "Southern troops would avoid the borderlands." He ground his teeth. "Or north and west to the coast? Though I thought north last night—" He paced a slow circle around the horse. "Or north and west." Another day's ride in that direction would bring him to Lian Calla.

He muttered to the horse as he stowed his gear in the remount's saddlebags.

He leaned against a tree, his cloak wrapped about him, and stared into the woods. Nikka, Nikka, he thought, you are in a bad way if a girl you slept with just one night does this to you.

"We need weapons," Hipolla said.

Keira thought of Roshannon's dagger tucked in her boot. "I don't know how to use weapons," she said slowly.

Hipolla flicked the reins. "No matter. I think we're near Lian Calla. We'll smell the sea tomorrow."

Keira's spirits lifted. Her mother had told her stories about seas full of red-sailed ships and waters that lapped the edges of the world.

That night they sat up late, propped against tree trunks, and whispered about Cartheon. "I do not believe you," Keira would say, having learned that this phrase would sting Hipolla into spilling another fantastic tale of the city—of great bathhouses with heated pools where people swam and lounged for pleasure in the afternoon; of trees grown from three trunks braided together, their branches forming a woven latticework that shaded the walkways in the spider masters' gardens.

"Ha," Keira said.

Hipolla laughed. "If you never believe me, why do you always demand more stories?" While she spoke she worked on a stout length of ash she had found in the woods. She peeled bark from one end and smoothed the wood with chips of quartz, until she had produced a long, serviceable club.

Keira reached into her boot, drawing Roshannon's dagger. She held it out handle first to Hipolla. "You need to carve a hand grip," she said.

"So I do." Hipolla looked at her a moment, then took the knife matter-of-factly, as if she had always known it was there.

Keira watched the grip take shape in Hipolla's hands. The club was a peasant weapon, but deadly enough, with a longer reach than the dagger. She had seen men fight with staffs at Kerlew Fair.

When the club was carved to her satisfaction, Hipolla showed Keira how to hold it two-handed, how to parry a blade, how to thrust it into a man's stomach and ribs.

Keira let Hipolla take watch. Hipolla handed the dagger back to her quite naturally and thanked her for its use, but Keira slept fitfully. A familiar dreamscape of fields and sky appeared, while ominous pikes bearing severed heads flowed toward her, not borne by human hands. She fled in panic. The pikes pursued her, hurled along on a demented wind. The dead mouths shrieked at her but the wind snatched their words away. Suddenly a tall, lean shape in a cloak appeared, the face unclear, walking toward her. Was it Roshannon?

"Wake up." Someone shook her shoulder.

Keira stared blindly for a moment before she recognized Hipolla's voice.

"You were moaning and kicking," Hipolla said. "Good dreams, eh?"

Keira sat up straighter. "Something was chasing me."

It was nearly dawn. Hipolla's eyes glittered. "What did you dream?"

Keira reflected that perhaps Hipolla felt bad dreams would pay back a companion who had kept a weapon to herself.

"I was running from something close behind me. I think my husband is chasing me," Keira said. As soon as the words left her mouth, they felt true.

"Why would he chase you?"

"He bought me and the mare. Any reasonable man would at least want the mare back, don't you think?"

Hipolla glanced from the mare to Keira and grinned. "Oh, at least." She considered a moment. "In the dream did he say anything to you?"

Keira shook her head.

Hipolla persisted, demanding what images and landscapes had appeared. When Keira said she could no longer remember the dream, Hipolla turned her back and fiddled with the pony's saddlebags.

"What is the use of dreaming, southerner, if you do not remember the dreams?"

Belly down in the fallen leaves, Keira watched as a double line of armed horsemen rode by. Foot soldiers trotted beside the riders, holding on to the horsemen's stirrup straps. Boys on ponies driving a pack of remounts brought up the rear. The riders' black banner was stitched with a plain silver wheel—Sanctum. Headed for the sea, Hipolla had said. Keira willed the sound of her heartbeat to nothing, willed herself invisible. Hipolla had spotted the men coming this morning and concealed their horses deep in the woods. Keira prayed no scout would ambush Hipolla.

The soldiers rode in tight formation, joking and laughing among themselves.

A lone man trudged along the road, bent almost double under a load of firewood. The column of soldiers, trotting two abreast, forced him into a ditch. As he scrabbled for a foothold, his enormous bundle of firewood flew apart, twigs snapping under the horses' hooves. He cursed them roundly.

Two soldiers leaned in their saddles, caught the man's arms as he staggered up, and, whooping, forced him to trot down the road between them. The man struggled, dragged along between the riders. A dust cloud eddied along the trail.

Keira spotted a boy hidden beside a rock pile overlooking the trail, as the woodcutter fell facedown in the dust raised by the soldiers' horses. Keira waited until the boy crept out from behind his shelter toward the still figure in the middle of the road. She crawled into the woods and raced to the glade where Hipolla held the horses.

"Twenty-five riders, heading north," Keira said. "With foot soldiers trotting between the ranks. I think they killed a woodman."

Hipolla whistled. "Twenty-five liege soldiers? All well armed, with fresh horses? Perhaps they are headed for Lian Calla."

The two women passed a valley where free-held farms lay on both sides of a stream. An empty watchtower loomed in the fringe of trees above the orderly strips of fields. Keira drew rein a moment. The settled areas cut from the hilly woodlands looked like wheels themselves: the heart, the hub of farms and outbuildings divided by a stream, then a ring of carefully tended orchards, the trees' pale blossoms standing out vividly; next the broader ring of planted land, narrow strips of pale green, or dark earth where the sown crops had not yet sprouted, the fields carefully terraced to hoard the stony, hilly land; and last the ring of dark woods bound the settled area like the rim of a wheel, closing it away from the rest of the world.

They cut through the woods, following the stream some distance beyond the village.

Hipolla gestured toward the tower. "I'll get a look while you water the mare."

"Take this." Keira drew the dagger from her boot and handed it to Hipolla. "The villagers may not like you climbing their tower." She didn't know a better way to show Hipolla that she trusted her than to offer her the dagger.

Hipolla watched her a moment but shook her head. She tucked the club under her arm and mounted the pony.

"Whenever we separate, we should both have weapons. Always." Hipolla trotted into the woods.

Kneeling beside the mare, Keira splashed her face with water, cupped her hands full, and let the water run down her face and neck beneath her dirty shirt until it wet the edges of the sash she had bound around her breasts. Her skin itched; she craved a bath. Suddenly the mare's ears pricked forward; she jerked her head from the water, splashing Keira's face.

Another reflection broke and ebbed in the water, a man's dark-haired image. Keira started, thinking of Roshannon, the dream, the story she had told Hipolla. The mare snorted, standing in the middle of the stream. Keira spoke soothingly to her. Don't bolt now, devious beast, she thought.

"Greetings." A lean, pale stranger touched his forehead and casually dipped his water flask into the stream not a dozen paces from her. Several days' russet stubble shadowed his face, and a sheathed dagger and a short sword hung from his belt.

"Greetings." Keira drew her flask from the water and stoppered it. Her hands shook ever so slightly.

The man grinned. "You are brave to ride these hills alone, lad." He scooped water in his palm and drank, his eyes never leaving her.

"So are you." Keira judged the distance to the mare and

listened for sounds of Hipolla returning. The mare whickered as she might at the presence of another horse. The still stream mirrored the overhanging trees, shards of sky, a hawk circling, and the shape of the man crouched beside the stream. Keira tasted her own fear and something else.

She watched the man's reflection wipe its hand across its mouth.

"These are dangerous times. We should travel together."

"You're kind to make the offer." Keira straightened. What was taking Hipolla so long? This one's companion?

"Does that mean you accept?"

"Travelers should not do anything rash," she said.

He smiled slowly, stretching. He had evidently satisfied himself that she had no weapon.

"Wise of you, lad. Now pay me for the water you've taken." He rose suddenly, his hand on his sword hilt.

Keira took one step back, yelling for Hipolla, and scooped up a handful of dirt. The brigand pounced, but Keira flung the fistful of dirt in his face and splashed across the stream toward the mare. He caught Keira's shoulder, tripped her, and sent her sprawling on the wet bank. She yelled hoarsely, saw the mare snorting and backing into the woods, and tried to crawl away, reaching frantically for the dagger in her boot.

The brigand jumped astride her, knocked her head into the ground, and twisted her arms behind her back. "Now, lad, I'll spare you. I just need the mare and your valuables." His dagger point pricked her neck just below her right ear.

"I have none, just the mare." Keira spat dirt from her mouth and tasted blood where she'd bitten her tongue. Her ears rang as he knocked her head into the ground again.

The mare whickered. Suddenly there was a hiss of wind, a solid, dull thwack like a melon splitting. The man slumped forward across her, and she jerked away as the dagger's point dug into her skin. Something wet and sticky smeared her neck. She scrambled from beneath him, twisting to look up.

Hipolla loomed over them both, looking like a madwoman in the flapping gray robes. The man rolled and staggered to his feet, still clutching his dagger, his right hand reaching for his sword. Holding the club two-handed, Hipolla rammed it into his stomach, thrusting upward. Something cracked. The man's fingers clenched and loosened on his dagger. It fell and Keira snatched it.

Her eyes met Hipolla's. The man sank to his knees, his eyes staring into some strange distance. He coughed blood and crumpled to the ground. Hipolla took his dagger from Keira and slit his throat. But his eyes were still open. Keira stared transfixed at the second wide red mouth pouring out his lifeblood.

The man's spirit, reaching toward her like a baby groping for her knees, his will to live, was clutching at her spirit, sinking, fading, and finally snapping.

Hipolla touched her shoulder. "Are you all right?"

Keira nodded, stumbling to her feet. The taste of vomit surged into her mouth. She gagged, grabbing for her water flask.

"You're bleeding," Hipolla said. She traced a line below Keira's ear.

"It's nothing." Staring in amazement at the man, at Hipolla, and the bloody dagger, Keira touched her forehead in salute to her companion. Only then did she notice that both she and Hipolla were blood spattered.

"There's an old horse in the woods," Hipolla said, "with full saddlebags." She looked dazed for a minute but quickly recovered herself, lay down the ash club, and unfastened the man's sword belt.

Keira helped, the throb in her tongue bringing her back to reality.

Hipolla pulled the sword belt from beneath the man's body and examined his quilted leather armor. Together she and Keira tugged it off, along with the filthy clothes that Hipolla decided were in better condition than her own. The two dragged the body, clad only in its bloody tunic, into the woods. Keira knelt and traced a wheel on one bare, dead instep. For a moment she had felt the man's spirit; it was only proper.

"Even for him?" Hipolla asked.

Keira nodded.

"I never killed anyone before," Hipolla said. "I thought he had you." Carefully imitating Keira, she drew a circle on the other foot.

Keira rose and wiped her hands across her pant leg. While she kept watch, Hipolla shed her robe in the shelter of the trees. She emerged looking like a mud-spattered, thoroughly disreputable youth. With the dead man's dagger she cut her hair, then dug a hole in the soft earth and leaves and buried it.

Keira ripped the cast-off robe into long strips and packed them in her saddlebags. Hipolla cleaned the man's dagger with a rag.

"It should be purified," she said, "now that it has drawn blood. I hope this will be enough." She adjusted the sword belt around her waist, sheathed the dagger, and gave the club to Keira. Then she opened the man's rakka flask, and instead of taking a swig, splashed a handful on the cut below Keira's ear.

It stung like a hundred needles biting. Keira cursed. "Why did you do that?"

"Our healers use rakka so. It helps wounds heal."

"It's meant to drink."

"Not among us. It defiles the mind, it takes away the will and dreams." Hipolla stoppered the flask without taking a sip.

In man's clothes Hipolla moved with a different rhythm, and Keira studied the difference, altering her own movements, thinking of how Roshannon had moved.

The highland pony balked when Hipolla mounted.

"It smells death," Keira said. She held a bunch of sourgrass under the pony's nose. It nuzzled the grass, lipped the tiny yellow flowers, and accepted the offering. The pony licked her hand for the taste of salt until it calmed. Briskly, she rubbed the broken star on its forehead, then moved to the mare and mounted in silence. There is no luck in a dead man's clothes, she thought.

"Lian Calla," Hipolla said.

She pointed to a lush green valley, where a string of horsemen rode along a hillside trail. Keira propped herself on her elbows, watching the road. They had hidden their horses among the trees and later realized that what they thought was forest was a vast tea plantation, built in terraces up the hillside, and interspersed with sweet-thorn and nut trees. The open blackflowers poured their resinous scent into the air, making Keira's mouth water; she had stuffed her pockets full of fallen leaves and flowers, hoping for a moment when she and Hipolla could brew tea. She tried not to think of Roshannon as she stared at the hills and valleys, all girded with terraced fields. She, who had grown up on the rich southern plains, marveled at the tenacity of farmers who had to hoard earth behind stone walls on steep hillsides.

She wrinkled her nose at the odd new smell that Hipolla said was the bay, an incredible odor with a backlash of salt and dyers'

vats, that wafted in from the west and challenged the more delicate scent of the tea flowers.

"It smells like a chamber pot someone was too lazy to empty,"
Keira said.

"Only when the wind comes across the bay." Hipolla laughed.
"Never seen the sea before and all you do is say it stinks. What
will you say when you see Cartheon?"

A breeze swept inland and tatters of fog that lay at the foot of
the hills dissipated. Beyond them, the countless terraced green
hillsides mounted like giant staircases into the blue sky, with each
layer of steps full of clustered settlements, fields, orchards, and
pastures. Keira flinched at the thought that Roshannon's eyes
might have rested on this same scene, or might soon do so. Last
night she had dreamt he was chasing her. He caught her, spun her
about by the shoulder. His face had been the brigand's first, then
become his own. His hands had closed on her neck. Maybe if she
swigged the rakka tonight, she would not dream of him.

Hipolla pointed farther westward. Far below, beyond a series
of hills and the sprawled shape of a city, a silvery line winked at
the edge of the land.

"The sea," she said.

A dull reddish stain hung in the sky, and smoke drifted along
the seaward ridges.

"Even if there is trouble here," Hipolla said, "maybe we could
persuade a trading ship to take us north." Hipolla nudged Keira's
shoulder. "What do you think?"

Keira started. "You think it wise to enter Lian Calla?"

"Just to the edge of the harbor where the fishermen keep their
boats. Just to persuade someone to take us north along the coast—"

Keira shook her head. "No."

"What do you mean, no?"

"He may be there."

"He?"

"My husband."

"Would he recognize you in men's clothes?"

"I'm wearing *his* clothes. And even if I weren't, he—he would
know me."

Hipolla looked at her. "He really scares you, doesn't he?"

"Last night I dreamt of him chasing and catching me. Just before I woke his hands were round my neck."

"I thought you didn't dream."

"I usually don't remember them. This one I did."

Hipolla laid a hand over Keira's. "Do you really think he might be here?"

Keira nodded.

"Let's skirt Lian Calla. I'd rather not go against such a dream, even if it is only a southlander's dream."

Since dawn Roshannon's hand had strayed to his boot top. The countryside had begun to look familiar, but his inner senses gave him no peace. Increasingly, visions of home, of the rich, timbered sea islands where he spent his boyhood, filled his head. But his visions of that girl had grown far stranger. Had it been an ordained turn of the Wheel that cast her into his path?

He twisted his fingers absently in the reins, then scratched the annoying spot below his right ear. He could have sworn someone had pricked his neck with a dagger while he slept. The annoying sensation had started this morning, after he woke from the dream of a dagger dripping with blood. Curious, he had first unsheathed his own dagger and examined it carefully, before saddling the gelding.

Impatiently, he pushed the wooden ring back on his little finger; the small act summoned Keira back into his thoughts.

The older loyalty to his home, which he had not seen in three years, and the mystery of the woman he had bought circled in his head like duelers in an even match.

He thought of the sea, the currents that surrounded the islands, each with its separate color, smell, and wave patterns. He thought of his cousin Ni'An, his dead uncle's child, gotten on a kitchen maid, but according to the laws of the clan, raised with every privilege granted a child whose parents were wed. Ni'An would have been an outcast, a bastard in the Sanctum. The Sanctum soldiers Roshannon served with had scoffed at the clans' extended families. "Is it true," they jeered at Lian Calla mercenaries, "that you men accept any child a woman drops as yours?" Roshannon had been baited thus many times.

"Is it true," Lian Calla men retorted, "that you men lock your wives and daughters away, making them wear clothes that hide their hair and faces, lest another man see them and try to steal them from you?" Sometimes daggers came flashing out, more often fists. Sometimes more men died brawling over differences of custom than in the actual fighting.

Folk were strange, Roshannon thought, and nothing was stranger than to see yourself, if only for an instant, as a stranger would.

The island clans formed allegiances with foreign peoples by marriage or leman contract. When blood mixes, spirits meet and mix, the elders said. Besides, mixed blood was held to keep people from becoming too puffed up, too arrogant, or sickly and mad.

He amused himself imagining what the clan would think of Keira Danio. His own child by the weaver Jeta would be walking and babbling now. He felt a sudden keen desire to see the child, or hear someone speak of it.

He drew rein and scanned the countryside, frowning. The land was awakening to spring, yet oddly still. Even the faithful hawks that had accompanied him seemed to flush little game. Story-tellers and players and traders, even peddlers bearing their merchandise on their backs, should be traveling the roads south of Lian Calla by this time of year.

Roshannon headed for the coast. The swift, surefooted gelding carried him through the hilly borderlands of Lian Calla province, where the free-held farms often bore the sign of the Wheel on their gates, while rounded god stones watched over their fields.

Roshannon rode hard, until the sweat on the gelding's neck was lathered into foam and the horse dropped its head, spraddle-legged, to drink from a brook. It was well beyond twilight. Exhausted, he tended the horses, hobbling both the gelding and the stallion. He built no fire and ate only tart, sour cress from an icy creek.

Before dawn he rose, vowing to smell the blackflower tea plantations by forenoon. He rode the stallion, driving himself and the horses through the hilly farmlands that bordered Lian Calla, past endless tiny strips of fields wrested from the woods, past the proud red gates of free-hold farms, past watchtowers and fortified stone holds.

By afternoon he reached the foothills that sloped up to the mountainside tea plantations. The wind from the sea carried the scent of blackflowers and the salt tang of the ocean. But another scent came as well, the smell of smoke.

❀ 7 ❀

Roshannon followed old hunting trails across the ridges and into the highest levels of the tea plantations. From the blackflower groves, a sweeping view of Lian Calla city-state spread out below him.

A green necklace of islands curved in from the western horizon, their names like a prayer sailors said, bringing home their ships: Farrayuan, where he had been born, Norr, Delithe, Ys, Kos, Ran, Merida, and Silla, the near island.

The rocky promontory of the city proper thrust into the sea, a giant arm almost meeting the islands. Lian Calla port was a great natural amphitheater, hands of earth and rock that cupped the fine harbor. Its sandstone walls shone gold in the clear afternoon light; taller than any structure inside the city gates rose the double towers of the clan citadel.

Roshannon rode through the blackflower groves, reining in, breathing in the sea smell and listening for its faint insistent roar. Fruit and lumber trees, flowering dogwood, and wild cherry interspersed the plantations. In this season shipwrights and apprentices usually searched the woods for trees that would yield the ribs and keels and hulls for island schooners. The warm sea winds brought spring on early, yet he encountered no one in the plantations.

Outside the groves stood a dozen god stones representing the united clans of the coast and islands. Each stone bore a clan crest on one side and a carved man and woman embracing on the other, the image of infinity, fertility, and increase. Roshannon touched the ancient stones as he rode by, for they were said to bring luck. Below the blackflower plantations, in tiers of broad terraces descending to the city and the harbor, stretched the fields and orchards that fed Lian Calla. Settlements of tea workers, freehold farmers, artisans, and peasants clustered nearby. But flames danced on house roofs and smoke rolled over the settlements like obscuring fog.

Smoke rose from the merchants' quarter of the city. The unmistakable stench of burning thatch filled the air. The eerie scream of a horse, the bellows of livestock, and the cries of people drifted up to him. In the tier above the orchards the tiny figures of a dozen riders galloped, the sun winking on their armor as they torched cottage roofs. A half-dozen men pursued the fire setters.

Sanctum men.

As Roshannon watched, horrified that another dream image had come true, a pursuing archer shot a Sanctum man, who slumped forward over his saddle.

Roshannon spurred the dun stallion through the labyrinth of fields. Maddened by the smell of smoke, the beast plunged over the stone walls between fields. The gelding followed, fighting the lead rein. The closer he came to the sea the more he saw of what his dreams had shown. God stones had been ripped from fields. In the final strip of land between orchards and fields, only three remained, like the last teeth in an old man's mouth.

But the earth and stone walkways between fields had helped break the fires. Mist rolled in over the seaward hills, damping the flames but spreading smoke everywhere.

At one cottage with a blazing roof, an artisan beat the burning thatch with bedding. A boy and girl drew buckets of water from the well, tossing them on the thatch and racing for more. Roshannon dismounted nearby, tying his horses to a wagon shaft and blindfolding their eyes with his sash.

A woman struggled to drag a chest and cooking pots from the house. Roshannon dashed inside. Flames had eaten through the thatch, opening the rafters and rooftree to the sky. The smell of damp, smoldering thatch and charred wood mixed. Sparks whirled in the air as the fire consumed the rafters. The wife, her lower face swathed in a wet rag, tugged frantically at an iron-bound chest.

"Outside," Roshannon said, choking on smoke. He hefted the chest onto his shoulder and plunged after the woman.

The man and his children flung water onto the flames, refusing to give up hope, but stood at last before four badly charred and roofless walls. A last bucketful of water hissed as it landed on the hearthstones inside the house. Half-dazed, the family sat on their mound of salvaged possessions. The children, their faces streaked with soot and tears, stared at the smoking remains of their house.

The man wiped his hand across his soot-streaked face, refastened the well bucket, and sent it down for fresh water. He offered Roshannon the first drink from a carved wooden dipper.

"I thank you, ka, for helping us," he said. "I don't believe I know you."

The woman looked up from her own dipper of water. "Why, don't you remember, Erdi, Roshannon-ka who went to war some years ago?"

"Gods, Lucky Nikka, they always called you?" The man's face twisted as if he wanted to grin, or thump Roshannon's shoulders, but was unsure what was permitted now. He touched his forehead. The intricate tattoos that artisans favored covered the backs of his hands. "Those bloody bastards."

"When did this trouble start?" Roshannon asked, undoing the dun stallion's reins.

"When the Sanctum appointed a governor here, this winter."

His wife put her hands on her hips. "They have no respect for women, either."

Erdi nodded. "They pressed the council for years. Some days ago southern soldiers entered the city. The council closed the gates, so that no one could enter or leave."

Roshannon took the blindfold from the stallion's eyes and mounted. His shoulder throbbed with a ghostly pain; he dreaded what he might find in the city. He undid the gelding's lead reins and tossed them to Erdi. "Take this horse. It belonged to a Sanctum man; perhaps you can find better use for it."

He passed another burned cottage with a family picking through salvaged possessions, and spurred the stallion on. He made out the red foresail of a witch schooner riding in the harbor, at anchor among the island fishing craft. The witches had always traded with Lian Calla, though trade had lapsed since his boyhood when more mercenaries began taking southern pay. A witch ship anchored in Lian Calla harbor would irk Sanctum delegates and merchants, though Lian Calla had maintained trade with the northern cities as well as the southern, all the while warily eyeing the two powers' conflicts. But no islander would serve the south

against the north, for that would violate the neutrality Lian Calla
had followed since the days of the Schism.

We are like the man who stands aside watching others duel,
Roshannon thought. Now the dagger's at our back and we must
choose sides.

He slapped the horse's flank, galloping through the town that
had grown up outside the gates, through the market and artisans'
quarter, onto the broad paved road that led to the south gate. Four
horsemen challenged him before the barred gate. He held his
hand palm up, in friendly greeting, relieved to spot the clan marks
on their shields. They had a prisoner, a Sanctum man with bound
hands, who sat his horse glumly.

"Nikkael Roshannon-ka?" one guardsman asked. "And no
ghost?"

Roshannon nodded.

Their chief stood in his stirrups and hailed the gatehouse
guards. "Open up, for a prisoner and a guest."

The massive bar creaked upward, and one of the great double
doors swung open. Roshannon rode through with the guard troop.
His right shoulder throbbed with a dull ache and he felt giddy
from the effects of inhaling smoke in the burning cottage. Marks
of skirmishing showed inside the gates: smears where blood spattered on the cobbles had been hastily scrubbed away; a half-
burned cart propped against the side of the gatehouse. One
guardsman had a bandaged arm.

"Where are my mother and cousin?" Roshannon said.

"Ka." The guardsman pointed to the towers of the citadel and
nodded. Roshannon rode with the guard and their prisoner into
the heart of the city. The streets were deserted, with all house
windows shuttered; their horses' hooves echoed on the cobbles.
No children scrambled in the streets; everywhere the reek of
smoke and damp, charred wood clung. Roshannon glanced up at
the banner over the citadel, pleased to see the circle of green and
blue waves, not the Sanctum banner of his dream. Near the great
market several tall, proud merchants' houses stood with caved-in
roofs and soot-rimmed windows. Beneath the market's red entry
gate, three clansmen had cornered a Sanctum merchant and
dragged him off, squealing protests. Two sailors carried away a
Sanctum soldier's body, the dead man's hands dragging on the
cobbles.

Roshannon dismounted, looking about for someone to take his horse. He called to a gray-robed healer's lad and held out the reins.

"Ka," the boy said, bowing to him.

Roshannon grinned at his formality. "Where is the lady of the harbor, my mother?" The peculiar sensation in his shoulder had not gone away; his arm felt stiff and numb.

The boy nodded toward the citadel as he stroked the dun's forehead.

The guardsmen dismounted, too, and marched their prisoner before them. "Come with us," their young chief offered. "I'm not sure the mess of them has been cleaned out yet. We've blocked off the entire Sanctum quarter, but some of the devils may have escaped."

Roshannon thanked him but went on alone, trotting up the maze of streets that led to the citadel. Riding here was impossible, and the narrowness of the streets could become a defense of final resort. The tunnel-like streets opened suddenly on plazas and carefully tended gardens. But the gardens before the temples and bathhouses were deserted. Collapsed market stalls littered the bathhouse plaza. A surgeon healer, from the middle islands by her dress, was speaking gently to a wounded man as two helpers eased him onto a litter.

Roshannon sped down the long, deserted porticoes of the bathhouse. A cat streaked out of his way, leaping an overturned ko board and scattering marker stones. Sunlight broke through the clouds and veils of smoke, making the vivid mosaics glitter underfoot.

Two at a time Roshannon took the stone steps behind the bathhouse into the uppermost level of the city. At the top of the hundred great broad steps, one for each island clan, was a garden of ancient blackflower and sweet-thorn trees with barbs as long as a man's fingers. Beyond this garden lay the moat that surrounded the clan tower. The drawbridge was down but guarded by twenty men. Some drew swords when he approached; others fingered the hilts of their weapons, their backs to the tower. One of those men he would have recognized anywhere: a man shorter than himself, with an unscarred face, who wore a pearl at his left earlobe.

"Ni'An Lia Roshannon," Roshannon cried.

"Cousin?" a shocked, familiar voice said. Ni'An's sword

snicked back into place. He ran to Roshannon. "Not a ghost and not dead in the wars?"

Roshannon shook his head. From the corner of his eye he watched the others relax. No one else in the garden looked familiar.

Ni'An embraced him. They kissed, then pummeled each other's back, rowdy as boys. Ni'An held him off at arm's length. "You smell of travel and of smoke, Nikka. And who dared change your face?"

"A man who no longer lives."

Ni'An grinned. "Your mother will want to see you. Come, they're all in the room that overlooks the harbor." Guards inside the tower started as if they had seen a ghost and waved the cousins on. "Your mother was hurt," Ni'An said quietly. "One of the island healers is tending her."

"How badly hurt?" Roshannon asked.

"Not badly enough to keep her from attending council."

Roshannon heard the grin in Ni'An's voice. "Only death will stop her from doing that. What has the Sanctum been doing? I helped a family drag their things from a burning house."

"Oh, aye, it's gotten bad." Ni'An stopped in the middle of the stair and pointed up. "Listen." As they climbed the stone stairs to the upper levels of the double towers, the sound of gruff debate had grown louder. "They're in the mapmakers' rooms. Your mother called the Ivarra together earlier, to reason with the Sanctum, but the bastards brought weapons into the court. They killed old Tain and one stabbed your mother in the right shoulder before we got him."

"This means war," Roshannon said. "The end of the neutrality."

"Oh, aye. That's exactly what it'll mean. You cannot reason with the Sanctum. Or what say you, after fighting for them?"

Roshannon watched his cousin's face. Three years had changed the boy into a man, and what else had three years done? "They think in a different way than we do, and I can't say I have much taste for their reasoning."

They crossed the antechamber and came face-to-face with the guards outside the double doors. Impassive, one guard stood back and pushed the great door inward.

Roshannon and Ni'An thrust in among the crowd. Everyone was talking at once, shouting and airing grievances. The low tables where mapmakers, shipbuilders, and navigators usually conferred had been shoved together to form a vast platform in the south end of the room. On this raised dais sat the Ivarra, the council members and elders who governed Lian Calla. Clansmen and traders, hotly debating the day's events, crowded around them. Roshannon slipped past a gray-robed healer who stood bandaging a merchant's arm. A pair of clansmen led away a loudly complaining Sanctum merchant.

Hands clasped Nikka's shoulder, people spoke his name, wonderingly. Faces of clansmen and comrades he had not seen in three years, along with the traditional mercenary welcome, "What, you in the flesh, not a ghost?" blurred by him. Roshannon lost Ni'An in the crowd, but suddenly spotted the straight-backed woman sitting on the dais near the window. He hurried toward her. She was talking with the councilors seated on either side of her, the chiefs of the Norr and Delithe islanders. She wore the councilor's black tabard, belted and girdled, and through her girdle was thrust the dagger of clan authority, the shey'na.

She turned from speaking to the man on her left. The moment Roshannon's eye met hers his shoulder burned more intensely. He noticed the slight tilt of his mother's head, the mouth pressed tight, as if pain were an unworthy annoyance she was trying to ignore.

His mother smiled. "Nikka."

He knelt, touching fingertips to forehead. Looking up, he saw her face twist in pain. Her left hand clenched and she slumped forward.

"Healer," he yelled, jumping onto the dais to support her.

A gray-robed man hurried forward, gesturing clansmen away, and pulled aside the folds of her cloak, revealing a bloody, bandaged shoulder.

Impressions of his mother's pain washed over Roshannon; his breath caught in his throat and the din of the crowd swelled. He lowered her into the chair, wondering if his sharing of her pain lessened the pain she felt. She came to, and with not quite her old impatience, batted away his hands and the healer's.

"Lady," the bearded healer said, "I warned you. And I cannot tend you here."

Lady Roshannon drew the sheathed dagger from her girdle and handed it to the man on her right: Vertis, the chief of the Delithe islanders. The crowd hushed, clearing a space to the door. Ni'An appeared at Roshannon's elbow; together they carried her through the antechamber and into the adjoining chamber, the old navigator's map room.

The room was bare and bright and the two cousins laid Lady Roshannon on the highest of the map tables, near the window so the healer would have plenty of light. The healer adept followed. He opened the leather haversack he carried, rummaged a moment, and selected lengths of spidersilk wadding and phials.

"We need fire and hot water," he said. "And some basins." He frowned in Ni'An's direction. Ni'An drew flint and steel from a belt pouch, laid it on the table beside Lady Roshannon, and disappeared out the door.

"Scalding water," the adept was muttering. "To infuse the potion." He pulled a small bottle of dark amber spirits from his pack. "Uncork it," he told Roshannon.

Lady Roshannon's eyelids fluttered. "Healer, you should not order my son about."

"Ah, lady. You should not have come to council dripping blood."

"You would always be the last tended, lady." Roshannon opened the bottle of spirits and recoiled at its reek.

The healer took it and placed it carefully on the table. He peeled the layers of blood-soaked cloth away from the wound. Roshannon watched in a sort of horrified fascination. He had seen many wounds and himself had many scars, but he preferred not to think about what the body was like beneath its thin layer of hair and skin. He exchanged a look with the healer and walked to the window.

The window offered a clear view of the harbor, the gatehouse, and the smoke-veiled hills. A sleek, red-sailed ship rode at anchor across the mouth of the harbor, and near the wharves a broad-beamed Sanctum merchantman was burning. A waterfront crowd cheered as its charred mainmast toppled, hissing, into the water. The ruined ship heeled over into the bay, sinking slowly. A pungent tang of burned, pitch-daubed wood filled the air while barrels, bales, and other flotsam rose free of the wreckage. Onlookers snagged loot with long boat hooks. "Save their barrels full of rakka," someone yelled. "The healers can use it." Scavenger boats flitted alongside and closed in, fishing out the cargo and surviving crew, including one frantic sailor astride a rakka barrel.

Roshannon turned back to his mother.

"What an unlucky homecoming for you," she said.

"Lucky that I am here now," he said. The adept had laid bare the still-bleeding wound, a slash that had raked across the shoulder and opened flesh to the bone. Roshannon winced and let his eyes go almost shut, while he took his mother's left hand. From his kit the adept drew needles and silk thread and the thin cauterizing wand.

Ni'An entered with a young girl carrying a basin of water. He set a small ritual brazier, obviously scrounged from the nearby temple, on the floor by the healer. The girl looked awed, but set down the deep basin without spilling a drop.

The adept set a small, covered basin to boil on the brazier, which was full of glowing coals. The palms of Ni'An's gloves had singed from the heat in the brazier's iron legs; he peeled them carefully off. The adept measured a dose of opiate into a tiny basin.

The drug's heavy, sweet smell permeated the air.

Lady Roshannon snorted. "That stuff gives me strange dreams, adept. I can bear pain."

"You've borne enough, lady." The healer dipped a sea sponge into the bowl of opiate, letting it soak in. "Hold it under her nose," he told Roshannon.

Roshannon did so, balancing the shallow basin beneath the sponge to catch drips. The fumes enveloped him, prodding him into a strange detached observation of the world. He watched the healer's jade earrings, the flash of his instruments, the quick, knowing hands moving in mysterious, soothing rhythms, and Ni'An and the girl mixing a solution of old spirits and sea salt under the healer's direction. The sickly sweet odor brought back memories of other healers working over him. The healer cleaned the wound, thrust the wand into the brazier, lifted it free, and touched it to Lady Roshannon's flesh to stop the bleeding. Her fingers dug into Roshannon's arm, then relaxed under the effects of the drug. His right shoulder twinged as his mother's head lolled back against his arm. The white streak in her hair had spread. Her slit eyes glittered under their lashes and her lips moved, forming no words that he understood.

The adept repeatedly washed the wound with steaming hot water. Then he painted a wash of spirits over the wound, pinched it together as if flesh were just a suit of clothes put on over the bones, and sewed it up with a needle and thread he fished with tongs from the boiling water. Then he applied layers of the sea salt and ancient liquor while Roshannon pinched his nostrils against the fiery stuff, thinking of all the southern rakka he had tasted and what excellent surgeon's potions it would make. The adept wrapped the arm in clean, spidersilk bandages and straightened from his task, smoothing his hands over his tunic.

He took the sponge from Roshannon, poured the drippings in the basin back into his phial, and grinned. "You will all make healer's assistants someday."

With great grogginess, Lady Roshannon shrugged off the effects of the drug. "But will I live and keep my arm, to prove your skill as a healer?"

"If you don't use the arm before you should and reopen the wound." The healer gathered his kit together. "I'll check it every day, ka. Rest, lady, until I tell you to be up and about."

"We will help you to your bed, Mother," Roshannon said.

She waved her left hand. "I won't be carried."

"Walk, then. We'll be one on either side of you." He raised an eyebrow at the healer, who stood by the door.

The man nodded. "Just see that she stays in bed when you get her there."

Roshannon supported his mother's weight on his left side as Ni'An paced by her right side. The girl held the door.

Roshannon glanced out the window. The sleek, northern schooner had lowered a ship's boat; the men aboard carried green truce banners. So we are going to talk with the witches and choose sides, he thought.

"Things grew stranger every year," Ni'An said as the two cousins paced by the bathhouse. They had returned to the council, listening to the arguments until midnight. Many favored executing the entire Sanctum quarter, some three hundred men, women, and children. But the quarter's residents stayed hidden in their houses, and with their two wells they could withstand a long siege. In every quarter of the city, the Sanctum residents had left marks, in mutilated relief carvings and defaced statues in the hall of justice where their main band of soldiers was imprisoned. In the streets, folk walked warily, and few carts rumbled into the market.

"They planned to usurp the city," Ni'An said. "One of the captured soldiers said they expected more troops, sent from Karda and A'Hrappa. For some reason those troops never came. If they had we would have been hard-pressed. The mercenaries that left with you to serve the Sanctum had returned a short time before, thinner in numbers. They were mostly far islanders and wanted to return home. When you weren't among them, we thought you were dead, though some recalled that you had set out to travel through the southlands on your way here." Ni'An looked at his cousin. "Did you learn anything to your liking?"

"I learned, but mostly not to my liking. I should have known the southerners would pull some trick such as this."

"Their merchants do not like our temple philosophers debating the nature of experience and letting men carry their private thoughts in their hearts. Their priests stood in the marketplace, haranguing people with their beliefs. No one listened much, because their doctrines do not appeal to us. They call us half-souled barbarians, but they worship a god who is all male and therefore only half a being. Then the merchants raised taxes on the goods coming from their lands to ours. They refused to pay rents for the traders' quarter we allowed them. They refused to speak with your mother, the shey'na-ka, because she is a woman. They called us traitors because our ships trade north as well as south." Ni'An threw up his hands in frustration. "They think only their own ways deserve respect. They call lemans whores who have no rights and should be whipped."

"What of Jeta?"

"She is safe. She put on widow's clothes."

"She is not married?"

"No, and her daughter is a keen little beauty, with your eyes."

"You have taken care of her?"

"The clan has done everything proper. Cousin, you should go to her."

"No. I can take her the gift of game but I cannot go for any other reason."

"Has war taken your taste for women?"

Roshannon grinned. "I hope only death will do that, cousin."

"What of the southern women? Is it true they are kept hidden away, with even their faces covered?" Ni'An leaned against the wall of the bathhouse.

Roshannon made a vague gesture, thinking of Keira: And also true they sleep once with a man, steal his clothes, ride off, and torment his dreams?

Ni'An watched his cousin's face, trying to figure what Nikka's trouble could be. A quirkiness of spirit, a sea change had come over Nikka. He insisted on going rabbit hunting that afternoon. If he fancied rabbit, any of the kitchen boys could have set snares, or any of the gamekeepers could have gone hunting as well.

The cousins spent an hour tramping in high meadows above the tea plantations, before Roshannon got two hares with his blowgun. He hurried home and with his own hands, skinned and dressed the two fat young hares. An embarrassed-looking stable boy interrupted him, saying he would dress the game, and three kitchen maids, giggling and incredulous at the sight of the shey'na-ka's son doing such work, made the same offer. Nikka waved them aside, also remaining deaf to Ni'An's offers of help.

Ni'An sat in a patch of shade, watching his cousin and chewing on sourgrass. A mystery had come back from the infidel wars with Nikka, a moody thing that wrapped him within itself and had turned him into a stranger.

Ni'An knew the rabbits were a gift for Jeta, and something more.

Mysteries had always drawn him, enchanted him, especially puzzles that had no answers or so many possible resolutions that they might as well have none. Good, deep mysteries were the best—such as why the child of a certain man and woman had different-colored eyes than either of its parents, when both swore they had slept with no others. Or why one man married a certain woman and not another, and why their love lasted or failed. Or why the leaf skeletons of certain trees followed always, unerringly, the same shape and exquisite pattern. Or why the limbs of creatures as lowly as frogs, when the meat was cooked from their skeletons, were shown to end in hands so like a tiny human hand that the similarities made a man's breath catch in his throat and filled him with wonder for days. Layers and layers of unknowns, thick as snow on the mountaintops in winter, mysteries entwining like the many-colored currents of the sea.

But the puzzle about Nikka concerned him more closely than any other and stirred in his heart. He and Nikka had shared everything: near death on a boar hunt, confidences about women and their first experiences of lovemaking, disagreements over philosophies and speculations about the nature of the world.

But now the mystery lay between them.

Roshannon took the two fat young hares to a weaver's cottage outside the eastern gate.

He stood outside Jeta's doorway, holding the trussed hares in a gloved hand. Her voice, singing an ancient ballad, was slightly off-key, just as he remembered it. The memory sent a hot trickle up his spine. The light slanting through her open doorway slid across her muscled arms and quick fingers as she beat down the latest line of color into the warp threads of a half-finished tapestry.

The girl child playing in the corner spotted him first. Her child eyes went big at the sight of a stranger come with a gift of meat. She ran to her mother and whispered in her ear.

Jeta turned to face him. She was beautiful, he thought, the ripe beauty of the woman come after the willowy grace of the girl.

"Roshannon-ka." She rose, touching her forehead and bowing her head, light sliding on her glossy black hair.

Her daughter, his daughter, imitated Jeta's obeisance, then stared at him in total innocent curiosity with eyes as black as his own.

"Which Roshannon-ka are you?" the child asked.

For a minute Roshannon and Jeta looked at each other, a smile forming on both their mouths. Then the moment faded beyond possibility into the complications and changes of the present.

"I am the Roshannon-ka who is your father," he told the child. He asked her name.

"I am Piri."

He read the curiosity in Jeta's eyes; Jeta, ever practical, was weighing him and her daughter on a scale of need and consequence, figuring the result.

She sent the child to wind yarn. "Have you come to take her into the tower?"

He shook his head. "It is for you to say when she will come to the tower." He suddenly wished the visit over, done, with all the possibilities of their future relationship severed and cauterized the way a battlefield surgeon would tend an amputated stump. He recalled their exuberant wrestling matches, and the beds they had shared. Jeta had bloomed, a rose open to the cycles of life. She made him think of a ripe wheat field with heat lightning shimmering above its surface. But she seemed faintly unreal, like a love from someone else's life.

He could not look at her without also seeing Keira Danio in his mind's eye—a boy-woman in his pilfered clothes.

He knew he would never touch Jeta again. Only the child connected them now. He watched her face, saw her absorb this knowledge that he was only just realizing himself. Jeta would not misunderstand. She would accept, forbear, send her child at the proper time into the clan tower to learn whatever would be of advantage to her, as any wise woman would.

"Take a husband from among the foresters or artisans, or shipbuilders, and forget me," he told her as he left.

8

Several days north of Lian Calla, Keira and Hipolla reached a short peninsula bounded by cliffs that plunged into the sea. Stunted trees clung to the cliffsides, gnarled and grotesque, bent backward by raking winds.

Bare patches of stonework glinted in the sun, and a carved stone face peeked through the mat of creepers.

The horses picked their way up a knoll. Blocks of carved stone lay scattered everywhere; any surface facing the sea winds was pitted and pocked with channels like those termites and beetles delved in wood. Stone columns rose among the scraggly bushes and trees.

Hipolla brushed her hand along the fluted shaft of a broken column as she rode past. "So it is real. The ruined city of the witches." She twisted the reins through her fingers. "Once this was Licarta, the mother city of Cartheon. It ruled the north before the Schism, before the borderlands lay full of dead men. Before the Sanctum had the power and the armies to destroy those who lived here, and plow the ground with salt."

Squinting seaward, Keira made out the patterns of ruined streets and the remains of tumbled walls, the outlines of a vast dead city being slowly buried by creeping plants and shifting soil and sand. Trees had rooted in the split blocks of once-great walls, and their creeping roots had buckled sections of mosaic pavement. Ruins full of wind-bent trees gleamed on half a dozen hills.

Lizards basked on the rounded fragments of a nearby god stone. Fat blue and green snakes sunned themselves on tumbled steps, their sleek bodies glittering like enamel in the sun.

"This would be the perfect place for soldiers to ambush us," Keira said.

Hipolla shook her head, her eyes sweeping the starker central ruins. "It is haunted, and unlucky to the Sanctum. Northern soldiers wouldn't come here. Only ghosts and lizards and snakes. And us. For sanctuary."

At the base of a high hill they dismounted and led the pony and mare. A blue-green lizard raced across their path, hissed, and spread miniature dragon's wings with taloned claws. It dodged Keira's boot toes, trilled, and disappeared among broken stonework.

A slow wind, like the voice of dead people in a dream, came whispering around the hill. Flashes of broken mosaic pavements and toppled columns spun in Keira's mind. She rebuilt the city in her imagination, a white stone citadel gleaming on the edge of the sea.

Hipolla left the pony to graze and went to explore. Keira slipped the mare's bit and hurried after her. She brushed her hand against the battered statue of a woman with a chipped nose and broken hands, smashed breasts and feet. It was one of many that remained in long rows, all casting blue bars of shadow across the remains of a mosaic temple floor. Leaves and earth had blown into the portico, and wild nasturtiums carpeted its floor. Collapsed roof timbers had dragged down against the columns. Mushrooms and bright orange fungus thrived in the rotting wood, and vines smothered the broken columns in green.

Keira walked by the columns, brushing her hand along stone legs and the carved folds of trailing robes. The Sanctum forbade the representation of the body—for the flesh was only the shell that held the spirit. To delight in it was to worship unworthiness.

The well-known teaching tasted bitter on her lips. In wonder she studied a subtly carved, smiling face the chisel had missed.

"Sppt! Slowpoke."

Keira trotted toward Hipolla's voice. The forest of columns opened onto broad crumbling steps, overgrown with weeds and thornbushes, and a plaza where a pool of water that dwarfed even the largest temple meditation pools reflected the sky.

Hipolla crouched at its edge, laughing and waving at Keira. "We can bathe, thank the gods. We reek of horse." She pulled off her boots and britches, sat down, and paddled her feet in the water. She peeled off her shirt and leaned back on her elbows with her eyes closed.

So much water was too much temptation to resist.

Keira tugged off her boots and stepped out of Roshannon's pants. The sun-warmed pavement burned her feet. She pulled off her shirt and unwound the sash bound about her breasts. A dark line of sweat and grime caked her skin above and below the sash. With luxurious ease she scratched the dirty skin above her breasts and across her belly and settled on the warm stone ledge beside Hipolla.

Hipolla cocked an eye at her and splashed her foot down hard in the pool. Water splattered them both. Impulsively, Keira pushed her off the ledge into the water. But Hipolla grabbed Keira's hand as she fell, and with a great splash, both toppled in. Sputtering, Keira flung water in Hipolla's face. They wrestled, dunking each other and emerging with dripping hair, sleek as otters.

Before the head cloth and ear tag had been put on her, Keira had swum in the creek near home, while her mother and Deva pounded clothes on the smooth wash stones. She paddled her hands in the water, remembering.

The girls pulled in their clothes, pounded them against the ledge to clean them, then spread them out to dry.

Hipolla splashed across the pool, kicking thunderously. Keira crossed more slowly, as the memory of swimming flowed back into her arms and legs. Water reflections danced over the relief carvings beside the pool. The figures of men and women, she saw with shock, were doing all the things Roshannon had done to her on her wedding night. The riot of carved shoulders, breasts, and legs, the hands lifted and outstretched, blurred as she turned away, flushing with embarrassment.

"You," Hipolla yelled. "What are you turning red about? Are you sunstruck?"

Keira ducked her head and swam to the other side of the pool, sick with worry again, sure that all the dreams of him meant she was with child. She floated on her back and closed her eyes until Hipolla ignored her. The sun-heated water rocked her. She had forgotten the good feel of it against her bare skin, the freedom of simply floating. Baths in her father's house had always been rare affairs, shallow basins of lukewarm water, except for the complete ritual bath after she bled each month and after her mother had given birth.

She touched her belly.

She struggled with the count of days, saying them over again in her head. By the moon and by the days she reckoned she was halfway through her cycle. Only when the full moon came again would she know if she was truly pregnant, and by then she should be inside the witch city. And there, among total strangers, it would be easier to lie.

A hand grabbed Keira's wrist. Hipolla coaxed her down to see fragments of a broken statue on the bottom of the pool. They broke the surface, splashed, and played tag.

"Our skin will be wrinkled as old crones," Hipolla said as they climbed out. Their clothes were stiff and dry, and smelled of the sea wind. The two girls basked by the pool until the sun slid toward the west.

"Who did that to your back?" Hipolla asked. "Your husband?"

"My father."

Hipolla plucked sourgrass, knotted it, and chewed an end thoughtfully. "Do you know that you are beautiful?"

Keira frowned, because Roshannon had said that, too. "It is of no use to be such a thing. It is flesh, not spirit."

"One and the same. Indivisible. Both holy." Hipolla grinned as Keira's eyes widened at the heresy. She touched Keira's shoulder. "I'm sorry. I've offended thee, and I owe thee much, but not offense."

The two put on their dried shirts and explored the ruins.

Hipolla pointed across the water and the spit of land. "Lyssa bay is beyond that headland, just another day or so, where the sea reaches into the land with five finger bays. Cartheon sits where they meet.

"I'll tell you how the world was created," she teased, "if you tell me how your priests say it was done." They perched on broken steps overlooking the sea.

Looking north, with the salt wind drying her hair, Keira told the story of creation: of the voice in the darkness and the spirit Wheel shaped from the breath of the voice, of the first man, the bearer of the spirit, and the first woman, his servant, who let evil into the world, and the turning of the Wheel.

Hipolla wrinkled her nose. "There is a meanness at the heart of that story, like a worm eating the heart of an apple." And she told the story of the voice in the darkness, and the spirit Wheel shaped from the breath of the voice, and the being.

"The being, both male and female, fertilized itself with its own imagination and lived in the cosmos countless time. Out of boredom and curiosity and loneliness, it decided to create beings unlike itself. So it dreamt and made: animals and plants and the bones of the earth itself. Into each creation it put a piece of its own spirit. And still it was not content, though it had divided its essence and was fading fast. At last, the being created two creatures, man and woman. But it discovered it had given away all but one morsel of its spirit to the winds and waters. So it divided this last bit of its spirit to give these creatures souls. But since both have only half a piece of spirit, they strain forever the one toward the other, and joining with the other to gain completion is their greatest desire. Now men and women have forgotten they each carry half of the complete soul. That is why they quarrel and why one can never please the other, you see."

"What an interesting heresy." Keira wriggled her toes in the sunlight, thinking about the cycles of her body while the sun's warmth pressed her down, down into the earth. How fascinating and frightening that what the witches thought about souls was oddly like the priests' doctrine.

She leaned back on her elbows. "But, what *does* happen when men and women join? Do they truly become one, two bodies and two natures bound into one spirit?"

"Is that what happened with your husband?"

Keira stared fiercely at her bare toes and felt her face go hot.

" 'Twas you who asked." Hipolla smiled slowly. "But I've heard that if two are joined truly, body and spirit, then the one can see through the other's eyes, feel through the other's skin, be where the other is, know all that the other knows."

"That is demonic possession." Keira folded her hands across her belly.

"No, it is a gift."

The archpriest sat alone in his tent, wrapped in meditation and misgiving and an ache of longing.

He had dreamt twice of the field where he had ordered his soldiers to take tithes from travelers stopped along the road. The scene engraved itself into his brain—the stark fields barely softened with the first green growth of crops, and the thick woods edging the highway.

Something in the leafed-out trees had raised the hair on the back of his neck. A presence.

Fool, he thought, I should have ordered the soldiers to search the woods near the highway. Instead he had tucked his misgivings away into the routine of squeezing goods and cooperation from the travelers. But the dream of the stand of trees whispering as the wind rustled their foliage left him uneasy. The dream prompted a keener desire to taste the strangeness of the witches, to travel the realm of visions.

He hated the witches because it was his duty, but yearned to fathom their abilities.

He had learned that pain, vigils of deprivation, and self-flagellation were his doors into visions. When he needed pain great enough to achieve the vision state that he craved more and more, he dismissed his servants and sent for the chief torturer.

The chief torturer was a soft-spoken man named Set who wore a fastidiously trimmed beard. He had worked among the novice priests, examining them for the taint of heresy, and, his job done, been recently dispatched to the archpriest's camp, where Lyrian appreciated his artistry.

"Those with blue and gray eyes tolerate pain best," the torturer had said. "I don't know about yellow and green eyes. Dark-eyed people seem to scream faster than any others. It is, of course, just something I have noticed in my work."

Lyrian had blue-gray eyes and a great tolerance for pain. He sometimes thought the torturer understood him better than anyone else. The man was an artisan of pain who played every bone and nerve of his chosen instrument, the human body, exquisitely.

The chief torturer, who camp rumor said had once been a healer, gave him what he needed—pains that racked bone, muscle, and nerve until he lifted from awareness of his flesh, leaving it behind like a flayed skin, and entered a territory of visions intoxicating as scraps of dreamscapes that tantalized a just-wakened sleeper in the morning.

Set was unorthodox—he disdained cutting, burning, and breaking bones—and might have been accused of heresy had he not been so effective in getting confessions from recalcitrant priests, prisoners, and hysterical women.

"But to cause pain and leave no mark," he said in his soft voice as he began work on the archpriest's legs, "that is true craft."

The archpriest screamed, a glorious release as pain flooded his body. He looked at his right knee, because it felt as if his leg had been snapped off there. His leg was whole but for the torturer's attentions.

"Thank you," Lyrian said. Gritting his teeth, he dismissed the torturer and surfaced in the land of visions, seeking the presence that had so disturbed him.

Lady Roshannon propped herself up against her pillows. The bed curtains and shutters had been opened so she could see both city and harbor. Navigational charts and a tapestry worked in dozens of blues and greens to resemble the changing currents of the ocean hung on the austere room's whitewashed walls.

"Sit down, Nikka." She indicated a flat-topped chest and the tea bowls on a table by her bed.

"I dreamt of you and the hills and harbor, ka," he said.

"So you should, as I did of you, though I was not sure I would ever see you again." She set down her tea bowl a bit stiffly, and held out her hands. They touched fingertips.

"The shoulder aches?"

She grinned. "No doubt in future winters it will sharpen my memory of these events." She settled farther back against the pillows. "Have you sent word to the shipmaster?"

He nodded. "Your word and my seal."

"They will want surety, a token of trust and goodwill to go to the witch city."

"A hostage, you mean."

"And it will be you. You've never been to the great city, of course."

"It's full of wonders."

"So the stories say. Your ears have always been sharp for stories." She sipped tea as she gazed out the window, and Roshannon thought she was looking at something far away or long ago.

"Have you ever been there?"

She raised her chin. "No, but the witch lords came more freely to our harbor years ago. You remind me of your father, the last time I saw him, when he sailed north." She set the bowl down. "Nikka, I wish you wouldn't go, but you are the best one to send."

He frowned at her choice of words, her hesitancy as she spoke. It was unlike her.

"Lady, is there something you would tell me?"

"Is there something you are not telling me?"

They regarded each other a long moment, until they laughed, leaving both questions unanswered.

"I would prefer that you get children on your own wife someday soon," his mother said.

"Women turn my eye, Mother, but not yet my heart."

"Aye, and the result of one of your turns of eye is now walking and thriving, showing a taste for letters and charts."

Nikka smiled, glad his mother's interest in his daughter was genuine. As they discussed the business of the harbor, trade between the islands and the coast, he wondered what she would make of Keira Danio.

She steepled her fingers. "We must ally with someone, yet keep a measure of independence. My heart shrinks from the south. The governor they tried to foist on us and his retinue of priests actually destroyed navigational instruments as blasphemous things."

Roshannon nodded. "My heart shrinks from the Sanctum, too, lady, and more so since I served them. Their minds travel places I don't want to follow."

"Indeed," his mother said. "Find out which way the witches' minds turn when you go among them. The disagreements that put north and south at each other's throats generations ago are legends now; no one will tell a straight tale. We counselors have questioned every Sanctum man and northern trader who has traveled here about the history of the Schism, and what sparked it. We need to know precisely what those old quarrels were, to figure where our advantage will lie."

Roshannon nodded, staring out the window at the harbor. "When I send dispatches to you, we use the agreed-upon code? The one that even Ni'An does not know?"

"Aye. It may save his skin if anything goes wrong for you—" Lady Roshannon exchanged glances with her son. Someone knocked lightly on the door. "Come in."

A maid entered carrying soup and bread, followed by the surgeon.

"One last thing," Lady Roshannon said as Nikka bowed to her. "Return to Lian Calla alive and well. And stay long enough so that your hand learns to know a boat's tiller again, and the plow handles in sowing season."

Roshannon had not stood so close to witches since boyhood, when the northerners entered Lian Calla freely and traded openly at the waterfront market. When the Sanctum began to hire more islanders as mercenaries, the witches had anchored their great schooners beyond Lian Calla's harbor and sent crew members ashore in ship's boats to trade.

With his clansmen, he bowed as the northerners stepped inside the council room.

This shipmaster was old beyond reckoning, but her golden eyes were clear and keen. A gold circle of rank gleamed against the dark skin between her brows. A raven, a ship's bird that carried messages between vessels, rode her left shoulder. A familiar bound by witchcraft, according to Sanctum belief. Beside her walked a young woman with silver hair and golden eyes. A gray hunting cat padded along between them. Daggers and thick, carved staves hung at their belts. A clerk gestured them toward the low tables where steaming bowls of blackflower tea waited.

"I am Irina Cathaya," the elder said, "and this is my niece and pilot, Isharra Lir."

The shipmaster glanced about, perhaps testing the room with her witch senses, before she sat down. The younger woman lifted her tea bowl first as a sign of honor and trust. She watched the assembly with careful, golden eyes.

Roshannon felt the hair on his arms stand up; he was sheathed in gooseflesh. With their silver hair and yellow eyes, the witches had an otherness about them that made men pause. But the exact quality of that otherness remained a mystery, because the witches and their natures were so wrapped in fantastic tales, rumors, and gossip. During three years among southern soldiers, his ears had been stuffed full of stories. Yet he could remember other times, long ago, when the silver-haired men with their yellow wolf eyes had sailed regularly into Lian Calla free port, trading stories of the far northern Ice Kingdoms along with bolts of spidersilk and coils of spider rope, and making the Lian Calla women laugh. Storytellers traveled with the trading ships, and he had joined the circle of children sitting spellbound at their feet whenever he could.

He had not feared the witches then, and he struggled with

himself to regain an almost childlike sense of acceptance, as he saw other men doing. The hunting cat paced a slow circle about the assembly room, then sat, blinking like an ordinary, lazy cat, grooming itself in a spot of sunlight.

The shipmaster coughed. "We wished to trade spidersilk for tea and pearls here, our usual business. We sail back to Cartheon, then north to Brink in the Ice Kingdoms, where the port should be ice free when we reach it. My cargo is almost loaded and I wanted to leave with the tide before dark. Yet my pilot says you want me to carry a message to the city."

"A message and a group of petitioners, including myself," Roshannon said. He wore his mother's shey'na through his sash and was conscious of the odd feel of it as he paced before the great window that overlooked the harbor.

He quickly bowed out of the proceedings, letting his mother's fellow councilors explain the situation. He looked out the window while the voices continued behind him. The witches' schooner, rigged in pale silk but for a bloodred headsail, stood at the harbor's mouth. Men in smaller boats skimmed around her, exchanging silk and tea, and tales, no doubt. In the room behind him other clansmen described how the Sanctum had violated Lian Calla's neutrality, honored since the time of the Schism. Roshannon stared at the northern schooner fore and aft, suddenly perceiving the oddity about the great figurehead beneath the bowsprit. It was a woman with her eyes closed as if she were dreaming or sleeping. Aft was a less elaborate figurehead of a dreaming man. He laughed to himself, marveling.

Roshannon turned his back on the view of the harbor and leaned at the window. The cat padded over, sniffed his hands, and stared with great round eyes into his face. It was unnerving.

The young pilot turned to look directly at him.

"The Sanctum considers that a man who does not follow its religion has no honor," she said. "Even that he is not truly a man. They consider that we have no honor and only half souls. Why should you who have served them so long and so well trust us?"

"We have always trusted you northerners enough to trade with you," Roshannon said. "And we do not bother with splitting souls. We have taken their pay, but we have not taken on their ways. We of the islands and the free port of Lian Calla have never had masters," he said slowly, "only contracts that we have honored." He looked about the room full of grim, waiting faces. "But for myself," he said, "I will be dead before I serve the Sanctum again."

"So will all the people of the islands and the free port," a councilor in the middle of the floor said. A chorus of assent rose, and half the island factions jumped to their feet.

The shipmaster raised her hands palm up, for silence. "The loss of your ships and your marshals will weaken the Sanctum armies," she said. "But you islanders and free porters have served too long as mercenaries for the lords in Cartheon to believe you will no longer ally with the Sanctum. I can take those who want to come to the city, to talk with the steward. I leave at dusk, the tide willing. With good winds, my ship should reach Lyssa, Cartheon's port city, by two days' nightfall."

Roshannon smiled to himself, thinking of the dream vision that had shown him Keira in the great city.

❀ 9 ❀

In the heart of the city of Cartheon, by the birthing pool inside the steward's bathhouse, the whisper of water and of women's voices echoed against the stone. Two midwife healers had been walking a third, much younger woman between them for hours, their sandals slapping the flagged stones as softly as a rhythm of rain. Now they escorted the vastly pregnant woman down the stone steps to the pool.

Aramit Leyto, the high steward of Cartheon, knelt beside his leman, Sira, as she stood in the pool. She clutched his right hand tightly, digging her nails into his palm. The birthing was going well, even though it was her first, but she was terrified of physical pain.

He stroked her forehead. He had mind-touched her to ease her pain and distress, but now he disentangled himself from her fears. He wanted to seek the one just emerging into the world, to touch the new spirit and know if it would be a dreamer, a miratasu, an awakened one.

"Ka." The two senior midwives stood on either side of him, watching Sira. The eldest sister touched his shoulder. "Ka. Let her bring the child forth."

He looked up into the old one's face. She knew his hopes, and his fears, and also her own business, better than any other. *My business first,* her eyes said. *Then yours.*

He pressed Sira's hand and rose. The wet hems of his cloak and his robes dripped onto his sandaled feet. He joined the court dreamers, the brother-sister twins Riva and Thaia, waiting at the end of the pool. His mind swirled with the images of Sira's swollen, water-distorted body, bringing forth life. Sira was young and modest, though he tended to forget that; he wanted to see everything.

120

The dreamers nodded to him and continued their ko game. Doubtless they had wagered on the child's nature. They doubted it would have the dreaming gift but were far too politic to contradict his hopes.

He paced past them, reciting a veda in his head, and sending it also into Sira's head, to calm her and give her strength. By the water clocks, it had been twenty-eight hours since she had begun, doubled over her belly and digging her nails into his palms.

"You could hasten this," he had said to the eldest midwife as he drew her aside earlier.

"Hasten, and maybe harm the child."

He eyed her. She meant, perhaps, that the drugs might rob the child of its dream self, if it were to be a dreamer.

"And potions could hurt the Lady Sira." The midwife had fingered the pouches of dried herbs on her belt and gone about her business.

He stared into the pool, sacred to women and to the mysteries, to the circle and the Wheel itself. He had not dreamt the child would be a dreamer, and that was a bad sign. Nor had he mindtouched the child in his leman's belly, because that was held to be dangerous and unlucky. Suddenly the three women at the edge of the pool cried out. He hurried over.

The child was emerging. The younger sister stood back, to let him see. The elder sister had waded into the pool, and half supported Sira in her arms. Sira crouched in the water, the surface of it just lapping her breasts. From between the water-distorted image of her legs, blood streamed up, a thin plume folding and feathering on itself. The child's dark head emerged between her thighs. Sira looked up at Aramit, her face joyous and triumphant, her hair plastered against her forehead in wet, dark tendrils from the steam in the birthing room. He knelt beside her while the child's shoulders and arms waved into the water, the tiny fingers curling and clenching, the attendant umbilical cord floating along the small, plump body, the penis like a strange bud tucked between the fat thighs.

He felt hope, watching the newborn child float unafraid above its mother's body. Sira balanced one hand under the child's foot, one hand against its ribs. Its eyelids fluttered but remained shut. Its forehead bobbed above the waterline, but it moved its limbs perfectly and needed to take no breaths, as long as the umbilicus fed it the stuff of life.

The child's head was above water now, and it opened its eyes. Aramit watched the baby closely, and took a breath. He said the first of the vedas in his own mind and sent a tendril of dream touch toward the new one.

The baby's consciousness stirred, waking to the world. It stared with blind, total curiosity at its surroundings, buoyant in the warm water, anchored to Sira by the cord of flesh.

Aramit probed inward and felt the world blur as he watched it through the newborn eyes. The unfocused eyes saw only motions and shadows, the ears heard only the comforting lap of water against stone and the low murmur of the midwives. The new mind, still embedded in the great interwoven cycles of the Wheel, still fed life's blood by the steady beat of Sira's heart, was tasting awareness. Aramit shared the wondrous tingle of pure newborn curiosity, the first great seed of the ability to travel into other selves, other bodies, other places.

The child flexed fingers and toes as he settled into its mind, ready to help it awaken. Aramit perceived the threads of connection rising from the child's self, because the awakening self is the center of the Wheel, threads wafting through water and air, glistening with the wonder of awareness, touching him, touching Sira, beginning to grow into them like the blind, tiny root hairs of a great tree probing unknown soil.

He drew a breath, murmuring the second veda that sounded like the lap of waves, the mimicked language of the womb.

Child, he thought, as he felt his son's awareness mesh into his own, dive into the river, leap the cliff, and fly, send your self questing now and your spirit will never be imprisoned in your body.

The child mind surged outward into the fragile, bridging threads. Aramit said the third veda as the root tips of his son's consciousness touched his own, a whisper touch, softer and more intimate than any caress between unawakened man and woman. His skin prickled with heat, sweat bloomed on his forehead, in his armpits, on his upper lip. He cradled his newborn son's awareness, ready to feed its tiny energy his own strength.

But something happened. The child mind recoiled as the tips of its dream self grew into the surface of a larger, older, vaster awareness. Its newborn mind clouded, filling with fear instead of

sheer joy, and its consciousness cringed, like a blind man staggering into a wall, and retreated, crumbling and diminished, becoming aware of itself as separate from the lapping water and
the murmuring voices, burrowing back into the lonely nest of
the flesh and blood, faltering and learning dread and eternal
aloneness.

There was no inward eye to open and fill with dreams, except
in a minor way, no inward dream self to outstrip the flesh.

His boy child was otherwise perfectly healthy and normal, and
for that he would rejoice in public, and honor the woman who had
given him the child. But in private he would mourn, that he had
fathered another who would never dream as he did.

He withdrew from the child mind, lest he frighten the boy, and
straightened by the pool. Emotions drained out of him, as if he
had witnessed the burial of a friend. The dreamers glanced up
from their ko game, watching him.

He kissed Sira's forehead. "I thank you, lady, for the healthy
son you have given me." He turned, summoning the dreamers. He
was suddenly tired and did not want to see the business of the
afterbirth, nor see the child taken from the pool, or see the cord
cut, nor hear the child scream as it took its first breath of air and
became awkward and unable to hold its head upright. He left the
midwives to their business and sent for the healers.

He walked slowly to his chambers. He needed to sleep, and after he regained his strength, search out that strange presence he
had felt in the south.

The steward, dream master Akitya Harro, and court dreamers
Riva and Thaia listened grimly to the spy's latest report. They sat
in the citadel at the heart of Cartheon, in the steward's chambers,
whose unshuttered windows overlooked the city.

The Bala Kothi agent, a stocky man in a trader's dusty, travel-
stained clothes, had just returned from his latest journey through
the borderlands and the south.

"Neither borderlanders nor southerners understand true witchery anymore," the spy told the high steward. "Anything the
temple priests disapprove of is called witchcraft in the southlands." He laughed bitterly. "Priests accuse people of witchcraft
for talking to animals, for not declaring a stillborn infant immediately dead, for not singing dirges loud enough. Ka, it is the truth.

They scare their children with stories of witches. They see miratasu as soul stealers, like weasels sucking the yolks from chicken eggs. They see women and outlanders as half-souled, and say that married men carry the poor half souls of their wives back to the Wheel when they die. They fear the mind link as demonic possession. They think pain is their lot, especially for women, and do not respect the teachings of pleasure. They are strange people, and tightfisted with their tors in the bargain."

"But there is something else," Aramit said slowly.

The spy rubbed his nose. "I believe—though I have no proof— the gift still lives among their priests. I overheard soldiers talking. The gift fascinates the highest-ranking priests; they reward soldiers who bring them live witches. They try to torture the secret of the gift from those poor devils. But they don't understand that women, too, bear the gift, or that it flourishses best between men and women, and works like a bridge between their minds."

The spy finished his tea. "The archpriest called Lyrian Sena pays Bala Kothi scouts gold to catch witches from the Blue Forest. The head of one of them, tortured until he willed himself dead, is on a pole before the archpriest's tent. But the archpriest not only wants to kill witches—he seeks to understand the gift and use it against us."

"Would he buy traitors?" the steward asked.

The spy grinned. "I don't think he has enough gold for that. But you should watch the lords on the borderlands."

Akitya Harro, the woman who was the chief dream master, smiled grimly. "Their fear and ignorance has twisted into blind hatred of us and all they think we are. But the dark side of amaratsa separated our peoples generations ago: the abuses, the wrong paths taken. Remember that. We cannot forget the men and women bound unwilling, used as spying eyes hidden in the hearts of rival households."

"Remember the darkness that we may walk in the light," Riva said.

"There is logic to their hatred," Aramit said, "if their stories preserve only memories of amaratsa's dark side, with some truth twisted into the fears. We must find the miratasu among them and discover how they use their talents."

The spy set down his tea bowl. "I've found one—that archpriest. I felt the talent in him and he seemed aware of me. Somehow he has awakened his dream self, but I felt no other bonded to him. It shook me so, I left the camp that night."

"What you say must be true, for I've felt strange things in the south." Aramit felt fear twisting his gut. He was ready to travel the void, though he knew each voyage might be his last.

He nodded to Akitya Harro, who waited beside the bed, and to his court dreamers, the twins who had been mind-bonded since birth and who, with Akitya, would seek him in the void if he failed to return. Whispering the first of the vedas, he lay down, still as a tomb effigy.

He envisioned the flat grain-rich southlands where austere priests held sway and those who might carry the gift were tortured and hanged like peasants.

He dropped his human skin like useless clothes, exploring the seductive mystery of the void, swimming its vast complex oceans, becoming one with it.

A vast wind vane, his spirit twisted: east, north, west, south.

North of the peninsula, rolling, forested hills folded away into blue distances. Late in the forenoon, the women emerged from the woods into a small valley. A long apple tree stood before a ruined holding; a body had been hanged from a high branch. The black-robed figure twisted slowly in the breeze.

Beyond the tree smoke rose from a wrecked house and outbuildings. The wind had not yet shifted and brought the smell of death.

Hipolla motioned Keira to stay, and rode ahead. She dismounted near the tree. The pony sidestepped and snorted at the odor of death and smoke.

Though the house was ruined, out of habit Keira kept the mare from trampling the rows of planted grain and broomcorn. She dismounted and sloshed through the long, wet grass to a row of sweet-thorn saplings. Something rustled in the field. She crouched in the shelter of the sweet-thorns, listening. A slight shape flitted through the gnarled fruit trees next to the bean field. Whoever it was had surely seen the pony and Hipolla, and Keira could not warn Hipolla without giving herself away. The mare snorted, her ears pricked forward. On hands and knees Keira crawled around the sweet-thorn, picked up a flat stone, and waited a heartbeat. Another presence, awash with fear and insatiable curiosity, lapped at her senses.

She flung the stone at the rustle.

A high, young voice cursed. A bent-over shape dove into the tangled orchard.

Keira gave chase, suddenly reckless. Tree branches whipped in her face and dead wood snapped under her hands as she ducked beneath the gnarled trees, slipping in the wet grass and getting snagged on brambles. Blossom petals flew into the air as she grabbed a tree to catch her balance.

The shape darted away and a stone whizzed by her head. Furious, she raced in the direction it had come from and pounced on her flushed quarry, who had slipped on the wet grass and fallen headlong. She grabbed a muddy, booted foot.

"Let go, you filthy bastard." The dirty, wide-eyed boy child kicked at her shins.

Keira yanked his leg, laid him out flat on his back, and sat on him. She slapped him, clamped a hand over his mouth, and grabbed one bony shoulder.

"By the Wheel, be still," Keira hissed, not loosening her grip. Her hand stung where she had struck him, and her left shin ached. He was a skinny child, probably not ten years old. Fear and shock filled his eyes and he was probably more scared than she.

"Be still. I won't hit you if you don't hit me."

"Get off me, you bugger, you weigh more than a hundred stones."

Keira snorted. She allowed the boy enough slack to scramble to his knees, but pinned his arms behind his back. He twisted to bite; she tightened her grasp on his arms, straightened, and marched him back to the sweet-thorns, wondering how long he had been hiding and what he had seen.

Hipolla trotted up and the mare whickered a greeting. Quick as a trapped animal, the boy twisted, bit, and kicked. Both he and Keira tumbled into the wet grass, rolling and kicking. He scrambled away but Keira pinned his legs.

"Good hunting?" Hipolla squatted near the urchin and pulled his head up by the hair. "What's this?"

"A brat," Keira said. "You belonged to this settlement?" She helped the boy up. He took her hand hesitantly, and his eyes slid from her to Hipolla and back.

"Yes." His lower lip quivered. "You with them?" His eyes fastened on the sheathed sword at Hipolla's side.

"You mean those who fired the settlement and hanged the priest?" Hipolla asked. "No, we're travelers."

Keira brushed a dew spider off the boy's filthy black cloak. Beneath the cloak, a sling was wrapped sashlike about his waist and his pockets bulged, probably with stones.

"Where are you traveling?" he asked.

Hipolla nodded toward the north. "How long ago did the reivers come?"

"Near dark yesterday. My mother hid me in the smokehouse."

Keira put a hand on the boy's shoulder. "We won't hurt you. We'll take you with us."

"A priest's son?" Hipolla said. "He'd be better here with some food."

The child's face turned from one to the other as he dug in his pocket for a stone. Keira pushed her hand firmly over his and exchanged a glance with Hipolla. "If you don't behave you cannot go with us." She stared the boy down.

Hipolla shrugged and walked along the orchard, brushing blossoms from the trees.

The brat trotted beside Keira, careful to keep his distance from Hipolla. He looked up at Keira. "I was going to steal your mare and get away."

"Enterprising brat," Hipolla murmured, but there was a catch in her voice.

"That mare has never carried anyone but me," Keira said, "and probably would have thrown you. How did you know we weren't soldiers?"

He brushed a tangle of hair off his forehead with a muddy hand. "You're tall for girls, but girls aren't soldiers. Everyone knows that."

Keira and Hipolla stopped.

The child smirked. "I saw you pissing in the woods," he said. "And everyone knows that—"

Hipolla laughed and tucked a handful of tiny green apples into her belt pouch.

Keira knelt before him, both hands on his shoulders. "You understand that we are dead if anyone but you knows that, don't you? It's a secret, like when you hid and saw what happened, and stayed alive. You understand, don't you?"

The child brushed her hands away. "I know, a secret. Now let me alone."

A shift of the wind brought the sharp tang of smoke and damp, charred wood, and the smell of the body on the tree. The brat stumbled and turned as if to run. Keira and Hipolla caught him and he pressed up against Keira's side. She drew the edge of her cloak over his face.

"You won't leave me, will you?" he asked.

She shook her head.

Hipolla touched Keira's hand. "There's some food and other things down there we can use. But we must go soon. Wolves may come, or other scavengers."

Keira persuaded the boy to stay at the edge of the orchard. He settled in the crotch of a low pear tree and wrapped his cloak around him. "Be our lookout," she whispered. He nodded solemnly.

She looked back once as she walked the mare down through the trampled vegetable plots. The brat in his dirty, burr-laden cloak was hard to see among the old, gnarled branches.

Hipolla searched the vegetable rows, snatching at tender young beans, yanking up young dandelions, anything edible. Stones bordered the plots, and a huge stone pile rose beside the well. The house's kitchen garden was destroyed. Horses' hooves and booted feet had ground the kitchen herbs into the dirt. Someone had kicked over the wattle-and-straw bee houses and trampled the little wooden troughs filled with honey and rosemary, set out to see the bees through a hard spring. Keira stooped, dipped her finger into a pool of herbed honey, and licked it off. The folk who had kept this holding had kept it well. Anger rose in her, a slow-rising rage at those who had destroyed so much labor, so much care.

The apple tree's blossoms, just ready to set fruit, shone pale and delicate against the bare, black limbs. Hipolla mounted and guided the pony beneath the tree. Standing in the stirrups, she cut down the body. Blossoms fell across her hands. As the corpse slid over her saddle horn and to the ground, the pony snorted and sidestepped.

"The dead cannot harm you, beast," Hipolla told it. She turned to Keira. "I have no love of priests. But the best and quickest thing we can do is pile timbers and stones over him and the woman."

Keira nodded, thinking she would have been glad to find the priest who had married her dead. This one had been young, his hair braided down his back in a style the Sanctum priests never wore. Keira knelt and drew wheels on the bare insteps.

"Someone took his boots," Hipolla said.

Keira shook her head. "A priest would wear sandals."

Hipolla beckoned Keira and paced around a corner of the ruined house. The woman lay on her back under a coppiced tree, a kitchen knife jutting from her throat. Her bruised, dead face was framed in a proper head covering. Blood crusted the left ear, where her spoilers had ripped out the silver ear token that marked her as a priest's wife.

Keira looked away. "How much do you think he saw?"

Hipolla's mouth tightened as she shook her head. She pulled the knife, laid it aside, and with Keira's help dragged the body to rest beside the priest. Charred timbers tilted across the well, and the hearthstones and flagstones of the floor still steamed with the heat of the fire that had destroyed the house. Ashes fluttered and swirled in the breeze. The thatch would have gone quickly. Careful not to look too closely at the bodies, Keira dragged charred timber and rubble over them. She worked quickly, thinking of the skinny brat huddled in the tree, then thinking of nothing at all.

The house's stone floor radiated heat like a bread oven, warming their boot soles as they shifted debris to cover the bodies. Fragments of earthenware crockery crunched under their boots.

"Why kill a priest so?" Keira asked. She nursed a scraped finger as she set a final rock into place on the priest's cairn. A strange world when I bury a priest, she thought, straightening from the rock pile.

"The borderlands go back and forth," Hipolla said as she filled their water bags at the well. "They've never been loyal to the Sanctum. People follow their own ways here. Sometimes they tolerate the priests. But when the priests tell them how to think—" She held a finger to her throat.

Keira tossed stones on the heaped cairn. Eight choruses should be sung at a priest's death, followed by the prescribed days of mourning and ritual bathing. Her mouth seemed full of earth; no words came.

"But we should be safer now, this far north," Hipolla said. "If the brat keeps his mouth shut."

"He would starve if we left him, you know that," Keira said.

Hipolla shrugged and busied herself scavenging in the rubble. They found a haunch of stringy meat in the smokehouse, sliced it on the spot, ate, and cached the remains in their saddlebags. They mounted and rode along the orchard.

"Brat!" Hipolla called.

The boy jumped down into the knee-high grass and wild herbs. Keira held a hand down to him, slipping her foot from the stirrup to let him mount. He pulled himself up behind her and clenched her waist. The mare sidestepped as if to question the extra weight.

"If anyone asks," Keira said, "we are your older brothers."

"Yes. A secret," he said solemnly.

Hipolla drove them north all day, making them skirt villages and the watchtowers that warned of settlements, hardly allowing them to rest. They hid in the woods to let other people pass by on the track, and ate only what they could snatch while riding: rose hips and the tender green spruce needles Hipolla said made fine tea. She would snatch a handful from a tree as she rode by, chew them, and spit them out when the flavor was gone.

The urchin grinned when Keira asked his name. "Brat. You said so yourself."

Hipolla laughed. "You like that name better than your own?"

"Well, Brat is better than priest's brat. That's what the other children called me."

Hipolla asked about the men who had killed his folk. But he kept silent, as if he wanted the memory of what he had seen and heard buried by a cairn of his own making.

At twilight they halted in the woods and sat propped against trees. Hipolla doled out the dried meat. Keira chewed slowly, trying to make the food last. Brat had washed at the stream, and his muddy, sooty, and tear-streaked face had become that of a fox-thin child, bony and angular. He would grow into a comely boy, she thought, if food finally stuck to his ribs. Brat sat pounding a circle in the soft ground with his boot heels, trying not to cry, Keira thought.

Brat spoke at last. "I was afraid they would open the smoke-house door and find me, though I was quiet as a spider. I heard my mother screaming and my father shouting. I saw the horsemen when I ran from the smokehouse and hid in the woods. Some of them had come before to tell my father to keep his religion to himself. They carried swords and sickles. The smith and the carpenter from the great hold over the hill were with them. I recognized their horses." He looked at Keira. "Will my mother and father be born again?"

"Of course," she said, though she felt unsure. "They are returned to the Wheel, and the Wheel does not end."

"Women shouldn't talk of the Wheel," Brat said.

Hipolla snorted, then began to whistle softly.

At last the boy slept, curled into a space between tree roots.

"He is bound to open his mouth with the wrong thing at the wrong time," Hipolla said. "Do you think the men who killed his parents would hesitate to kill us if they spotted him in our company?"

"He knows how to keep his mouth shut."

"Believe me, I pity him. I sometimes almost forget he's a priest's brat, though I see how he looks at me, how he fears my green eyes. Borderlands folk sometimes have green eyes, but what do you think he would do if he knew who I was? We've been so lucky, but three stretches the luck."

"How much farther do we have to go?"

"Cartheon lies north and west, another two days' hard travel at least. Yet if the borderlands are allying with the north at last, our travels may be easier."

"You *have* been to the city, haven't you? Why lie to me?"

"I haven't lied to you since then. How did I know that I could trust you, slowpoke?" Hipolla rolled her shoulders and stretched.

"And I trust you, Hipolla."

Hipolla nodded, almost a bow.

Keira settled beside Brat on a bed of needles and brush. He bumped against her shoulder and she slipped her hand over his. His fingers twisted in hers, and he seemed to sleep more easily now that he was clutching something.

Keira focused on the mournful hoot of an owl and prayed she would not dream, neither of Roshannon nor of the heads on the pikes. She wondered at how strange the world had become, that she traveled with a ka'innen northern woman, whom all the teachings of her childhood told her to hate. She had seen no magic, though Hipolla had hinted at these things. But Hipolla had saved her life, killing a man who would have robbed her and left her dead. She hesitated, gathering the words in her mind, to blurt out to Hipolla all that had happened, then all that she had dreamt or imagined between herself and Roshannon. But just when the words might have poured out, her heart froze. She stared at the skinny new crescent moon setting through the trees like a ghostly scythe.

"You'll take first watch?" she asked instead.

Hipolla nodded.

The next day they rode hard until forenoon and stopped to rest in a shaded, tiny meadow beyond a village. A green haze of buds softened the stark silhouettes of the poplar trees that fringed the meadow. The sun came out, burning away mists and warming the land. Though their stomachs were tight with hunger, all three lifted their faces toward the sun, soaking up its warmth. Keira foraged for potherbs to eat raw and rationed out the last of the dried meat. Brat rummaged on the far side of the meadow, digging stones for his sling. Hipolla washed her face at the stream, letting the water drip down her neck. Keira drank from her cupped hands and splashed water on her face, savoring the rest and the sun.

She grinned at Hipolla. "Another day or two, and we'll truly be in the city?"

Hipolla nodded. "But I still think it's a mistake to bring the boy with us. This is a fatter land than some we've passed through; everything is blooming. It might be better to leave him here."

"We promised him."

Hipolla wiped her hand across her mouth. "What kind of life do you think there will be for a priest's son in the north, when he's been taught to hate and distrust everything there?"

"It's no different for him than for me. Why do you accept my going there and refuse to accept him?" Keira felt the brutal truth in Hipolla's words; they stung her with doubts about what life she would find in the north.

"I think you need to go there, and truly want to," Hipolla said fiercely. "That makes the difference."

Keira touched Hipolla's shoulder. "I don't want to quarrel with you, not now. Do you want to separate?"

"No. Give me some time alone." Hipolla strode away and began vigorously rubbing down the pony. She glanced up curtly when Keira and Brat stepped into the trees.

"What's wrong with her?" Brat asked.

"She's worried. We're out of food and there's still a distance to go." Keira took the mare's lead in one hand and Brat's muddy hand in the other. They wandered farther into the woods while Keira swallowed her own anger and considered Hipolla's words. It would be difficult for Brat to live among the northerners, but even stubborn children were young enough to forget old ways. She wondered about herself. If in a day she and Hipolla reached the great city and walked among the witches, would she be an outcast, too, jeered by the people among whom she sought refuge?

Keira glanced through the treetops at the sky, where a pair of hawks glided in lazy circles. While she was deciding that Hipolla was just too stubborn about some things, and wondering what it would be like to be a hawk, spying with hawk eyes the land below, she spotted a patch of wild strawberries on a sunny bank. She tethered the mare in a gully and she and Brat climbed to the patch, scanning the grass for snakes. The fragrant, sun-warmed berries made her mouth water.

Suddenly a horse whinnied on the other side of the bank. Keira froze, and she and Brat stared at each other. He had stuffed a handful of strawberries in his mouth and his lips were stained red.

Noiselessly, Keira scrambled up and peeked over the bank. A black and a chestnut, still saddled, were tethered in the meadow beyond, grazing on the sparse new grass. The black raised its head and snorted.

She glanced at Brat and slid unceremoniously down through the luscious bank of wild strawberries. She jumped into the saddle, gave Brat a hand up, and raced toward their encampment.

She heard a yell and a muted clash.

Through the trees that screened the meadow, she saw three figures. Hipolla and two men circled each other, fighting with short swords and daggers. Blades flashed, clanging together.

Keira swung Brat off the mare.

Hipolla was the center point of a deadly circle, parrying the blows of the man on the left with the dagger, and of the man on the right with the sword. The men taunted her like two cats playing with a mouse. The man on Hipolla's left was using the longer reach of his sword to get under her guard.

Keira slipped the ash club from the leather thong she had rigged to carry it on her saddle. One-handed she guided the mare, kneed her into a trot, then burst from the shelter of the woods. She rode down the man on Hipolla's left, screaming and cracking the club in his face. Its blunt end caught his jaw; she heard something snap. The man stumbled backward, away from Hipolla, his short sword dropping from his hand. Falling, he snatched frantically at Keira's foot in the stirrup. She kicked him in the face, and guided the mare in a tight circle around him, clubbing him on the shoulders and head. He collapsed and lay still.

She reined in at the edge of the meadow. The mare screamed like a warhorse and pranced, worrying the bit.

But the other man, a tall bearded fellow in a helmet, had struck through Hipolla's guard. A dark red stain was spreading on her shoulder. She advanced, slashing at the man's head with her sword, spinning to slash at his belly with her dagger, and lopping again at his feet with her sword. He dodged, stepped backward, and hopped over the sweeping sword, and while he was regaining himself, bringing sword and dagger back to warding position, Hipolla stumbled onto one knee.

"Hipolla," Keira screamed. Her hands shook. She rode close to the two duelers, hoping to retrieve the fallen man's short sword and club the man who faced Hipolla.

Hipolla's opponent caught her sword on the flat of his dagger, parrying her blow as she righted herself. He drove his sword in through her guard; she rolled backward out of his way.

Keira swung the club. He thrust up an arm to ward off the blow, yanked the club from her, and stumbled backward. Hipolla closed in and hamstrung his left leg. Cursing, he sank to his knees, swinging the club in one hand and his sword in the other. He struggled upright and jabbed the club toward Hipolla. The edge of it clipped her knee and tripped her. The man laughed, staggered drunkenly, and ran her through.

Time froze. Keira, on the mare, had no weapon but the dagger now. Her eyes met Hipolla's. She felt Hipolla dying, felt her own death coming for her, tasted the man's triumph looming over her. She could not ride the mare into a sword and a club. She calculated how many precious seconds it would take to dismount and sweep up the dead man's sword, which she did not know how to use. Her vision focused in merciless clarity—she saw clearly every possibility, every consequence, every line on the man's face as he cursed, wrenching his sword from Hipolla's body and pushing her limp form aside.

At the edge of the woods Brat fitted a stone into his sling, and his arm whirled in a blur. The slingstone whistled through the air and slammed the man's armored cheek piece. He spun aside, cursing, dropping the club.

The stone skipped and struck the mare's fetlock. She reared frantically. Keira slipped sideways, clutching the saddle horn. Her fingers lost their grip. Her foot twisted in the stirrup and came free. The ground rushed into her face. She landed on her side, her right shoulder and face thudding into a patch of wet grass. Her head reeled, her mouth tasted full of blood.

Wasp stars buzzed through her brain. The man loomed over her, holding a sword in one hand, a dagger in the other. Blood was dripping down his cheek, and he laughed at her. She was going to die and find out if she had a place on the Wheel.

"Now, lad, any tricks left?" he roared.

Roshannon's hand stopped in midair, the ko stone raised to make a move. He was winning the game, but suddenly the board and stones looked like nothing he had ever seen before. He clutched the edge of the table, sagging as if someone had punched him in the stomach. The cabin lantern swayed as the ship plowed through a trough. The ko stone fell, scattering the other player's pieces as Roshannon staggered upright. The room blurred, the familiar faces of Ni'An, the shipmaster, and the pilot dissolving into a queasy fog.

He waved a hand blindly into the air, then clutched his stomach.

"Poison," the shipmaster's low voice said. "Or perhaps we should throw the new cook overboard."

Another voice inside Roshannon's head was calling him *lad* and laughing at him.

"Art seasick?" Ni'An's voice asked.

He stumbled to the cabin door and started up the steps. A vast wave crushed down on him, grinding into him a clear vision of death. He tripped on deck, gasping for breath, and leaned against the foremast, then bolted for the rail, leaned over, and retched.

Roshannon sagged against the rail, glaring at the skinny

crescent moon riding the western horizon. The heave and pitch of the deck underfoot magnified the emotion that swept over him.

"Wast never seasick before," Ni'An said, as he laid his arm along his cousin's shoulder.

Roshannon braced himself at the rail and breathed in the cold, salt air. Behind him, a sailor laughed softly, amused, no doubt, at an islander who was seasick. "Cannot help me now, Ni'An. Go below and play another game."

His cousin left and the watchman approached. "You'll go below now," the man said.

"And retch a cabinful? I need the air."

The guard muttered something and retired.

Clutching the rail, Roshannon knelt on deck and pressed his hands over his eyes. Damn you, woman; damn you, Keira Danio.

The two sailors whispered, laying wagers on whether he would be sick again. Coins clinked together in the darkness behind him.

The sword plunged at her; she rolled aside.

She kicked the swordsman's shin, tripping him. His sword and dagger arced above his head and flew wide. He landed on her, bare-handed and furious, his knees bruising her ribs, his weight crushing her to the ground. He scrambled for his own dagger in the grass as she wrenched Roshannon's dagger from her right boot. His left hand closed around her throat, his fingernails dug into her skin. She stared at him, fascinated and terrified. His will and hers struggled for life, his terror and rage dragged over her, a vast net, stifling her.

Stab him in the ribs, Roshannon thought fiercely. Stab him in the neck if the ribs turn your blade. Stab him.

She twisted her head, worked the knife free, and drove the blade between his ribs again and again, until his hands unclenched from her throat and his wide, dead eyes stared at her.

Frantic, Keira shoved his deadweight off her. She rolled away, pulling the knife with her, and staggered to hands and knees. She pushed the man onto his back and made sure he was dead.

Keira crawled to where Brat knelt over Hipolla. The earth seemed to slope up at her, then tilt crazily away. Stars buzzed like wasps through her vision.

Hipolla's fingers curled like white claws in the wet grass. She lay twisted at an odd angle, settled on her shoulders as if looking into the woods. Keira was anxious to straighten her leg, her arm. She leaned over her friend.

"Slowpoke," Hipolla whispered hoarsely.

"Hipolla." Keira touched the pale, sweated face.

Hipolla coughed, a terrible gurgle. Red froth edged her mouth. Her eyes closed halfway. Her blood-spattered knuckles clenched around a tuft of wild garlic and her boot heel dug convulsively in the wet grass.

Keira bundled her cloak to pillow Hipolla's head.

"North and west one more day." Hipolla clutched Keira's hand. "Take my earring. In my boot. As surety. If any of Tanta clan—tell them—"

Keira shook her head. "Hipolla." She smoothed the hair from Hipolla's neck and forehead. The bloodstain spread on the leather armor. She opened her mouth but no words came.

Hipolla opened her eyes. The pupils had become huge. Keira saw her own reflection in them, a tiny self.

"Earring," Hipolla said.

"Hipolla."

"Thou, for love of me, take the earring."

Roshannon lay on deck, listening to the wind and the creak of the ship's timbers.

"Keira," he whispered.

Keira started, wrapped in darkness, annoyed by the voices prodding at her. He cares whether I am dead or alive, she thought in wonder. But that cannot be, she thought, retreating from the touch of his emotions.

Brat crouched beside her, tugging her shoulder. "Up, Keira, up." Sunlight was slanting across the meadow. The shadows of the trees reached eastward.

Keira rolled onto an elbow and laid her face in Hipolla's hair. Gently she pressed the dead eyes closed, and kneeling, crossed the hands on the chest. Her throat felt raw, her hands curiously numb. She bent over Hipolla and kissed her.

Brat was standing beside her when she rose, her shirtfront smeared with Hipolla's blood. The meadow slanted away from her, ripped with hooves and boot tracks. The three bodies in the grass seemed to recede from her, as if already taken up on the Wheel and spun away. She swore she could count every blade of grass. She watched a black thread of ants march across her boot toe. In cold fury she rubbed her boot into the grass and stamped them.

Brat stared at her. He had tethered the mare and the pony across the meadow. She watched him back away from her until he stood with his face buried in the pony's shoulder, and clung to the saddle.

She touched his shoulder. He turned to face her.

"They'll get us," he said.

"Maybe." When she looked toward Hipolla, the ground rushed up at her. She raised her chin and took Brat's hand. "Quick. Fetch candlewood for a pyre. I don't want anything but fire getting at her."

"You won't leave me, will you?" he asked.

The fox-thin face swam before her eyes. She shook her head.

She retrieved her cloak and put the dagger back in her boot, after cleaning it in the grass. She gave Hipolla's dagger to Brat and gathered up the short sword and club. At the last moment, Keira remembered Hipolla's insistence over the earring. Gingerly she slid her fingers inside Hipolla's boot and pried it out. She turned away and retched into the trampled grass. A minute later she forced herself to draw two careful circles on the soles of Hipolla's boots. Quickly, she and Brat gathered dead wood and stones to make a cairn over Hipolla, spiking it with lit twigs of resiny, fiercely blazing candlewood.

No words came, only the terrible feeling that her heart had turned to stone.

With curious detachment she inspected the other bodies. From the first man she stripped a wide red sash and a worked leather belt pouch. Next she stooped over the man she had killed with Roshannon's dagger. Blood crusted his half-open mouth and teeth. His eyes were wide open. An ant was crawling in his ear. She straightened up and spat.

"Mount up," she said to Brat. They rode back through the woods the way they had come, and Keira pillaged the saddlebags of the brigands' two horses. She left the horses there, saddled and snatching mouthfuls of sourgrass.

She brushed her hand through her hair. Her fingers caught in a clump of knotted hair and a wet, sticky patch on the side of her head. She rode with the cloak wrapped tight around her, concealing the crusted blood on her shirt. At a stream she washed her head wound and combed her fingers through her blood-matted hair. She dribbled some of the contents of a plundered water bag over the cut on her head, wincing as the liquid seeped into raw skin. It was rakka and stung like fire. Cursing, she took a swig. The rakka burned her tongue and throat, but prodded her into a semblance of life. She swished it about her mouth, feeling the place where she had bitten her tongue.

She splashed water over the bloodstain on her shirt, scrubbing it as best she could. Brat retreated into silence as they rode on, his eyes dark and wary.

Keira rode in a half trance. Every leaf, every tree, every furrow of every field, each rustle, murmur, and scent was clear to her, with wintertime sharpness or the clarity of dreams.

That night she sat watching over Brat as he slept. She turned Roshannon's dagger between her fingers, picking at a line of dried blood on the hilt.

❀ 10 ❀

Someone grabbed a hank of Roshannon's hair, raising his head, and pulled his eyelids open. He cursed, flailing at the annoyance and the lantern light that splintered in his eyes.

"Dose him with ginger and ginger tea," Irina Cathaya said. "I don't want anyone puking on my cargo or on my deck."

Two sailors carried him to his cabin belowdeck and laid him in his bed. When he regained consciousness, the ship's doctor and his sailor assistant were in the cabin shaving gingerroot—pungent enough when freshly cut to make lips curl and nostrils burn. They brewed the infernal ginger tea and poured it down his throat. Ginger was the time-honored remedy for seasickness among the islands, too. Every sailor carried some in his sea chest, but Roshannon privately suspected that it worked simply because its powerful smell and taste distracted one's mind from the seasickness. At regular intervals in the middle of the night, the captain and her niece poked their heads in the door.

"The ambassador isn't going to die on us, is he?" Lady Cathaya asked, sounding half-amused.

Roshannon wondered if everyone on board had laid bets on whether he would be seasick until they made port. The captain and the doctor eyed him, then held a muttering conference outside the door, while Isharra tried coaxing more of the wretched tea down his throat.

He caught her wrist as she reached for another bowl of steaming gingerroot brew. "Enough, lady; the treatment will kill me before the sickness does."

Isharra grinned. "You're better, then?"

"Better yet if I never drink ginger tea or eat the stuff raw again. Last night I had a nightmare of a banquet where every dish set before me was gingerroot—boiled, roasted, made into soups, sweets, puddings, and teas. The people sweated ginger, even the candles reeked of it."

Isharra laughed. "Oh, I must tell the cook. My aunt thought his cooking might have made you sick. The crew threatened to toss him overboard once. But don't think badly of my aunt's remedies."

"Oh, aye, she just doesn't want anyone puking on her cargo or her deck."

"You would not either if this were your ship." Isharra's eyes narrowed as she leaned closer to him. "Were you really seasick, my lord?"

But her aunt and the ship's doctor entered the cabin, with Ni'An close behind, so Isharra went abovedeck with her question unanswered.

Keira lay watching the inn for some time, reassured by the solid stonework and air of prosperity. Smoke drifted up from the chimney and carried the smell of food to where she and Brat lay hidden in the woods. A caravan of three pilgrim merchant wagons lumbered past, the iron-shod wheels rumbling along the rutted track. The lead wagon flew the black-and-white penance banner that proclaimed all the goods were meant for the Sanctum, and supposedly warded off brigand attacks. Brat would have hailed the caravan, but Keira pulled him back.

All day she had ridden in moody silence, teaching Brat some of the secret hand signs Sanctum women used to communicate without speaking. Brat learned quickly, proud of his dozen signs, and he, too, seemed relieved not to talk.

"Food?" Brat signed.

Keira nodded. A vision of hot tea made her mouth water. All day they had eaten things grabbed between riding: tart, crunchy, water-holding purslane and sorrel in bare, sunny meadows; chickweed and mallow and rose hips. When Brat found a patch of wild strawberries, she had turned her back and let him gorge himself. Strawberries reminded her of Hipolla's death.

Brat's eyes looked older, as a soldier's eyes might. He carried his sling wrapped around his saddle horn, always fitted with a stone, and his pockets bulged with smooth stones. He had demanded to know where she was going.

"North," she said, wanting to tell him no more. The less he knew, the better for him, if they were caught.

"If we go too far north, we will run into witches."

Keira had grinned to herself, hoping they would soon do so. She longed to find the witches who wielded the magic that made the priests hate so blindly. Only a truly great magic could provoke such long-simmering hatred.

The caravan's lead wagons had reached the inn gates. When she was sure the rutted path between the giant, long-needled trees was empty, Keira signaled Brat and they followed.

The mare pranced and snorted, having caught the scent of other beasts. Outbuildings and a watchtower nestled like arms about the settlement. Cows grazed a fenced clearing beside the inn, and quick, thin pigs rooted in a grove of oaks. In the huge inn yard, a pup that looked half-wolf stalked a pair of plump hens and came face-to-face with a red rooster, who spread its wings, its hackles raised, and pecked the pup smartly on the nose. Brat laughed as the pup retreated, yelping. A stable boy with unruly black hair rushed from filling the water trough, snatched the pup by the scruff of its neck, and carried it inside the inn.

The merchants' slaves were unhitching the horse teams from the wagons, whose eight-spoked, iron-bound wheels stood as tall as Brat himself. Their silver earrings shone against their copper skins as they spoke together in a strange language. They reminded Keira of Roshannon.

She dismounted and called the stable boy. The landlord strode across the yard, grinning welcome, his quick black eyes appraising the mare and pony as the stable boy led them off.

"Will your woman's food wake the dead?" Keira asked.

"Indeed. If not the dead, then the barely living."

"Are there fleas in your beds?" She winked at Brat.

The man grinned. "None that have killed a man yet."

Before he could sling his arm about her in sudden friendship, Keira hefted her saddlebags onto her shoulders; the landlord hurried off.

Inside, the caravaneers had claimed the choice area by the hearth and were supping on crusty dark bread and stew. Keira found a bench in a corner, so she could watch the door and the company, and hear their talk. She shared bread and stew and a bowl of spiced ale with Brat, while the strangers appraised her from the comfort of their own circle. They were discussing Kum, the holy city perched on a mountain in the borderlands. Kumini priests, they said, traveled as far as the Ice Kingdoms, where the yellow-eyed people lived, and to the lands of Bala Koth, east beyond the inland seas. The southern priests called suspected heretics "those who have tarried too long in Kum." But witches and Sanctum alike protected the pilgrims who visited the holy city. The pilgrim party was large: a pair of prosperous-looking merchants; their sons and apprentices; hired guards; and three women—two matrons and a comely girl who was embroidering a sash. The flash and pull of needle and thread made Keira brood: would she ever again sit sewing by a kitchen fire? She smiled. She had never thought she would miss sewing.

The merchants' women wore their headdresses folded back on their necks like high collars. Heavily adorned ear tags flashed in the light as they laughed and talked. The stout, richly dressed graybeard who appeared to be the leader laughed at something his wife said and his glance flicked over the corner where Keira sat.

Keira sipped the ale, which was as fine as any she had made. One of the landlord's sons scattered ko stones on the table, enticing Brat to play.

"No wagers," Keira muttered, ruffling Brat's hair. The boy played well enough, from what she understood of watching the game over her father's shoulders. She listened to the click of the ko stones, glad that Brat was enjoying the moment. *Take comfort now, for there may be no comfort tomorrow.*

She could not endanger Brat further, Hipolla had been right. Staring at the fire, she spun a comforting daydream: the highland pony tied on behind a merchant's wagon, with Brat safely inside among the women, being coddled and pampered.

The air in the room seemed to quiver, making the colors of the people's clothes bleed into the space around them. She blinked in annoyance and took a long draught of ale. The gray-bearded merchant approached.

"Ka." She nodded.

"Ka." He nodded. His pilgrim's garb was cut from shimmering spidersilk. "Would it please you to join our company?"

"This corner suits me well, for I am tired and given to melancholy," Keira said as graciously as she could while Brat kicked her foot under the table.

"My slaves will shortly make music, and my youngest daughter's voice may remedy the melancholy."

"I would gladly hear songs," Keira said, glaring at Brat as the merchant rejoined his party. The youngest daughter's eyes flicked up and met Keira's; the girl blushed and bent over her work. A moment later she exclaimed, "I have lost the needle, pulled it off the thread," and the embroidered sash fell to the floor.

The girl and her mother searched the folds of material.

The merchant waved his hand. "Put away your work that you may sing. You've not lost your voice, have you?"

The girl rolled up her work and drank deeply from the ale bowl she shared with her mother.

"You would be safer with the merchant's wagons than with me, Brat," Keira whispered.

"We'd both be safer with the wagons. Will you ask to go with them?"

Keira shook her head.

Four male Bala Kothi slaves carrying long-necked luthas entered and sat on a bench facing the fire. As they played, a mysterious current flowed in the room, through the quick, dark fingers of the Kothi players, through each note sung. Keira's blood stirred. No wonder the priests forbade such singing and the long-necked Kothi instruments.

The relentless drums and shrilling flutes of the priests made music like the heartbeat of a trapped thing. This music tantalized, making one's feet itch to dance. Brat pushed his stew bowl aside, propped his chin in his hands, and stared dreamily at the Bala Kothi. The musicians' fingers blurred across the strings as the music quickened, becoming wilder. As wild as the rhythms of a knife fight . . .

Slowpoke, a voice inside Keira's head hissed.

The music leaped and sprang, as an opponent would. Under the table, her fingers clenched on an imaginary dagger hilt. Her thoughts and the music twined together. She was dizzy and quickened, far removed from the aches in her ribs and thighs, and the sore, bruised heel of her hand.

Something like a butcher's quick knife slit her from throat to belly. Body and spirit ripped like stiff new linen, and for a moment her breastbone seemed split in two. One deft twist of will freed her from the flesh, like a snake casting an old skin. From the rafters she looked down at herself and the company gathered there.

She had two separate awarenesses.

Her dream self buzzed around the room quick as a fly, while her real body stiffened on the bench, its stomach queasy, its skin sheathed in gooseflesh. Her spirit self, light as ash and drunken with exhilaration, did a cartwheel under the rafters.

Her spirit vision flitted with dreamlike fluidity to the top of the gray-bearded merchant's head, with its bald spot big as a ten-tor gold piece, back to the rafters and its fringe of cobwebs; from the girl's hands folded in her lap, to a young apprentice who sat scowling at the girl.

Eerie skins of light clothed all the people in the room, as if candles had been lit inside their flesh. Fears and passions that she could taste clung to all the bodies except her own. Her counterfeit boy's body slumped on the bench below, gray and ghostly. The merchant and his wife, the girl's parents, were twin sparks revolving each around the other, while the landlord shimmered with fears of soldiers pillaging and plundering. The attendants and apprentices sparked with varying degrees of ambition, weariness, and resentment.

With real eyes and dream eyes, Keira watched the merchant's daughter stare too long at her boy's body and blush.

Waves of emotion overwhelmed her. She floated through the inn's roof, soared over the forest, through the darkening sky. Wind wove through her; she forgot where and what she was until a vast low voice murmuring in the rocking darkness below reminded her of other beings, and she smelled wet salt.

Two sudden pinpoints of light blinded her dream eyes as she drifted down toward a fully rigged ship with bloodred foresails full of wind. A raven screamed and flapped past. She swooped, brushing its feathers with her dream self. On the deck below, tiny figures moved through the flickering light of the ship's lanterns. A man leaning at the rail suddenly looked up.

Him.

Unable to resist, she hurtled down from the top of the masts.

Roshannon frowned at the top of the mainmast. One of the shipmaster's ravens, perched in the rigging, spread its wings and screamed. One black feather brushed Roshannon's cheek and drifted across his chest. His skin turned to gooseflesh and his legs braced wide at the rail to take the heave and roll of the waves.

He clutched the rail as the ship slid into a trough. A presence filled him. For a split second he was blind, deaf, overwhelmed. He took a step backward, grabbed the rail, and braced his legs wider; his skin flushed with heat. An immense wave of sadness engulfed him.

His eyesight blurred yet his other senses sharpened. Through the immense wave of sorrow—her sadness, he realized—came the smell of a wood fire, the sounds of a crowd, and a compelling thread of music.

Her emotions tasted familiar. The same numbness had overwhelmed him after he killed his first man.

She plunged more deeply into him, like a child burrowing under covers. He was a cup; she filled him to overflowing. He was her and himself, man and woman, joined in an eerie oneness.

Keira, trying desperately to make herself *fit,* swam in the rich, strange otherness of him.

Through Roshannon's eyes she watched the sea currents weave endless hypnotic patterns and the red sail fill with the night wind. Through his eyes she saw the great city growing on the horizon and the blurred stars of lanterns along its shore.

Hands dug into his shoulders. "Nikka," a voice said. Isharra's face swung into view, her silver hair whipping across her mouth, her lips moving, the roaring in his ears and the thread of wild Bala Kothi music drowning out her words.

Through his eyes Keira stared at a beautiful green-eyed woman whose long silver hair whipped about her face. The woman spoke to Roshannon, he murmured indecipherable answers. Was this woman a witch? Another man, whose unscarred face was almost the twin of Roshannon's, leaned at the rail, peering landward. Behind him, the lantern light showed billowing sails and the lithe dark shapes of sailors crossing the deck. She drank it in, feasting.

Roshannon bit back a laugh, savoring the strange inebriation. He had not understood a word of what Isharra said. This joining was curiously like making love, yet more intense. Just as keenly, he felt Keira's fear at sharing his body. The longer she stayed, the clearer grew the image of the crowded inn, the swirling music, the vast hearth, the hard bench she sat on. Something stirred between his legs. His embarrassment and his arousal burned like brands into Keira's consciousness. Horrified, yet bound to the mysteries of his body, she panicked.

"Damn you, woman." Roshannon leaned against the rail.

You mean me, Keira thought.

"What ails thee? Art sick again?" The silver-haired woman leaned closer to him.

"Ni'An," Roshannon yelled. He bit his lip and slammed his fist into the rail hard enough to bloody his knuckles. Pain jolted through Keira's dream self. He leaned hard over the rail, his fingers clawing into the wood while the pain throbbed.

"Woman, woman," he said, glancing at the top of the mast. Isharra, he saw from the corner of his eye, was glaring at him.

Her spirit self tore free and fled into the darkness. He reached for her; she flew on, forgetting all in the thrill of soaring the night sky. She struggled to remember what she had been before this glorious flight; a thin, rhythmic thread stitched itself into her awareness. The music, pouring through to her from her physical body, hooked her and pulled her back to the inn.

Keira bit her lip and stared with fierce concentration at the music makers' earrings, their sashes, high leather boots, and broad, dark faces. Their eyes were turned inward, into the heart of their music.

She shifted on the hard bench, feeling the solid wood beneath her thighs and buttocks. Her body felt feverish and stiff and her hands shook. But Brat sat calmly beside her as if nothing had happened.

"Brat," she said hoarsely. "Did anything strange happen?"

"What do you mean?"

"Anything. My—attention was elsewhere." Her stomach was still on the ship, by the feel of things.

He yawned. "That girl stared at you and her face turned red. Girls are strange, aren't they?"

The merchant's daughter sang, her voice melding with the clear, liquid notes, and piercing every smoky corner of the room.

One of the merchant's attendants glowered at Keira over the rim of his ale bowl. His eyes slid to the merchant's daughter.

Keira called the landlord's son and paid her account. Brat protested, but she gave him a deadly look. She craved aloneness, escape from the others.

The merchant rose. "What do you think of my daughter's singing?"

"The music and her voice are a salve for melancholy."

"High praise from a stranger."

"Ka, no higher praise than you yourself gave. You are a lucky man to have such a daughter."

"A lucky man will have such a wife," he said. He reminded Keira of the horse trader she had haggled with for the mare, and suddenly she liked him.

"But I see that she will be well and truly wed, if her husband values her as much as you do." She bowed to him, thinking of her own father and Roshannon.

The thin-faced attendant and a ruddy-faced friend were waiting at the foot of the stair. The attendant touched Keira's sleeve as she moved past.

"Ka," she said to him. "I bid you good night." A sudden vision of the merchant's daughter and this man as a wedded couple wavered in the air between them; she struggled to focus on his real face and the tiny muscle twitching in his lean cheek.

"Indeed, and carry off my lady's heart with you." His face darkened, but his friend laid a warning hand on his arm.

"I think not. Your lady's heart is where it belongs."

"With you, are you saying?"

"No, here, with her family and those she knows."

"You got your fill of staring at her."

"A prudent traveler would notice everyone in a room," Keira said. "If your lady noticed me, it was only idle curiosity, I'm sure." She stood as she remembered Roshannon doing, apparently at ease, offering no notion of threat or of fear. Calculating the seconds it would take to reach her dagger and sword, she slipped her hand from Brat's and put her body more solidly between him and the men.

"You ogled her." The young man thrust his face into Keira's. His friend grabbed him.

Keira held her ground. His jutting nose reminded her of the beaks of the ravens aboard the ship.

"I looked at the merchant's daughter as any man would look at something of beauty. You are a lucky man, if she is to be your wife." She put her hand on the young man's shoulder. "We are both too young to be courting trouble or death. It will come for us soon enough."

"You are right," the more sensible friend said. Hothead let himself be led away. He watched Keira take the first step up the stairs. They nodded stiffly to each other.

Keira climbed the stairs slowly, overwhelmed by the flood of other people's emotions.

"Weren't you afraid?" Brat asked. "You really fooled them, they really thought you were a man they shouldn't fight."

Keira clapped a hand over his mouth. "Hush, lest anyone hear!"

Keira passed the large common rooms and chose a small cell whose shuttered window offered a view of the stable yard and road. She shifted a stack of lumber from the corner to bar the door, in case Hothead had further thoughts. Wrapped in her cloak, she sat on the pallet without removing her boots.

"A bed," Brat whispered reverently. He curled up, his hand in hers.

"Yes, a bed. Imagine traveling to Kum in the merchants' wagons, with that girl to sing you asleep at night. Promise me that if anything happens to me, Brat, you'll ask that merchant to take you to Kum."

The Kothi music below became mournful, with deep, rolling choruses. The sound seeping through the floorboards reminded her of the sea she had flown over in her—dream? Madness? Possession? She shook her head, struggling to name that experience. Never in dreams had she smelled the sea, plunged from the top of a ship's mast, felt the rushing shock of joining with another body.

In the forest an owl hooted. Brat had fallen asleep holding her hand. Gently she slid her fingers from his grasp and stared into the darkness, afraid to sleep, and so to dream.

Roshannon leaned hard against the rail. Damn it if Isharra had noticed the peculiar bulge in his tunic. By the Wheel, he could not help laughing to himself at his predicament.

He groaned inwardly when he saw the shipmaster herself approaching. But she immediately crossed tongues with her niece, continuing the endless argument whose gist he had picked up before, something about Isharra's responsibilities to clan Cathaya, and her duties to provide another house with a child.

The young pilot always chafed and blazed at her aunt's blunt reminders, which was just what Roshannon needed.

He nodded to Ni'An. They paced beside the rail, leaving pilot and shipmaster to their squabble.

Ni'An grinned and slapped his cousin on the butt. "That is a fine salute for a woman you said you had no interest in, Nikka."

Roshannon hit Ni'An on the shoulder; Ni'An cuffed him back. They feinted, jabbed, and circled on the rolling deck, laughing at each other.

Keira waited until the stable yard was absolutely silent. She knelt by the bed, touching Brat's shoulder; he did not wake. She said a prayer for him and for herself.

Climbing out the window and to the ground by way of a tree espaliered against the wall, she crept into the stable, saddled the mare, and rode off.

Near dawn Keira was trotting down the road through the towering trees. She cut back into the woods and drew rein. Her heart sank. The sense that had blossomed last night so strangely in the inn told her she was being followed. She waited and soon Brat rode into view at the edge of the path.

"You should go back," she said slowly as the boy reined up beside her. The mare whinnied at the highland pony and nuzzled its neck. The horses at least were glad to see each other.

"You promised not to leave me."

"I cannot take you into more danger; I must go on alone."

He was pale with anger, trying to take a man's manner and look down his child's nose at her. "You promised not to leave me. You sneaked off, after you promised. Of course, women have no honor."

Keira wanted to hit him or laugh at him. Instead she laid her hand over his. He pulled it away. "It would be safer for you in the merchant's train to Kum."

"We would both be safer in the merchant's train—"

"The holy city is safe, it has been a refuge for many generations. Even if the armies clash, the city will stand. Go back to the inn, and ask the merchant's protection. Tie your pony on behind his wagon, go to Kum and live a long life in safety. Please, Brat."

"If you go to Kum, I'll go to Kum."

"I must go north, Brat."

"My name is not Brat. It's Beren SanDyllin Harth." He raised his chin. "And I'll go where you go."

"Beren, you don't understand. We may be killed. I want you to live out your life. That's why I left you."

"I don't care. You said you would take me with you. You promised." He twisted a finger in the pony's mane. "If you don't take me, I'll just follow you."

Over the small sounds of morning, drums rose from the east in a vast heartbeat, the sounds of armies preparing to do battle.

Keira shook her head. "Very well."

Beren grinned.

In a hut in the middle of the Blue Forest, Xian Tanta woke and stared around him. He decided he must be alive—for his surroundings were surely too dowdy, too unglamorous to be any of the halls of paradise. He squinted around at the big, one-room hut, felt the bedding beneath him, and watched the woman bent over the hearth.

Xian Tanta closed his eyes, not sure he wanted to be alive.

When he opened them, he was staring at an out-of-focus face that was neither young nor old—did the woman belong in dreams or reality, in past or future?

"I thought you were a ghost when I found you," she said.

"Am I a ghost?" he asked through cracked lips.

The woman smiled. "No danger of that this time, ka. You will live, whether you want to or not."

"You say that with authority. Are you a healer?"

She grinned. "I healed you. That should make me one." She thrust a horn ladle brimming with steaming broth at him.

The scalding chicken broth burned his lips and tongue and dribbled down his chin, burning that, too. Further proof that he was alive.

"Hipolla," he said. "Polla."

"My name isn't Hipolla," she said. "My name is—" She held another ladleful of broth insistently at his mouth.

He caught her wrist with his hand, halting the spoon's progress.

"Reyna," he said, remembering. The long, staggering march,

the fever and the soreness in his ribs, the sight of himself, like a demented scarecrow, reflected in a stream, his hair stiffly matted with blood. He had called this woman Hipolla when he first saw her. She had cut his tunic away and pressed a family of fat white maggots to his side to clean dead rotting flesh from the live flesh so that the wound fever would not poison his whole body. Only nirikan healers used maggots. He was, if not among his own people, at least among people who followed similar ways.

"Reyna," he said. "I cannot eat now." He let go her wrist, noticing that his fingers looked like talons.

Her hand was so steady, she had not spilled any of the broth on him. She looked at him and nodded, taking bowl and spoon away.

"You know what the southerners would do to you if they found me here. But you helped me."

"I am a healer, and the southerners do not rule these forests," Reyna said.

If he had not splashed rakka on his wounds he would be dead of wound fever, she assured him. The hunting cat had come with him. How long he had lain on the battlefield and wandered, she could not say. But he had lain in her hut a week.

"A week? I must find Polla." Cursing, he reeled out of bed and fainted.

His body mended rapidly after that day. His spirit was another matter. He had lain a long time in dreamless fever in the healer's hut. Normal dreams would have given him some knowledge of Hipolla. He questioned Reyna about recent battles, the Sanctum's inroads into the Blue Forest, where raiding soldiers were burning settlements, and where she had found him, for time and his dreams had become tangled. Often he woke to find the hunting cat curled by the healer's hearth, blinking impassively at him as if it wondered whether he would decide to be up and about the business of life again.

In a few days his left side began scabbing over, the newly forming scar tissue pulling stiffly when he moved his arms in even the simplest swordsman's gestures.

At last Reyna asked about Hipolla. He saw she thought Hipolla had been his lover, so he explained. But that night he dreamt Hipolla dead, laid on a hasty pyre, with flames eating her. Before dawn he rose, calling for a horse.

"I saw your house earring," Reyna said, "but order me about all you will, I have no horse."

"Then get me one or I will walk, back to my land, into the city, for I must get there somehow."

He walked. The healer went with him, alternately cursing him for his stubbornness, yet supporting him when he got dizzy. By the second day they reached freeholders who had no sympathy for the Sanctum and willingly lent Tanta a horse.

✸ 11 ✸

In the morning haze the witch schooner reached Cartheon and its five great headlands folded away into the distance. A continuous ribbon of city walls crested the bluffs, and bustling waterfronts lined all the bays below. Swarms of gulls and terns glided along the shore, swooping to peck at refuse on the beaches or quarreling with the ravens in the schooner's rigging. Skinny children combed the beaches below the city walls, poking at litter with bone-white driftwood sticks, while fishermen pulled their boats onto the sand and mended their nets.

Roshannon and Ni'An exchanged glances, grinning. Roshannon shaded his eyes against the sunlight sparkling on the waves. From where the schooner stood offshore, he could see five finger bays reaching into the land, five headlands meshing with the water, like two giant hands joined in a firm compact of sea and earth here at the edge of the world.

Isharra, her silver hair flying, ordered the deckhands to trim sail.

The schooner glided by the second bar of land, a finger of beach and rock that held another segment of walled city and the remains of a forest. The first bay was a tangled maze of fishing boats, rafts, cargo barges, and high-prowed canoes that skimmed the water.

Thousands of roofs and towers crusted the hills beyond the beach, and sunlight flashed from windows, tiles, and bronzework. Warehouses with red peaked roofs and blinking windows sprawled at the edge of the water, while dozens of feluccas were tied up at crowded wharves. Stout walls and gates rose above the weathered huddle of the waterfront. Great bridges of dark red stone that Isharra said were walkways soared up to the high city on the rock. The sound of hundreds of people talking, bargaining, and yelling orders and bids wafted over the water as the schooner drifted by.

"This is Cartheon proper," Isharra said. "Lyssa low town is what we've passed."

Ni'An whooped, but Roshannon felt apprehensive. The inhabitants of this vast city would think Lian Calla of no more account than a gnat on its endless flanks. If Keira came here, she could easily disappear.

As the ship rounded the third finger of land, the city's vastness grew overwhelming.

Enterprising gulls lit on the schooner's carved rail, watching sailors and passengers with keen, greedy eyes. Sleek, moon-faced seals bobbed in the water, barking like dogs, begging for fish.

The crew anchored the schooner near a floating pier. There raftsmen and canoemen waited to carry ship cargoes and passengers to the city itself. Isharra, grinning, unfurled a green banner and ordered crewmen to lower the ship's boat.

Irina Cathaya emerged from below, carrying a satchel and wearing her sword at her side. She and Isharra invited the Lian Callans into the ship's boat, called for a pair of oarsmen, and climbed in beside them. Cathaya-ka cursed one of the waiting canoemen amiably and promised him twenty silver tors if he and his relatives hauled the *Nightwind*'s cargo of tea and lumber into the docks.

They entered the main harbor through a great triumphal arch set at the lip of the fifth finger bay. One side of the great arch was firmly set on the edge of the shore; the other side rose from the water, as if remnants of a sunken city were rising from the sea to meld with the living city.

Roshannon's senses prickled. "It looks like a piece of witchcraft."

"Oh, aye," Ni'An said. "It makes a body wonder if they brought us in this way just to overawe us."

The water gate made Roshannon think of a half-finished city, built out to the edge of land until the sea encroached on it. Below the lap of the waves it was hard to tell if the images were reflections or fragments of underwater building.

The old shipmaster smiled. "It stood so in my grandmother's day, and in her grandmother's day before. It remains from the times before the waters rose."

The oarsmen rowed swiftly through the tangle of smaller craft and canoes entering the water gate. Ancient stone faces and inscriptions decorated the gate, while a stylized carving of a man and woman embracing showed on the great arch's keystone.

The sailors lifted their oars, letting their boat nose against the steps of a vast stone pier where a market was in full session.

The Lian Callans stepped ashore, glad to go unremarked in the throng. City dwellers elbowed their way through the mob, their eyes bright with bargaining fever and curiosity, calling each other oafs if they bumped shoulders or trod on their neighbor's feet.

Lynxlike cats with black-tipped ears and golden eyes darted among the merchants' booths and dragged off entrails from the butchers' shambles and fish guts from the fishmongers' baskets. Roshannon paced the pier, getting the feel of land back in his legs. Isharra raised the green banner and Irina Cathaya led them up a narrow street beside the pier's bustling market. People who spotted the green banner moved aside and let them pass.

They marched up narrow, cobbled streets and steps cut into the cliff, into the upper city, where Cartheon lay open to their view. Each headland held another quarter casting its reflection into the water, and each narrow bay was alive with smaller craft skimming like water insects among incoming ships.

Roshannon traded a glance with Ni'An. He felt small and provincial, and less a guest than a prisoner.

The copse that Keira had chosen as refuge offered a good view of the two armies facing each other across the valley. She rummaged in her saddlebags while Beren, who had slipped the pony's bit to let it graze, perched in a tree for a better look at the action below.

She fed the mare a handful of grain and stroked the gray's neck. Sporadic gusts of wind snatched the sounds of men and animals away, the silence making the armies seem more toylike and unreal.

Keira knew she should flee, but watched entranced. The Sanctum troops, which she recognized from her previous near encounters, moved in great bunched masses, with separate wings straying into the surrounding countryside. Small troops of mounted men circled the larger mass, darted at it on one side or the other, then withdrew. These were the northerners, the blasphemers. Watching this strange demonstration of the art of war, she thought of ants or flies swarming into a vast patch of honey. The northerners were badly outnumbered.

Beren twisted toward her and pointed. "Eastward, across the valley, what is that?"

"It must be Kum, the holy city on the mountain that the merchant spoke of." Keira peered through the screen of trees.

"Look, they're moving closer," Beren said. "I want to watch them fight."

"If either army catches us, they would probably kill us—we have no value as hostages."

"You could say you were my mother, a priest's widow. The Sanctum army would never kill you then."

"I could say you were my brother. But what if the witches caught us?" Keira shook her head, remembering Otella, the southern camp follower she had questioned. Getting caught by the Sanctum army meant sure death. She wondered if the Red Man was with the army below and if he had taken more witches captive. But circling the armies and surrendering to the witches would be dangerous with Beren along. Reaching the city still seemed the best idea. She suspected the witches who lived there could explain her dreams and her mysterious bond with Roshannon—and perhaps sever it. The memory of the city seen through his eyes and her awareness of his body still haunted her. Damn him.

A drumbeat rose from the valley, insistent as the drumrolls that plagued her dreams. The tree branches on the edge of the overhang quivered and rustled. Suddenly the branch Beren was standing on cracked, and he fell. She grabbed for his foot, got thin air, and stumbled against the sapling. He tumbled down the bank, his wild, ashen face staring up at her. Below him, the vast, crawling armies had come much closer, and a line of helmeted foot soldiers detached from the main body was climbing uphill. One carried a banner tilted downward, a thin red pennant writhing like a snake in the air about his knees. Keira cursed. It was like one of her dreams coming for her, but real, implacable. For a heartbeat the red pennant swelled into an archpriest's red cloak, whipping about the lean figure of a faceless man walking toward her. Abruptly the image shattered.

She scrambled through the undergrowth. Beren had stopped himself by grabbing a gnarled tree, but his slide loosed a rain of pebbles. A few bounced and skidded downslope toward the approaching men.

Beren looked up, his face a dirt-smeared mask.

Keep still, she signed him, and pointed down, fearing he was within bow range. For now, the band of archers and shield bearers were intent on the terrain.

Below, a white-haired man with a raven riding his shoulder raised a hand to shade his eyes, and glanced toward where the boy lay.

Hurt? Keira signaled Beren. He shook his head from side to side and craned his neck, trying to look down over his shoulder. He inched up the slope, hugging the ground and dragging his cloak along beneath him. Keira pointed to where the slope leveled out to meet the scrubby woods. Safer if he went that way—she would bring the horses.

Drumrolls surged up from the valley.

The mare snorted as she might at the presence of other horses. Keira scanned the small sheltered meadow and the line of trees as she picked up the lead reins. "Quiet, beasts," she said, rubbing the mare's neck and twisting her fingers in the pony's mane. She led the horses to the edge of the trees, hoping the foliage hid them from the soldiers' view. Crouched in the underbrush, she motioned Beren to keep crawling, and prayed he would not rise and show himself against the slope, a perfect target.

Her senses prickled. A vast wave of emotions that dizzied and sickened her washed over her.

Below, the wind caught the serpentine red banner and flung it straight out. Its pattern showed three trees, their crowns and roots interlaced, surely a witch thing. Then she spotted the southerners hidden halfway up the slope: crouching men in dusty leathers with sun glinting on the metal studs of their armor.

The raven on the standard-bearer's shoulders screamed. Its dark wings beating, the bird shot up. An archer in ambush shot at it, but the bird soared beyond the arrow's range. The archers downhill took cover behind their shield men. A second later, a half-dozen arrows hissed upward, one catching an ambusher in the throat. Another arrow flew wide, striking a rock near Beren and shattering it into fragments.

Keira crawled to the edge of the bank, bracing herself around the sapling's trunk and holding her right hand down to him.

The two groups screamed taunts at each other. An arrow hissed into the red banner. Its bearer and his companions flattened against the slope, their shields covering them like giant tortoiseshells. Another exchange of arrows hissed through the air.

Beren clasped her right hand with his left, kicking frantically to get a toehold in the crumbling bank. He slipped, sending a rain of pebbles and dirt downhill, his face white as death.

Keira ground her teeth as his entire weight dragged at her arm. She kept her grip by an effort of will, slowly hoisting him upward. Looking in his panicked eyes, she tasted his fear. It invaded her. She closed her eyes, concentrating, willing his emotions away from her. He clutched the sapling's trunk with his right hand and scrambled onto the bank. He and Keira crawled through the thicket on hands and knees, her right arm nearly giving out under her. She handed him the reins, boosted him into the saddle, and mounted, pressing her heels into the mare's flanks.

Time roared by yet infinite details crowded in on her senses, as they had when the man jumped her with the knife.

She grinned. "You should fast a year before you expect me to haul you over a bank again. You felt like you weighed a hundred stone."

"A hundred stones? You're crazy." He slapped the mare's flank.

The whistle of arrows ripped the air. Both tensed and cringed at the sound.

The mare tossed her head and snorted as a chattering squirrel fled up a tree, a blur of gray. From below came the sound of men screaming. Keira slapped the mare's flank, leaning low into her neck. An arrow hissed through the trees ahead of them. A stray arrow, she hoped, glancing back wildly over her shoulder. No one was pursuing them.

They crashed through the undergrowth, fleeing blindly until the drums faded behind them.

"We could have hidden and seen the whole battle," he said. "If I had not fallen."

"We are lucky to be alive and not captured." Noting his stubborn chin and his eyes flashing with excitement, Keira wanted to thrash him, except that she shared his excitement.

"It was like watching a ko game," he said. "The armies looked like ants."

Keira looked back. Against the top of the hill, a rider was coming fast. She cursed, slapped the pony's rump, and whispered a prayer into the mare's neck. Where had the rider come from?

"We may have to separate," she yelled as a dip in the hills hid the rider from view.

"No." He smacked the pony's hindquarters with the flat of his hand, urging it close beside her.

Over the hills the rider came into view again, dust flying from his pony's hooves.

Beyond the meadow they were crossing stretched a wood. The last fold of hill hid the rider again.

"Into the woods," Keira said. Without looking back, they plunged into the forest, riding deeper and deeper among towering trees and blue shadows. The trees had shaded-out undergrowth, so they could ride fast. Only bars of light filtered through the treetops, touching a branch here and there. Keira saw no light to mark the fringe of the woods behind or ahead.

"Is it safe in here?" Beren asked.

Keira touched his hand. A sudden misgiving struck her: what if the rider had paced them, herded them into the woods?

The carpet of fallen needles drank up sound. Keira kept the mare at an easy trot, scanning the trees and ducking in the saddle to avoid low branches.

The shadows here were darker than in the southland woods. The biggest trees bore needles as long as brooch pins, and the bases of their broad trunks formed vast moss-covered knees where tiny wildflowers and pale orchids grew. Invisible insects buzzed in their ears, nostrils, and eyes. Beren swatted and cursed. She slapped her neck and put up her hood.

By what she judged to be noon, the clouds of insects had diminished and the air smelled sweet and sharp. But Keira knew she was lost. She hesitated to tell Beren. The straight, tall trees went on forever, blocking the sun. Branches creaked in the wind as the needle trees whispered among themselves in the murky forest.

If the horseman knew the woods, she was doubly lost. She dismounted at the foot of a giant tree, left the mare with Beren, and began to climb. Fruit trees had always been easy. This tree hindered her at every step. The broken stumps of its lowest branches made fine footholds, but higher up the branches closed like a woven net. She bundled her cloak in a sturdy crotch and struggled on. Higher still, a chattering, gold-eyed creature with delicate black hands and dark eyes skittered over her arms. If this was a nesting tree, what lived in the nest? She felt dizzy yet strangely exultant. The hundred scratches on her hands and ribs stung, but the sting told her she was still very much alive.

At last the blue roof of the forest appeared, the thousand tree-tops glimmering in the sunlight. She braced herself and looked about, glad of the sun on her face. To north and west, fog lapped the edges of the forest, making it impossible to see how far the wood stretched.

"Oh, piss," Keira exclaimed. The view only told her how lost she was.

This must be Hipolla's home territory, the heart of the witch-land, the Blue Forest, home also to the great, wild hunting cats Hipolla had talked of.

She scrambled down, blinking bark dust from her eyes. Her boots slipped on a few footholds, and the jagged stumps of branches scraped her hands and ribs. Far below she made out the dim shapes of the mare and pony.

"Come down," Beren called.

The boughs of the tree obscured the boy's shape, but through the last screen of foliage, as she retrieved her cloak, she saw the wrongness, the reason for the strain in his voice. Other horses and men waited below.

A litter of bark and brittle twigs rained down as she slipped choosing another foothold.

"Come down," a man said.

They had circled the foot of the tree. Poor Brat peered up at her from beside his pony. She retrieved her cloak and carefully put it on.

"I am coming." With a sick taste in her mouth, she picked her way down through the maze of branches and dropped from the tree, waiting for arrows to pierce her flesh. Like a cat, she landed on hands and knees in the forest litter and looked up.

For a moment, she expected to see the Red Man standing before her.

But a pair of brilliant green eyes appraised her from a face painted like a wolf's.

The witches dressed in patched clothes streaked green and

brown, and had painted their faces to resemble beasts'. The other men had wary eyes as golden as cat eyes.

The green-eyed man grabbed her and jerked her to her feet. Another man, his face painted like a hunting cat's, wore a strung bow over his shoulder and held the mare's bridle, stroking her chin and addressing her as *thou*. The mare did not even show her teeth. Keira felt betrayed by the creature. She stared in fascination at the beast masks. They must be Blue Forest witchfolk.

Beren, his hands bound, stood beside his pony and looked terrified.

Suddenly a man grabbed her from behind and twisted her arms behind her back. She bit her tongue, and the metal taste of fear filled her mouth.

"They made me call you," Beren said. The bowman clamped a hand over his mouth. But she was proud that he had not revealed her as a woman, and nodded to him, hoping he understood that.

Keira twisted experimentally in her captor's grasp. He twisted her arm more tightly behind her back.

"Do not make me hurt you, lad," he whispered against her neck. "I do not like to hurt."

"But you are hurting me and hindering me from my journey."

Cat Face and Wolf Face smiled grimly.

"What are you doing in our woods?" Cat Face asked.

She looked up, wordless, and spotted the hilt of Brat's dagger protruding from the cat-faced man's sash. They pushed her against the tree trunk and searched her boots and sash.

"Off with that boot you've got the dagger in."

She heaved and kicked, sliding sideways so the rough bark scraped her shoulders. The cat-faced man yanked off her boot.

The dagger in its thin leather sheath fell to the ground. Its presence seemed to satisfy them; they did not search further and find Hipolla's earring. Cat Face wrinkled his nose at the smell of her boot and hastily put it back on her foot. His companions snorted.

Green Eyes picked up the dagger, drew it, and flourished it in the air. "Ah."

Wolf Face whistled. "A pretty thing." There was a little moment of silence among them.

"Ehh!" An archer yelled as Beren bit his hand, kicked his shin, and scrambled away. In two strides the man caught the boy up like a sack of goods and tossed him halfway across his shoulders.

Beren kicked and screamed. Keira wished she could laugh; it made a fine sight until another bowman gagged the boy.

"Let him go." Keira kicked wildly backward, felt her boot connect with shinbone.

Her captor grunted and cursed, pushing her face into the tree bark. She smelled sap and bark dust, her own sweat and that of the men who had caught her.

Someone slid a blindfold over her eyes, a gag over her mouth, and jerked both tight. Through it all, like an eerie taunt, one of the men whispered to the mare, soothing her and calling her pet names.

❀ 12 ❀

Something ailed his cousin. And that something was the most annoying mystery Ni'An Lia Roshannon had encountered for some time.

Normally he relished puzzles, for mysteries touched the heart of life. Why a woman chose one man and not another was a good one, worth much thought. Or why some babies were born with cauls, harelips, birthmarks, or twisted limbs. Or how the city's silk masters had coaxed the dozens of different species of silk spiders into spinning for them. Good mysteries these, satisfying as a draught of water from a deep well, worth many hours of conversation before the bathhouse, in the inns, over games of ko and bowls of tea.

The Sanctum priests would say, god's will, the turn of the Wheel. They would simply not poke into such delicious mysteries.

But this latest puzzle unsettled him.

Something lay on his cousin's spirit, a something Ni'An had never seen before. Nikka had fallen into a perpetual state of distraction from the business at hand. He often let silences fall between his words, musing on something inexplicable. Sometimes he abruptly shrugged his shoulders and walked out of their richly furnished rooms, giving no explanation.

Ni'An first suspected his cousin had fallen in love with Isharra, but abandoned that theory when he saw absolutely no evidence of it. In fact, since his cousin returned, he seemed to have little interest in women.

This morning Nikka had caught Ni'An looking at him and grumbled that the damned steward was taking his time about seeing them.

Ni'An, who knew his cousin so well and felt so restless himself

164

in this city of marvels, doubted his misgivings, and thought, of course, the frustration of waiting for an audience is what ails him. But later, watching his cousin, he realized the ailment truly had come with Nikka, into Lian Calla.

Ni'An watched his cousin even more closely.

First, he took the changes for the malaise of a soldier who had served in foreign lands. Nikka barely discussed his time in the southern armies or the southerners themselves. Perhaps he had simply seen too much.

One day as they wandered in the marketplaces, through the mazelike artisans' quarters, he caught Nikka staring at a tall, slim boy in a gray cloak. They were sitting in the courtyard of an inn, sipping spice tea, and playing a leisurely game of ko, when between two moves Nikka froze.

Ni'An glanced in the direction of Nikka's sudden rapt attention—a boy with reddish hair, cut straight at the shoulder, was sipping tea with a companion at an adjoining table. So smoothly did Nikka shift his gaze and decide on his move, setting down his counter and capturing a pair of Ni'An's stones, that Ni'An thought he might have been mistaken about the object of his cousin's interest. Ni'An watched and waited, feeling Nikka, who had always been so close to him, recede into some strange private territory.

The second and third times he caught his cousin staring at a tall boy in a gray cloak, Ni'An thought someone was following them—but any shadower who knew his business would hardly send a person dressed in similar clothing to tail them day after day.

The fourth time Ni'An had a troublesome thought that he first dismissed but reluctantly reexamined. This tall lad was comely, at the last edge of his youth. In many lights it would be hard to determine from a single glance whether he was man or woman.

Nikka was frowning at him. "What is wrong?"

Ni'An shook his head, embarrassed. He fiddled with a ko stone. His whole game strategy had drained from his head in that instant, as he wondered if his cousin had become a fancier of boys while in the Sanctum army.

From the towers of the steward's citadel, Roshannon scanned the city spread below like the orb web of a fantastic spider. And we are the hostage guests of the chief spider himself, the high steward, he thought.

The dream masters' and the spider masters' quarters surrounded the tower, while the spokes of great thoroughfares radiated from the city's heart to its many gates. The finger bays and Lyssa low town lay southeast, with the forest gate at the eastern boundary and the Blue Forest beyond it.

Roshannon was restless. Neither he nor Ni'An, Irina Cathaya, or Isharra had yet seen the high steward. Apparently the high witch lords considered the question of the bothersome Sanctum armies at their leisure, as if it were something their artificers had made, a faceted jewel they turned in their fingers, curious to observe its subtle shifts of color from all sides.

For such an invisible man, the high steward's hospitality was generous—Roshannon and Ni'An had been given rich apartments. But today their rooms felt like a cage, a box where the steward kept delegates until he deigned to pay attention to them. Only the high steward could order out an army, or give outlanders rank within it, and Roshannon was in no mood either to wait or to play at politics.

He finished writing the day's dispatch to his mother—larding descriptions of everything he had seen with the slang of the islands where he had grown up, making the job of the steward's man who must intercept and read the letters ticklish—folded and sealed it and called for Hiri to deliver it to the captain of the fastest schooner sailing to Lian Calla.

Hiri was a youth from Kos island who never spoke unless spoken to. Ni'An affectionately called him The Mute. But after delivering the first batch of letters, Hiri had hidden near the docks and watched men board and question each ship's captain who carried the dispatches.

"So the high steward's spies know we exist and have arrived in the city," Roshannon told Ni'An sarcastically.

He expected no less. He filled the dispatches with minute observations of the city and its inhabitants and several agreed-upon sentences to indicate whether he had an audience with the steward and what transpired. He visited the marketplaces where the spider masters showed off their breeding spiders, kept concealed in ornate, covered cages, and mined as much information as he could from the tight-lipped guildsmen about the silk industry. He visited the historians and the dream masters, coaxing them to discuss the history of the Schism and the witches. It was a thankless task, for their lips were tighter than those of the silk guild.

Ni'An wandered the city, losing his heart to the marvelous toys of the artificers' quarter. Roshannon envied his cousin his enthrallment with the witches' devices.

With Ni'An, he explored the markets to ease the feeling of being a beast in too rich a cage. The city was a great net, to catch a man and all his wondering as easily as the spiders that made the silk would catch a fly in their own webs—a great wheel following the path of its own mysteries.

The dream masters' quarter, the ancient heart of the city, was the only area the witches had forbidden to them. Its maze of narrow streets circled and twisted, sometimes completely concealed by roofs and balconies that touched across the street. It would be ideal defensive territory if the city ever fell and invaders sacked the outer quarters. Despite his frustration, Roshannon admired the city's outer walls and watchtowers and the nested walls of the separate quarters. Docks, seaweed plantations, and fish ponds lined the inner bays, promising a harvest of food to withstand the longest siege. The outer bays bustled with ferries and fishing boats, and fleets of red-sailed ships patrolled the coast, watchful as sharks. The wonder of it would stagger any who tried to assail it. Such a city could only fall by betrayal.

Or perhaps by sheer indifference to events in the outside world.

Roshannon raised the far-seeing glass to his eye. In the forest above Lyssa beach, smoke rose from dozens of glassmakers' ovens. He swung the tube across the ocean of roofs, squares, and glittering domes, to the patch of woods inside the eastern gate where the tanners had been situated to keep the stench of their trade from polluting the city.

He peered down at the dream masters' quarter again. The maid who had brought brush, quill, and ink told him that only initiates passed through the gate of the maze. "All others get hopelessly lost in Dreamtown," she said.

Dreamtown.

Its convoluted alleys echoed the twisting of his own heart and mind. Slowly he turned the wooden ring on his finger, brooding and scanning the vast city through the glass.

Roshannon recalled his own first experience with the far-seeing tubes. At first it defied his hardheaded practicality that by squinting through a tube with two glass lentils winking in either end, a man could see three miles distant the tiny characters on a merchant's awning, the young girl leaning out the window above to watch the market hubbub while she brushed her hair, even the flower tucked behind her ear. He learned to appreciate the tube as an enhancement of his eyes. All the artificers' toys pricked at his senses and thoughts and unsettled him. The witches made much better seeing tubes than the islanders, but the artificers bought glass from the glassmakers, worked it in secret, and guarded the details of their manufacture.

Ni'An had returned one day excited by a map of the moon that a man had shown him. "He said he first dreamt the moon's mountains," Ni'An said, "and so turned the glass toward the moon. Strange, isn't it, how these people are led by their dreams?"

"Aye," Roshannon said, grinning to himself, "because they use dreams as another sense." But he thought uneasily that the tube, at least, was a fundamentally harmless, honest thing, letting a man see only what was physically there. It had no power to summon dream visions or reveal *them* in sharper focus.

In the darkness Keira smelled boot leather and horse sweat, heard hoofbeats and the creak of harness. She came to, knowing the thing pressed into her neck was a rider's knee. Blindfolded and slung over the horse like a sack of grain, she was bouncing and rolling against the horse's withers. Her stomach heaved. She did not want the rider to know she was awake. Her fingers were swollen, her arms and feet numb.

She strained to hear Beren or perceive him with that other sense.

She wriggled her toes; hot needles shot through her flesh. She sneezed, and the gag dug into the sides of her mouth.

The rider laughed and shifted her over the curve of the saddle horn, which dug into her ribs and made her glad she had scarcely eaten in the last days. Her throat burned. She choked on the saliva-soaked gag, tasting horse sweat and dust. The sun's sudden warmth on her back, buttocks, and legs told her the scouts must have come to a clearing in the vast woods. Almost nightfall, she thought, sniffing and feeling a chill in the wind.

The rider drew rein. "Off with you," he said. A hand yanked

her numb feet. She slid across the saddle, until her feet hit the ground. Her cloak hung against her, crumpled and sweaty, with all its hidden wealth pressed into her skin. Her whole body ached. She swayed against the horse's shoulder. A strong hand righted her.

The rider cut the cord from her wrists. The air stung her rope burns. "Put the horse piss to good use," one of the men said. Stinging liquid fire poured suddenly over Keira's abraded wrists. One man laughed as she gasped. They retied her wrists, leaving a short length of cord between her hands. She would be able to feed herself, but otherwise her hands would be useless. She sensed Beren nearby and began to wonder what the limits of this sense were.

They would question her and then kill her, she supposed. For being a southerner, a spy in northern territory. Or if she showed them the earring in her boot and demanded to be taken to Tanta clan, would they kill her for being a thief and take the trinket?

Someone loosed the gag, pushed it away, and thrust a water skin to her lips. She drank greedily and choked, the corners of her mouth sore. Water dribbled down her chin. "Where is my mare, you thieves?" A hand pulled the gag back in place.

A familiar whicker caught her ear, and she jerked about to face the sound. She sensed where each of the four men and Brat were, but only with the blindfold removed would she know if her guesses were right. Being blindfolded had seemingly sharpened her ability.

"Up you go," the rider said. Her captor gave her an abrupt leg up and sprang into the saddle. She twisted her covered face to the sun, craving the warmth.

East, they were heading east, for the sun's warmth struck her on the back and the back of the head now.

Pain screamed along her nerves until it became an entity separate from herself. Her consciousness swung around the physical pain, bound like a beast tied to a pole, only able to stretch so far.

A memory of music, awful sorrow, the rush of her spirit leaving her fleshly body behind, prodded her. A curious hollowness grew at the center of her being, and her flesh seemed to split like a seedpod from breastbone to navel. She swallowed, squeezing bit by bit from the pinched shell of her physical body. Every hairs-breadth of progress hurt. She fought the pain. What was effortless in dreams or a more relaxed state, tortured her battered, bruised body. The spirit body reflects the real body, she thought in weird, detached wonder.

Abruptly she tore free, like a scab ripped from the edge of a wound. The sound of her heartbeat, her aches, the clop of the horses' hooves, dissolved.

She shot straight up, light as feather or ash, so quickly the speed dizzied her. Her dream self observed rolling blue woodlands below, clearings, bands of horse archers, and settlements. Time and place spun, wrapping and unraveling around her. She drifted through clouds. A whirlwind suddenly snagged her spirit. The powerful tow swept her along, faster and faster, farther and farther north.

Keira found herself moving through a great market as in a slow dream, peering at all the wonders.

An oddly familiar voice led her into a crowd milling about a leather worker's booth. From the center of the throng came a laugh so like Hipolla's that she turned, compelled, toward the laugh.

Through the swarm of faces and voices, one face came clear for a moment.

The tall man's elusive profile shifted, the haunting voice rose and fell, bantering with the leather worker. He turned on his heel after trading a final insult with the merchant, and slipped into the crowd.

Sun glinted on the earring dangling from his left ear: two wheels, jade and amber, joined by silver. The sun blinded her; she was no longer sure what the earring was.

Only a flicker of silver hair and the sun catching on the magnificent earring led Keira on. The voice danced on ahead of her, Hipolla's laugh, Hipolla's tone, but deeper, pulling at her, a lure impossible to resist.

He flowed as swiftly and surely as a ghost, his way made magically sure through the crowds. He passed a carter's horse. The wind ruffled the silver hair. Sun sparked on the earring against his dark left cheek and glinted on a collar around his neck as he turned his head. His profile taunted her, so like Hipolla's that tears burned her eyes. His image glittered and blurred. Keira blinked. He had disappeared behind a loaded cart.

Keira darted onward.

Perhaps she chased a ghost after all, a demon ghost sent to torment her. She remembered Hipolla's words. "Slowpoke."

For a moment, there he was again, a tantalizing glimpse, luring her. Her mother and Deva had whispered ghost tales. You could not catch a demon ghost, they said, but only follow and follow until your heart broke. For a demon ghost would not forgive you or free you as a normal ghost would, but only lead ever onward, taunting and torturing.

Keira went on. She would know whether this was a man or a ghost, whatever the price. Suddenly all the faces and buildings around her blurred as she floated upward.

Below her the city became the size of a child's toy. She looked down on it and saw its pattern, all its thoroughfares and rooftops and gardens, like a glittering spiderweb with a dark center the color and taste of dreams.

Exultant, she soared above the city. Unable to resist the temptation, she drifted closer and closer to its walls and rooftops, dizzy with the joy of finally seeing it.

The high steward sat up in bed with a start. His arms were sheathed in gooseflesh, every hair erect.

Joy washed over him, fierce and soaring. He grappled with it, embracing it, seeking to discover what powerful, unknown dreamer was abroad.

He grabbed a cloak and his short sword, slipped on sandals, and stepped onto the balcony that overlooked the spider masters' quarter. Outside, the joy of a dreamer floating over the city enveloped him, infectious and exuberant.

He grinned, studying the sky.

Someone of great, wild power had awakened recently in his or her dream self.

He breathed in, said a veda, and a second veda, and loosed his dream self. It soared above the exact center of the city, above the moon-silvered rooftops, above the heart of the dream masters' maze.

It had not long to wait.

The mysterious dream self swooped in a triple circle, faster and faster, like a boisterous child spinning itself dizzy, getting closer and closer to him, and at last, careening like a drunken hawk, brushed his dream presence. He sought to meld himself into the new presence, to follow and see what body it had slipped from.

But it knew he was another, and fled, leaving a string of images in his mind: three bodies hung on a gibbet, a body hung in an apple tree, a scar-faced man, and a curious vibrant redness.

The instant of touching told him the dreamer was a young woman who had slipped from a tired, bruised body, while thinking she would soon be dead.

Aramit leaned against the parapets. The image of a man with a scarred face lingered, piquing his curiosity.

He said another veda, to keep the aftermath of the contact from causing headache, and went inside, planning to confer with his court dreamers. He needed to identify the troubling presence in the south, which might be the archpriest the spy had mentioned, and find this other dreamer. Perhaps they were bonded.

If the two presences were not one and the same, where had these wild, full-blown dreamers come from? Agents dutifully sent dispatches from the Blue Forest, from Bala Koth, from Kum and Lian Calla, reporting births and marriages in families suspected to carry the gift, curious happenings and rumors. For generations, their lists had traveled back to Cartheon, into the hands of the stewards and dream masters, and proposals of alliances had gone out, to marry that provincial daughter into this city clan, this son into that provincial clan, to nurture the gift and keep it strong. But how, by the Wheel's thousand names, could agents so carefully in place have missed these talents?

Unless the agent in Kum had been subverted or killed since the dispatch a month ago. Unless the gifted ones had blossomed in the south's heartland, where few agents dared set foot.

He said a veda to check his frustration. The agents were low-level talents—keen enough to spot the gift; ironically, the first wave of Sanctum witch hunters had been similar talents, eager to point out the miratasu among their people and send them to the gallows. Perhaps the gift itself, which once flourished among both northern and southern peoples, had transmuted in the veins of disbelievers and emerged in a form even agents would not recognize.

The first time he had accidentally touched another awakened

one, he had been a youth, a solitary who prowled the city streets from the sea gates to the citadel and back, dressed in old clothes, exploring the home quarter of the harvesters who worked the kelp fields, the fish market, and the tanners' gate, dipping into the minds of the people, tasting the salty rivers of their dreams, fears, and lusts.

One hot day he had been losing a ko game to an old bathhouse philosopher. Suddenly another mind had brushed his, netting him in a joyous whirl of sensations. Aramit sat bolt upright, like a hound scenting a trail, or a lutha string quivering before the musician's hand falls again.

It was none of the well-disciplined minds of his schoolmates who studied at the dream masters' feet, but an unknown mind. A woman. A soaring mind, darting like a kite or a fish.

He walked blindly, as the dreamer touched him again, feeding him images of sky, clouds, birds in flight, shadowed walls, the masts of ships swaying back and forth against the sparkle of the harbor waters.

At noon he found himself at the great fish market beneath the second headland. Silver-bellied fish glittered everywhere in the sun, heaped in baskets, piled on tables, pegged onto boards, and being scaled by the fishmongers' women. Some swam live in huge glass bowls. The smell of drying seaweed and an underlay of rot mingled in the air. The barefoot fishwives stood on wharves smeared with fish entrails, their aprons spattered with blood and winking fish scales, their quick knives darting, their strong, work-hardened hands gutting and filleting the catch for merchants and artisans' wives. Sly, greedy cats darted among their worktables, dragging off fish guts or snapping up handfuls of roe tossed aside.

The dreamer stood behind a long table smeared with blood and fish scales. Her feet were planted firmly in a mound of seaweed strewn with fish bones and bits of cake salt, and she wriggled her bare toes from time to time.

She wielded a little, moon-shaped fish-gutting knife with amazing skill and speed. But her mind soared like a gull.

He observed her quietly for a long while. The sun and heat intensified the market's smells. Sweat beaded the girl's upper lip and forehead. At last she looked up, meeting his eyes. Startled, she lost her concentration; the knife sliced her thumb, and her blood oozed out to join the fish blood on the table.

She stared at him, perhaps a little afraid.

Her mother cursed and threw a fish head at a skinny brindle cat that was dragging a carp off by its tail. She grabbed her daughter's hand, squeezed the thumb, and sucked the blood, then reached into a basket and sprinkled a handful of salt into the wound.

The fishmonger's daughter widened her eyes at the salt's sting, riding the pain. Aramit rode it with her, halving it. He laid his hand over hers.

Her mother and father eyed him warily.

"I will honor your daughter," he told them. It was the truth. Those who sought out gifted ones explained as little as possible, because the uninitiated often distrusted the gift and commoners were wary of their social betters. But few commoners would refuse a chance for one of their children to be trained in the dream masters' quarter. Because the gift came to man and woman, lord and commoner alike: the gift was no respecter of rank, and wise men sought it among all people.

"Would you come with me?" Aramit asked the girl.

The girl's mother frowned at him, then pushed her daughter toward him. "Be sweet to the lord if he fancies you," she had said.

And that had been the beginning of his twenty-five years' acquaintance with Akitya Harro, now chief dream master in her own right. He had taken her back to the dream masters' quarter to study with the other awakening ones. And when the dream masters deemed the time ripe and safe, Aramit and Akitya slept together, thus truly awakening their second selves.

But Akitya's pregnancies, by him and other men, yielded only miscarriages or stillbirths. The healers had no remedy. After Aramit was elected high steward, he dutifully formed alliances with many women, hoping for an equally gifted child. He still longed for such a child, and, in between his dalliances and state matings, as he called them, shared Akitya's bed. When their minds met in private, they soared. But when they met in public, as steward and dream master, they battled each other for the good of their respective offices.

The next morning, the steward stretched at the window, glad of the sun's warmth on his back. A servant filled tea bowls and left silently, bowing to the court dreamers.

Thaia sipped carefully from a tea bowl. A dream master's silver finger sheaths covered her fingers from the second joint to the fingertips and ended in curved claws, symbolizing the often beastlike nature of dreams. Gestures transformed her hands into an eerie blur of light and shadow.

"Last night I touched a miratasu, a strong talent," the steward said.

"The same one we have felt in the south?" Riva leaned forward, only the tiny line at the edge of his mouth betraying the fact that he was fighting the pain that plagued his joints and sometimes crippled him, forcing him to stay in bed. Thaia laid her hand on his. She would be sharing his pain, dividing it into a burden both of them could more easily bear.

"I don't know." For a moment the steward envied them the perfect union the gift had allowed the twins, joined in spirit in their mother's womb. "A young woman dreamer soared above my citadel. Whether she was, or is, what we have felt in the south, I am unsure. But the contact felt different."

Riva nodded. "What we felt in the south before was a clouded spirit, like one not fully awakened. It was impossible to know if it was male or female." He sipped his tea. "Is it possible that the lineages are gone astray, and that many talents awake in the south?"

"A message came from a pair of linked scouts not long ago," the steward said. "It said one of their team members was captured, then tortured and killed by a southern miratasu. The woman linked to this captured scout died not long afterward. Yet our Bala Kothi spy's description of the head the priest keeps on a pole by his tent was of a different man."

Riva sat forward. "So this priest killed more than one dreamer. Curse him. Could a southerner kill with the gift? As in the old days?"

"We have used the talent that way," Aramit said. "Awakened ones with strong enough talents can kill, but the killing often taints their spirit. The ancient assassins twisted the minds of rulers, forcing them to kill themselves. That's one of the reasons the southerners hated us. And I think someone who did not understand the talent could kill inadvertently."

Riva coughed. "But southerners would hide the talent, would they not? Seeing it only as a shameful thing, an evil to be stamped out or strictly controlled by the priests."

"The histories say that is how they used it before. Would they have learned to see the gift in other, better ways?" Thaia asked.

"Using the gift against us would surely interest them," the steward said. "Just as we have our histories, so do the southerners have theirs. An ambitious priest could learn from the old history books."

"But such wild dreamers in isolation, without training—" Riva spread his hands. "—what could they accomplish?"

Thaia laughed. "Never underestimate a dreamer or an enemy, especially if the enemy is a dreamer."

"Seek these dreamers, then discover if they are enemies," the steward said. "I don't trust myself to spend any more time fishing the void for them. Meanwhile, the Sanctum armies are harassing Blue Foresters and borderfolk near Kum. I suspect your talents are needed there."

"When do we ride into the borderlands against the Sanctum?" Riva asked.

"Soon."

A courier appeared at the door and discreetly cleared his throat. Aramit beckoned him inside.

"Ka. Lian Calla's man sent dispatches at dawn to the captain of the *Red Gull,* which sails for Lian Calla today. The letter describes the silk guilds, the warehouses, how the silk winders dress, and so on. Rather boring. They seem only interested in trade possibilities, ka. You wish them followed again?"

"Do not make it obvious today," Aramit said.

"My shadowers will be discretion itself." The courier bowed and departed.

Aramit cradled his tea bowl, considering the two diminutive warriors before him. There were those who drew blood, broke bones, killed outright; then there were the more subtle warriors of the mind. The idea of southern miratasu wielding like powers frightened yet fascinated him. He was still young enough—and foolish enough—to crave a worthy enemy.

"See what you can touch in the city. Tonight I will decide if I want the dream master's help." The steward watched Thaia's eyebrows raise. The dream master, Akitya Harro—who wore her old fish-gutting knife tucked through her sash to remind herself and everyone else that she had been born in a narrow house that overlooked the fishmongers' wharves—was Thaia's old teacher.

But no matter where Thaia's personal loyalties lay—and he wondered sometimes—she was devoted to her twin brother, the city,
and the sanctity of the gift itself. There was comfort in that.

Brother and sister rose in unison, and for a moment again, envy
for the unity of their spirits piqued him. He thought of the four
stillborn infants that had resulted from his young passion for
Akitya, and their agreement to live apart. He thought of Sira's
child, the perfectly healthy, perfectly normal son who would
never dream as he did.

Thaia glanced at him. "We share your grief, ka, that your son is
not a dreamer."

"Ka," Riva said. "I have reason to believe House Ayello would
welcome a leman contract."

"You mean to harness me to my duties as a stud, friend?"
Touching fingertips to forehead, Aramit grinned at them. As they
left, he wondered what range of talent the wild ones possessed.
The business of governing seemed irksome; he wanted to dive
into the void and not emerge until he had found the strange
dreamers, tasted the world through their eyes, and learned
whether they meant Cartheon good or ill.

On impulse, he called a courier to summon the Lian Callans.

❀ **13** ❀

"Keira," Roshannon said into the dark.

The sounds in the blackness around him resolved into familiar things: the fountain splashed in the garden outside; in the bed beside him, Ni'An shifted and mumbled in his sleep; crickets chirped; and a hunting cat called softly in the courtyard.

Roshannon blinked and stared away from the chink of light at the courtyard door until his eyes adjusted to the dark.

Closing his eyes, he saw her again—sprawled on a rug, staring up at him, catching her balance. A magnificent earring, a wheel of jade and a wheel of amber joined by a silver clasp, swung against her cheek and into her hair. In his old clothes she made a comely lad. She crouched facing him, her dark eyes full of secrets and pain.

He folded back the covers and drew his dagger from his boot. Naked, he slid from the bed. He stood listening at the courtyard door. Shadows filled the courtyard. Bare plum branches scraped the stonework, and water hissed softly in the fountain. The stillness taunted him.

"Nikka," Ni'An said at his side. "Hast seen something?" he asked in the island dialect they used around the steward's men.

Roshannon shook his head.

"The dreams come again?" It was not really a question. Ni'An had been with his cousin when the first visions came, that day they had gone hunting in the woods overlooking the fields and the sea. "Do you fear an assassin?"

"No. Why should the stewards dispose of us before they know exactly what we want?"

Roshannon slid into the bed and lay staring into the darkness. It was hours before dawn. The courtyard's smell of water and wet stone poured into his senses. He struggled not to close his eyes, not to let the waking vision of her creep up on him.

He woke to a din of knocking and shouting. Roshannon and Ni'An opened the door of their chambers, finding four green-clad men, who hurried them before the carved, bronze-bound doors of the great council chambers.

Isharra and her aunt, both wearing swords, nodded greeting outside the council chambers.

The steward's men cleared a pathway through the crowds that had pressed toward the doors with petitions and complaints. Loiterers jammed the hallways, telling their troubles to any willing ear or the air in general.

At last the doors were thrown back. A throng swarmed out through the area the steward's couriers kept open. Knots of Silktowners talking about guild business gestured with their red-gloved hands, the heels of their red boots clacking on the mosaic floor. Roshannon stared in puzzlement at men with fringed leather collars about their necks.

"Tanners," Isharra whispered to him with a grin. "Leathertowners." She gave him an ironic little salute. "The masters in their dreaming masks should interest you."

"Dreaming masks?"

Isharra would have answered, but Cathaya-ka put a firm hand on her niece's shoulder as the crowd behind pressed them forward. The steward's green-clad couriers herded everyone inside the high chamber.

Roshannon stared over the heads of the jostling crowd at the great chamber's arched walls and vaulted ceiling. In the eastern wall a stained-glass window rose from floor to ceiling, catching the sun. Its lead tracery formed a giant wheel, and inside the wheel lay a web, in whose center hung a wondrous, graceful image of a silk spider. Sunlight pouring through the glass splashed all the window's colors across the crowd, which had formed into orderly ranks at the couriers' signals. He got a crick in his neck from staring. More couriers closed in on Roshannon and Ni'An and hustled them to a series of box seats along one wall. Isharra and her aunt disappeared in the crowd temporarily, only to appear again in seats nearby.

A dozen steward's constables rapped their green staffs on the mosaic floor as the last of the guildsmen and their cronies left the hall.

Spectators crammed the galleries built along the hall's north and south walls, while light blazed through the wheel-shaped window, scattering colors across the mosaic floor.

Isharra leaned forward, looking excited. "There are the stewards, on the seats of honor."

"Seats of honor? They're pillows," Roshannon said, glancing at the twenty-five stewards seated in the front row against the northern wall.

Isharra made a face. "They are sacks, true, stuffed with a thousand skeins of wound silk and shaped like a silk spider's cocoon." Her tone implied that he was pathetically ignorant.

The steward's constables rapped on the floor three times.

A line of figures wearing masks carved in the likeness of sleeping or dreaming faces took seats above the stewards. These latest arrivals cocked their eerie masks above their faces like visors. The masks reminded Roshannon of the figureheads carved on the witches' schooners, and of his own disturbing dreams.

He leaned toward Isharra. "Where is the high steward?"

She shook her head. "Not here. Because you are summoned to the high council does not mean the high steward will be here himself." She pointed to the dream master sitting closest to the great window. "But that is *the* dream master herself, Akitya Harro. Consider yourself honored."

Roshannon gritted his teeth, wanting to curse. Would this be a condescending show of status, with no progress made? He jammed his doubled fists between his knees. Lian Calla would be overrun until these strange, stately folk made a decision, and an army of howling Sanctum fanatics would be scaling the outer walls of this city before these folk realized the danger. He began mentally composing an irritated dispatch to his mother when two black-robed constables arrived, rapped their staffs on the floor, and the session began.

Cathaya-ka, called on first, rose, and in a ringing voice declared why she had brought the Lian Calla men to the city, and what she had seen at Lian Calla harbor.

One of the silver-haired constables approached Roshannon. The man's house earring was a silver disk set with a black, glassy pebble, and the silver hair made it difficult to guess his age. His eyes were green as sea ice. Roshannon frowned. Could the man see all the way through him to the heart of his visions, he would believe in magic indeed.

"State the petition of Lian Calla, ka," the judge said.

Roshannon rose and did so, quickly and cleanly. Very simple, he thought: a treaty with Lian Calla, two thousand troops to keep the Sanctum from overrunning the city-state, and for him, a commission in the northern armies to fight the southerners gathered near Kum. "My services and all my knowledge, gathered while I served the Sanctum, in exchange for these other things," he said. "Along with open trade in tea, ship timbers, and silk."

As he spoke, he studied the earrings of the other lords present in the chamber. Nowhere did he spot the dream earring, the wheel of jade and amber.

Black Robe coughed and steepled his fingers. "So you know our enemy and would turn that knowledge to our use, you who have fought as a southern liege man?"

"It is only wise to know an enemy," Roshannon said slowly, "whatever the source of that knowledge may be. Better you break their armies in the field than let them gather at your walls." He imagined a shadow in the courtyard, a knife in the dark—if the lords of this grand city decided he was enough of a nuisance to assassinate them, then dump his and Ni'An's bodies in the ocean.

Several restless spectators in the gallery muttered loudly.

Black Robe paced. "And only wise to test loyalty. Do you not fear us; do you not think we are a danger to you?" There was infinite patience in his eyes, a kind of amused, philosophical detachment that reminded Nikka of his mother, his father, all the old men on the council.

"A sensible man must fear a worthy opponent," Roshannon said. "But my battle is not against this city." I'm lying there, he thought with grim amusement. "And this city is less danger to me or Lian Calla than to itself, if it does not take the Sanctum threat seriously." He scanned the gallery, grasping for a sense of what lay in the hearts of these men. But this was not an army camp, whose soldiers he led into battle and fought beside, who had seen their comrades die and who slogged through mud and rain, whose shoulders he could touch in the silent watch around the campfires before dawn, whose labors he could share, and beside whom he might one day die.

"What is your price, mercenary?" the other black robe asked.

Nikka ground his teeth again. What did Lian Calla, the green jewel that was his home, mean to these lords and officials in this greatest of all cities on the edge of the world? Their unconcern stuck in his throat.

"Do not think of me only as a mercenary," he said.

The dream maker leaned forward, suddenly. "How should we think of you, then?" she asked, in a beautiful, low, compelling voice. "As a teller of doom? The south has sent no true army against us. These border skirmishes have gone on since the priests declared us damned, in body and spirit, many generations ago, and we fought the great battle, and the Schism came between our two peoples. Every year, I understand, the southerners pray for our doom, calling for our city to sink into the sea." She paused. Some of the assembly snickered.

"Our doom has not yet arrived, and I think it will not arrive through means of the southerners," the dream master went on. "You must have served the priests' army well to earn that strategist's sword you carry. Why should we trust you to serve us? If only our price is higher?"

The woman looked directly at him, and for a moment, Roshannon had the disconcerting feeling that his skull had been sprung like a treasure chest and was leaking all his emotions and dreams. He jerked his attention away from her and focused on the great window and its thousand blazing colors.

"I honor my word," he said. "If I say I will serve you, it is so."

The black robes paced. "Bought loyalty is no loyalty in the end. There is always someone who will pay a higher price."

A man rose in the gallery behind him and cried out, "Sail back to Lian Calla and fight the priests yourself if you are so skilled a strategist."

"If you, brave one, will sail back with me and fight under my command," Roshannon said. "There are other prices than gold to buy men with. In the end you in this city will have to face the priests' armies. It is not wise to underestimate them, and their fear and hatred of you." He glanced angrily at the dream master. "Yes, I have fought in the priests' wars. I have seen them destroy what they hate and fear, what they do not or cannot understand. They hate the infidels, the people beyond the islands, who worship other gods and think other thoughts than the Sanctum approves.

"In the infidel lands, the priests traded at first, their eyes gleaming at the natives' gold, silver, and jade. But they ordered soldiers to plunder the shrines of strange gods, topple statues, ruin those with any sensuous detail, and burn holy writings, so nothing but their own book would exist. Destruction is their passion, and they seek death rather than fear it, for death to them means escape from the world of flesh into the realm of spirit."

He thought of Keira, her tagged ear, her bowed head, the scars on her back, the hanged bodies on the gibbet, the priest lecturing her. A rush of images filled his head as he spoke. Not until he bought her and wedded her had he truly understood how much he detested the Sanctum.

How could he explain this to these skeptics sitting smugly in their great city? Further words caught in his throat. He stood silent, waiting for them to decide.

The two black robes conferred, and the one who steepled his fingers said, "We can let you prove your loyalty." The sea-ice eyes weighed him, as they might weigh the middle of a ko game, ki'tarse, the point of critical balance. "Messengers from Kum say a Sanctum host is camped north of the city on the Dara plain. They pillage into the Blue Forest, and threaten to burn some of the woods."

A man laughed harshly in the upper gallery. Roshannon turned to face the sound. From four tiers up, a tall man in shabby clothes shouldered his way past other lords. He vaulted over the partition between the tiers, worked his way to the first level, and leaped to the floor.

"*Have* burned, you mean," the man shouted. "And massacred my entire clan! But perhaps the great city of Cartheon does not care about its loyal subjects in the Blue Forest."

The stewards rose as the newcomer bowed mockingly in their direction. His silver hair slipped over his shoulders, and he brushed it back impatiently. "If we sit here talking much longer, the Blue Forest will be a smoking ruin. This islander speaks true about the southern armies."

Roshannon leaned forward. Swinging against the man's left cheek was a great jade-and-amber earring, two wheels bound together with a silver clasp.

* * *

The high steward had entered the hall through the door in the dream masters' gallery, his court dreamers pacing beside him. By habit, he scanned the petitioners for the sincerity of their emotions.

He stared across the great hall at the Lian Calla strategist who wanted support for his city-state, and a place for himself in an army sent against the southerners. Something familiar about the man's face pricked the high steward's mind.

As the lord in the gallery shouted and leaped to the floor, another gifted one focused on that lord with incredible intensity, and for an instant a keen vision of three bodies hanged on a gibbet and of a great wheel of jade and amber blazed in the high steward's mind. Dozens of lords had risen from their seats, shouting in chorus their approval of this rash one's disdain, thrusting their fists into the air.

The roar in the hall echoed off the ceiling, engulfing everyone, and subsided raggedly as the couriers pounded their staffs on the mosaic floor.

Suddenly remembering where he had seen the strategist's face before, Aramit rose. He called for silence, excitedly searching the faces of the milling crowd in the south gallery for the one he knew already, the one the unknown dreamer had left in his mind a night ago.

There, the scar-faced mercenary from Lian Calla. Aramit summoned a page, who told him the man's name, and the name of the witch lord who had leaped onto the floor.

"Roshannon-ka, Tanta-ka," he called, rising. "You will be informed tonight of my decision. Clear the hall and let council deliberate."

He nodded to his dreamers, smiling. He had already made his decision.

☸ 14. ☸

Pain dragged at Keira. Returning to full awareness of her body was like crawling into a cramped hole after soaring free. Her bruised ribs ached. Every scratch on her forearms stung, and the place where she had bitten her tongue burned. Her legs remained clamped around the horse's sides, and her buttocks ached. She felt fevered, as if she were dying of thirst. She wanted to float away again.

But she remembered the other, the unknown presence above the city, and she was afraid.

The rope had numbed her wrists and fingers; hot needles shot through her hands as she clenched them. Someone clamped a rough hand over her mouth and tugged the knot of the blindfold loose. The cloth fell from her eyes and she squinted against the light, feeling sick.

"No noise, or you're dead," Green Eyes whispered. He nudged her to dismount.

Beren was standing by a tree, his hands bound behind his back, his eyes flicking from one to the other of the witches. Because of her numb hands, Keira lost her balance dismounting. Green Eyes caught her, and her body slid against his before her boot heels hit the ground.

He frowned at her thoughtfully. Suddenly he thrust his gloved hand under her chin. She tensed. He dropped his hand, touched her knee, and ran his hand quickly up her thigh into her crotch.

Kicking at him, she jumped backward. Beren yelled and charged their captors, using his head as a ram. The bowman hauled the boy off his feet and clamped a gloved hand over his mouth. Beren bit the man's hand hard, and the bowman, cursing, staggered into Green Eyes. Keira lost her balance and landed on her backside.

Green Eyes grinned, holding out his hand to her.

She glared up at him, her face hot. "Is this how you greet prisoners after they have spent a day slung over a horse?"

"I mean you no dishonor. That was only to satisfy my curiosity. Ka." He offered his hand again.

Brief smiles played over the faces of the other men, though whether they were laughing at her, Beren, or themselves, she could not tell.

"Well, is your curiosity satisfied?" Keira demanded.

Green Eyes smiled. "No, now it's worse. You are a much more interesting prisoner now that I know you are a woman. Who are you, and where were you headed?"

"I am a traveler."

"So are we all in the journey of life," Green Eyes said.

"A traveler set on by brigands." Keira dug her elbow into the ground, rose to her knees, and staggered up without his help. She noticed the new, carved-leather rakka bottle that swung at Green Eyes' belt. It was not the one she had taken from the brigands who had killed Hipolla. The scouts had probably killed another Sanctum soldier.

Green Eyes paced in a half circle before her. "Are you a camp follower, strayed from the baggage train with your brat?"

"She's too young for that to be her brat. Look at her," Cat Face said, stepping closer. "By the Wheel, I could have sworn she was a lad."

"Hardly any breasts," Green Eyes commented. "Lady, what are you? Which army do you serve?"

"I serve no army, not as soldier's wench, or anything."

Cat Face looked thoughtful. "Say 'serve' again."

She hesitated. "I serve no army."

The scouts grinned sourly. "No northern army, surely," Green Eyes said. "Your *r*s sound southern, though you hid them well."

Cat Face held her arms behind her back and shoved her between the shoulder blades. "Did your soldier tire of you, lass?"

"Or is the southern army so desperate it uses camp followers as scouts?" a bowman taunted.

Keira kept silent, wondering if they would use her as they thought she had been used by the southern army. She closed her eyes, recalling Otella with her bulging belly, squatting alone against a tree, the lucky piece of silver hair hanging between her sweaty breasts. But a thin hope consoled her. If they raped her, she could escape them, or at least escape her own body, as she had so recently done.

But the witches appeared to take no further interest in her as a woman. The men talked quietly, joking among themselves as they made a fireless bivouac among the knees of a giant bay tree. They had brought more horses, two bay geldings, likely taken from dead men to use as remounts. She sat braced against the tree trunk, with Beren beside her. They fit neatly side by side, shoulders touching, in a hollow formed by two of the ancient tree's huge roots. At least she and Brat were still alive, and the blindfolds did not reappear. The witches divided the little pile of belongings taken from her saddlebags. They poured the grain into their own saddlebags, and Cat Face found the ear tag she had stuffed in the bottom. Turning the copper triangle over in his fingers, he tossed it back in the saddlebag. Apparently it was too poor a thing to interest them.

Keira puzzled over whether the witches' studied indifference should outrage or reassure her. Hunger and pain had made her ears sharper, but only scraps and murmurs of their captors' conversation reached her.

After finishing the camp chores, the witches drew apart, their voices rising and falling in argument.

"You want to kill a woman?" one voice asked, so low Keira barely heard.

"What will they do to us?" Beren whispered.

Keira shook her head, easing her shoulders against the rough bark of the tree trunk. "Be brave," she whispered.

Crouched nearby, the man left to guard the horses coughed. "Shut up," he said. Beneath the paint his face was unreadable, but the part of his hair gleamed silver, where new hair was growing out into dark, dyed hair. If Sanctum men caught him, that silver hair would be a death warrant. He checked their bonds and rejoined his fellows.

Cat Face sauntered toward them.

"What are you going to do with us?" Keira asked.

He put his fingers over her lips. "No questions." His eyes shone golden as wolf eyes, while he munched dried fruit from her saddlebags.

"You are nothing but a thief, stealing from me."

"I steal from no one. We only share your provisions." His mouth twisted a little as he considered the withered apple slices in his palm. He held his hand before her mouth. The sweet, dried smell made her mouth water. Feeling like a beast, she ate from his hand. He gave her and Beren water, then gagged them both and checked their bonds. Another man slipped in among them. Bowman and Cat Face slipped away. Darkness fell. There was nothing but the murmur of the woods and the horses, and the quick, elusive voices of the men as they came and went.

The army came closer. Drumrolls moved with them like thunder across the fields.

Her bare feet were bloody from having fled across the stubble of the newly threshed field. She could flee no farther and turned to face them.

The lead riders carried tall poles that grew into the very edge of the sky. Atop them, silver and black banners waved in the breeze.

Her dream eyes traveled up. It hurt to raise her eyes so far, as it sometimes took great effort of the will to make her dream legs move.

The banners floating in the wind were human hair.

From the top of the poles, the severed heads of a man and a woman looked down on her, their eyes staring. Their mouths opened.

Keira stared blindly into the woods. The gag choked her and someone had clamped a hand over her mouth.

"Have you dreamt well or badly?" the witch voice asked. In the cold, gray light of dawn, Green Eyes' painted face looked frighteningly beastlike. He cocked his head as if he were studying her yet listening intently to the forest sounds. Her heart pounded. For a second she feared, worse than a Sanctum army overrunning them, that he could see her dreams reflected in her eyes. Behind the line of Green Eyes' shoulders she watched his companions stirring. Beren slept beside her, curled in a ball like a hedgehog. The place where his shoulder touched hers was the only spot of warmth in her body.

"Bad luck to wake with a bad dream, even if you are a spy," Green Eyes said.

* * *

"The trading winds won't wait for us, though the steward dallies," Cathaya-ka told Isharra outside the audience hall. "We must get our cargo cleared." She asked her niece to accompany her to the spidersilk guild.

Isharra asked Roshannon along. Ni'An and Roshannon agreed, Roshannon glad to focus his restlessness on something, since the witch lord Tanta had disappeared in the crowd leaving the great hall. But the cousins followed the shipmaster and her niece warily through the streets, expecting an argument to spark between the two women.

The main spider masters' guildhall was as grand as the stewards' hall. Sunlight poured through the stained-glass window in the east wall, dappling the vault ceilings, arches, and mosaic floor with color. The window, made in the pattern of an orb web, blazed like a jewel set in darkness. Beneath the window, spider masters conferred with Bala Kothi merchants in fur-trimmed robes and scarlet boots.

Isharra and Cathaya-ka strode down side aisles, past the banners of merchant adventurers and money changers, past rows of carved columns and soaring, filigree arches. It seemed that a spider had built the place, spinning the great window web to catch the sun, then changing its habits, retreating into the shadows to spin out fragile arching ribs and join them into vaults, and let down silk cables that solidified into pillars. Spiders had built the hall, Roshannon thought, because the wealth from the spidersilk had paid for the fitting of each stone and the carving of each column.

Isharra and Cathaya-ka trotted up narrow hidden staircases to the cubbyholes where the guild accountants worked.

"Certain spiders give silk used for cordage," Isharra said, "others for the silk that makes sails, others for the finest clothing silk."

Irina Cathaya admonished the clerks. "See that you have my cargo loaded with care. Don't let any porters drop bales into the harbor then toss them aboard, and try telling me they are first quality. Folk are particular about their goods in Brink, and I must answer to them. So you must answer to me."

Two skinny clerks drew up her bill of lading, hastily copied the document, stamped the copies with a seal, and trotted behind her down to the storerooms clustered around the guildhall courtyard. Red-gloved silk workers thronged the crowded courtyard,

wending their way among women and men carrying huge baskets
full of fat ivory cocoons. "That is the raw silk," Cathaya-ka said.
She explained that centuries ago the silk workers had bred spinning spiders that encased their prey in cocoons, that could be
gathered, boiled in vats, and unwound into single long filaments
of the precious silk. For generations, she said, the guilds had controlled the spiders to maintain the most special, secret grades of
silk. The breeders had even recorded the lineage of the spiders,
exact crossbreedings, and the shapes of original webs.

Like breeding horses, Roshannon thought.

Ni'An glanced at him as if they shared the thought.

Spider breeders, who carried their prime specimens in tiny,
domed cages cased in embroidered covers, held court in the
atrium's sunniest corner, touting their spiders' prowess at produc-
ing cordage or clothing silk. Skeptical spider masters quizzed
them on the virtues of their creatures, examining the spiders, offering bids, haggling, throwing up their hands, circling the crowd,
returning, settling on their haunches in patches of sunlight,
switching to philosophical debates before darting back into the
realm of prices.

Isharra wandered with the cousins back into the Silktown quarter. In a wide square where a storyteller held a crowd enthralled,
Roshannon spotted Tanta dropping a coin at the storyteller's feet.

"Ka," Roshannon said, touching the man's shoulder.

The tall witch lord turned to face him, his green eye and his
gold eye blazing.

"The Lian Calla strategist from the steward's court," Tanta
said. "What do you wish of me?"

"What you wish of me—allegiance in the battle against the
Sanctum."

Xian Tanta eyed Ni'An, and his glance rested a moment on
Isharra. "If you wish the Sanctum to fall as much as I do, you are
surely my ally." He touched his fingertips to his forehead.

Roshannon watched the earring turn against Tanta's cheek as
the witch lord accompanied them, his hunting cat beside him.

Roshannon's dream made him doubly intrigued yet wary of the
lord with mismatched eyes. He glanced at the great clan earring,
wondering if his dream had shown him a piece of past or future,
or was simply playing him false.

Tanta was courteous but aloof toward Ni'An, and after raking a head-to-toe look over Isharra, affected an elaborate, almost angry indifference toward her. Despair masked the man's presence, bitterness like a subtle incense. His hunting cat Shadow, a gray beast with black-tipped ears, whose muscled shoulders reached almost as high as a man's thigh, stalked beside him, twitching its tail back and forth, its moods seemingly as volatile as its master's.

They explored Silktown, speculating on the reasons for the abrupt dismissal from the steward's hall. In a deadly quiet voice, Tanta recited the names of all his family the Sanctum soldiers had slaughtered.

In an alleyway they encountered a pack of red-gloved women shoving a lone woman against the wall. The brown-haired woman raised her arms to protect her face, and one girl yanked her hair. Two others tugged off her red gloves.

"Counterfeit! Imposter!" one silk worker yelled.

Roshannon stepped forward. Tanta laid a hand on his arm. "Do not bother. It is not our affair."

One silkwinder waved the woman's glove aloft. "Look at her hands. They have never worked silk. These are the hands of a tanner's girl or a baker's daughter."

The accused woman raised her chin. "Let the guild accuse and punish me," she said. She snatched her red gloves back, her face flushing as she noticed spectators. The other women adjusted their cloaks and collars and led her off.

"What was that affair?" Ni'An asked.

Tanta scratched his hunting cat behind the ears. "The Silktowners, with their red gloves and their collars as badges, have run of the city. Likely that girl dressed so to catch a better suitor than she might have otherwise." He shook his head. "The silk workers guard their rank jealously. At midsummer and midwinter they stage mock battles with the other guilds. In between they skirmish, like hunting cats patrolling their territory."

"But what will happen to that girl?" Isharra asked.

"The silk guild will fine her," Tanta said, "and send her home through her own quarter's gate with red chalk slashes on her cheeks."

The four companions hastened through the square.

In the spice sellers' street nearby, frugal housewives haggled with merchants over the weight of tiny pyramids of peppercorns.

A gang of boys raced along the cobbled street, rolling painted wooden hoops.

They found a sword yard shared by fledgling fencers and masters, and spent their frustrations in exercise. Ni'An and Isharra ended a match and leaned along the wall watching.

Roshannon and Tanta dueled until their skins shone as if oiled. Still the image of Keira with that earring against her cheek nagged at Roshannon, like a worm gnawing at his spirit. But he relished the weight of the weapon, and the burn in the corner of his eye as sweat trickled down his forehead, for the physical exertion distracted him from inner misgivings. He and Tanta circled and feinted, parried and thrust, the practice bout transformed into deadly meditation.

The sword master and his pupils ringed them, cheering.

Keira stared through Roshannon's eyes down two arms' lengths of flashing steel, past a flickering, wrapped sword point and into the face of the gold- and green-eyed man from the marketplace.

The shock of the meshing ruined Roshannon's timing. Cursing, he sidestepped Tanta's sword a bare second too late, and the edge of the blade stung his forearm. Muttering under his breath, he regained himself. Keira shared the pain and burrowed deeper, riding him, tasting his thrill and his exuberant agility as he lunged now sideways, now back, then circled the intent silverhaired man who reminded her so much of Hipolla. Tears that would have burned her eyes stung his eyes instead, blurring his vision.

Roshannon cursed again, blinking, catching himself, compensating, strengthening his guard. His eyes were her eyes, his sight her sight, and his sweat stung the corners of her eyes and clung to the upper rim of his lip until her tongue licked it away.

Her heart soared. This latest melding had required only a fuse of desire, the twist of a thought to be done. Being in his body was a relief, a refuge, an intoxicating distraction from her own worries, much more exciting than getting sore buttocks from riding all day, blindfolded to boot.

Dizzying knowledge poured into her, filling her brimful: the sureness of a swordsman's stance, the tireless strength of his sword arm, the glorious stretch and play of every muscle in his body, and a sweeping awareness of the people watching them.

The sight of lordly earrings pricked Keira's consciousness and
cost Roshannon another stinging hit from Tanta's sword. As if in
apology she slid more deeply into him, focusing on his opponent's eyes, the set of his face, a distracting movement of his hand
as they spun and clashed together, a sudden glimpse of onlookers,
a rushing blank expanse of wall as he pivoted back to face Tanta.
During a clear beat in the rhythm of the fight, she spotted the
woman who had been aboard the ship standing in a sweat-stained
tunic among the spectators. The woman reminded her of Hipolla,
drew her attention, and ruined Roshannon's timing.

He bit his lip and cursed her, and the pain plowed her consciousness more deeply into his. She glimpsed the man who
looked like Roshannon's twin, and the silver leaf and twisted sea
pearl gleaming at his ear.

By the Wheel, they were all ka'innen. In despair, her spirit
twisted inside Roshannon like a captive spark.

The troublesome wench fled again. His heart pounding,
Roshannon almost lost his balance. But his automatic responses,
honed over years of swordplay, combined with Xian Tanta's
slight stiffness on the left side, saved him.

He struck through Tanta's awkward guard, rapping him
smartly across the ribs, drew back his blade, and bowed to his
opponent.

Tanta bowed in return. "Ka." He clapped Roshannon on the
shoulders to show he did not lose sorely. The sword master
bowed to them both.

Roshannon glanced around self-consciously. No one, by some
quirky miracle, seemed to notice anything amiss with him. But
Ni'An said, "Cousin, you seemed to falter twice." Roshannon
grinned, blaming it on the week he had spent without a sword in
his hand. But he knew Keira had, for the first time, enjoyed the
connection, even though, as usual, she had shied away. He
assented heartily when Tanta suggested they visit a nearby
bathhouse.

Isharra disappeared inside the women's bath, but Tanta lingered at the portal of the men's bathhouse, unable to resist the
charms of a trio of silkwinders. Roshannon relished watching
these women who took obvious pleasure in the company of men.
Tanta bantered with them, trading barbed repartee like the rapid

exchange of archers. The silk workers flirted back, as if they thought it fine sport to exchange teasing fire with lords as they strolled the silk quarter's prosperous streets.

"Lady," Tanta told one fetching, black-haired flirt, "I warn you: if you lose your heart to me I will not give it back."

The red-gloved woman laughed. "My heart is steady. I am too careful to lose it to you, Xian Tanta." She winked at him and pranced off arm in arm with two red-gloved companions.

The frivolity lifted a weight from Roshannon's heart, though he had been so long around things southern that he felt awkward. The silkwinders' merry faces blurred before him. He thought of a thin face framed in red-brown hair, shadowed under the brim of his old hat, the face of a woman who had fought for her life. Inside he was shaking with an urge to invade Keira's consciousness as she did his.

He bowed to the silkwinders and stepped through the bathhouse door.

"Do you tire so soon of flirtation?" Tanta asked.

"Today I have no taste for it."

Tanta grinned. "I would rather flirt now and philosophize later. There is nothing stirs the blood so nicely as crossing tongues with a Silktown girl."

Inside the bath the men stripped, revealing among them a collection of old and not so old scars, a concise history of adventure and misadventure such as soldiers carry on their bodies. Roshannon felt a strange stirring of emotion at sight of the ragged scar that hooked over Ni'An's thigh like a jagged fishhook. It marked the cousins' battle with an ancient boar. The beast had nearly killed Ni'An, its tusks furrowing his right thigh as Roshannon rammed his boar spear into its chest down to the stopping bar. The animal's hot breath hit Roshannon's face like a furnace blast, and its glittering, dying eyes focused blindly on him as it died on his spear. The creature's dying torment and Ni'An's pain twisted horribly through his awareness. Ni'An had limped badly for months after he healed, and winter chills brought an aching stiffness in the leg and a faint limp.

But the memory was too vivid. Keira had stayed with him, fastened into his awareness, drawing on his emotions. He shook his head and told himself he was not in that forest glade, still diving in the path of that charging boar and holding the spear with all his might.

Through the veils of steam rising in the room, he focused on the great reddened, puckered scar across Tanta's ribs and left side. Out of honor Roshannon did not ask what had befallen. A man told the history of his scars in his own time. The three sat on the sweat-room benches, while cleansing steam hissed up from the red-hot rocks in the sweat pit. Roshannon glanced at Tanta while he was picking a spot to settle. His heart pounded anew. Swarms of fat, glistening white maggots were crawling over the witch lord's side, feeding on his wounded flesh.

Roshannon sat down abruptly, telling himself it was a trick of the steam and the scarcely healed scars themselves, a fatigue brought on by squinting at the sun in the fencing yard. Or the effect of the link with Keira.

He closed his eyes and leaned against the sweat-house bench.

Keira rode Roshannon's consciousness, enthralled by Xian Tanta, and tasting his sorrow for Hipolla. Everything will be all right, she told herself, if I can reach this man, show him the earring and tell him my story.

She basked in these convictions, savoring the steam baths through Roshannon's body. Her wariness returned. She refused to dip into his emotions, for that meant he and those other troubling presences could tug more fiercely at her.

But in the cold room, an abrupt, immense weight bore down on Keira and Roshannon, forcing her more deeply into him, threatening her with oblivion and dissolution into his awareness. She felt like something in a mortar while a giant pestle descended, ready to crush her being. Something sought her, uncurling vast probing tentacles, scenting and longing to taste her essence hidden inside his body.

Remembering the other she had touched unwittingly, she ripped herself free and fled.

At twilight, Cathaya-ka was still haggling with the guild suppliers and supervising the packing of bolts of the finest white silk that would be loaded on her ship. She waved to Isharra, walking along the dock.

"Gone all day, girl? You are supposed to be learning the

business of trade." The older woman stooped to examine the contents of a chest. "Not getting yourself killed on a battlefield where you do not belong, and failing to honor your obligations with House Ayello to boot."

"Ka," Isharra said. "I would honor those obligations afterward. If an army marches south, I want to serve in its ranks."

"You were hot to sail to I'Brin last winter, girl, to see the islands of ice and the yellow-eyed northerners, to see their bone daggers and their conjurers and hear their storytellers. If your passions don't stay hot any longer than your mother's soup ever did, beware them. They will betray you."

"Then that is something I must learn to stomach," Isharra said.

The older woman grunted, fingering a bolt of silk. She closed the lid of the storage chest, sat down a bit heavily, and grinned at her niece. "Don't think I am blind. I see you fancy that Lian Callan."

"Humph." Isharra looked quickly away.

"He is a strange, troubling man. Not that Lord Tanta would be any less trouble." The older woman grinned at her niece. "Follow your heart into battle if you must, girl, if it is truly a taste of the battlefield that you want, but not because you pine for some man. Battles leave a certain taste in your mouth, and nothing will ever be the same to you again."

"Ka. I suppose my aunt has always been proof against men and adventures."

Cathaya-Ka smiled wickedly. "I've never been proof against either, girl. But my head got level on my shoulders when I was a bit younger than you. And I always chose my men and my adventures carefully."

Isharra embraced her, but Cathaya-ka shrugged off the embrace with seeming embarrassment and waved her niece away from the packing.

"You are little use here anyway," the old woman said. "Your heart's not in it, and may not be until you've gotten a bellyful of fighting. So go adventuring with those men. My blessing on you, hardhead."

The dream readers' quarter was honeycombed with narrow, spiraling streets that opened suddenly into private squares centered around fountains. Tall, narrow houses overshadowed the streets. Tiny booths curtained with black and white silk lined the squares, and Roshannon and Ni'An watched a steady stream of men and women of all ranks duck inside to have the adepts decipher their dreams.

At one booth, Roshannon glimpsed a tripled reflection of himself in a three-paneled, hinged mirror set up just outside the doorway. The triple image seemed to manifest the fragmented selves he felt inhabited his body when Keira's awareness meshed with his.

An aged hand pulled back the curtain, and a woman, dressed in the dream readers' black robes, with the single vertical silver slash between her brows, stood regarding them.

"Dreams reflect the self," she said. "Self of flesh, self of spirit, and the bridge between the two. Propitious dreams, ka'in. Know thyselves." She nodded to Roshannon. "May I serve you, ka?" Her eyes were clear, the large hands folded before her knotted with veins. She seemed to look through him with a gaze that recalled the far island proverb about a blind storyteller seeing the tale most clearly.

"If a man dreams a woman he knows wearing the clan earring of another man," he said abruptly, "what does that dream mean?"

The skin around her eyes crinkled as she smiled. "My lord, that is an old dream, an old situation. Is the woman or man well known to this dreamer?"

"No."

"Does this dream reappear?"

"It has only come once."

She gestured around the darkening square. "Perhaps the dream means nothing, perhaps it embodies a fear. And perhaps, ka, this man who dreams is a jealous man."

Roshannon decided she was a charlatan, and had said only what anyone might have said.

Ni'An, keeping one eye on his cousin, gave her a coin.

Jealous, Roshannon thought, how can I be jealous of a woman I have only seen once? The hag had cheek. He stalked away.

Ni'An followed him in silence, matching him stride for stride as they strolled along the waterfront. Noisy taverns lined the piers, the reflections from their lighted windows sliding into the blackness of the bay, their customers' raucous songs mingling with the steady slap of the waves. Beyond the tangle of gaming-house and tavern rooftops, a forest of masts rose against the sky.

The two cousins paced over the water gate, pausing midway to look across the harbor where the lights of Lyssa low town glittered. A sound of argument and snatches of song drifted from the taverns, muffled by the creaking song of boats rocking at their moorings.

Ni'An touched his shoulder. "Did you dream of Isharra, cousin, wearing Tanta's earring? She fancies you."

"Never mind what I dream, Ni'An." He twisted the wooden ring and the silver ring from his fingers and handed Ni'An both. "Take these. I do not wish to wear them."

Ni'An turned them briefly in his fingers, shrugged, and slid the pair inside his belt pouch. "A strange mood's on you, cousin. That dream really was yours, wasn't it, not just something to test the reader with?"

"Forget that, Ni'An." Roshannon stretched and breathed in the sea air. Far below the arch of the water gate, the ebbing tide revealed the bones of the ancient city that had sunk into the edge of the sea. "Keep the rings, and your questions, just now."

The cousins strode back to their lodgings, where Roshannon fell asleep at once and had a strangely satisfying dream of strangling Keira.

The man laughed. He pounced on Keira, lithe as a cat.

His face was clear as a mask, the wide brow, the pale blue eyes, the mouth twisted grimly up at the corner. The man who had killed Hipolla, and come for her, was coming for her again. Her legs went numb. She could not flee. The perfectly remembered details of his face horrified her, rooted her to the spot.

The edge of the short sword blazed with light as it sliced toward her.

He laughed, a triumphant, murderous peal. His callused hands closed on her throat.

She twisted, fumbled in her boot top, but her fingers refused to work and could barely grasp the dagger hilt.

She could not breathe. Her vision blurred.

Suddenly the face, inches from her own, changed. The mouth softened, the eyes darkened. The hands dropped from her throat and became thin hands flicking reins.

Brat laughed at her. "Women should not speculate on the nature of god," he said as he slapped the pony's flank. A stem of half-chewed sourgrass hung from his mouth. He laughed again, taunted her from horseback, and spurred the pony into a gallop, challenging her to a race.

Wind rushed against her skin and through her hair as she chased him. But the mare by some caprice never gained on the pony, though she soared over bushes and streams, past screaming gulls.

Too late Keira saw the jagged chasm opening in the ground. The mare hesitated at the great barrier that widened every second, bunched herself, and leaped. Her hooves struck the opposite edge. She landed badly, screaming, faltering to her knees. Keira flew from the saddle, her eyes open as she floated through incredible cloud formations. She tumbled into a patch of sweet clover.

The muffled thud of the pony's hooves drew near. She propped herself on an elbow and squinted into the sun, embarrassed. How Brat would laugh at her for falling from the mare.

He dismounted and walked toward her, silhouetted against the sun, which rode like a blazing star on his shoulder and blinded her. But he was too tall.

She shaded her eyes. The outline of the face came clear, dark hair whipped across the scarred and unscarred jawline. Roshannon. His face held no expression she could decipher.

His shadow fell across her legs, her knees. She dug her elbows and heels into the clover as he looked down at her.

He grinned as he stooped, and neatly pulled the grassy hillside out from under her.

Furious, she clutched at air and kicked. She floated away from his touch, which at first pleased her, until she realized she had drifted into the chasm, into a mysterious, endless void beyond all human touch.

❧ 15 ❧

By the Wheel, they are ready to come to an agreement, Roshannon thought when he saw the plain room that had been chosen for the stewards' latest parley. It had the matter-of-fact look of a general's tent the night before a battle.

Roshannon frowned at the man pointed out as the high steward, Aramit Leyto. The city's ruler had seemed anonymous yesterday among his fellow stewards and the dream masters. Of average height and average build, he seemed venerable one moment, youthful and impetuous the next. Yet today, though he and the dream masters wore austere citizen's robes, the high steward could not go unnoticed, for he shone with presence.

But, true to form, the stewards, dreamers, and their hangers-on sipped steaming tea and haggled over points of strategy all morning.

Roshannon knew his mother would certainly not want a force large enough to take on the air of an occupying army and block the clan assembly's attempts at self-rule, much as the southerners had already done.

"From the greatest city in the world," he said, "what is one thousand men? It is merely the best guarantee that your new trading partner remains safe from Sanctum threats, and that shipments of tea and ship timber reach you faster."

He cradled a tea bowl as the witch lords debated. They wanted their tea, after all, and the fine wormproof ship timbers hewn from island trees, and these goods would come at a cheaper price from an ally than from a city-state ruled by an enemy.

Several hours later Roshannon found their terms acceptable. A force of one thousand picked men, to be reduced to five hundred when the war with the Sanctum ended, would be dispatched to Lian Calla city-state. Citizens would house the soldiers inside the city walls and Lian Calla clansmen would command them. The soldiers would also help rebuild what Sanctum soldiers had damaged.

He and Ni'An embraced in the audience chamber.

Roshannon promptly sent a letter to his mother, after asking for and being graciously given one of the steward's own green-clad couriers to bear it. The letter contained the agreed-upon innocuous sentences, salutation, and closing phrases that meant he thought the northerners could be trusted. The steward's courier, more than the letter itself, would lighten his mother's heart and show her the depth of the witch city's pledge.

But Roshannon's latest remembered experience of Keira in the Blue Forest pricked his contentment throughout the rest of the meeting. Upon waking this morning, he had tried linking his awareness with hers. He came close to touching her, but his body began aching tremendously, especially in the buttocks. A terrible, dry taste filled his mouth, choking him. Something blinded him, thwarting his attempts to see through her eyes.

Roshannon caught the high steward studying him. He felt disoriented, as he had in the bathhouse when Keira shared his eyes and a sudden invasive presence crushed into them both. He ground his teeth and returned the steward's gaze, angry yet fascinated. Was the high steward trying to breach his mind, slip inside his awareness as Keira seemed to do so effortlessly? Had his been the invasive spirit felt yesterday right after the sword match? But Roshannon's spirit and the steward's grated, like two hopelessly ill-matched millstones.

Somehow, Roshannon thought, Keira could keep him from her mind, except during a crisis. A useful skill, that; but how did the girl create an impregnable wall in her mind? He imagined stones of outrage, mortared by the need for privacy. Suddenly the steward's touch, which felt nothing like Keira's, retreated, and the steward, looking puzzled, spoke to a dream master.

Roshannon recalled his own uneasiness when he first realized he was tasting people's emotions. First he felt moonstruck, full of strange fancies. Gradually he saw the peculiar talent's uses. Then in pity and a kind of wonder, he grew to perceive other folk as deaf or dumb, lacking some fundamental capacity. All his life he had wanted to find another like himself, one who carried the strange gift, one with whom he could share its rich mysteries.

He suspected that he and Keira were either true witches themselves, or hybrid creatures with similar blood running in their veins. The thought that the thin-lipped Sanctum priest might have unknowingly married two witches made him smile.

He closed his eyes, remembering the silver-haired trader, the storyteller who had visited his mother before the trade agreements had given the Sanctum a firm base in Lian Calla. The stranger performed marvelous tricks at table with knives and goblets, tricks that made young Nikka, sitting beside his mother, laugh and be glad that she was laughing, too, sounding hearty as one of the scullery maids flirting in the kitchen with a soldier. Nikka had always called Kirin the shipbuilder father—and not thought about the matter for years. He recalled his mother's peculiar tone of voice when she had said perhaps he was the best man in Lian Calla to send to the witch city.

What a rich joke that would be, if he were a half-breed witch, considering how long he had fought among the Sanctum armies as a mercenary.

The steward watched him intently. Roshannon shifted in his seat, concentrating fiercely on the patterns of the mosaic floor, the colors of the window.

The high steward rose, raising his hands for silence. "Troops will be dispatched from the city this morning, the one thousand to Lian Calla from the western gate; and forty thousand pony archers toward Kum through the eastern gate."

A wild hubbub broke out, a tumult of amazement and eagerness. Lords rose and pledged to accompany the army with their own troops. Isharra exchanged rapid-fire whispers with Cathayaka, and pledged to accompany the troops. Roshannon rolled his eyes and caught Ni'An and Tanta grinning. What council could meet at dawn, yet mobilize an army by morning?

But several hours later, from the balcony of the great justice hall, they saw the truth of the steward's words. Here the high steward exhorted his constables and marshals to battle honorably and well. They cheered him and saluted, touching fingertips to foreheads. He offered Roshannon and Tanta a spyglass and pointed toward the eastern gate.

Roshannon steadied the glass and squinted. Masses of men, wagons, and animals choked the streets of the tanners' quarter and swarmed the great triple-arched gate.

Roshannon felt uneasy as he lowered the glass and handed it to Tanta. Aramit Leyto must have made his decision in advance. But why had the man let him and Ni'An stew so long beforehand? Merely because he could?

Tanta stared his fill and passed the glass to Isharra.

The high steward embraced them all and drew wheels on their right palms. Two strangely fragile figures attended him, a man and woman so slight they resembled children, though their eyes looked old as the sea. Both wore swords little longer than those boys carried.

"His court dreamers," Isharra whispered. "He shows no higher approval than to send them with us." She embraced Cathaya-ka, bidding her farewell.

The old woman appraised her niece at arm's length. "If you die on land, you will get a landfolk's pyre. I will probably not be able to retrieve your body and give it to the sea."

"So be it, aunt. May the Wheel turn well for thee."

"Stubborn girl," the old woman said, but she grinned. "I must be gone, the tide is in." She embraced Isharra again, then without a backward glance strode away, her silent helmsman at her side.

"Fair winds, sweet seas," Isharra called, brusquely wiping her eyes with the back of her hand.

Roshannon dashed off another quick dispatch to his mother. Before noon near the tanners' gate, he, Ni'An, Tanta, and Isharra joined the main column of the army, trotting past caravans of bowyers and fletchers, cook and smithy wagons, pony trains laden with baggage, troops of foot soldiers with gray hunting cats stalking beside them, and a straggle of sutlers' and healers' caravans, until they reached the command ranks.

The soldiers sang as they marched. A strapping lad in the procession ahead stood balanced on his saddle and stroked the eastern gate's ancient keystone as his horse passed beneath. Women in the crowd lining the street cheered him on. He bent his knees and slipped easily back into his saddle. Two men behind him applauded his daring and grace.

"So they say farewell to the city and wish themselves luck," Isharra said. She raised the tip of her unstrung bow to the gate.

Roshannon and Ni'An did likewise. Anything for luck: a soldier always needed it. Nearby flew the streaming green banners

that marked the steward's constables, but Aramit Leyto did not
appear among them.

"Does the steward not accompany his army to war?" Roshannon asked.

She hesitated a moment, her eyes darkening. "He does. They
say he travels in disguise and that no one, not even his constables sometimes, knows where he will be until the army halts
at night. He often wanders the city dressed as an old dotard, walking through all the gates and neighborhoods, to see things for
himself."

Just beyond the gate, a flock of red-gloved silk workers and
seamstresses presented banners to the companies of men trooping
through. White-robed adepts from the spider masters' guild held
high the city's great banner of three green interlocking wheels,
letting the lines of horsemen and foot soldiers pass under it as a
blessing. The eldest dream master sacrificed a hare in the army's
path, letting the animal's blood drip onto the ground.

Outside the eastern gate the court dreamers and the raven masters—whose message-carrying birds formed a tight net of com-
munications between the troops—joined the command ranks.
Files of field strategists and couriers parted and rejoined, forming
a protective circle around them.

Tanta drew rein beside Roshannon. His hunting cat rode balanced over his saddle horn, its black-tipped tail switching back
and forth. "If the high steward sends his dreamers," the witch lord
said, "he must suspect there are dreamers in the southern army."

In two days, using relays of remounts, the pony archers
reached the edge of the Blue Forest and the wooded foothills that
sloped up to the mountain citadel of Kum. The rich land they tra-
versed promised a good harvest. Spring was touching the land,
and blossom-laden fruit trees stood out white as ghosts against the
great, dark forest.

Roshannon's command was a motley crew of veterans yanked
from retirement and supplemented by raw boys. The veterans
would invariably compare him to their old commanders, and per-
sist in their set ways, while raw boys were always unpredictable.
But he had expected no better. He reviewed the ranks and rearranged them, putting older men beside boys, staggering them
like the squares of a ko board, hoping to steady the boys and keep

the veterans from grumbling together. He had Ni'An try to dig out a history of the veterans' former commander. He ordered his men to spare fields and orchards and to divert action away from planted land if possible. Farmers would hold no goodwill toward an army that destroyed their harvest and their future. Sparing fields and villages had won the Lian Calla mercenaries many unexpected allies in the infidel lands across the sea.

Xian Tanta rode beside Roshannon and described the erratic, skirmishing warfare the pony archers and Blue Forest men waged against the southern armies. The outnumbered archers worked in roving bands, living on a few hours' sleep and whatever game they could shoot. They ambushed wings of the large and lumbering southern army, or harassed the southerners and stole their horses and cattle in places where archers could dispatch the more heavily armored enemy with relative ease, then melt into the wooded hillsides.

Tanta told Roshannon how his family's borderland hold had been overrun. "We who escaped became skirmishers. We lived like gypsies or tinkers, a band of men, with the women and healers in a wagon train. One day our luck died. Somehow a huge force found us, circling us and our women in the wagons. They slaughtered us—my brother fell beside me before I went down. I woke, thinking I was dead, yet crawled free of the bodies of my kin. A healer found me wandering in the woods and helped me reach the city to ask for help.

"We have fought like a pack of little dogs," Tanta said. "Running down a huge beast, nipping its heels, but unable to draw enough blood to bring it down."

Roshannon nodded. "You do not use infantry, or heavy horsemen?" They rode side by side in the close-packed ranks, their boots almost touching.

"Only after an onslaught by the archers," Tanta said. "In mass it wastes the lives of too many men, costs too much for armor, and grain to feed the greathorses that carry armored men. It beggars the land, so my grandfather said. Few men can pay for a greathorse, and the gear, but any man can keep a pony and a bow. In the woods, we have all grown up hunting with the bow." They moved at a trot, in looser ranks, and his gray hunting cat, Shadow, leaped from the saddle horn and ran beside them.

Roshannon grinned. "It is gadfly war you folk practice."

"The gadfly drives many a beast mad and brings it down, eventually." A peculiar gleam lit Tanta's eyes once the blue fringe of forest came in sight over the folded hills. Roshannon saw tears glistening in the witch lord's eyes and wondered if he would himself ever look on Lian Calla again.

While Nikka rode, his mind turned inward on the intricate moves of battles and the mysteries that united or sundered armies. And he sent his mind questing after Keira. A few times he was sure he touched her consciousness, just the barest shiver of contact that did not provoke the walls that blocked him from her spirit. Again he sensed only hot, sweaty blackness, a dry, choking sensation in his throat, and a monumental ache in thighs and buttocks from riding hard all day. No visions came. He pondered that blankness: had she simply closed her eyes, or was she somehow deprived of sight? Meanwhile, he felt her will nibbling at the edges of his consciousness.

It is subtle revenge on you that if you now visit my awareness, Keira Danio, you will share no better pickings from my senses than I have gotten through yours for the last week. Nothing better than a sore butt, a stiff back, and a mouthful of dust.

But if she had been riding hard enough all week to make her rear end ache, where by the Wheel's thousand names was she? With Bala Kothi nomads, or horse traders? With scouts or couriers of either side?

He dismissed her from his thoughts as best he could.

From the wooded hillsides, couriers, scouts, and tiny bands of archers straggled to join the army, practically doubling its size. All told of farms and holds pillaged and burned.

Bunches of hard-bitten fighters drifted in from the woods, joining the columns briefly, or getting food from the cook wagons. By the time Roshannon and Tanta, far back in the line of march, saw the troops ahead of them stop and ordered their own men to halt, scouts were returning to the hastily set-up camps.

At twilight Roshannon swung down from the saddle of the fourth horse he had ridden that day. Only when his boot soles touched ground did he notice the aches in his knees. A few weeks in the city had made him soft.

Tales of a huge Sanctum army camped on the plain before Kum spread from tent to tent like fever. Citizens from Kum and the valleys and forests beyond had swollen the numbers of the

Army of the Book, the whispers said. Rumor said an archpriest commanded the host, with veteran Bala Kothi marshals under him, and priests marching like berserkers among the foot soldiers, killing as lustily as demons because they did not fear their own deaths.

Theus, the veteran appointed as Roshannon's aide, gestured to the tent he and two boys had erected, and the red strategist's banner flying from a tall pole before its doorway.

Roshannon touched palms with the man. "Theus-ka, if you or the men have any news or problems, wake me at any hour."

Theus nodded. "Ka. I'll fetch your food in a minute."

Roshannon shook his head. "I'll see to the men first, and eat later." Surely, Roshannon thought, Theus should be dandling his grandchildren on his knee by now, not campaigning. But a soldier who had lived to grow so old must know his business.

Roshannon's men encamped high above a riverbank, a scant mile from the main encampment. Campfires flickered like fireflies among the pale tents pitched on the gentle hillside. The sound of men joking, cursing, wagering on ko games, and remembering their sweethearts overwhelmed for a moment the whispers of the river. One of the cooks cursed, a fight broke out, and Roshannon, down to the marrow of his bones, was back in the army again, waiting for the eerie thrill of battle. With Ni'An beside him, he walked among the tents, speaking to men, watching them mend their gear or their horses' tack, and stopping to listen to a storyteller and a home remedy for a saddle-weary backside.

The leading strategists gathered in the tent of the steward's high constable, a tall, solemn man named Loreth Keya. Roshannon felt them appraise him warily.

In one corner of the tent, Tanta and Isharra argued with each other about the joint command they had been given.

"You are no soldier, but a sailor," Tanta protested. "Your mother's sister was right to try to keep you at sea. You may get yourself killed."

"So may you, but I do not tell you to stay out of battle."

"I have vengeance to take."

"And I am no stranger to battle," Isharra said.

"Just follow my orders tomorrow."

"Make certain your aide sets up a separate tent for me." Isharra's eyes flashed. She nodded civilly to Roshannon and Ni'An.

Tanta made a face and scratched his hunting cat between the ears.

A few other women's faces showed around the tent: those who had ridden in with scouts and reported on the positions and strength of the enemy, and those seasoned to fighting with the bands of pony archers—farmers' and horse breeders' daughters, sisters of holdsmen killed, all transformed into warriors.

The strategists spread maps and charts on low tables pushed together in the middle of the council tent. At the far end of the table sat the steward's dreamers, so frail and withdrawn they looked like children. All the northern strategists lowered their eyes in reverence to them. The woman of the pair met Roshannon's eyes and nodded. He glanced away, feeling chilled and only concentrating halfway on the words of the other strategists afterward.

Roshannon did not spot the high steward among those gathered in the tent. But the dreamers were his eyes and ears.

The strategists who reported first were men of local clans and holds, who had been fighting the Sanctum along the southern fringes of the Blue Forest for a year. They used the woods to make emergency bivouacs and cover their movements, and retreated into the dense, shadowed forest to heal their wounds. Southern soldiers avoided the deep forest, where invisible archers could ambush them from among the trees. Though these skirmishing bands harried the larger Sanctum forces constantly, the enemy ranks seemed to swell with an inexhaustible supply of men.

"Their women breed like spiders," one man said. "There are always more of them to come against us."

Not a few claimed that the archpriest who commanded the southerners had somehow instilled in his soldiers the belief that they could not be beaten, while others said that factions in Kum had swayed folk east and south of the citadel to the Sanctum cause. According to others, the Sanctum priests had proclaimed the world would end after a great battle on Hara plain, and that all who died fighting with the southerners would go straight to the heart of the Wheel.

"We are on them like fleas on a dog," one grizzled veteran said.

"But we need to divide their main body and chew at it." He eyed Roshannon warily.

Roshannon and Ni'An stood out conspicuously among the witches, their long, sleek black hair like banners proclaiming their seacoast origins. That Tanta and Isharra stood beside them helped, but perhaps not enough. The first battle will be the worst test, Roshannon thought. Either my men will follow me, or they won't.

Keya, the steward's constable, said officials from Kum and priests under the protection of sanctuary banners had parleyed with some of the bands of pony archers. "They ask us to spare the city and its liege lands," he said. "Already the scouts report folk from the outlying districts swarming through the city gates, seeking refuge, but swelling the number of defenders and mouths that would gobble the citadel's supplies if it were besieged.

"But is Kum acting more for merely political reasons than holy ones? And so violating its neutrality? And can we attack it on those political grounds without stirring up another ten generations of hatred between north and south?"

"With all the years of hatred between us, what does another generation more of it matter?" one strategist demanded.

The woman dreamer laughed. "There will surely be more years of hatred no matter what we do. Hatred, once learned, is a hard habit to lay down. But the high steward does not want us to add to that burden if we can help it. He asks you to remember that we were once one people, and that the gift ran then in as many southern veins as northern ones."

The dreamer's words intrigued Roshannon. "Does Kum openly aid the Sanctum?" he asked, conscious that every eye focused on him as he spoke.

"Kumini men have joined the southern army," another man said. "But then so have seacoast men."

Tanta leaned forward, staring at the man who had offered the insult. "Kum is a crafty place. It aids only itself. But how we deal with that city could turn all the borderlands for us or against us."

"Then leave the city in peace," Roshannon said.

"So says a man who served the southerners how many years?" someone in the back of the tent demanded.

"The city is not what we must crush," Roshannon said, "but the armies in the field. Without them the city cannot stand anyway.

It will be an island in the midst of our army if we defeat the southerners."

Keya, the steward's constable, stroked his chin. "Kum would not consent to siege. Kum would buy its freedom with its temple treasuries."

Isharra nodded. "It is rich as Cartheon, in its priestly way."

When the strategists departed, Ni'An went to talk with the healers and Roshannon returned to his own tent. Summoning Theus, he asked for a handful of scouts. Six men appeared at his tent a short time later, a one-eyed veteran, two skinny boys, and three woodsmen from the wide screen of spies and skirmishers the pony archers absorbed into their army.

He questioned them until the candles in the horn lantern guttered and he was ready to drop into bed.

"One thing more," he said, glad that Ni'An had not yet returned. "If you find a boy, with dark, reddish hair about so long—" He touched the base of his neck. "—with a pockmark in the middle of the forehead, wearing a linen shirt, breeches, and a gray cloak, a boy riding a fine-blooded gray mare, bring this one to me alive.

"Even if you find such a one dead, bring me the body."

Roshannon woke before dawn. He lay thinking about luck, turning its possibilities over in his mind, deciding what detail might be the magic thread that would keep him alive and whole through the day. Battle's peculiar realities seemed cut from different logic than ordinary life, and remained more elusive and mysterious than the workings of a dream. Finally, he decided not to cut his hair.

Theus, come to attend Roshannon, nodded with an old soldier's total acceptance. He knew what games men played when they decided what carried their battle luck, and carefully made no comment about his master's hair—that would be unlucky. He helped Roshannon put on the silk undertunic that Tanta swore was better than mail against arrows.

"You do not have to go with me today, cousin," Roshannon told Ni'An, who had just ducked into the tent. Better that one of them, at least, should remain alive and could get news to his mother.

Ni'An shook his head. "But aye, today I do. Tomorrow I will

ride with the healers. I spoke with them until midnight last night about their arts, and left my far-seeing glasses and scopes in their care."

Roshannon hesitated before drawing on his gloves. "Ni'An, give me back the rings that I gave you. Today I'll wear them."

When the cousins stepped outside, Tanta was reining in his pony before the tent, appraising Isharra, who rode beside him. With her wheat sheaf of hair tucked under her helm, she resembled the score of young men arming in the dawn. She and Tanta looked oddly like brother and sister, Roshannon thought.

"We aren't going into the exercise yard today, lady," Tanta said. "And it's no good thing to die, even if you think it is for a right cause. I would not think less of you if you stay behind."

Isharra laughed at Tanta, tossing her head. "But I would think less of myself if I did, after all the trouble I gave my aunt. That you try to dissuade me persuades me all the more strongly, ka." Her eyes met his as she gathered the reins.

Tanta seemed cloaked in an even thicker despair than the one that had haunted him in the city, yet yesterday he had seemed eager for battle. Perhaps a premonition of his own death had touched him, Roshannon thought, feeling sudden sympathy for the man. His concern for Isharra was curiously touching, and her annoyance at Tanta's attentions oddly amusing.

Grinning, Isharra touched heels to her horse's flanks and joined Tanta's file of mounted archers.

"Isharra left her aunt behind, only to have Tanta take up scolding her," Roshannon told Ni'An.

Ni'An grinned. "I'll wager those two are lovers before long. What do you say to five silver tors?"

"Done." Roshannon clasped his cousin's hand to seal the bet.

Roshannon's men looked distressingly battered and disreputable in the light of morning but saluted him heartily.

"Aye, they don't make heads turn," Theus conceded, "but the old ones know their trade."

He nodded with approval as Roshannon checked the riding order, making sure the boys were staggered in among the older men. Theus checked the arrow supplies, the remounts.

The steward's constable, Keya, had ordered Roshannon to harry the Sanctum's right flank, cause havoc, and withdraw if he could not break the line. "Seek weak points in the ranks, then circle and harass them and escape them to fight another day. We must cut them hard, sink their spirits before we stand a chance against their main body."

Roshannon, his men hidden on a wooded knoll, saw the truth of Keya's words as he surveyed the right flank through the scope. The main southern body was many times the size of the entire northern force. The right flank was a solid line of infantry supported by heavy cavalry six or eight ranks deep, possibly two thousand men against his hundred. This wall of armored horseflesh and men would crush foot soldiers and thinly armored pony archers like a millstone grinding living flesh into pulp—but only if its opponents were foolish enough, or unlucky enough to have to meet the armored wall head-on.

He studied the edge of the line closely, searching for a mass of young, beardless faces, or the sight of bandages showing white at the edge of armor, any sign that might indicate potential weak spots. He put the glass away, thinking of the other way he could test the enemy line, using the special sense, probing for places where fear festered and might dissolve the men's orderly ranks. So much depended on luck. He had seen battles turn on a single man wavering in a line at a critical instant.

Each archer carried two full quivers of twenty arrows each, and pack ponies laden with arrows followed in the rear guard. If every man shot twenty times true, the right flank could crumble, but that was an impossible dream. His situation, Roshannon knew, was a bloody-minded exercise in seeing how good he was at keeping himself and his men alive. His forces were a reed cast against a solid wall. Well, let the reed find the chinks in the wall. Passing the glass to Theus, Roshannon said a prayer for himself and the old men and boys.

"Luck," he said. "Luck and courage be with you."

Thinking of one last chance, one last stand before they would be overwhelmed by the enemy's superior numbers if caught between the southern infantry and cavalry, he ordered them to fill their girdles with sling stones before they rode out. A soldier never knew what might save his life.

Before noon the line of the enemy flank extended, combing its way through the wooded hills for its foe. A young commander hot to pursue the pony archers, maybe. But the heavy cavalry had moved forward beyond the screening fire of their infantry archers.

Roshannon sent a dozen pony archers to lure the southerners into a more vulnerable position, down a defile shielded by rocky slopes that his scouts reported ahead.

Roshannon decided he should conserve the arrow supply for real trouble, and called the most confident slingers forward. The heavy cavalry of this end of the flank was only a hundred men, which he had counted through the glass. White traces of bandage showed beneath many of the men's mail shirts. If he failed to scatter these men, the pony archers, in their lighter armor, had only one choice: to outrun the enemy. The southern cavalry followed the creek along the valley. Above them Roshannon waited with two dozen slingers in anxious silence. When the men filled the defile, he ordered fire.

A hail of pebbles rang against armor and sunk into horse-flesh. The frantic screams of men and horses echoed eerily up the slope. The slingers sent a second and third volley of deadly stones into the cavalrymen before the Sanctum foot archers loosed an answering hail of arrows. Four slingers fell, one caught through the throat.

But the rain of stones had made the cavalrymen fall back, many now riderless, trying to re-form their ranks. Riderless horses raced screaming along the valley. It seemed butchery, and too easy. Roshannon closed his eyes a second, thinking of the feast the wolves would have tonight. *And what are strategists, what am I, but a wolf who thinks?*

Many younger boys, now eager because the enemy seemed overcome, clamored to chase the southerners back to their lines. "Hold the line," Roshannon yelled. "No chasing them." Some older men grabbed boys who would have plunged into the valley and gone at their foes hand to hand, cursing them, slapping their faces, but keeping them from rushing headlong after an enemy they saw as vanquished. The older men had seen how hopelessly they were outnumbered, how easily they could be lured to their own deaths and crushed by the greater southern numbers. They knew the value of living another day to get in another shot tomorrow.

The northerners dropped back rapidly, carrying their companions' bodies with them, racing for their ponies before the Sanctum forces could encircle them. Roshannon vaulted onto the dun, glad that the precious arrow supply was still intact. He ordered his archers into staggered lines.

The fear of the men below washed up to him, weaving into the excitement of his own troops, a tantalizing sensation. He raced his archers into position above, where the remnants of cavalry were rejoining their infantry. At his signal, a rain of arrows swept the sky, black and whistling. Below, Sanctum infantrymen screamed and raced into the ranks of the cavalry as the sheet of arrows fell toward them. They raised shields and some just bare arms against the steel-headed rain of death. The ragged line retreated, scrambling for their lives.

Roshannon ordered his own archers back, out of range of the returning volley of enemy fire. In the confusion and terror, the extended flank had lost its order. Roshannon saw the enemy strategist exhorting his men, a black cloak flapping about the man like raven wings. He ordered the best of his archers to target practice, but they missed.

He felt the wave of pride surging through the boys and old men. It was then, searching the hilly meadows with the glass, that he spotted a six-wagon southern supply train in a meadow ringed by gentle hills. It lay practically open, thinly guarded by a handful of foot soldiers and horsemen.

Green Eyes and his companions left Keira and Brat bound and gagged and concealed on a treetop hunting platform one day. Keira wondered if she could follow the scouts on their raids by using her dream self. Ever since she had touched the other presence over the city, she hesitated to let her dream body seek Cartheon. But images of the city tugged at her senses. Since that last encounter she feared touching Roshannon, even though she might see wonders through his eyes. She had contented herself letting her consciousness drift above the treetops. Beyond the forest, the land crawled with armies joining battle, and the soldiers' emotions seeped into her bones like winter chill. She idly considered drifting away from her body and not returning.

The witches returned from their foray sweated and bloodied, minus Watcher. Green Eyes and Cat Face argued about having left Watcher's body.

"Risking all our lives," Green Eyes said, "to keep one dead man's body out of southern hands is not wise."

"They'll hack his body into trophies, put his head on a pole, and give his hair to their whores as trinkets," Cat Face said bitterly.

"But he was dead. Whatever else they did to him he could not feel." Green Eyes splashed rakka over long cuts on his left arm and shoulder, pouring the pungent liquor from another ornate, carved leather flask.

The scouts divided the contents of captured saddlebags full of spiced, dried meat. They solemnly splashed rakka over their wounds and mourned Watcher in sullen silence. All complained of strange dreams lately. At dawn, while they roused themselves, they discussed their dreams with as much assurance as they discussed things that actually happened to them. That night the witches built a campfire.

That they risked a fire meant they were close to home or felt safe, Keira knew. Beren took great comfort in the fire, turning his face to it and stretching his bound hands toward its warmth. Keira said nothing to him, but the dread in her heart grew.

Green Eyes and Cat Face played ko on a tiny, gridded peg board. They playfully insulted each other's strategies as they clicked pegs into the tiny holes on the board. A new man joined them that day. He looked well fed and rested next to these men, and joked and spoke of battle.

"We play gadfly with them, darting at their flanks, stinging and stinging them and flying away. Their right flank is battered, but our boys didn't lose many. One of Lucky Nikka's raids got fifty horses and provisions wagons with the archpriest's personal gear." The new man's eyes flickered over Keira and Brat with great interest. He squatted on his heels before her, studying her face and thoughtfully chewing a strip of spiced jerky.

"She interests you?" Green Eyes asked.

"She?" The new man frowned and rejoined the others. Their voices lowered to conspirators' whispers as they discussed something, glancing now and again toward her.

She moved her shoulder closer against Brat's. The scouts would soon be safe, among the familiar comfort of their own army camp. What she and Brat were heading for she had no notion.

Green Eyes settled against a nearby tree to take first watch.

"Propitious dreams," he told her.

The Red Man approached Keira, moving swiftly through the vast dreamscape. His open robes revealed a great wheel-shaped scar burned into his chest. He halted not two paces from her and watched her, his mouth curving upward in a slow grin.

She looked into his eyes and was hooked. She could not look away, caught as she was in the great well of aloneness that was his spirit. His spirit battered at the walls that protected her self, wanting inside, wanting to taste her and share the world through her eyes.

She stared at him, horrified. Her will slipped, struggling to keep her defenses up.

"Greetings, brother," he said, staring her down.

She almost laughed, pleased that he had mistaken her for a boy. But he laughed at her, his eyes burning with the spirit hunger. A sudden wisp of smoke rose from the deep scars on his chest, and fire flickered along the brand in his flesh, forming a wheel of flame. His laughter pealed on until the fiery circle filled the world.

She clawed her way through blackness and fire. She woke staring into the dawn woods, hugging to her chin the blanket meant to cover both her and Beren. Her chest felt as if a white-hot millstone had landed on it, crushing her breath away. She blinked, her vision bleary and unsteady, until she made out individual tree trunks and branches and the huddled shapes of the witch encampment. She smelled a campfire and tea brewing.

Green Eyes was watching her as he whittled a twig with his dagger, his eyes glittering. "Do spies only have bad dreams?"

"Why do you care about my dreams?"

"They are not good if they make you thrash in the night."

"How do you know I have bad dreams?" She straightened her shoulders and glanced at Beren, curled like a hedgehog beside her and breathing softly. She lifted her chin, watching Green Eyes. She had the sudden urge to confess all her dreams to him, just to see what he would do.

"Do you fear what you see when you sleep?" he asked.

Keira's heart pounded. "Why should I?"

He waited for her to say something.

She kept silent. She had dreamt the heads on pikes every night since the scouts captured her. Every night the dead faces in the vision had changed, their features twisting into horrible leering grimaces, their voices becoming a shrill, sibilant keening, though she could never remember what words they hissed at her when she woke. But the Red Man and the wheel of fire was a new dream. She stared over Green Eyes' shoulder at the woods. Tatters of her dream visions overlaid her view of the trees for a moment, then dissipated, swept skyward by the campfire's smoke.

Better for me to end up in the witch encampment? she wondered. Or better for the Sanctum to capture me, better to live among what I know, than to flee into the presence of something I have no knowledge of?

Green Eyes grinned at her. "You do not believe in dreams, you southerners? That you can see what will come and what has been, and maybe the face of someone you will meet tomorrow?" He shifted. "You know, my dead grandfather has given me good advice in dreams."

She snorted. "Your dead grandfather." She wanted to hurt him, to puncture his faith in his world, because her own faith in everything was dissolving.

"Whoever or whatever visits you in your dreams," he said almost gently, "is not giving you good advice, I think."

Keira glared at Green Eyes, unable to think of a suitable retort. Something in his eyes and manner reminded her of Roshannon, which infuriated her. Something in all these blasted witches, she thought, reminded her of that man who had bought her. She wished they would simply ignore her, allow her the invisibility that a southern man would. Pointedly ignoring Green Eyes, she reached over and shook Beren's shoulders to wake him.

The scouts broke camp before dawn. The new rider carried Keira, handling his mount one-handed, his right arm crooked about her. His dagger hilt dug into her back. Sun burned through the blindfold on the right side of her face, numbing her, casting her into a trance of timeless darkness. But through it all she smelled the sweet, resinous scent of the woods.

She licked her parched lips. "Where do you take me?"

"My business is to take you there, not answer your questions. Did you dream well?"

"My dreams are no business of yours."

He flicked the reins. "You have a right to keep your dreams to yourself."

Keira snorted. "Because they are probably my last, you mean?"

He made no answer, but began telling the other scouts about a strange dream he had had last night. "A vision of a red-cloaked man, with the shape of a wheel burned into his chest."

Green Eyes said hoarsely, "I had a similar dream, but dreamt other things as well."

Keira stiffened in the saddle, as the Bowman and Cat Eyes muttered of similar visions. "Ask the cub," one said. Beren, reluctant to say anything about dreams, admitted to the same thing in a small voice.

The new man drew rein and tapped Keira's shoulder. "What did you dream? Did the Red Man visit you, too?"

She nodded stiffly.

A hand touched her shoulder and Green Eyes' voice asked, close to her ear, "What are you, lady? For I think you brought the dream, with such force that it even touched the boy's mind."

Keira said nothing, wondering herself if what he suggested were true. Green Eyes snorted to himself and the group rode on.

At least I am still alive, she thought.

Sometime in late afternoon, the new man removed the blindfold. She blinked. Nothing looked familiar, but, ironically, nothing looked different from before her capture. They were still riding through a labyrinth of great, dark needle-leaved trees. She glanced at Beren, whose blindfold had also been removed, and nodded, hoping to reassure him. Even he looked suddenly wary of her, as if he believed he had been betrayed. He raised his chin and did his best to look through her, as a proper, grown southern man would.

She wanted to slap him, shake him, most of all to explain to him. But she knew the witches would grant them no time alone together. The knowledge of how alone she was pressed in on her. The idea of slipping into Roshannon's awareness tempted her, but she was afraid to try it now, uncertain of what might happen. Willing herself into calmness with a great effort, she studied the forest: the great tree trunks, the tangle of branches blocking the sun, the wild grapes and creeping vines that wove among the undergrowth, the carpet of leaf cover that drank up the sound of their passing.

How appropriate that god had dreamt the world, she thought. It made sense that creation formed in dream thoughts rather than waking ones, for waking thoughts were not fanciful enough to encompass creation. Miles and miles of forest and mist unraveled, one of the first and strangest dreams of creation.

Before dusk, they came to the edge of a great encampment. The smell of cooking fires and horses, the hum of thousands of soldiers' voices, enveloped them. Sentries took the scouts' horses after they dismounted. Grimly Keira wondered if some officer would appropriate the mare. Her memories of southern army camps rushed back.

Huddled in her cloak, her hands still bound, she paced between her captors, alert for rocks and tent pegs that would trip her. The cords binding her wrists chafed her skin, which was slick with sweat and grime. Brat walked beside her, staring about him with more boyish enthusiasm than fear.

"Unbind our hands that we might at least walk freely," she said.

Green Eyes' hand prodded her back. "Keep moving."

The vast encampment sprawled over hillsides and valleys along a narrow river. Rows and circles of tents with banners flapping in the breeze spread to the horizon. Many earth-colored tents clustered among trees hung with saddles and cooking gear. Herds of ponies, like the one she had bought for Hipolla, were corralled at intervals throughout the camp, others hobbled outside tents. A litter of equipment and wagons covered the sheltered meadow and hillsides. The smell of cooking meat made her mouth water.

"We're late," the new man said.

Green Eyes jerked the cord that bound Keira's hands. "Keep a move on. I'll be glad to deliver you and end this business."

Keira swerved around a tent peg and flung her leg over a guide rope. A hunting cat stared at her from the doorway of a tent. The men called to it, crooning, but it switched its tail and blinked at them. A thin thread of flute music drifted through the camp. A woman with a child stood by another tent flap, watching the wind comb its way across the meadow and ripple the tent covers.

Soldiers were everywhere: sitting cross-legged by fires, playing ko at makeshift boards, racing their ponies, practicing archery or fisticuffs, mending tack, trading stories, and laying wagers. They wore knives in their sashes or belt sheaths. The long, curved shapes of sword sheaths rode their hips and trailed below their cloak hems. Everywhere the shapes of great, double-curved bows slung across shoulders and saddle bows caught Keira's eye.

The new man led them around the side of a smithy wagon, past tubs of water used for stanching blades. The smell of molten metal turned Keira's stomach and made her think of executions.

They reached a low hut of wicker withes and logs that smelled of resinous sap.

Green Eyes nudged her forward. "Bathe yourself, lady, ere you go before the captains and they decide what to do with you."

An old woman came around the side of the hut.

"This prisoner," the new man said, "goes to Lucky Nikka's tent afterward."

They led Beren off. Keira demanded to know where they were taking him. Green Eyes said, "I cannot tell you, lady."

Beren looked at her a moment as if he might say something. His mouth tightened, his face seeming older, leaner, sadder. He squared his shoulders, as if carrying the weight of the world on them, then turned his back on her. He walked stolidly off between the new man and Cat Face.

Inside the steam house, Keira tried not to consider that this might be her final bath.

In the bath's entry, a cauldron of water bubbled on a coal fire. On the other side of the entry was a wall full of pegs for bathers' possessions. The attendant, who wore a dagger tucked in her sash, eyed Keira thoughtfully when she shed her clothes, exposing her bruised ribs and scarred back.

The crone laughed when Keira took off her boots. "Ah, lass, you really need a bath, you do. They sending you off to be one of Lucky Nikka's bedgirls, eh? I hear he's a finicky man and turned the offered ones all away."

Keira frowned, wondering who this odious Nikka creature might be.

The steam bath itself was a circular pit with a round hut built over it, its bottom a fire pit covered with heated rocks. Wooden benches encircled it, and here Keira sat while the crone ladled boiling water from a cauldron onto the rocks. The steam hissed up, and Keira slid into a pleasant lethargy as the hot vapors enveloped her. Her muscles lost their knots and aches and her body ran with sweat. She imagined herself flowing and dissolving into water and steam.

The attendant cleared her throat. "The guard is waiting." She dumped a final ladle full of hot water over Keira.

The spell of comfort broke. Keira stared at her bare feet a moment, thinking how white they were against the rough stone floor, then lifted her eyes. The woman studied her, curious, and turned away when she realized she would get no story.

"If Lucky Nikka takes you, he really does have peculiar taste," the crone muttered.

Keira refused to dignify the woman's speculations with a response and pulled on her clothes in silence. Their worn material was full of the smell of forest and sea, wood smoke and sweat. She dug in the lining of her boot and pried out Hipolla's earring.

She folded her fingers over it, said a prayer, then opened her hand. Tears suddenly stung her eyes. The earring lay gleaming in her palm, the only thing she had left of her friend. Better to go to her death wearing something of Hipolla's, something to give her courage. Especially because it was a lordly thing and she, a freeholder's daughter, had no right to wear it.

She tilted her head and fitted the wire through her pierced lobe. Smooth and cool, the two circles swung against her cheek.

The bath attendant gasped when she saw the earring but said nothing. She handed Keira over to the guard outside—only Green Eyes himself, who bound her hands again with a leather strap.

But he stared at the earring and at Keira as if she had played some unspeakable trick on him.

"Who are you, lady?"

"I am only myself." She raised her chin; the talisman swung against her cheek. "Take me where you must."

It was a cool, windy night, with moonlight and shadow dappling the sea of tents. Wind ruffled the many standards and swirled the aromas of cooking fires through the tents. Lanterns lit inside the many tents turned their occupants' activities into a shadow play on the hide walls.

Keira stumbled and sidestepped a stake and guide rope. Uphill the ground cleared before a large pavilion.

A plain green banner hung from a pole before its door flap, and a horn lantern was hung below. Knots of people, soldiers, even women and children, idled in the clearing before this tent, and everyone stared expectantly at them as they approached.

"Way, way, a prisoner for the captain." Green Eyes shouldered

his way through the crowd. People moved aside leisurely, eyeing
her and her escort. One woman touched the earring Keira wore.
"Stop that!" Green Eyes said, pushing the inquisitive one away. A
fresh round of whispers buzzed behind the hands of the gathered
idlers. Their earrings and armbands caught reflected firelight,
which seemed to wink mockery at Keira.

Damn all you lords, I refuse to show fear before you, she
thought, raising her chin.

A guard stationed before the tent nodded. "He is within, bring
the prisoner."

Someone held the tent flap and Keira ducked inside. She
straightened in wonder, and was bumped forward by the press of
people coming behind. Thick rugs spread on the ground made the
tent floor spongy as a carpet of moss. Lanterns hung from
crosspoles illuminated the inside, and the roof shimmered in the
wind. Chests and cushions were set against the walls, beneath a
litter of parchments.

On an inner partition of spidersilk the shadow play of figures
bent over a table fragmented suddenly as the guard approached.

A stocky, fair-skinned man stepped up beside Green Eyes to
take her in his charge.

"Propitious dreams," Green Eyes whispered to her, and slipped
away in the crowd.

The stocky man laid a hand between her shoulder blades. Keira
shuffled forward, her eyes busy on the colored patterns underfoot.
Her new guard's hand dropped away as his fellow nodded briskly
to one who appeared from behind the partition.

Keira noted the new pair of boots settling in the rich geo-
metrics of the rugs. She raised her eyes.

Not three paces before her stood Roshannon.

☙ **16** ☙

"Ros—" Keira choked. She stared, her breath caught in her throat. It was no dream indeed, but he himself standing there before her.

The crowd pressed closer. He stared at the earring, at her. She turned her head, and the earring slid across her cheek. Her pulse climbed as she felt the hot flush of the connection begin.

Someone pulled Roshannon aside.

Someone shouted. Suddenly the man with mismatched eyes that Keira had seen in her dreams, his face much sterner and leaner than Hipolla's, darted forward and snatched at the earring. "Murderer," he growled. Keira twisted and stumbled backward, her ear throbbing with pain. He grabbed her shoulder; his fist flew at her face. She ducked, tripped, and went down, biting her tongue.

Keira rolled and kicked, struggling to right herself with her bound hands. She fell on her face, drew a knee up under her, and tried again to rise.

There were shouts of encouragement. A man yelled hoarsely for order.

The silver-haired man yanked her arm, flipped her over, and sat on her, pinning her shoulders. His nose not an inch from hers, his hair flung forward over his green eye, he stared at her. She screamed in his face, bit his finger, and scrabbled backward, digging her feet into the rugs.

"You filthy, mother-damned bastard." His fingers closed on her throat.

She spat in his face.

Roshannon hooked an arm around the man's neck and chopped at his forearms, yanking him backward off her. The two men thrashed about on the rugs together. The spectators, little more than a bleary thicket of boots to Keira, retreated, forming a rough circle. Finally the silver-haired man came to his senses and lay still, cursing Roshannon.

Roshannon staggered up, shaking hair from his eyes. Someone hauled Keira up backward to her feet. Roshannon's eyes met hers; for an awful instant she thought his spirit would seep into hers and drink up her emotions. But he only touched her shoulder. She stared at him, frozen. Someone pulled Roshannon back. A shorter man whose face was brother close to Roshannon's tried to calm the witch lord down. Keira's eyes narrowed: the man I saw aboard the ship, she thought dizzily.

Roshannon stepped backward into the press of people. Keira noted the plain clothes he wore, the sword at his side, the rich sash worked in silver thread, the jeweled dirk sheathed on his hip, the single gleaming pearl bound in silver wire that dangled at his left earlobe. Just as she had feared, he was a lord, no common soldier at all.

A silver-haired woman archer touched his arm and whispered in his ear, her lips almost touching his pearl earring. For an instant Keira's eyes met his, then she glanced to the safer faces of total strangers. She felt sick: she had seen the faces of these people through Roshannon's eyes, but the familiarity was no comfort, for her dreams had not revealed what would happen when she saw them. Roshannon's spirit pressed at her, like a wind probing the chinks of a house's outer walls, eager to get in.

Staring at his earring, she remembered how he had kissed her hands and the whip marks on her back.

Someone announced the steward's constable. A man with a beautiful, ringing voice, spellbinding as a priest's, called the mob to order.

"Who is this prisoner, Nikka?" the silver-haired woman asked. She stood between Roshannon and Keira's attacker, her hand poised on the ornate swept hilt of her dagger.

Nikka? Keira almost laughed. Was Roshannon himself the odious Lucky Nikka with the odd taste in bedgirls? She felt hollow and drained, remembering how she had watched this woman through Roshannon's eyes aboard the ship. She licked her lips and waited, wondering what the witches would do with poor Brat. Doubtless, she would be killed. It was only a question of how.

"Murderer." Keira's attacker wrenched himself free of the men who held him. "No Tanta would freely give up that earring. And what brigand could resist such a trophy?" He glared at her. "I demand justice: this one's life for my niece's life."

Roshannon put a hand on his shoulder. "The prisoner will be questioned, and justice done. You have no right to attack anyone in this tent, Xian Tanta."

Xian Tanta. Keira said his name over to herself, thinking what a strange way this was to find Hipolla's uncle. He watched her coldly. The witch woman reached to touch the earring. Keira's eyes met hers. The woman drew her hand back, but her fingers brushed Keira's cheek in an almost mocking caress.

Green Eyes slipped up to Roshannon and handed him the sheathed dagger. "We took it from her boot when we caught her," he said loudly enough for all to hear; glancing at Keira, he nodded to her.

"Her?" Xian Tanta frowned intently at Keira, his mouth twisting.

Someone tittered nervously. "If you cannot recognize a woman when you are sitting on her, Xian Tanta," a man quipped, "you must be getting old."

Tanta's face paled, but he laughed raucously with the others at the joke turned on himself. The witch woman smiled slowly.

What strange people, Keira thought.

Roshannon held the dagger aloft, carefully concealing the ornate hilt in his hand, then tucked it into his sash.

A final insult, Keira thought; they will kill me with no concern for the truth. But he does not want it known that he bought me, and if someone saw that the dagger I took matches his own, they might guess the connection between us.

She hated him. Hated the inevitable feel of being someone he could dispose of as he wished.

While the witch scouts had kept her blindfolded, she had learned to slip into him as easily as she could stick her foot in a stream and withdraw it again. She had become defiantly proud of that ability.

But her pride that she could weave through him, tasting his life at any time, simply to relieve tedium, without letting him share her emotions, began to evaporate. She saw the danger. She craved merging with him again, because it gave her pleasure, power, and knowledge, and she had acquired the habit of it.

Yet she hated his calm, his unreadable eyes, hated the ka'innen clothes he wore, hated the obvious calculation with which he had palmed the dagger—hated the notion that to him she was possibly just a ko stone that he might move anywhere he pleased, that she, and the mare, and even Beren were his property, his ka'innen chattel, to dispose of as he wished. He was far more dangerous than her father. She would never escape him, for he would own her body and spirit. Idiot, she thought, you should have gone to Kum, traded the necklace for gold, entered one of the hermit or traveling orders, and had a safe place for Beren and yourself, with food in your belly.

Numbly, she let herself be led behind the silk partition, where a makeshift council chamber was set up. A lantern hung from a ridgepole illuminated the low tables that had been pushed together. Parchments, maps, tea bowls, and a tray of still-steaming meat pies crowded the table's surface. Tanta seated himself brusquely. His clenched, white-knuckled fist poised on the table's edge shook so slightly it seemed to Keira a trick of tiredness or the light. A red-haired man with a red armband on his right arm sat beside Tanta, the witch woman on his other side. Keira sat directly opposite Tanta. They both stared at each other. Keira felt strangely betrayed: her dreams had shown her these people but suggested nothing of what would happen when she encountered them.

"Murderer," Tanta said softly, his voice Hipolla's, but lower and more stinging, his face Hipolla's, but merciless.

"I am no murderer," Keira cried. "Hipolla Tanta gave me this earring before she died."

"We will question her." A dark-faced man in a long green tabard stepped forward, planted himself by the partition, his hand on his dagger hilt. "Go fetch the dreamers," he told a boy, who nodded and left.

Roshannon kept at bay the crowd trying to sneak behind the partition and stare at her. "Out of here," he yelled. "All those of you who are not concerned in this, out. We must question this prisoner in private."

A tall graybeard saluted Roshannon, then barked orders, chasing onlookers outside. Keira overheard two men wagering on whether she would be hanged or beheaded at dawn. A knot of people left, grumbling to themselves after staring their fill at her.

She wanted to scream at them, *if it is public spectacle you crave, you should get a bellyful when they execute me.*

Keira strained to see the maps, the shapes and names of foreign places, wondrous territories that she would never see. The man with the red armband swept the papers into a bundle that he laid beside Roshannon at the head of the table. Every eye turned toward Keira.

"By your honor, Xian Tanta," Roshannon said, "do you pledge not to attack this prisoner in this tent or anywhere within the authority of this camp?"

"Ka." Nodding curtly, Tanta touched the fingers of his left hand to his forehead.

The green-clad man stooped beside Keira. "I am Loreth Keya, the head constable of Cartheon's high steward. Simply tell the truth. You need fear nothing while you are being questioned. Do you understand?" She nodded.

"Did the earring you wear belong to Hipolla Tanta?"

"Yes."

"How did you know Hipolla Tanta?"

"I bought her at A'Hrappa market on the temple steps. The army had captured her and left her there for the temple to sell. Folk called her a witch and pelted her with kitchen garbage."

Tanta's face went ashen.

"What were you doing in A'Hrappa, a Sanctum stronghold?" the constable asked.

"I was riding north."

"Why?"

"On my own business." She heard the crowd outside jesting and whispering. Her head hurt and her stomach felt hollow as she considered her judges' shadows on the gently shifting tent wall. If a soldier outside strode between a campfire and the tent, his softer, dreamlike shadow wove through the shadows of those judging her. *But this is not a dream.* She tried comforting herself with the thought that, being soldiers, if these men decided to kill her, they would likely be quick about it, unless they first tortured her . . .

"What did you do in A'Hrappa?" the constable asked.

Roshannon turned his empty tea bowl in his hands and signaled for fresh brew. Distracted, Keira watched the pale crosshatch of scars on his forearms catch the light, the old lines faint as shadows against his skin, the new lines cut over the old as if a scholar practicing writing had drawn stroke after stroke upon his skin. Each was the mark of knife or sword, of death faced. Hipolla had pushed back her sleeves to show the same pale marks on her own forearms.

"I bought Hipolla and the pony for her to ride," Keira said, "and left the city."

The constable rubbed his jaw. "Why buy her?"

"Because I wanted a guide to Cartheon."

The constable snorted. "Do you southerners make pilgrimages there now, to celebrate the great Schism?"

"Your wit is sour," Keira said. "I headed for Cartheon because I wanted to go there."

"Why?"

She carefully avoided looking at Roshannon. "I was curious. I wanted to see if you witches are soul suckers, as the priests say."

Tanta rose; Isharra drew him back down.

The constable frowned at Tanta and strode around the table. Isharra leaned forward, her shoulder brushing Roshannon's. With her dagger, she speared one of the tiny meat pies on the platter in the center of the table. She raised it to her mouth and ate it, stabbed another, and offered it to Roshannon on the point of her dagger. He shook his head. Keira watched in fascination, her mouth watering at the smell of the meat pies, her stomach twisting with a strange stab of emotion. Roshannon's long fingers drummed a slow rhythm on the table. He wore the silver wedding ring and the wooden ring she had tossed away, one nested next to the other on his little finger.

The constable, standing behind Keira, bent close, and spoke almost in her ear. "Why did you ride north?"

Startled, Keira lost her temper. "You creep behind me like an old lecher. Ask me your questions face-to-face, not from behind my back where I cannot see you."

The company burst into uneasy laughter. Xian Tanta fixed his mismatched eyes on her.

The steward's constable stalked to the end of the table, his face dark, his eyes black. "Answer my question."

Keira gritted her teeth.

"How did Hipolla die?" Tanta asked.

"Two men attacked her while we were separated. When I returned she had wounded them, but was wounded herself. I got the one, the other killed her."

"And?" Tanta leaned forward.

"I killed him."

"With what?"

"The dagger they took from me."

Roshannon coughed. "The scout who brought her gave it to me." He waved it in the air to satisfy their curiosity, keeping the distinctive hilt hidden in his hand.

"You tell a strange story," Tanta said. "Did both of you travel in men's clothes?"

Keira nodded.

A messenger slipped in and whispered in Roshannon's ear. He spoke briefly to the man, scrawled on a piece of paper; the man took it and left.

"Where did you get the clothes?" Tanta asked.

"Hipolla got hers from a dead man. I *bought* men's clothes. I am neither spy nor thief, and I did not murder Hipolla."

"But all those who can prove otherwise are dead or far away?" Tanta insisted.

"Not so. The boy could tell you if he were here. What have you done with him?" She stared all of them down but avoided looking at Roshannon. "You have already decided that I am guilty. Why should I say anything?"

On and on it went. Their questions were a sea of sound eating away at her. Every time she looked at Tanta, peering into his green and gold eyes, she thought of Hipolla and reproached herself. Slowpoke, Hipolla had said as the red froth darkened her mouth. That image will haunt me forever, Keira thought. But she remained steady and her answers did not change. The questions circled, stalking not the truth, but her, like wolves, clever, persistent, untiring hunters.

At last the constable indicated a frail-looking couple standing in grave silence at the edge of the partition. "These are what you would call witches," he told Keira. "They are truthsayers, or as you might say, soul stealers. They can enter your mind to see the truth. You can end this questioning now if you let them into your mind."

Keira stared at the two. Sweat etched its way down her ribs, and her head throbbed. "No. Don't let them touch me."

The constable conferred with the fragile-looking man and woman, called for silence, and ordered everyone from the tent but Roshannon, Tanta, Isharra, and Ni'An. "We must know the truth. They must examine you."

"No," Keira said. "Do not do this to me."

"Ka, is this wise?" Roshannon rose. "I served the south long enough to know how truthsayers and 'soul suckers' terrify these people. There is no reasoning with them about it. It's abomination to them. This girl was raised with that doctrine filling her ears from the cradle. Consider what harm this truthsaying examination may do her."

"Ka. You defend the southerners?" the green-clad man asked softly.

"I offer you my understanding of them, ka," Roshannon said just as softly.

Keira frowned at Roshannon. Was he defending her, protecting himself, or maneuvering her into a game of his own? Mentally, she tightened the walls that she had built in her head to keep Roshannon out, and got ready for an assault. The strangely frail-looking twin brother and sister seated themselves at the table and watched her. Suddenly their wills rippled toward her and enclosed her like a net, seeking to invade her consciousness.

"No." She screamed, all her senses suddenly blazing black and red, as if a circle of fire burned in the depths of her brain. "No, no, no." Her ears filled with roaring; her sense of balance fled. She clawed at the table, feeling herself slip backward into utter blindness and dumbness, the strange void she had felt in her last dreams. She struggled to keep herself upright and reeled dizzily. Her head thudded down on the tabletop. Pain laced through her body, releasing her from the pincers of the twin alien wills. She tasted blood on her tongue. When her vision cleared and she looked up, the brother and sister were staring at her, their lips parted, their faces full of horror.

A stranger stood at the partition.

"This truthsaying has gone quite far enough," he said in a deep, low voice.

The truthsayers bowed their heads, and the constable knelt, whispering something that sounded to Keira's dazed senses like "any more rat soup." Keira narrowed her eyes at the man who was dressed like a common soldier, hoping her bleary vision would clear.

He nodded to Keira. "You are in my custody and under my protection. There will be no more tampering with you."

"By the Wheel, you carry the gift," the tiny white-haired man whispered. His eyes narrowed as if he had a terrible headache.

She closed her eyes, her head throbbing in time with her heartbeat.

"By my honor, I pledge surety for the prisoner," Roshannon said as casually as he could, "and will keep her safely in my tent. If you all agree."

The high steward smiled slowly at him, then abruptly left the tent with the dreamers, glancing only once at Keira.

Keira's chin rose; her face was a mask. Xian Tanta glared at her. Mutely, Keira offered him the earring. He made the gesture of the broken wheel at her outstretched hand.

Loreth Keya scooped the earring from Keira's palm. He looked at it thoughtfully, grabbed Xian Tanta's shoulder, and pressed it into his hand. "You keep it." Tanta left the tent without a backward look. Isharra hurried after him, her long hair and her cloak flying.

Roshannon turned back to Keira. She twisted a tea bowl around in her hands, withdrawn into herself as the others filed out. Roshannon signaled even Ni'An to leave.

But they were not yet alone, for a messenger had just come to give his report. Roshannon offered the man a water skin and praised his keen observations. He ordered the messenger back to his lines with the word to advance ten columns of horse archers ready to attack the Sanctum wing before they marched at dawn. The man bowed; Attal, he was called, a Blue Forest woodsman who could creep close to the enemy as a ghost and remember everything he saw. The Sanctum troops had killed his two wives and children when they burned a forest hold. He was lean as only a man who thought revenge was food could be.

Roshannon watched the man leave. He closed his eyes, wishing away the headache that was probably only a fraction of what Keira had suffered resisting the dreamers.

Facing her, he laid on the table the sheathed dagger the scouts had taken from her.

His fingers curled on the table, and her eyes followed the motion of his hand. Did she expect a blow, he wondered with an awful sadness, a crashing fist, a palm slapped hard across her cheek? He could feel her fear, but it was a far more complex fear than that of mere physical violence.

She rose, a creature at bay. She seemed taller. Perhaps it was that she stood straighter, her head no longer bowed, her eyes no longer focused on the ground or inward, but outward and on him. She looked thinner, too, as if she had been honed and tempered.

She was furious with herself that, facing him now, she recalled his touch on that long-ago night, as he traced the lines of the scars on her back, first with his fingertips, then with his mouth. He stared at her as if he, too, were trapped in some mysterious compulsion. Surely she was carrying his child, surely, she told herself, this is why the connection began and he has such power over me. Surely that must be why the encounter with the dreamers made her feel all her senses would spin from her body like unraveled threads, leaving her numb.

He drew his dagger and cut the strap that bound her wrists. Red marks showed on her skin, but she was too stubbornly proud to tend her hurts before him. The leather strap fell to the rugs.

"You have led an interesting life," he said, "since that night we shared a bed. There are many questions I would ask you, w—"

"You are not the only one with questions to ask."

He poured tea and pushed a bowl toward her. She considered throwing it at him, then felt oddly sure he knew her thought.

She clutched the tea bowl to keep her hands from shaking. She downed the bitter brew and licked a piece of tea leaf from her lip.

"You have not forgotten your questions, have you?"

She shook her head, feeling sweat trickle down her side. "Do you believe I did not kill Hipolla Tanta? I am merely curious."

He leaned across the table. "I was, hm, with you at her death, though I did not know it at the time. I saw a small meadow, you riding a man down, a hamstrung man, a boy with a sling—"

She dropped the tea bowl and jumped up.

"So that was true?"

"Deviltry. You are a demon."

He laughed and was on his feet in one smooth, fluid motion, coming after her. "I? No woman ever disturbed my dreams so much. When you faced death, sharing your struggle made me seasick for the first time in years." He grinned. "*You* are the demon."

"If you saw in a vision that I did not kill Hipolla, then why didn't you say so? Or do you want me killed and out of the way, since it would be mightily inconvenient for you to have a southern wife?"

"True, it is inconvenient for me to have a southern wife. But you ran away from me. Do you remember? Besides, the cityfolk don't think many others dream true. I am a new liege to them; they do not trust me."

She twisted the tea bowl in her hands, furious. Whether she looked at him or not, memories of their wedding night hung in the air between them, confusing everything.

"Why did you not claim me as your husband?" he pressed. "They would have questioned me; you would have spent an easier time."

"And ended up in your charge so much sooner." She sat down, scraping her thumbnail along the table to keep her hand from shaking.

He leaned forward, intent on her face. "Which do you fear more, lady, yourself or me?"

"Don't flatter yourself into thinking you have such knowledge of me."

"But I do. I do. As you have vast acquaintance of me from the many visits you've paid me." He let himself laugh at her. "You are one of them. You are one of the witches that you were so curious about, one of the soul suckers the priests rail against. We both are, but they seem not to know about me for some reason."

Abruptly, she stumbled away from the table as if searching for a place to run. He leaped over the table and caught her by the shoulder. The moment he touched her, a torrent of twisted emotions surged in her veins. She stared at him and slapped his face. He caught her to him, but tripped; they tumbled onto the rugs.

"Stay away from me," she said. "Stay out of my dreams. Stay out of *me*."

He wrestled with her, straddling her.

Her skin crawled with heat, with the tantalizing memory of sliding beneath his skin and seeing through his eyes. Every image and sensation she had shared through him flickered through her veins. The memory of his touch scorched a merciless dizzy path up her spine, across the curve of her breasts, the back of her neck.

He smiled at her, the smile of a ka'innen lord who would re-claim his runaway possession totally.

She shuddered, seeing on his face that he wanted to feast on her as she had on him. She clenched her fists, feeling suddenly tired, old, adrift, helpless before the force that would marry them truly, bind one irrevocably to the other like alloyed metal. Panic-stricken visions flicked through her mind—once his spirit merged with hers he would know everything—that Beren was a priest's son, that she was likely pregnant. She bit her lip until the pain gave her some room to think. A man who knew a woman as he would know her once their spirits joined could jail her more com-pletely than any other man. Yet perhaps her thoughts were safe, for the sharing had let her tap only wild surges of emotion, sud-den joys or sorrows or pains. Her terror at having him know everything of her warred with the strange desire for him. Desper-ate, she thought of provoking him into punching her stomach and ridding her of the child she was sure she carried. Wild plans formed in her mind: get the ring, get other clothes, burn those of his she had worn, escape the camp with Beren, and reach Kum.

She stoked all her emotions into hatred of him and ka'innen ways, of the Wheel's turning that threshed down women, free-holders, and others under the scythe of lordly men's desires.

When he touched her, she gritted her teeth.

"What do you want of me?" he asked.

"Ka. I have not the right to want anything of you." She practi-cally spit the words at him.

"Then by what right did you enter my awareness like a thief climbing into a house? Again and again you came, tasting the world through me. Did you worry about my will and my wants? I think not, yet you will not let me enter you."

Her fists shot out at his face, she kicked at his shins. Her wild-cat scream cut short as he clamped a hand across her mouth. Fran-tic, she bit his thumb, but his pain curled back into her. He yanked her up, one hand twisted in her hair.

"Is this what you want?" he whispered. "Is this all you understand of men? To be beaten or kicked and given another set of scars to match the ones on your back?"

She twisted in his grip, frantic to shut out the sound of his low, relentless voice.

Two young guards poked their heads around the partition. "Trouble, ka?"

"The day that one foul-tempered girl is too much for me," Roshannon said, "I will call, I assure you. Leave us."

The guards obeyed without question, but Keira thought their faces were masks of amused speculation, and she hated Roshannon for that, too.

She jerked her legs, trying to work her knee up. Abruptly he slid off her, yanked her to her feet, twisted his fingers into her hair, jerked her arms behind her back.

"I would stay out of your dreams if you stayed out of mine," he said.

She jammed an elbow into his chest. His grunt of pain gave her a certain wild satisfaction, but his pain flowed back at her.

He pinned her again. "If you struggle much more you will be hurt." She writhed, got a hand free, and punched wildly. He swerved aside and grabbed her hands, watching her. His mouth twisted. His arm shot out and he cracked her cheek, openhanded.

Keira stared, frozen. Her right cheek burned as if branded. The blaze of pain dropped her bluntly back to earth, and she saw that he shared it. The pain built a wall between them and ended the lapping of their spirits one against the other.

"When you need to punch someone, Keira Danio," he said coolly, "fold your thumb out over your fingers so—" He showed her, forming her hand into a proper fist. "Else you will break it."

She flushed, yanked her hand away from his, and scrambled up. "What are you going to do with me?"

He grinned. "What do you want me to do with you? But the real problem is what the steward is going to do with us. We are in this mess together now."

Her mouth twisted. She stepped over the low table, to have that between them. "Well, whatever comes, kill me quick rather than sell me. I can't be anyone's slave after the freedom I've tasted."

"Women are not sold among the clans, or killed for running away. That is not the way. Do you want to be dead?"

"You have those rights."

"Tell me what you thought of my rights when you stole my clothes and dagger, and dropped that ring by the piss pot?"

Her jaw set. "I paid you back for the things I took; besides, the clothes are old."

"You took my lucky shirt," he said softly.

"If you want the dagger back you can have it. Perhaps *that* I did not pay you for."

"Did it serve you well?" He looked at the sheathed dagger, which lay like a reproach on the table between them.

"It saved my life."

He shook his head, drew it, and flicked his thumb across the edge of the blade. "No, you saved your own life. Remember that and keep the dagger. Though you will probably never forget the face of the man you killed."

She frowned at him. "You know everything, then?"

"I know you in ways I have never known another. As you know me. In some ways it isn't pleasant, but in other ways there is no greater pleasure."

She felt herself redden. There was so little between them, a clutter of tea bowls, a candle, and the scarred tabletop. Only air between them, and a space a hand might reach easily across. She stared at her white-knuckled fist on the edge of the table.

Staring at the silver ring and the wooden ring nested together on Roshannon's little finger, she thought of the simple magics Deva and the other woman had sworn by: a hair, a nail paring, a thread from a cloak, kept nearby to encourage a certain man; the same item burned with your back turned to a door to keep one off. She had found a thread of Terrak's cloak, burned it with her back turned, reciting every curse she knew, and his interest in her had waned. That was not real magic, anyway, but just a women's game.

"Give me the wooden ring," she said.

"I see how your thoughts run. But it will not work. Even with the ring back, my clothes off your back, it will not break the connection between us. What is between us is not in things, but in spirit."

"But the ring was my mother's, so I want it. The other thing—I do not want. I never wanted it."

"Nor did I. That makes no difference. If you want to be rid of it for a while, drink a bellyful of rakka, until the world slides out from under your feet. You will not dream, or touch others, or see through their eyes for a week. Though the rakka may make you feel like dying."

She stiffened. "Is that true?"

"I did it once," he said, somewhat bitterly. "But now I would rather dream."

"Why do you tell me this?"

"We are alike, strangers with the witch gift. We should be allies."

"What of the ring?"

He slipped it from his finger and laid it in her hand.

"Do you think I bought you from your father on a whim?" he asked suddenly.

"Fair fever, maybe. At Kerlew I've seen men buy cattle, cloth, or spice, just so another could not have it."

"I've seen that too." His voice lowered. "Damn you, I bought you because you wanted me to."

His words were like a dagger in the heart, pinning her. She stared at him in horror as she recognized their truth.

"How many men have you known, Keira Danio? Only your father, who decorated your back?"

His soft insistent voice folded open too many wounds.

"There's the brat, Beren," she said huskily. "I trust him."

"So you can trust. That's good to know."

"You are a mystery to me. I don't understand you."

"I know," he said.

"Where is Beren Harth?" she demanded.

He spread his hands. "We have done nothing to him."

"Nothing you say can equal the sight of him."

"I cannot let you see him."

"Then I have nothing more to say to you."

"So be it. Propitious dreams."

Roshannon rose and left without a backward glance. He ordered the guards into position and paced off thinking about that slip of her tongue, and of his own. His breath plumed around his face and he drew his cloak tighter. He ordered food brought to Keira, and decided to visit the boy taken with her.

In the tent beside the cook's area, the child glanced up at Roshannon with a brief flicker of appraisal. He sat at a low table, playing a solitary game of ko. He was a skinny boy, all knees and elbows, with dark curly hair that caught red lights.

"Where is she?" he asked, keeping his eyes on Roshannon. "Have you come to kill me?"

"No, I have not come to kill you," Roshannon said, admiring the child's forthrightness. "She is under guard. She asks about you."

"Who are you?"

"A strategist."

The boy studied his plain clothes and dusty boots. "You do not look like a strategist to me." He swung his legs below the table. "Strategists dress finer."

"Only after the fighting is over," Roshannon said.

A cough outside the tent flap announced the cook's boy, who entered bearing a platter full of game cooked in savory herbs. Roshannon saw the boy's eyes widen, and his own mouth watered; he had not eaten since dawn.

The boy sniffed. "Is that food for you?"

"It is for both of us." Roshannon dismissed the cook's boy after he filled the tea bowls.

The boy snatched his hand away from a lid. "It's poisoned," he said quickly.

Roshannon laughed, dipping out stew. "I will eat it all if you suspect my hospitality."

That settled it. The boy attacked the food like a starveling, sating his hunger, then asking if Keira had eaten.

Unless she is a proud fool, Roshannon thought as he nodded and sipped tea. He studied the spot of gravy on the child's nose; the boy caught him looking and wiped at it with his sleeve.

"My name is Beren, but she calls me Brat. I can't talk to you any more if you don't tell me your name, ka."

Roshannon set down his tea bowl with as much solemnity as he could muster. "Nikkael Roshannon."

Beren wiped his mouth on the back of his hand. "What are the northerners going to do with me and her?"

He shrugged. He wished he knew that himself.

The boy looked uneasy. "She said that if anyone found out she was a girl and I, ah, that we'd be dead."

"You aren't, so maybe she was wrong," he said as the boy ladled out more stew. "Did you know she was a girl when first you met her?"

Brat mopped his bowl with a hunk of waybread. "I saw them pissing in the woods. They were mad as hornets and made me swear." He tore another piece of bread and suddenly paled. "You won't tell her I told you?"

Roshannon shook his head. "Them, you said. Who was the other one?"

"Hipolla. But she was a witch." Brat spit out a piece of gristle. "I can't talk to you anymore."

Cold air rushed into the tent as someone opened the flap. Xian Tanta stood at the doorway. The child peered warily at the witch lord over Roshannon's shoulders.

Tanta asked to speak with Roshannon alone. He stepped outside, his boots crunching in the gravel. Roshannon dipped his hands in the water bowl and wiped his mouth. The child made a sign in the air.

"Have they magicked you?" the boy asked, as Roshannon stood to leave.

Roshannon shook his head. "I am only a soldier. I know nothing of magic."

Outside, Tanta argued that Keira should be held in custody in his own tent; since she had traveled with his niece, his honor, he said, demanded that he now offer her a place in his quarters. Roshannon was in no mood to grant Tanta's request or bargain with him.

"Let things remain as they are for a while," he said finally.

By the stars it was past midnight when he returned to his tent. Cloth partitions had been added to his tent, to provide sleeping areas for Keira and Ni'An.

He could sense Keira's sleeping presence, but evidently Ni'An had not yet returned. Roshannon pushed aside the tables and spread his pallet in the partitioned nook, trying not to think of her in the other end of the tent.

❀ 17 ❀

Roshannon knelt and brushed his free hand over the mat of wildflowers and grass roots. The damp scent of roots, the promise of fertility, rose from the earth. Digging his fingers into the earth, he took up a pinch of soil and ate it. All around him, the men in his command bent their heads in silence and ate their own scant portion of earth.

It was good earth, with the sweet taste of cropland that would bear well, with or without the bodies of men to nourish it.

With or without my body in particular to feed it, he thought. He had eaten earth a hundred times, surely. He recalled the sour, salty tang of the water-poor, infidel land.

He brushed the back of his hand across his mouth and rose. Around him, men murmured that the earth was good. An old soldier's superstition, the partaking of the land: soldiers' food, the soldier's last meal, the veterans called it. And it was the joining of the cycle, a fitting thing. "So I feed on the fruits of the earth, and it at last feeds on me, and is fruitful." He whispered the words, the phrases the island farmers spoke when they circled their god stones and plowed their fields in the spring.

The ritual comforted the younger recruits. They all knew the taste of good cropland, had all bent from their plows in the fields, or in their mother's kitchen gardens, to taste the earth and decide if marl or manure was needed.

The man in the corner of the tent cut his finger, held a tube above the bloody slice, and stared into the tube. He cursed, turning into the luminous gray light pouring through the tent flap.

Keira had spied on him some time through half-open eyes. At first she thought she dreamt, then she knew that he was working magic.

240

He cursed and wiped his bloody finger on his pants, then crept over to her. She muttered and shifted a little, feigning sleep. That scared him off a while. But soon it seemed a spider crawled across her hair. He plucked a single hair.

She stirred and he retreated. Fascinated and a little frightened, she watched him through half-open eyes as he fussed with the tube again.

What kind of magic was he making? He bent over the tube, his eye tight against its end, his hands cradling the shallow white bowl that the tube was aimed into. Light poured through the tent flap and struck the bowl.

"Gods," he cried. He sounded pleased and awed.

Keira kicked at the covers and sat up. "What are you doing?"

Startled, he dropped the tube. It rolled onto the rugs. The curved glass in the end—a bit of glass shaped like a great lentil bound fast in the tube, winked like the eye of a strange beast. He snatched it up before Keira could touch it.

The sunlight dimmed, dampened by clouds, and the two of them faced each other in the filtered gray light of the tent.

Keira watched him put the tube in a satchel, wondering how he had magicked her and why.

Face-to-face with the woman who he suddenly suspected might be Nikka's ailment, Ni'An coughed.

"Watch her. Let no harm come to her," Nikka had charged him. His elder cousin had put on his gear, kissed Ni'An farewell, and gone to reconnoiter the Sanctum's right flank before dawn.

"Ka." Ni'An nodded to her, somewhat amused. She wore an ancient shirt that had seen better days. She had soldier's eyes and a wary unwomanly poise. In fact, when he looked directly into her sea-gray eyes, he could doubt this was a woman standing before him. The stance, the dark eyes, the line of the jaw, the dusty boots, all hinted this was a determined lad facing him. Only when her eyes flicked aside for a moment, when her attention was diverted from him for several seconds, could he see clearly that for all her lean height, this was a girl with glimmers of beauty about her but none of the comforting curves of womanhood, who had hacked her hair into a fringe that shadowed her face and hung unevenly to her shoulders. Yet the minute he looked into her eyes again, the illusion of boyhood made him doubt his senses and his previous observations. He wished Roshannon-ka had given more definite orders about her, and wished he knew exactly what his cousin's relationship with her was.

It was some comfort, he thought, if Nikka's ailment turned out to be a woman. But this woman? This strange southern witch? The few southern women he had seen had been the priests' and merchants' women who inhabited the special quarter of Lian Calla set aside for the Sanctum envoys—silent women their men never introduced, dark-cloaked shapes scurrying into or out of rooms, doing the bidding of this Sanctum man or that, and rendered almost faceless by the stiff-sided hoodlike headgear they wore.

Nikka had once commented that Sanctum women reminded him of the shy, black-hooded gulls that flocked in the foamy edges of the surf but fled into the dunes or took flight the minute a man set foot on a beach. Yet this girl was another creature entirely.

Ni'An fetched the roll of gear Nikka had left for her and dropped the bundle by her side. He packed his satchel while she watched.

"Ka," he said to her. "The camp is disbanding. Part will stay here, part will re-form. These clothes should fit you, and my cousin bids you wear the armor." Calling her *ka* was softheadedness, he thought, but addressing her as *lady* seemed somehow facetious.

She studied him awhile, as if considering whether calling her *ka* had been mockery. Then she ducked behind the partition and soon emerged clad in his own shirt and pants, but holding the silk body armor before her in puzzlement. Ni'An played dresser, prodding her into the gear and tying the side fastenings as if he were her squire. She stooped to fasten one of Nikka's sheathed daggers in her boot—the dagger Nikka's father Kirin had given him after his first hunt, before he sailed north.

Ni'An flushed, staring at the dagger. He looked sidelong at her. Her connection with his cousin was very close, else she would never be carrying it.

She turned to face him. He was sure she had noticed his attention focused on the dagger.

"He permits me to have it and said that it may save my life," she said coolly. She had an astonishing rich, low voice, neither man nor woman's.

"Aye, that it may." Ni'An nodded stiffly, feeling suddenly stung and ashamed that he had been so transparent to her. His clothes, being of slightly smaller cut, fit her better than Roshannon's, but only increased the disquieting illusion that she was a lad. But the thought of her allowed a dagger that not even he had ever been permitted to carry offended his sense of order and convinced him that this changeling creature was the heart of Nikka's ailment. The queer, fey mood had gripped Nikka ever since she arrived in camp.

He nodded curtly to her.

The tall, thin girl drew her battered old cloak around her. It was a thing a man might be ashamed to let his hunting dogs bed on, yet she gathered its folds as if it were a regal robe.

"Where is he?" she asked.

Ni'An wanted to laugh at the impossibility of her, but something in her eyes stopped all notion of laughter.

"To battle," he said, wondering if Nikka had bedded her.

Her eyes darkened. She retreated into herself, wiping emotion like a mask laid away.

He led her outside. A crew of gear handlers and camp followers entered quietly and began stripping the tent of furnishings, pulling down the vast frame, collapsing the pavilion cover, and rolling it into a neat bundle. She paced around the handlers in curiosity as Ni'An walked beside her.

"Ka. Exactly who are you?" she asked.

"Ni'An Lia Roshannon."

"What does Lia mean?"

"That my mother was a kitchen maid who took a clansman's fancy and shared his bed, but died before I was grown. The clan adopted me. I am Roshannon-ka's cousin." Ni'An grinned, curious how she would react.

"Ka. I am Keira Danio, a freeholder's daughter."

Ni'An nodded, impressed by her quiet dignity. If she thought, like many southerners, that a leman's children were soulless bastards, she was tactful enough to keep all traces of that thought from her responses, or proud enough not to react in a way she might know he would disdain.

She peered at him. "Are you like your cousin?" She studied him with an unnerving intensity, and her eyes seemed full of old knowledge. Then she smiled. "I see that you are not."

Utterly perplexed, Ni'An gave her an ironic little bow and steered them through a maze of half-laden wagons toward the cook fires, all the while noting that this girl even managed to pace like a man on those long legs of hers. Once he put out a hand to guide her, but she shrugged it off.

From the west the sound of drums rolled in snatches across the plains. Ni'An stiffened, facing that sound a moment. The girl did, too, then she met his eyes and looked away.

A half-dozen mounted healers armored in quilted silk, their bows and gear tied before them, were riding westward. They led a string of remount ponies, fitted with the special saddles the healers used to carry the wounded back from the battlefield.

Knots of people milled about the cooks' wagons. Scouts and healers sipped tea and breakfasted on chunks of waybread and leftover roast meat.

The girl took a tea bowl gratefully and downed the steaming brew. She devoured a chunk of waybread and observed the camp with eager interest while she licked crumbs from her fingers.

As Nikka had told him to, he showed the girl the mare, tied apart from the strings of hobbled ponies. She asked after a pony, a wiry highland beast. Ni'An wondered if she had stolen the mare. It was, beyond question, a fine beast.

In the distance, drumrolls moved like thunder through the air. Far over the plain, like a child's strange toys, flew the banners and great windsock kites that commanders used to guide their archers' fire. Here and there a raven darted, bearing messages.

The mist had not lifted this morning. In the west puffs of smoke drifted across the sky and dissolved into the gray dawn. In the distance the handgun fire sounded sporadically, like huge raindrops beating stone.

The girl cocked her head at the sound.

"Handguns," Ni'An said. "Long, cast-iron tubes loaded with shot and set off by touching a splint to a hole in the end. The southerners use them mostly to scare horses and scatter lines of men." He watched her. "Very poor range they've got and they often misfire in the damp."

They crossed a makeshift bridge to a wooded knoll off from the main camp.

"The healers' camp. Let us make ourselves useful." Ni'An gestured upslope toward the gray tents, pegged out low to the grass, almost invisible in the misty dawn.

A gray-clad woman raised her hand in greeting. Ni'An paced by tents full of men lying in crude beds, their faces twisted in pain or slack with drugged sleep. From behind one tent flap came the sound of a man muttering, cursing a dream.

It amazed him how well the witches held those who should die back from death and sometimes snatched them away entirely. Nikka had told him that wounded Sanctum men would often be routinely killed by their own troops, as a mercy to help them rejoin the Wheel.

Beyond the tents, healers were loading their ponies, preparing to move out. He spotted Yrena, who turned and waved at him when he called her. Though she was young, her thick dark hair was already streaked with the white the witches prized as a sign of their mysterious gifts, and she wore a short sword and dagger at her waist. He had made her acquaintance in the healers' quarter while he and Nikka were in the city, then discovered yesterday that she had accompanied the army.

"I go to the western lines today, Ni'An," she said, tightening the girth strap and rubbing her pony's flank.

"Do you wish companions, Yrena?"

"Only if they have strong stomachs and steady hands."

Ni'An and Keira carried the wounded man slung between them in a net of spidersilk cord.

Why the healer bothered, Keira could not fathom. The dying man should have wheels drawn on his insteps and prayers and earth thrown over him. But Yrena paced beside the litter, one hand entwined in the dying man's, the other holding a sea sponge soaked with sickly sweet liquor over his nose. He was breathing raggedly. His free hand twitched and brushed Keira's thigh, making her shudder. The touch of dying men held no luck.

From beyond the woods came an awful, ragged sound, like logs or pitch balls exploding. Keira stiffened.

"Hand cannon," Ni'An said matter-of-factly.

Somehow naming the odd sound made it less frightening, less mysterious. Keira wondered if Ni'An understood that hearing the names of the battlefield engines and actions would reassure her. This was the kind of instinctive knowledge of her that Roshannon

himself could express so unerringly that it frustrated and unnerved her. She had not been wrong to think the cousins alike, yet
unalike. Ni'An's eyes, like his cousin's, missed little. Behind
those black eyes she felt a thousand questions waiting, but she relaxed, feeling easier under Ni'An's frank, curious glance than in
Roshannon's presence.

"Gently, gently. Lower him." Yrena indicated a sunny knoll
where another team of healers was working over a man farther
upslope.

Keira averted her eyes as she lowered the net. A broken arrow
shaft stuck from the man's shoulder and a circle of blood as broad
as a melon had spread across his loose, silk undertunic.

Keira felt Ni'An watching her, perhaps only wagering with
himself whether she would be sick. She wanted to take off the
wounded man's boots, draw two proper wheels on his insteps,
and go be sick under a tree.

But Yrena's strange calm was compelling.

"My kit," she said. Ni'An spread the bundle open. A collection
of knives gleamed there, more than a soldier or a cook would
know what to do with, wicked instruments with needle blades,
thick curved ones, and others with jagged saw teeth.

"Keep the sponge over his nose and mouth," Yrena told Keira.

She is no older than I am, yet she defies the Wheel and works
over a dead man, Keira thought. She held the sponge near the
man's nose, curious to see how the young healer would wrestle
death for the man. He stopped screaming after taking a few
breaths from the wet sponge; that seemed miracle enough.

"Hold down his arms," Yrena said.

Ni'An and Keira moved to do her bidding, and Ni'An stroked
the man's arm, whispering a few hoarse words of encouragement
to him. Keira felt queasy. Her senses had been left mercilessly
open to the sharp, hot smell of the wounded man's blood and
sweat and the tendrils of his agony curling toward her. All the
myriad realities of the battlefield, the cries of the wounded, the
weight of pain and fear, built into a relentless tattoo that kept
rhythm with her heartbeat and threatened to break through, to
pour over her and transform her.

The healer cut away the quilted overarmor to get a free view of
the wound. Keira blanched at the thought of her digging the
arrowhead and shaft out of the man's shoulder. She lowered

her eyelids until her view of the world was a slit barred by her lashes.

The young healer tugged and rucked up the spidersilk under-shirt until she had a good grip on the material around the arrow-head buried in the man's flesh. She whispered something, a prayer maybe. Gently she worked at the material, first on one side of the arrow, then the other.

Keira watched in fascination. The man passed out, his fingers clenched into fists when Yrena started working the arrow-head free.

Yrena worked with total, calm concentration. Sweat had plastered tendrils of her hair to her neck. Patiently she tugged, and bit by bit, the silk-encased, broken arrow shaft moved outward in the man's flesh. She gripped the spidersilk tautly on both sides of the arrow and pulled steadily, her knuckles white. The great pucker of bloody material that had been carried into the wound smoothed out. The reek of fresh blood hung in the morning air all around them.

Ni'An shook his head to chase away a droning fly. His eyes narrowed as he peered into the grass and away into the woods, but his hand stroked the wounded man's arm.

"Almost out." Yrena rocked the material back and forth in short, rhythmic tugs. The broken arrow shaft wobbled. She caught it, held it, with its gory point up, and tossed it aside.

Keira stared transfixed. Magic?

The section of spidersilk shirt lay, bloody but not pierced, over the man's shoulder. Yrena folded it back, laying open the wounded shoulder.

A healer from the group upslope brought bowls of steaming water and crouched over the man, conferring. She bathed the wound with a balled rag of spidersilk, laid a dressing of spider-web soaked in pungent old wine and salt over it, and bound up the shoulder in more spidersilk.

Keira rocked back on her heels. She averted her head, dizzied by the sick, sweet smell of the sponge. Battlefield impressions invaded her consciousness—her own shoulder throbbed as she imagined what it would be like to have an arrow pulled from a wound. Twisting her fingers into the grass, she drew a quick wheel.

"Magic," she whispered. "It is magic that the silk does not break."

Ni'An's hand came down over hers. "It is lucky, but not magic. It is in the nature of the silk."

Kneeling over the man, Yrena told him in a fierce, low voice, "You will live, live and grow strong again." She touched his forehead and brushed her fingers over his mouth. Smoothing her skirt, she straightened and summoned attendants. Bloodstains, mud, and grass stains spattered Yrena's clothes, and her face had that look of strained alertness that branded the face of everyone Keira had seen on the battlefield.

The attendants, healers who were not yet adepts, were left to watch over the man. One girl held his hand while a youth talked to the unconscious man, telling him that he would live and regain his strength, and reminding him of all the things yet to do in his life.

Keira eavesdropped on this performance in fascination. "Do you think he hears?"

Yrena nodded. "We see and hear in dreams, don't we?" She gathered her tools. "It does encourage him to live. Those left alone, those that no one touches, slip more quickly into the daze and die. The will to live must be kept strong so that he can help himself heal." She lifted her chin and glanced at Ni'An.

"There is more work. Will you come?"

The healers gave a quick mercy stroke to those mortally wounded, but only if they had given up hope that the man could be saved, or if it was asked of them. They were stubborn and methodical in their defiance of death.

"If a man has given up the will to live, they know it," Ni'An told Keira, "and will not hinder him on his way into death."

She spent the morning with the healers, dashing across meadows and through lines of soldiers, becoming expert at hoisting the wounded into the cord litters, and fastening the litters to the special saddle horns the healers used, so that wounded soldiers could be carried more quickly back to the temporary healers' camps that dotted the fringes of the battlefield. Sweat rolled down her body, plastering her hair to neck and forehead, but she thought that Ni'An and Yrena, working beside her, approved of her. She felt annoyed she would even worry about anyone's approval, then equally peeved she had no time to stop and scratch the furiously itching bug bites on her arms and legs. Though the silk tunic might save her life, it made her sweat like a winded horse. For her, the battle was a jumbled mosaic of impressions: masklike faces of men wounded and dying; sudden retreats as the enemy advanced too close to the healers' camps; columns of pony archers sweeping by; fletchers' wagons thundering past in choking dust clouds; a thousand separate details that she observed with merciless clarity but seemed to float above. Yet the actions she witnessed seemed to fit no orderly patterns, and she marveled that commanders could understand what to do on the field.

By midafternoon an apparent lull in the action allowed them to stretch out before a patch of woods on a grassy knoll behind the line of battle, while a company of archers set to guard them kept watch.

Stretched out in the grass, Yrena yawned as she turned the pages of a thick, leather-bound book pulled from her saddlebags. From the corner of her eye, Keira glimpsed pictures and tiny handwriting.

She leaned closer. The pictures showed parts of the body, like diagrams of what a butcher cutting up meat might see, lines of sinew and muscle attached to the bone.

With a few quick strokes of a reed pen, Yrena sketched the round shape of a shoulder with the angled lines of muscle coming off it. Keira probed her own shoulder as she watched the drawing form. Beneath the sketch, the healer made notes in a tiny hand.

Yrena glanced up. "Would you like to look at it?"

Keira nodded, and Yrena passed her the heavy, open book. Its drawings filled her with the same wonder as the maps she had glimpsed in Roshannon's tent. Many were quick sketches. Grass stains, dirty finger smudges, even bloodstains marked the margins, but the sketches always lay in the clean center of the page. Age had faded the earliest drawings. The pages made a soothing, whispery sound as they turned, and the book fell open to a fine, detailed drawing of a human skeleton—a woman's, according to the tiny characters in the margin. She recalled a skeleton left hanging on a gibbet and picked almost clean by birds and swarms of insects.

Keira studied the carefully drawn bones of the hand, flexing her fingers and summoning up a vision of her own body stripped of flesh. She frowned over the lines of rib cage, thigh, and leg bones, so like the bones of animals she had helped butcher and prepare for food. Several pages stuck together. The book fell open at a picture of a pregnant woman with a child nested inside her body. Keira's fingers traced the lines of the drawing reverently as she thought of the maps she had seen in Roshannon's tent. Which of the two explored a stranger territory? she wondered.

"Did you tend this woman?"

Yrena shook her head. "She and her baby died. The family gave the bodies to the healers' school. After we had learned what we could, we burned the bodies on a proper pyre and strewed the ashes in the sea."

"Why did they die?" Keira asked.

Yrena frowned. "There are many mysteries. The woman was young but suffered fevers. Her hips were narrow, her labor long. Then she went into the daze and did not return. The cord may have strangled the baby, which was breech."

Keira bit her lip, thinking of her mother's stillborn babies and of Mistress Treya accused of witchcraft. "When a baby's born dead, or seeming dead—" She flushed, remembering her haste to see the man on the litter as dead, with no chance of holding on to life. "—have you ever breathed into its mouth?"

"Yes." Yrena glanced curiously at her. "And often we pass them quick from a basin of warm water to one of cold. Many times that starts them breathing. But the adepts at the school have better answers than me."

Shouts came from downslope. Keira handed Yrena the book, and the healer stowed it in her satchel.

Lines of pony archers with bent bows rode into sight through the scattered trees. Looped over their saddle horns the riders carried cord nets used to bring wounded comrades to the healers. But they were carrying no wounded.

Men on lathered horses raced after them. Xian Tanta galloped up and reined in his black horse. "Enemy's broken through," he yelled. "Go west. We'll form and cover you."

His eyes met Keira's. For an instant she thought he would ride her down. He cursed, wheeled his horse, and chopped a hand signal in the air. A lithe gray hunting cat rode perched across his saddle bow.

The pony archers formed ranks in the thin cover at the edge of the woods. In a flash, the healers mounted and lifted the nets bearing wounded between their ponies. Tanta ordered them behind the lines of archers. The healers drove their pack ponies with the precious supplies of rakka and spidersilk bandages into the woods, trying to keep them quiet. Yrena stowed her gear, quick as an old soldier, touched the knife thrust through her sash, and drew her bow. Beside her, Ni'An touched his own dagger, the kind of gesture that was meant to summon luck. Then he stooped to dig a pinch of earth and ate it from his fingers.

Keira glanced through the cover of trees, past the lines of archers to that still spot at the edge of the woods where the enemy would appear.

The enemy. *My own people whom I have fled, whose ways I have put aside.* The earth seemed to draw in and hold a vast breath. A horse snorted and someone calmed it. In the meadow they had left, the healers' campfires still smoldered. "Perhaps they will settle down to tea," an archer whispered, and a ripple of laughter stirred among the men.

Xian Tanta had dismounted and paced silently along the line. On his signal, every bow in the line swept up. Tanta mounted, holding his pony in tight rein, and raised his hand. Fifty hands drew and nocked arrows in one smooth gesture. The hypnotic sound of southern drumbeats rolled upslope, mingled with the sounds of approaching troops. Armored riders appeared at the lower edge of the meadow. Tanta's hand dropped. A hissing sleet of arrows arced to meet the foot soldiers just moving into the open. The skin on the back of Keira's neck crawled. Arrows thudded home, and men and horses screamed, slumping headlong or sliding to their knees, twisting and writhing in confusion among the southern ranks. Foot soldiers who turned to flee stumbled into the ranks of their own advancing horsemen. A few of the armored cavalrymen in the back ranks had slid from their saddles, struck by the archers' volley, and one bay greathorse screamed in its death agony with an arrow in its throat. The purpose of the footmen archers, the logic of their array, this ultimate working out of the Sanctum acceptance of death and sacrifice came clear to Keira: the men before formed an expendable wall of human flesh to shield the riders behind on their thundering greathorses. Somehow, though many had crumpled beneath the northern arrows, the footmen archers reformed their ranks and came on again, nocking arrows to their own long bows. But Tanta's archers had each drawn second arrows.

Ni'An pulled at the bridle of Keira's pony, then slapped her pony's rump. "By the Wheel, go, follow the healers."

But Keira drew rein, unable to move. Tanta signaled his archers to fire. A second rain of steel-headed death sliced from the trees toward the southerners, whistling eerily. She shuddered; the deadly arrow song seemed to rip her spirit from her flesh. Her fingers tightened on the reins, and the healer's pony pranced nervously. Shock waves of horror from the men downslope buffeted her, along with the fear and exhaustion of the pony archers. She wavered in a maelstrom, compelled to stay. There was no reality beyond the sound of the arrows, or the transfixing taste of fear, no place where she would ever again fit so completely as here and now, waiting for the possibility of death to crash down on her.

Cursing, Ni'An cracked her pony's rump with his riding whip, and the beast plunged headlong.

Around them ponies crashed through the undergrowth. Archers swept by, retreating through the scrubby woodland. Coming up beside her, she heard a familiar voice.

Tanta drove his horse beside her. "What is *she* doing here?" he yelled at Ni'An on her left side.

"I am trying to make myself useful," she snapped.

Tanta grinned. "To which side?" The cat perched on his saddle bow snarled and leaped free, racing among the pack ponies. Behind them the southern pursuit diminished to a ragged fringe of sound.

Ni'An rode between them. "This woman is under my cousin's protection and my own."

"You are all under my protection now," Tanta said. "Not that I welcome it."

With an abrupt arm signal, he halted the men in his command. They reined into a loose fan around him.

Beneath her anger Keira marveled at the precision of their movements. Tanta drove his horse again between her and Ni'An. His leg brushed hers as he tightened the rein. Keira wished she were riding her own horse instead of the pony.

"Form a tight wing and travel west," Tanta said. "It's safest there now." He motioned to the healers. They dug their heels into their ponies' flanks as the sound of drums came closer.

A wider ring of horse archers swept up.

"Fall back again," a section leader who rode up behind Tanta yelled. "Into the hills, where they cannot move so fast. They've tripled their ranks."

"We've met a stronger spoke of their army than we thought," Tanta said. "What of Isharra?"

"We lost sight of her. Their wing cut us off."

Tanta cursed, then raised his arm and barked out an order. Keira was nearly jerked out of the saddle as he grabbed her bridle. She beat his arm with her left hand, forced to keep her right on the reins. Cued by Tanta's signal, a line of men galloped through the space between her and Ni'An, closed ranks around her, and swept her off.

Turning in the saddle, she saw Ni'An lashing at three of Tanta's men with a whip handle, trying to beat his way through to her. More pony archers closed in behind them and he was lost to sight.

The troop of archers raced their ponies flat out, heading for the sparsely wooded hills where they could take cover. The archers herded the pack ponies and healers ahead, keeping always between them and the southern pursuit. The rear guard periodically slowed and peeled off from the main body, loosing more arrows into the enemy ranks.

For a moment Xian Tanta was nowhere in sight in the scattered throng of riders that surged around Keira like a market-day race. She began to hope she could elude his attention and rejoin Ni'An and the healers.

On broken terrain, Keira's pony suddenly stumbled and threw her. It lay screaming and thrashing, its leg broken in a badger hole. Groggy-headed, on hands and knees, she looked up to see Xian Tanta leap off his horse. He jogged up, the huge gray hunting cat at his side, just as Keira was drawing her dagger to finish the suffering horse. He drew a sign on the pony's forehead, muttered something, and slit its throat with his own dagger. Keira crouched in the grass, her stomach heaving, her head throbbing. Her tongue smarted where she had bitten it. Tanta's sleek, gray, golden-eyed hunting cat circled her, its tail twitching back and forth. She staggered up as he remounted, wondering if he would leave her for the southern soldiers.

But he trotted over, kicked his foot from the stirrup, and held a gloved hand down to her, his eyes cold.

Her head buzzed, the air full of the smell of blood and dust. The hunting cat crouched by the dead pony's shoulder, licking the blood still oozing from its slashed throat as delicately as a kitten sampling cream. Keira put her hand in Tanta's, her boot toe in the stirrup. Brusquely, he swung her up behind him.

"Stay on without grabbing my waist too much," he said.

"Let one of your men carry me if it annoys you."

"But I have further business with you and they do not." The cat left its feast to lope beside them, and Tanta rejoined the main body of the horse archers.

Ni'An, Isharra, and the healers were nowhere in sight. The archers glanced uneasily at Keira, and a murmur of speculation passed along the line. Tanta ordered another elaborate retreat and listened to a scout's report as the man rode alongside him.

An understrategist with a red armband trotted up.

"Ka." He saluted Tanta. "We can relieve you of that burden."

"There are too many questions I would put to this burden," Tanta said.

The understrategist glanced at Keira. "The steward himself spoke for this woman. Is it seemly for you to question her further?"

"Surely more seemly than for you to question me." Tanta gave another hand signal, wheeling his horse abruptly. Keira grabbed his waist with one hand and the saddle roll with the other to keep her seat. She wanted to elbow him in the ribs and see him sprawl in the grass. He flicked his long hair over his shoulder into her face. A strand caught across her lip. Shaking her head, she glared out over the formation of men.

Again and again, Tanta's men loosed sheets of arrows from beyond the range of the enemy archers, then retreated into the shadowy, wooded hills, like quick insects that taunt a large, slow beast and fly away to swarm over their prey in another place.

"Why do you not stand and fight?" she asked.

Tanta shrugged his shoulders and laughed bitterly. "I do, when the ground gives me the advantage, when too many of my men will not die. Now we are too badly outnumbered. And I'm not ready to die yet. But first, I must question you again."

"I told the truth before."

"So you say."

Keira snorted, irritated by his voice that sounded so like

Hipolla's. She bit her lip. "If you are truly a witch, can't you see I did not lie?"

Her words might have been an arrow that had caught him between the shoulder blades. He reined in his horse abruptly on a sheltered knoll.

The view made Keira catch her breath and forget her quarrel with Xian Tanta. Below them the battlefield spread, a vast, painstaking embroidery crawling with strange life. But she recognized the plain as that she had seen many times in her recurring nightmares of the Sanctum army pursuing her. She watched many bands of archers scatter into the hills, falling back before the thick, endless columns of Sanctum soldiers. She shook her head and raised her hand against the whipping strands of Xian Tanta's hair.

A sudden eerie calm engulfed her. The troop formations on the battlefield were a string of irresistible possibilities, like counters on a game board waiting to be played. She wondered where Roshannon was. A windsock kite in the shape of a red dragon rippling in the breeze above a troop of archers caught her attention. Its undulations prompted the bonds that fettered her body and spirit together to unravel. Feeling the familiar hollow sensation in the pit of her stomach, the dizzying, exultant otherness of her body, she floated above the troop of pony archers, up where her vision offered her a hawk's-eye view of the field, and tethered herself to them, like the archer's kite.

Xian Tanta's voice held her like a kite string, anchoring her to the other reality of her physical body.

She observed the land spread below her while the priests' drumbeats resonated through her and hammered at the earth in ritual sequence, once for birth, once for death, a third time for the Wheel that broke the flesh and returned it to the world of spirit.

The wash of emotions from the two opposing armies tugged her in like a whirlpool gathering leaves and twigs and pebbles to itself. Her dream body cast itself to the very end of the kite string of human voice that tethered her to events below. It yearned to merge far above the battlefield with the air itself and the blue, beckoning void above the clouds. But her second body, by reflex, craved watching the world through the other whose eyes she had already shared.

Her vision focused on the pony archers weaving and re-forming in mysterious ranks among the hills and scrub. Then it sharpened, giving her new vantage points. Every action and reaction of the troops fed into her awareness. Each flicker of color that was a war kite aloft, each line of men, each ravine, each wooded hillside, each piece of rocky ground, each puff of smoke that wafted from a line of hand cannoneers, imprinted itself in her consciousness. The armies crashed together and ate away at each other like ocean waves eating at shores, clashed and seeped away backward like a tide withdrawing, leaving a wreckage of dead men and horses across the landscape. She floated still higher, straining at the leash of Tanta's voice.

Her dream eyes saw Tanta's voice as a silver thread twined and thickened by her memories of Hipolla and stitched through her awareness. She had merely to think of ripping stitches to soar beyond sight of the battlefield, into the tantalizing mysteries of the void beyond.

But Roshannon's awareness tendriled after her, lapping at her spirit as gently as a caress. And having tasted the distinctive patterns of his awareness before, she knew that other, unfamiliar spirits also sought her, persistent as hounds. A massive cold weight tugged suddenly at her and for a moment, intrigued, she gave herself up to it, let herself be impelled toward this new presence that wanted to taste her. Images filled her consciousness, splintering shards of reddish light and darkness, resolving into the stately, crushing turn of a vast wheel. She had touched yet another awareness.

Those who had tried to breach her mind last night? Or the Red Man? Panicking, she struggled, resisting this other as she had learned to hold her spirit closed to Roshannon: she pictured herself as a blank wall impossible to scale, a locked door, a fish eluding a closing net, a sparrow evading a hawk. Giddy and terrified but excited that she had discovered others like herself, she plunged by reflex into Roshannon.

Tanta was talking to her, the fleshly her left behind him in the saddle, and his words twisted into the haze around her like a strange language whispered behind a door where she was eavesdropping.

Her ears were stopped with the intensity of what her dream eyes saw.

The taste of earth filled her mouth. Her heartbeat rang in her ears. She rode a furiously galloping stallion, her ears full of the screams of a hundred men, her whole body trembling to the mad rhythm of a charge.

Tanta twisted sharply in the saddle, catching her by the shoulder as she slid sideways.

Roshannon, his knees pressed tight into the dun stallion's sides, his mouth tasting of the pinch of earth he had eaten before he ordered the charge, was riding straight into the face of Sanctum heavy cavalry, an action he had done everything this day to avoid. He had sent a contingent of infantry with hunting cats downwind of a broken arm of the Sanctum army to harass them, and rushed up hand cannoneers for a barrage to stampede horses and obscure the fronts with smoke.

The battle seemed at a standstill; the overwhelming numbers of the southerners poured eternally against the meager northern forces. Something was going profoundly wrong. Old tricks no longer worked, and the enemy seemed to anticipate their actions. Then his unpracticed boys faltered during a retreat, leaving half their number trapped between southern foot soldiers and heavy cavalry. Rather than let them be ground between the millstone forces of the southerners, he decided to counterattack and give them a chance to get away. Theus had nodded, saluting and giving him a knowing look as they rode into place, distracting the heavy cavalry, drawing the greathorses into a facedown.

His men fired volleys of arrows into the enemy ranks. He ordered the line to wheel and halt, ordered the arrows nocked again, coaxed the boys to take careful aim. While the arrows hissed upward, he dismounted, dug a pinch of earth and smeared it across his lips, full of sudden dreadful intuitions about his own mortality. A second later he was in the saddle, watching their arrows cut gaping holes in the ranks of the southern greathorses, slowing the survivors, some of whom had to leap their fallen comrades. He spotted the ragged line of his left wing, rallying now under a bellowing veteran.

But the Sanctum leader, astride a blood bay, was grinning like a wolf about to cut down a stray sheep as he came on in the front rank of his men. It was better to counterattack than to flee and be pushed onto the broadswords and pikes of the foot soldiers, Roshannon knew. If by luck they survived the cavalry, they could herd the southern survivors back on their own footmen.

If the luck held.

Luckily they matched the Sanctum heavy cavalry almost man to man. Halfway to the enemy line, Nikka slid his sword from his scabbard, all his body singing with the mad thunder of the stallion's gallop. Theus rode on his right hand, and the roar of on-coming Sanctum riders filled his ears, the balance of life and death glinting on the edges of the hundred upraised blades.

Suddenly his consciousness, for an indescribable liquid mo-ment, was snatched, pinned to the blue sky overhead, to the ele-gant dance of the archers' dragon kites drifting up against the sun and disappearing. Heat sheathed him from head to toe.

A familiar finger of wind stroked itself across the back of his neck. Gooseflesh sheathed his arms. Keira abroad again, paying him a visit. Damn the girl. He struggled to hold his seat in the saddle, thinking that the joining might end with both their deaths. This time it offered an eerie, game-board clarity. Keira's vision pouring into his turned the hills inside out, revealing what lay be-hind them as clearly as what lay before. Through her eyes, his fragmented view of the battlefield became whole. He saw his sal-vation—another troop of pony archers circling on the battlefield toward them, if only they could last until the others arrived.

A scream ripped from his throat, from the throats of all the men around him. He swung his sword at the onrushing enemy ranks as the lines clashed together. A head toppled over the dun stallion's neck, spattering blood. The beheaded rider's horse plunged franti-cally sideways, colliding with two Sanctum riders, throwing off-balance the first Sanctum rank and opening a chink for the pony archers.

Roshannon cracked the dun's rump with the flat of his sword to get himself and his horse free, raised his blade to parry a blow from the right. He plunged into the wedged opening in the south-ern ranks, slashing and thrusting with his sword, feeling her rid-ing him, tasting and sharing battle madness, learning the first and last lesson of the battlefield—that madness was the only reason-able answer sometimes. Then there was nothing but redness, blackness, and the rise and fall of his sword arm.

The sound rumbled until it filled her awareness. It became a voice that insisted, like one prodding her out of a dream. She wanted to close her ears and refuse to hear, so comfortable had she been floating above the battlefield, satisfying her curiosity with bits and pieces of Roshannon's experience. The annoying voice insisted. She opened her eyes. Xian Tanta knelt beside her.

A man with a red armband stalked into her circle of vision and crouched by Tanta. "We are vulnerable here and the calm won't last long." His voice roared and grated at her ears, and he stooped, peering at her. "Is she sick?"

Tanta shook his head, showing his teeth in a slow smile.

Keira sat up, struggling against the profound weight of her own body that dragged her down to rock, to earth, to pain and fear. She wanted to speak, to scream, but her mouth had forgotten the form of words.

Tanta bent closer, his yellow wolf eye, his green summer eye studying her. The austere shaping of the bones beneath his face was clean and hard. In fascination she stared through him to the pattern of woods and hills and waves of men pouring from another set of eyes into hers.

He cursed softly and sat back on his heels. "What do you see?"

Keira shook her head; her voice caught in her throat as she dug her fingers into the grass. She felt as if she were hanging upside down from a tree while her mind struggled to turn what she saw right side up.

Abruptly, Tanta drew his dagger, and swung it slowly by its thong back and forth before her. The lines of the beasts etched on its blade blurred and spun into a thread of light.

"What do you see?"

The voice asked and the point of light spun through her hoarse answers, over and over again.

Two cracks sounded. Her cheeks stung.

"You slapped me," she said irately to Tanta, who was crouching by her.

"The quickest way to break the bridge, the mind link." He nodded and rose, holding a hand down to her.

She stared at her own hand, seeing instead Roshannon's gloved hand wielding a saber, then her own small callused hand, then Tanta's outstretched hand again. Fragments of many worlds shifted and seethed inside her, shifted and turned again. Is this how a woman about to give birth feels? she wondered idly. She put her hand in Tanta's, focusing on his face again, studying his mismatched eyes, feeling queasy, dizzy, dry-mouthed.

Green eye, gold eye. Summer eye, wolf eye.

Suddenly all that he was, all his pain and sorrow coalesced between them, meshing into her awareness. She was a sieve straining his experiences through her own spirit, and the act tasted of infinite pain and joy. Her fingertips curled in Tanta's hand. She saw the battlefield he had survived, the tumbled nest of dead men that had served to hide him from the southern soldiers, the buzzing, iridescent blanket of flies coating the bodies of the dead, and the maggots the healer had let feed upon his wounded side. Images of Hipolla leaked from his mind to hers and back again, shared memories, fragments floating on the void of his endless sorrow.

His eyes widened. He leaned even closer to her.

She withdrew her hand. Sympathy struggled with a growing horror of him. He, too, was like Roshannon, like the others who had tried to net her spirit above the battlefield. He had seen her in that shared moment as clearly as Roshannon had. Yet he was not the one who had touched her above the city. There were still others to face. She thought of the frail-looking twin brother and sister who had tried to enter her mind. She found herself staring into the yellow eyes of Tanta's hunting cat, which was pacing back and forth in a spot of sunlight.

The man beside Tanta put a hand on his shoulder. "Tanta-ka. We cannot stay here longer. A line of riders and foot soldiers is moving uphill and we are nearly flanked."

Tanta's mouth twisted. He held a hand out to Keira.

Afraid to touch him, Keira scrambled to her feet.

Tanta snorted and turned on his heel, the set of his shoulders just like Hipolla's.

Tanta insisted on carrying her before him on the saddle when they mounted up. Keira shrunk from his touch, exhausted, and struggled to build walls around herself. But this way of acquiring knowledge fascinated her too much for her to reject it outright. The connection with Tanta was frailer than the one with Roshannon, much easier to lock out. She puzzled over the vagaries of this strange ability she often cursed, while Tanta reined in on a wooded knoll above the line of southern soldiers who had pursued them.

The Sanctum riders carried lances and pikes, their armor dull under a sheen of dust. The lead rider's horse had apparently thrown a shoe or gone lame, for the rhythm of its hoofbeats rang unevenly.

A few longbowmen with half-empty quivers slung over their backs walked between the riders.

Tanta made a noise in his throat. "We will kill you quickly, at least."

The pony archers loosed a rain of arrows on the southern men. Armored cavalrymen and their mounts went down, screaming. One horse went down with an arrow in its throat. Its rider took shelter behind his dead horse as the survivors fled back the way they had come.

The red-haired understrategist rode down for a closer look at the carnage. The end of a longbow poked above the dead horse's flank, an arrow whistled, and a black-fletched arrow thudded squarely into his chest. His horse reared as the understrategist slumped forward in the saddle. He slid across the horse's withers and slipped from the saddle, held only by a foot caught in the left stirrup. Tanta, still carrying Keira before him, caught the horse's reins as it plunged back into the archers' line, then swung off his pony. Keira shifted into the saddle and dismounted.

Calming the understrategist's horse, Tanta freed the man's foot from the stirrup and crouched over him. The understrategist stared wide-eyed, blood frothing on his lips.

"Kill me," he whispered in a hideous gurgle.

Keira watched Tanta brush his fingertips across the man's forehead, press his eyes closed, and slide his dagger into the man's neck, to the base of his brain. The body shuddered, and the spirit was gone.

"Greet me, friend, when I return to the Wheel," Tanta murmured.

Keira wondered whether Tanta's Wheel was the same Wheel the priests referred to. Numbly she watched two archers methodically pick off the Sanctum longbowman behind the dead horse before the troop rode on.

As the nearly full moon rose over the plain, they reached camp with the understrategist's body slung over his horse.

Tanta rode in silence, unbroken until they spotted the tents and corralled ponies of their own encampment. He asked her quietly to tell him how Hipolla had died.

Keira thought again of her friend and that distant meadow. She closed her eyes and said simply, "She died bravely. Perhaps there is no better death than that."

"Perhaps."

Ni'An felt a rising sense of resentment as he paced, picturing Tanta carrying off that girl. He sometimes thought that her coming had brought madness on the entire camp.

Just then Tanta swept up on his fine-boned black pony, reining in right before the tent, with that girl wrapped in her ragged cloak riding pillion before him. Ni'An's mood sunk even lower.

"A neat trick you pulled," Ni'An said.

At that moment Roshannon-ka flung open the tent flap.

Tanta barely turned in the saddle, regarding them both levelly. "No trick. We were overrun."

"Has any harm befallen you, Keira Danio?" Roshannon asked.

"There's no harm done, so nothing to answer for." Tanta nodded to the cousins. "If you cannot keep one woman within eyesight that is no fault of mine." He sounded quite pleased with himself.

Ni'An watched his cousin's face, half hoping Nikka would pull the witch lord from the saddle and thrash him. The girl, the trouble itself, was the calm center of it all, the hub of the wheel. Seeing the awful stillness in Nikka's face as he regarded the girl, Ni'An suddenly had no doubt his cousin had bedded her, that she was indeed Nikka's trouble.

Ni'An stood by Tanta's right stirrup, and Roshannon at the horse's head. A knot of onlookers had gathered, he noted with relief, and Isharra and the steward's constable were elbowing their way through the crowd.

"I am not harmed," Keira said.

"That does not matter," Nikka said coldly. "You were given into my charge and no one else's."

Tanta laughed. "She speaks true. No harm done, whatever harm you imagine. Yet if you value this prisoner so much, why did you put her in the hands of your cousin who let her be taken away from him?" He jerked his reins, and his horse pranced in a tight circle.

"Enough, you two!" The steward's constable, his green tabard bloodstained and ripped, strode forward, grabbing Tanta's bridle and laying a hand flat against Nikka's chest. "If you two wish to fight over a bedgirl instead of planning strategy for tomorrow's fight, you are little use to the northern army." He gestured to Keira. "Off with you."

The girl dismounted and faced the constable. The glamour that had clung to her early this morning, the film of illusion that made one see her as a lad, had dropped from her now, leaving her revealed as a tall, thin girl with a pockmark in the middle of her forehead. "I am no one's bedgirl," she said hotly.

Ni'An laughed, admiring her spirit, realizing she was bone tired.

"Then see you never are," the constable said coldly.

"There are other things she is, though," Tanta said. "And I think that is a matter of importance to the whole camp."

Roshannon moved closer to Tanta's horse.

"Indeed it is, but damn you both for quarreling over her." The constable turned, his dark eyes blazing. His eyes fell on the witch woman who stood among the spectators.

"Isharra, I charge you, take her into your custody."

❀ **18** ❀

Several days later, Roshannon returned from the battlefield and ducked through the flap of his tent. He jerked with numb, stiffened fingers at the ties of his quilted armor. He gestured Theus away and sat on a folding stool to take off his boots. Suddenly too weary to do that, he slumped with his head in his hands.

He struggled with the sense of wrongness he had felt all day. His left thigh ached where the flat of a Sanctum broadsword had crashed into him in the confusion of battle.

But he was bone tired, too weary to take off his boots.

Wincing at the aching bruise that stretched from just above his knee to the point of his hip, Roshannon walked slowly to his pallet, lay down, and stared into the peak of the tent.

He gritted his teeth at the taunting vision of Keira riding back on Tanta's horse. Something had gone profoundly wrong from that day on, not only for him, but for the other strategists as well. Midnight and dawn raids no longer caught the southerners by surprise, and Sanctum troops anticipated northern moves, as if guided by a master ko player. Morale had fallen, the fighting had stagnated, and rumors of treason abounded. And when Keira linked with him now, despair and visions of death tainted her awareness. She looked thin and drawn and Isharra said she woke from bad dreams. Roshannon suspected the steward and his dreamers would soon seek him out, with hard questions about his link with Keira. But, just now, he was too tired to care when they would come for him.

The battlefield had become a nightmare. His men skirmished honorably, harried more lines, cut off stragglers, stampeded more horses, and made off with more baggage trains, as did the other strategists' troops, but these actions merely annoyed the vast, crawling Sanctum army, as a cloud of hovering gnats would provoke a bull into flicking its tail along its broad back and scattering the lot of them.

The pony archers needed the full force of their actions bound together somehow, and driven in one vast assault against the Sanctum. These gadfly skirmishing tactics failed to strike at the Sanctum's heart, while the vast army continued northward. At least the northerners had weakened the connections between Kum and the southerners by ringing the city and keeping potential southern allies out, and had captured couriers and supply wagons.

Patience, he told himself. He had to admire the troops he fought against, too. Their lines had re-formed countless times today with a ruthless resilience, and they fought with a seeming intuition he had not encountered before in the Sanctum ranks. It might be one of the Bala Kothi generals, or the archpriest himself who inspired such toughness.

Roshannon lay with his arm flung over his eyes, not sleeping, but drifting into strange territory. He opened his eyes to see two guards standing at the foot of his bed.

Keira was mending tack in Isharra's tent when the guards came for her, demanding that she accompany them to the steward's tent.

"For what reason?" Isharra rose at sight of their drawn swords and grim faces.

The guards shook their heads. "We cannot say," the youngest said. "Now quick."

Isharra insisted on accompanying Keira, and finding Xian Tanta, asked him to come, too.

The guards announced themselves outside the high steward's tent. Roshannon waited there, flanked by two more stone-faced steward's men.

"Bring them inside together," the steward called.

The steward's tent was simply, even austerely furnished. He and the two dreamers sat behind a low table set with tea bowls. He indicated that Keira and Roshannon should sit facing them. The guards stood behind, just inside the doorway.

One guard cleared his throat. "Ka. The woman appointed to guard this girl is outside with Xian Tanta. They insisted on coming."

The steward nodded. "Keep them outside. This is the business of no one but these two, myself, and the dreamers."

"Ka," Roshannon said. "Are you arresting us?"

"Not exactly." The steward gestured a servant to bring tea. "Sit down. Make yourselves as comfortable as you can. It's time for a truthsaying."

Keira shook her head, staring at the dreamers. "If it is to be that again, you had better kill me now."

The male dreamer, the one called Riva, grinned slowly. "Lady, we won't try that again. But we need the truth from both of you."

"The complete truth," the steward said. "It's vitally important now. Though you both have not actually lied, you've avoided much of the truth."

"Tell me what you charge me with and I can answer you," Roshannon said. "Otherwise, you speak in damned riddles."

"The riddle of the two who become one, who see through each other's eyes, share each other's senses and experiences. Very simple: the riddle of amaratsa." He sipped from his tea bowl and carefully set it down on the table. He looked from Keira to Roshannon.

"You two are wild miratasu, which interests me very much. In the city I realized you were bound to an awakened one. And from your mind," he said to Keira, "I saw several images, among them Roshannon's face."

Thaia, the frail-looking woman, leaned toward Keira. "We need to know when you two met and bonded. Do you deny it, that you have shared the world through each other's eyes?"

Keira stared at the table, conscious of the sound of her own breathing. Roshannon also remained silent.

"Does either of you deny meeting before Keira Danio was brought to this camp?" the steward asked.

"We could torture you," Thaia said, "overcome your minds and strip the information from you. Don't make us waste your lives."

"Those tortured will confess anything," Roshannon said. "So looking for truth in their words is not wise, which you know. But I am a subject from an allied city-state and have the right to know what I am accused of. Explain."

"We have sensed a spiritual pollution," the steward said, "a darkness in the turn of battles. We believe an awakened one leads the southerners, a powerful wild dreamer. We believe our enemy has a foothold in this camp, in one or both of you. Do you two deny being acquainted?"

Roshannon laughed. "No, I don't deny it. I bought this woman from her father, and slept one night with her. That, until now, was our acquaintance."

"Why an acquaintance of such short duration?" the woman dreamer asked.

Keira snorted. "Because I ran away and headed north."

The dreamer Riva raised his eyebrows. "You slept together only once?"

Keira flushed. "It is none of your business. What has that got to do with anything?"

"Everything," the woman said. "It is the best way to begin a bridge between two awakened ones. The joining of flesh helps spirits merge."

Keira's flush deepened and a horrible thought occurred to her as she stared at the twin dreamers. "Is it true, then, what the priests say—that some of you even sleep with your brothers and sisters?"

Brother and sister both laughed. "We were together in our mother's womb," Riva said, "joined in spirit from birth. There was no need for us to couple since the bond existed from the first."

"The priests kill twins," Keira said, "especially brother-sister twins, which they say are an abomination."

"Doubtless they say that," Thaia said, "because brother-sister twins seem like the original image of god, male and female contained in one body, one womb. Some of our strongest dreamers have been brother-sister twins. During the Schism the priests, in memory of how the gift sometimes occurred among us, killed all the brother-sister twins they could find."

"Once," Riva said, "we were one people and the gift flourished. But the priests feared the gift and remade the images of god, destroying the twin image of male and female together, suppressing the gift. They discovered that rakka suppressed the gift and after long generations suppressed even the minor gifts in whole families."

"But how can one night with someone cause such a bond?" Roshannon asked.

Thaia smiled. "It is how the gift works. The dream masters tell newly awakened ones to be very careful whom they sleep with."

"What happened when you first felt the gift, before you two slept together?" Riva asked.

"Fever dreams that left me dizzy came at the end of my

boyhood," Roshannon said. "They brought visions. Of my father sailing north to explore the Ice Kingdoms, of my first love."

"I had a long fever, too," Keira said, "full of strange dreams."

"About the time you began to bleed?" Thaia asked.

Keira nodded.

"That is how the gift usually comes to women. What were the dreams?"

"Small things first. Then I dreamt stranger things, and always a part of the dream became real: my mother's death, three women hanged as witches.

"I thought I was going mad."

"If you had not fled north, you might have," Riva said. "Or the archpriest might have caught you and tortured you to learn the secret of your mystery, as he has tortured others we have heard about."

The steward looked from Keira to Roshannon. "Adepts caution young dreamers to be very careful in choosing whom they sleep with after their gifts wake, for once forged the bond is not easily broken." He sighed. "But your bond intrigues me, because of its complexities.

"The scouts who brought you in, Keira Danio, complained of particularly strange dreams: of a Red Man, with a circle of fire burning on his chest. Did you dream of such a man?"

"Yes. What does it mean?"

"Trouble," the steward said. "We think the southern archpriest somehow shares your awareness. Did you encounter the Red Man, after you had slept with Roshannon?"

"Do your questions have a point?" Roshannon demanded.

"A very good one," Riva said. "A recently awakened one is especially vulnerable to other presences."

Keira stared into the steward's golden eyes. His will raged around her, yet refrained from touching her. "Yes, I saw him once, when I skirted a Sanctum army and hid in a tree. He burned with presence, like a lit candle. A camp follower I met later told me about how he tortured captive witches, and had scars in the shape of a great wheel on his chest."

Keira remained silent, knowing the steward's suspicions were true. Too many presences had probed her spirit; she remembered hiding in the tree, watching the Red Man, and feeling the eerie heat of his spirit.

Roshannon said slowly, "And this link explains why the battles have turned against us lately?"

Riva nodded to him. "Yes. Because the archpriest's spirit must have snared Keira's—in a much different way than when you two joined. Both Keira and the priest awakened where the talent must be hidden, or may be seen as madness. But the just-wakened dream self is a vast lonely net, casting itself far and wide, seeking kindred spirits. Like is drawn to like and two awakened ones often recognize each other. That is how the Red Priest can spot witches. And when Keira, just awakened completely through Roshannon, watched him from that tree, he was drawn to her presence, and she to his. As neither is trained in the use and control of the gift, both snared a bit of the other, so that he now invades her dreams and consciousness. And through her, because the link between you two is so powerful and so unguarded, he sees what Roshannon sees of our battle plans."

"You see us as traitors, and will execute me after all," Keira said, unable to hold the words back.

The high steward studied them both as he sipped tea. "I see the situation as the supreme test of both your loyalties. Where will you cast your gifts in the end, a runaway and a former mercenary? The head of the dream masters' guild would try to salvage you both because you are powerful dreamers. She'd isolate you, and have her adepts enter your minds and force the Red Man's spirit from you; then the dream masters would judge you.

"Granted, a more conventional soldier would execute you both within the hour. But I offer a reprieve." He smiled. "Because I see a way to catch the archpriest, who seems to be the southern army's heart, the keystone of their strength.

"The question is: Are you willing to risk your lives to help us catch him?"

"I favor that over the other choices," Keira said.

"That is my choice, too, if the sword or the invasion of my mind is the other choice," Roshannon said softly. "What game do you play?"

The steward sipped his tea. "A fishing game, to see if the fish will bite."

"We have touched the Red Man's spirit," Thaia said. "He is obsessed with finding others of his kind, other dreamers. His aloneness, his fascination with the mystery of his nature, is his great weakness. In reality, he is our brother and we hesitate to destroy such a great gift as his. But he uses the gift in dark ways. Here is the plan.

"You, Roshannon-ka, enter the southern camp. Act disgruntled with the northern cause and say you want to change your allegiance to the south. You are familiar enough with southern ways, having served in their armies, to figure a way of getting into the archpriest's presence. Once there, you are in danger but will have many chances."

"Killing him outright would never work," Roshannon said. "I would be killed."

"If the plan works," Riva said, "we will not kill him at all, but get him alive, so the steward can question him. The spirit link works best between men and women. A kind of holy marriage, if you will. Keira will let my sister's spirit enter her, then link with Roshannon. Otherwise my sister would spend too much energy linking with him herself. Once Keira meshes with Roshannon, she can return her spirit to her own body and be out of danger. Then Thaia will tackle the archpriest and spirit duel with him, dragging his dream self from his body. That disables his physical body, enfeebles it to the point where he will be suggestible as a child, easily led and manipulated."

The steward leaned forward. "The body is vulnerable when the spirit travels out of it. Thus Thaia, once she defeats the archpriest's spirit, can control the archpriest's body briefly, until he and Roshannon-ka get beyond the camp, where rescuers can sweep in. But we must keep the archpriest's spirit subdued and out of his body. His spirit learned power in total aloneness, never knowing the balance and joy of joining with another—it's a slightly mad spirit, perhaps, a powerful, deadly enemy. And through Riva, still meshed with his sister, the rescuers will know where to meet Roshannon and the archpriest."

"It's a madman's chance," Roshannon said. "If we succeed, what then?"

"I will honor you and consider you my true allies," the steward said.

Roshannon glanced at Keira. "I accept if you grant me time to speak with Keira Danio and with my cousin."

"I accept," Keira said. "There is no one I need speak to but the boy Beren."

"Speak to no one of this." The steward raised his hands. "My dreamers can instruct you both in the vedas, the measures of control that we use when we spirit travel. I wish you both well."

Isharra and Keira walked back to Isharra's tent in silence. Keira felt numb with exhaustion.

One horn lantern illuminated the inside of Isharra's sparsely furnished tent. The moon, full but for a sliver on the left side, cast an eerie light outside the tent's doorway, where a campfire flickered and two guards sat, trading tales.

"Do you want women's clothes?" Isharra asked.

Keira shook her head.

"Is that really yours?" The woman indicated the dagger in Keira's sash.

"Yes, it is mine."

"Do you know how to use it?"

Keira met the other woman's eyes. "Not really."

Isharra shrugged. "Then I will teach you sometime. You should not carry something you don't know how to use." She yawned, stretching. "And remember, if you get by me, there are two guards outside." She divided the bedding and tossed half in Keira's corner.

Keira was glad Isharra did not ask what the steward's business with her and Roshannon had been.

With a sigh Isharra sat on her pallet, stripping off her gear and tunic. Her muscled back was brown and unscarred. Her hair spread across her shoulders like a fan of bleached wheat.

A sudden memory of how Isharra had whispered in Roshannon's ear, her hair fallen across his shoulder, twisted through Keira's mind. Like an image of light and dark, they had looked beautiful next to each other. She had watched them together with a strange still wonder in her own heart. She could not understand why that should bother her.

Isharra was a soldier one moment and just a woman brewing tea the next. She mended tack in the lantern light, using a bodkin and her dagger. She looked eerily like Hipolla sometimes, but half of Keira's heart wanted to hate her. Though glad of the other woman's comradeliness, Keira still felt apprehension. *If I grow to like* you, *then surely you will be killed, as Hipolla was.*

Keira quietly mended tack. The count of days she kept in her head got jumbled again. She started over, craving that twinge of pain low in her abdomen that told her she would bleed with the moon as she always had.

The women had started a ko game when Roshannon arrived. Isharra granted him some time and, putting on her cloak, left.

"I would speak with you," he said.

"Do I have any choice?"

"You always have a choice," he said. "And I think you know that."

She watched him in silence. Both sets of ko stones were evenly matched, in a tight promising game. Unable to resist, he moved Isharra's blue stone. She moved a black.

He glanced at her, then looked quickly away. "I will not touch you in any way, my word of honor. But there are things you must know if I do not return alive from the steward's 'fishing trip.' "

She opened her mouth as if to say something, closed it.

"I'm bait for the steward's dreamers to draw the archpriest into a spirit duel. Bait is disposable. You are not stupid, you know that. If I die, my cousin Ni'An can protect you; if he cannot, go to Xian Tanta, who would adopt you into his clan in memory of his dead niece. If neither of those choices appeals to you, make your way to Lian Calla and present yourself to my mother, the mistress of the harbor. Tell her you were my wife. She would help you, though she might first refuse to believe you.

"Show her the dagger—my father gave me the pair of them, along with my first clan earring, the day he set sail with my elder brothers. They never returned from the voyage." He watched her. "As for the witches—"

"We are both witches," she said, taking a step closer.

"Oh, aye. We are and we are not. We don't see the world quite the way they do. But the steward's dreamers call you the most powerful wild dreamer they have encountered in many years. You are a prize to them, though they would not admit it to you."

"A sort of brood mare," she said matter-of-factly.

"It's not so simple as that. They venerate the gift, but twist it to their purposes. As I imagine they would treat you well, yet use you for their own ends."

"Ka. And how would you bend me to your purpose and that of

your people?" she asked, while she, a freeholder's daughter, still
dared ask a lord such a question.

He watched her gravely, as if unable to answer. Maybe it was
his hesitation on that question that finally made her trust him.

"If I die, it's none of your worry, lady. If I live and if you truly
become my wife, you would have to divine the answers. I cannot
say how we would each use the other, in pleasant and less pleasant ways." He grinned. "You've used my eyes, my body, more
than I have yours. And you took pleasure in the using."

"Ka," she said. It was true, but the idea of his entering her mind
as completely as she had his still frightened her.

"You must choose."

"I will." She moved another stone. "But I must see Beren
Harth."

"Tomorrow I will have him brought to this tent."

"How do I know I can trust your word?"

"You can." He clicked a stone down and captured two of her
counters.

She captured two of his stones. He countermoved so rapidly
that his hand brushed hers. She looked down but countered his
move instantly. The stones clicked on the board, a pleasant comforting sound. Middle game flew into endgame. By two moves,
he won.

Isharra stepped back into the tent.

"I will send the boy to you tomorrow," Roshannon said.

"Because you won and feel generous?" she asked.

He rose. "Because you play well and it is time you see him."
He turned to her. "What kind of ally will you be in this strange
fight, Keira Danio?"

"As good an ally as a freeholder's daughter can be, ka'innen."

Her dream self knew the land, for she had been here before.
Riders came over the hill. They wore Sanctum armor of antique
fashion. The two lead riders carried poles held before them like
talismans. Her dream eyes traveled slowly up the length of the
pikes. Floating hair caught her eye, but she could raise her dream
vision no farther. She stared at the horses' harness and the hard,
lined faces of the soldiers.

Her dream self staggered and fell before the oncoming riders.
A weight pressed her down until her backbone merged with the

earth. The weight atop her was warm and live, a man pressed belly to belly with her. They wrestled, turning over and over. Roshannon, kneeling over her, laughed at her. He bent over her, his hair brushing her belly. They began feasting on each other, as dark feasts on light, defines and changes it, and seeks to dissolve the line between the two.

She twisted in the nest of covers. Tears burned her eyes as she stared at the tent's peaked roof. Harnesses jingled outside as horses snorted and champed their bits, their shod hooves trampling the hard-packed ground. She flung off the covers and pulled on her clothes.

Isharra was gone, her weapons and overarmor missing from the neat stack of gear, but her aide coughed in the doorway. He led a skinny boy into the tent as Keira finished putting on one boot.

"Lady, I was ordered to bring this one to you," the aide said.

"Beren-ka." Keira sat up straight on the pallet and reached for the other boot. She frowned toward the aide, but he did not leave.

Beren knelt by her pallet, and they embraced. She held him at arm's length. His face had begun to fill out, and he looked less solemn.

"I'm the cook's Brat now," he said. "The cook makes me work, but he feeds me. What do they make you do?"

"I've helped the healers," Keira said, almost whispering in the hopes that the stolid young guard would not hear every word. "Could you wait outside?"

The man looked abashed but, astonishingly, did as she asked. She and the brat exchanged a grin.

Beren settled on her pallet. "When can we get away? I've seen your mare and my pony among the remounts when the cook sent me on errands. They haven't been ridden or given to other soldiers. They're getting fat and frisky."

"Good, gorging themselves on grain." Keira's fingers curled through the hair on the back of his neck. "So you have the run of the camp and a full belly every night?"

He grinned. "Do they give you enough to eat? Maybe I can sneak you a pie from the cook."

Keira mockingly swatted at him, and he ducked. "You want me to get fat, too, and not just our horses? Brat, you know they have captured a priest."

"I know. The cook sent me to take him food last night." His mouth suddenly twisted. "Do you want to stay among the witches? I thought you wanted to ride off, far away from this battle."

She nodded. "So I do. But there are things I must do."

"What?"

She shook her head. "Beren-ka, listen. If anything happens to me, go to the woman Isharra, whose tent this is. Or to Xian Tanta, or the strategist Roshannon's cousin Ni'An. Can you remember that?" She reached for his hand but he snatched it away.

"What do you mean? Are you running away again?"

Keira shook her head. "Not this time. I am going to do something that may be dangerous, but I can't tell you about it."

"Some people here say you are a witch. I've heard them. Is that true? Did you lie to me?"

"I never lied to you. And people call others by many names. But I am only myself," Keira said slowly. "And I'm trying to protect you."

He frowned at her, chewing his lip. "Oh, you're just a girl. I don't have to stay with you or listen to you." He glanced toward the tent flap and the guard outside. He made a face. "You should wear dresses now." He scrambled up and ran out the door, nearly colliding with the guard.

Beren walked through the great forest alone. Nothing and everything looked familiar, in that odd way dreams had. Somehow he knew where he was going, his footsteps soft as the settling leaves. He smelled and heard water and came at last to a stream partly pooled behind a natural rock dam.

He knelt to drink. The water was mysteriously sweet. He peered at his mirrored image, caught by something odd he had not noticed before.

His reflection stared back intently at him, with yellow beast eyes, yellow witch eyes.

Beren woke sweating, staring at the wagon staves that supported the canvas top of the cook Thoren's wagon. He suspected the dreams were Keira's fault. He crawled from the covers and peered into the beveled square mirror hung by a leather strap from a peg set into the end post.

He stared at his own image, turning his head this way and that, letting the dim morning light play over his eyes. Frightened and fascinated, he could no longer say what color they were, or if they were changing their hue.

He scrambled into his clothes and climbed outside to help Thoren.

"What color are my eyes?" he asked the cook. He stirred the stew pot so vigorously a gob of steaming spicy meat slopped over the rim and hit a passing hunting cat, which hissed and bolted.

Thoren grabbed Beren's wrist, halting his stirring, and looked at him a long moment. He snorted.

"They're brown as nuts, the best I can tell, sort of golden brown, like chestnuts." The cook tossed another handful of spices into the pot. "What ails you anyway? Have you taken a fancy to a girl at your age?"

Beren shook his head adamantly. Girls were worse than gold eyes, as far as he could tell, except for Keira of course, who wasn't exactly a girl.

The cook shook his head and sent Beren to the healers' tent with a huge shallow bowl of stew. On his way there, picking his way around sleeping troopers and hunting cats grooming themselves, Beren spied Liet, another cook's boy, coming from the area of the captains' tents.

Liet feinted at Beren's head with his empty stew bowl, but Beren dodged smoothly, used to the ritual and proud that no stew spattered his clothes.

Liet laughed; his eyes narrowed. "They've caught one of your people, pup. A priest, no less. I took him stew this morning, and he wrinkled his nose at it as if it were poison."

"Liar," Beren said, as Liet dashed by, playfully slapping the younger boy's shoulder. Beren made his way to the healers' camp more slowly and thoughtfully.

The smell of the cook's concoctions wafted to every corner of the camp, and every rumor in the camp found its way back to the cook's wagons. It was a good place to be among the witches, he thought, if one had to be among these strange people. While carrying food through the camp yesterday, Beren had overheard men discussing "that southern woman" and referring to her as a witch. And as a bed warmer for both Roshannon-ka and Tanta-ka. With a shock he realized the soldiers meant Keira.

The whole world slid from beneath his feet, sending him into strange territory. He wondered if Keira had not ridden straight for the witch scouts. And ever since that morning the scouts woke saying they had each dreamed visions of a red-robed man with a wheel branded on his chest, Beren, too, had dreamed. The Red Man, and now this latest dream of himself with witch eyes. And it was all Keira's fault.

He shook with anger at her.

He remembered wondering whether or not the cook was a real witch. The man had neither white hair nor beast eyes, nor did he beat the boy or call him names. Though Beren had been raised to distrust the witches, to hate and fear them as half-souled men, he could not forget their kindnesses.

Beren did not want to like a witch, so he convinced himself the cook was a war captive. But the cook had smashed that fancy by recounting his boyhood in the spicemongers' quarter in the great city of Cartheon, describing the ships and markets, and the wooden hoops he had rolled along the cobblestone streets with his brothers and sisters.

Beren tried to hate the cook, because hating witches was part of his duty. But Thoren fed him, and the food was good. The cook worked him hard but fairly, treating him no better or worse than the other helpers. He gave Beren a place to sleep in his wagon behind the braziers that were lugged out at dusk to cook the soldiers' food. Beren kept his sling wrapped around his waist. He made an eight-spoked wheel from long wood shavings scavenged from the camp carpenters, binding it with a bit of broken bowstring. He hung it inside the wagon, over the spot where he slept. One day he overheard Thoren scolding Ule, another cook's boy. Ule had found Beren's wheel and favored destroying it. Thoren stopped him, saying no one should destroy another's god symbols.

"But the southlanders break our god stones wherever they find them," Ule said.

"Lad, they're ignorant," Thoren said. "There's room in the world for all the gods man or woman can imagine. And those who don't know that are plain stupid."

Beren touched his makeshift wheel on the wagon's wall that night before he went to sleep, haunted by the image of his watery reflection smiling at him, its eyes shining yellow as wolf eyes or witch eyes.

The next day he traded with another boy to take food to the captured priest.

Inside the dim-lit tent the priest lay with folded hands, staring at the tent roof and muttering prayers. A tray with tea bowls and waybread lay on a chest beside the bed. The man sat up.

Beren turned with sudden misgiving. "Ka. Excuse me."

"Child, you are not one of them."

Beren turned to face him. I'm no longer one of my own kind, he was thinking. "Ka, I came to ask your advice."

The priest eyed him, gestured to the waybread, and lifted a tea bowl. Beren saw no signs of torture or mistreatment on the man, yet he had a dark, hunted look.

"No proper boy should be bound to a half-souled master." The priest sipped tea, regarding Beren carefully.

Beren nodded assent, but the notion turned in his heart that a woman and a half-souled man had treated him better than many a man who claimed a complete soul.

"I dreamt last night," he said, and blurted out his nightmare. "What does it mean?"

"Child," the priest said, "it does me good to speak to one of my fellows. But the dream is evil. You are wise to fear it. Indeed, I think it shows some truth. Fear of pollution brought this dream, pollution beyond hope of redemption. For the sake of your soul, you should flee this camp, before you are sullied past reclaiming."

Beren's hands clenched into fists.

The priest raised his tea bowl, sipping slowly. "I am Kumini," he said. "A sanctuary priest. Of course, the new order had some political disagreements with the patriarch of the sanctuary. Many of us older priests were turned out, to march in the infantry ranks and provide good examples of martyrdom." He looked at Beren. "Many refugees and pilgrims from the southlands fled into Kum. Some had accents like yours," he said softly.

Beren watched the priest smile at him. He felt suddenly like a fox cub facing an old hound. But he thought of Keira leaving him at the inn, after telling him he would be safer in Kum. He thought of the things he had overheard about her. "If I showed you a way out of this camp," he asked the priest, "could you take me to Kum?"

"By the Word," the priest said.

❀ 19 ❀

The ground under her sore and bleeding feet reverberated with drumbeats, like a vast heartbeat.

Her body stuck fast to the earth, heavy as a stone. Drumbeats boomed through the ground and shimmered the air. Unable to struggle any farther, she turned to face what was coming for her.

Wind poured against her back and her legs, a great hand pushing her toward her pursuers. It howled in her ears, flattening the grain and billowing her skirts.

The black banners of an army appeared over the hilltop.

She thrust her hands in her skirt pockets to keep them from trembling. Her pockets were full of stones. Frantically she flung the stones away, feeling herself grow lighter, more able to fly.

The riders in the front ranks carried incredible tall poles. She stared up their lengths to where long black and silver hair whipped in the wind; a row of severed human heads rode on the ends of the pikes.

She struggled to yank her feet free of the ground, but sweet, heavy clover heads brushed her knees as she sank deeper into the earth.

The warhorses snorted as their riders spurred them on. Their harness trappings glittered as they surged closer. The middle rider was the Red Man, who screamed curses at her.

Transfixed, knowing that she was going to die under those advancing hooves, she stared at the heads on the poles.

The eyelids of all the severed heads flickered open. The dead eyes regarded her and the dead mouths twitched and began to speak.

"Witch," they mocked. "Sister, witch."

Silver hair, black hair, whipped through her dreams, and she woke haunted by visions of the Red Man carrying Roshannon's head on a pike.

The taste of blood filled Keira's mouth, as if she had bitten her tongue. Isharra, who was donning her armor, greeted her and explained that Roshannon had left the camp very late last night.

Keira knew he was in trouble. She excused herself and raced through the camp, as if trying to shake demons clinging to her. The sounds of soldiers dicing and laying wagers on horse races, and the groans of a woman in labor in an isolated tent, touched her awareness briefly.

Keira found the mare among the remounts. The gray whickered a greeting, tossing her head. Keira calmed her, glad for the warm horse breath against her skin, the long tongue across her palm. With shaking hands, she braided pale yellow sourgrass flowers into a lock of the mare's mane.

"Good-bye, old friend," she told the beast.

Tears burned her eyes. She brushed them savagely away, seeking Beren.

He was nowhere to be found. But near the stream that flowed by the picket lines, she suddenly felt a presence, a will struggling to regain its place in the world. She parted the reeds at the stream's marshy edge and stepped forward. Dragonflies bright as glass shards, with yellow eyes and lace wings, drifted by.

Muck squelched around her boot toes and wetness seeped through the worn leather. With a thunderous clap of wings, a wild duck flew from the reeds. She stopped, shifting her weight to get the best purchase on the marshy ground. She thought she heard someone groan faintly. She slipped on a tussock of marsh grass, her boot hitting the water. A panicked bevy of newborn ducks hidden in a nest of dead reeds plopped into the water and paddled frantically around their mother, who twitched her tail and led them gliding off across the sluggish stream.

Keira found solid ground and stumbled through brambles, swatting gnats away from her face. Her boot toe caught against something. She catapulted forward, catching herself on hands and knees.

The thing she had tripped over was Beren, bound hand and foot, his hair matted with blood. His eyes widened as she turned him over. His lips were blue, his teeth chattering.

She chafed his hands and untied his bonds.

"Who did this to you?"

"The captive priest. He took my dagger, killed a guard, and sneaked by the remounts. He promised to take me with him to Kum. I had a bad dream of myself with yellow witch eyes, and I told him. He said I should leave this camp because I was polluted."

Keira wrapped him in her cloak and carried him to the healers' tents. Anger lent her a surge of strength. Looking into Beren's shamed face, she grew even more angry.

"I was stupid to trust him," he said. "But he told me about Kum."

She watched Beren thoughtfully, wondering why her dreams could not have shown her this. Or Hipolla's peril, so that she could evade it. And was the dream of Roshannon beheaded still in the future or already reality?

She left Beren with the healers, embraced Yrena, swiped the tears from her eyes with her doubled fists, and marched to the dreamers' tent. She felt hollow and light but ready to do battle.

At the Sanctum picket lines, Roshannon turned himself in as a disgruntled Lian Calla mercenary. After arguing among themselves, the sentries confiscated his weapons, pressed a dagger to his ribs, and ordered him to march. Four men escorted him, jostling him roughly; the dagger pricked through his clothes and drew blood. When they reached a gaudy pavilion, one kicked him behind the knee, so he sprawled facedown in the mud.

His escort dragged him to his feet, brushed him off, and presented him to a Bala Kothi general.

The Kothi—a bearlike man with gold threads braided into his neatly trimmed beard—greeted Roshannon as an equal, one mercenary to another. He pinched Roshannon's left earlobe between thick, ring-laden fingers.

"What house, and why don't you wear its token?" he asked.

"Nikkael Lia-Farrayuan, of the Farrayuan islands," he said, because Sanctum delegates posted in Lian Calla rarely traveled to the outer islands. The outer island houses would likely be unknown to them. "I wagered it in a ko game for a woman."

The Bala Kothi smirked. "You won the woman?"

"Indeed." Roshannon felt the other men believing his story, for his years among the Sanctum soldiers had taught him their pervasive, amused scorn for the islanders' weakness over women.

The general conferred with a sentry. A few minutes later,

Roshannon's escort dragged him to a larger tent, where a stark wheel banner fluttered from a pole before the doorway.

The two stakes on either side of the flagpole bore severed heads. The head on the flagpole's right side was half-mummified, the eyes long ago pecked out by crows, the shrunken mouth pulled into a horrible rictus that exposed the bleaching teeth. Hanks of long white hair hung from the scalp. A witch, captured and tortured. The head on the banner's left side was fresher, Roshannon saw, stiff and puffy from bruises and battering. It was the head of Attal, the Blue Forest scout who had disappeared, the man he had thought of as one whose desire for revenge on the southerners was his only food.

Roshannon ground his teeth.

One young sentry sneered, noting his reaction. "A friend of yours, I take it?" He shoved Roshannon forward. "Well, you may end up as pretty as he did."

Nikka said a prayer for the peace of Attal's spirit and straightened as he entered the vast tent.

A thin man sitting behind a low table indicated the sentries should bring the prisoner closer.

The Red Man. How aptly the name Keira had laid on the archpriest fit—as she had said, he wore a long scarlet cape over the black priest's robes, and a shimmering quality of redness bled into the air around him, setting Roshannon's nerves on edge. The man's presence seemed like a banked fire that could rouse itself into flame instantly. Roshannon felt repulsed yet impelled toward him. The moment they looked each other in the eye, Roshannon knew the Red Man recognized his gift, as a lean winter wolf does the scent of prey.

But the archpriest appeared in no hurry. First, the Red Man let two other priests and the Bala Kothi general question Roshannon. The priests sat one on either side of the general, solemn blackrobed men as austere and impersonal as crows picking over a battlefield. In sharp contrast, the Kothi wore a strand of pearls braided into his warrior's locks. His tunic shone with rich embroideries of the mythological beasts beloved of Kothi astrologers. The general's cloak buttons were fashioned from the coinage of a deposed Bala Kothi emperor, Roshannon noted, trying to remain calm and observant.

An honor guard crowded into the tent, and tea and rakka made the rounds. The priests spilled single drops onto the tent floor before downing the contents of their shallow bowls. Roshannon wet his lips on the leather flask that was passed to him but swallowed little.

He wanted his senses about him. He focused on the black robes of the priests, the simple wheel brooches that fastened their tabards at the shoulder.

"We welcome you, who have been our worthy opponent," the Red Man said, in a rich, low voice. He raised his hand. Roshannon felt, rather than saw, a man step up behind him, caught a blur of movement. A club smashed into the back of his head and the world winked out.

Outside a warm wind swirled the aroma of the cook wagon's spiced stew through the camp, making Keira's mouth water. But her sense of connection with Roshannon had abruptly ended, like a campfire crushed into darkness, or a candle pinched out. Keira imagined Roshannon dying as the camp follower Otella had told her a captured witch had died, taunted by the archpriest, who toyed with him, cat and mouse. Yet by simply walking away now, she could rid herself of this man who had bought her and wed her, bedded her and asked her questions she did not want to answer. With him dead, she was free to go her own way, for the witches respected the gift she carried. By itself, it was a dowry that could ease her way into their mysterious city. But it marked her like the brand on a prize animal, and would imprison her in their politicking.

The dreamers and the steward had given Roshannon to the Red Man the way they would sacrifice a counter in a ko game to secure a more favorable position for later moves. The memory of Roshannon's last words stung her. He, the ka'innen lord, had suggested she was a coward.

She rushed into the dreamers' tent.

"The Red Man is torturing Roshannon-ka and will not stop until he puts his head on a pike," she said in a rush. "It is time to help him."

"Yes, but we must be careful," Riva said. "You and Roshannon-ka are not trained, though he awakened before you and has great control over his gift."

Thaia touched Keira's hand. "Do you love him?"

Keira frowned. "That is none of your concern."

The dreamer turned aside, a little smile hovering at the edge of her mouth. "Listen well if you want to help him," she said. "If he dies you will feel his agony, and may die yourself. The gift is no easy burden. Yet to help him, you must share his pain and rise above it.

"When you enter Roshannon-ka's body and share his pain, he will think more clearly and be more able to control the archpriest's body.

"Remember," Thaia said, "if your spirit merges with the archpriest's, you could be lost in the void."

"You can die if you are too long gone from your body or slip into a daze," Riva said.

"It is dangerous," Thaia said gently. "Do it only of your own free will. We will enter you to be carried to Roshannon; once there, you can return while we battle the archpriest."

"I must do this," Keira said.

The dreamers had been downing syrupy tea and thick waybread and urged Keira to stuff herself. They pressed food on her until she felt eager to escape the discomfort of her body. They licked every crumb from their fingers and wiped their mouths. "Eat well," Riva urged her. "You will need it."

"Do you trust us?" Thaia asked.

Keira looked at the twins and nodded. "We must trust each other," she said. She thought of Hipolla and Isharra, and last of Roshannon's farewell. "I am ready."

She lay down, closing her eyes as the dreamers directed. Their voices crooned hypnotic vedas to her, sounds that eased the split of body and spirit.

Last came Riva's voice. "You are a falcon, soaring from the falconer's wrist, an arrow loosed from the bow."

She became two, became three, all folded back into the oneness of herself. Her spirit shot between treetops and cloud, merging into wind and sunlight, a concentrated spark of will.

"The falcon set free," the dreamers whispered into her ears of flesh.

Keira's spirit, bearing the dreamers with her, outstripped her flesh, while their wills and the impressions of their lives strengthened her and focused her concentration.

Tethered by the cord of connection to her physical body below, she traveled higher and higher, faster and faster. Her dream body reeled, drunken with excitement. Then she remembered her purpose.

She sought her target.

The archpriest discussed the philosophy and theology of the Schismatic Separatists while his subordinate priest removed Roshannon's boots. He paced around the raised pallet where the Lian Callan was bound, and casually beckoned the priest by the door, who held a bundle of thin willow rods.

"Pain is a very interesting phenomenon," the Red Man said, toying with the wheel brooch on his cloak. "It must be doubly so to those who believe the body is a holy thing. But I believe a proper man transcends the flesh and the limitations of the body. I can transcend pain, you see, and how others deal with it interests me." His cloak fell open. Wide scars forming a rough, eight-spoked wheel marked his bare chest, many old and fading, some fairly new and still puckered.

The young man selected a rod from his bundle and handed it to the archpriest.

The archpriest paused beside Roshannon. "The spirit is holy, and the flesh dross. Don't you agree?"

"I am not a philosopher, but a soldier."

"But even soldiers philosophize."

"We disagree on philosophy. The body houses the spirit, as a temple houses the vision of the Wheel. The temple is as holy as what it houses."

The archpriest frowned. "Blasphemy."

The thin willow rod hissed through the air, biting the soles of Roshannon's bare feet. He strained against his bonds, cursing. His curses and the hiss of the wands continued in counterpoint, forming an eerie rhythm. Each time the rods struck, he fought against screaming, but fighting the pain meant focusing on it and magnified its impact. His hoarse words rang in his ears, until he drifted like flotsam from a shipwreck, letting pain flow through him as if body and senses were a battered old sieve.

The archpriest shook his head like a man observing a wayward child. "Your doctrines do not seem to serve you. You have not learned to transcend the pain."

Tears leaked down Roshannon's cheeks. He closed his eyes.

The soles of his feet burned as if a thousand coals were embedded
in his flesh. Something in the archpriest's words struck him as
strangely familiar, but the fire of the wand biting the soles of his
feet was burning his thoughts away.

The archpriest ran a finger back and forth across the bottoms of
Roshannon's feet, with slow, almost tender deliberation. Then he
raised the rod and struck again.

Roshannon screamed until his cry gained a separate reality. It
poured from every inch of his body, through the tent's roof, and
into the sky.

The scream lanced up to Keira, who followed it down to earth.

Roshannon tasted blood in his mouth. He must have bitten his
tongue. Don't give up hope until you're dead, Nikka, he thought,
laughing bitterly.

The archpriest studied him. "Something amuses you?"

Roshannon shook his head no, trying to find among the waves
of pain a resting spot where he could gather his wits and recall the
plan the witches had laid before him in the tent last night. The
plan that sounded like the ravings of a cracked mystic . . . We will
enter you now, they had said, let our spirits taste you now so that
we can enter you more easily when you are with the archpriest.
Then we will tackle him and wrestle his spirit. With his spirit occupied you can overcome his body. How we do not know, but
you must think of something. Roshannon braced himself, thinking that he was in such pain he might be unable to tell when the
witches entered him, even though the entry last night had been
grating and harsh, not at all like the way that Keira slid into him.

"You have seen their evil," the archpriest said. "Don't you
wish to see them punished and killed?"

"I have seen their strangeness, and felt it," he said. "But if you
think their talents evil, then you must think yourself evil, because
you bear their gift. You are brother to them and to me, whether
you want to be or not."

The archpriest's eyes darkened. Roshannon despaired for a
moment, thinking he had taken the wrong tack. For a moment he
tasted the archpriest's loneliness, so like what he himself had experienced when his own talent awakened and he thought himself
completely alone in the world.

"What did they teach you about their cursed gift?" the priest demanded.

Roshannon laughed grimly through his teeth. "Not much, because they trust me only a little more than they trust you." He watched the man's face. "Rakka stops it, as you must know. A man with a bellyful of rakka does not dream—" Roshannon paused. "Tell me, is that why you southern priests make rakka and distribute it to all your estates, to keep the priests and novices from dreaming, to keep the people in general from dreaming?"

The archpriest bent over him, smiling slowly. "For a common soldier who said he does not philosophize, you presume much."

"War is my business, not philosophy."

The archpriest chuckled. "Fascinating." He gestured to his guards. Roshannon winced, trying to get a better view of the tent from the odd, flat angle allowed him. He counted six men present—the young priest and five guards—noting their uniforms, their arms, and their deference to the archpriest simply to distract himself from pain.

The archpriest asked a guard to open Roshannon's shirt. With his fingertip, the archpriest traced a wheel in the middle of Roshannon's chest.

Roshannon ground his teeth. None of the guards so much as blinked, and he wondered how many times the archpriest had gone through this performance. The guard, a stocky graybeard, walked casually to the brazier in the tent's right corner, drew his dagger, and thrust the blade into the coals.

"Sooner or later, the other one who shares your eyes will come to you," the archpriest whispered. "I feel the hellfire in you, calling to your demon familiar. But if you are in pain enough, your spirit will flee your body and you will die. I've seen it happen before. Yet I'd heard you islanders love life and all its impurities."

An old guard approached at the archpriest's signal, and studied Roshannon's face. The guard avoided Roshannon's eyes as if embarrassed. Maybe, Roshannon thought, he believes something of the hellfire inside me will contaminate him.

"Ka. He's not going, not nearly. I told you it was hours before the other one went into that daze," the gray-bearded man told the archpriest. A bead of sweat slid down his lined forehead.

The priest smiled slowly at Roshannon. "Then we have plenty of time to talk, you and I. Ample time, because the witches have just thrown you to me like a piece of meat to keep a dog busy for a while. You islanders always served the Sanctum well, always men of honor and fine soldiers. But I didn't think you would be stupid enough to believe the witches honorable. What are they planning, eh?"

He nodded to the older guard who handed him his dagger, its tip glowing red. The air filled with the odor of heated metal.

"To destroy you, as you would destroy them," Roshannon said, and closed his eyes, suddenly drained. He wondered how long they had tortured Attal. The red-hot tip of the knife dug a sudden furrow across his chest. He screamed hoarsely, watching the priest's eyes, feeling the wash of the Red Man's emotions, his fascination, his strange twisted brotherhood with Roshannon himself and the northerners he wanted to destroy.

Then a veil of other sensations settled in Roshannon, until pain became a distant annoyance occurring to someone else. His body flushed with heat; all the hair on his arms and the back of his neck stood up. A powerful current seethed through the tent.

The figure of the torturer looming over him blurred and shifted. "Keira," he whispered.

Through Roshannon's eyes Keira regarded the Red Man. She noticed the wheel brooch at his shoulder, the richly embroidered sash at his waist. Memories left behind in her fleshly body stirred, and she recalled the man she had first seen on the road to A'Hrappa, the alluring presence so like a steady flame that drew moths to their doom.

Joining with Roshannon brought fear and knowledge as their two consciousnesses meshed. A line of fire seared the flesh across her right breast, eating into her concentration, the pain surging and cresting with each heartbeat. She sunk more deeply into Roshannon, trying to comfort him, while the dreamers' spirits wafted around her, and the Red Man's spirit bruised her like a tightening net.

A thousand images poured through her, a river of memory and life that communicated in an instant the light and shadow of every soul inside that tent.

Tangible as a serpent, the Red Man's hatred slid toward her, a will vast enough to snare her spirit feet and topple her into a maelstrom, while Roshannon's pain laced through her. The vast swarming of energy inside the tent made her feel like chaff caught in a wind, hollow, light, buoyant, and strangely detached.

The archpriest peered at Roshannon. "Fascinating," he hissed. "There is witchery here now, I feel it." Impatiently, he motioned the guard outside. He gestured to the young priest. "I feel the hell-fire increased twofold, because the familiar is come. Come look at this man's eyes."

Steadily, through Roshannon's eyes, Keira watched a puzzled-looking young priest standing beside the Red Man, her enemy. This is my fight, she thought fiercely, my enemy. He is mine, leave him to me.

"Demon, you have come," the priest whispered, staring into Roshannon's eyes.

"I am come, priest," she answered through Roshannon's mouth.

Her will expanded, flickered against the Red Man's spirit, tasting his hatred and fascination, his aloneness, deep and compelling as a whirlwind, his emptiness that craved knowledge of others like himself, yet because of his doctrines, forever shrank from that contact. And knowing him, she feared yet understood him, and knew she could battle him.

He was an old enemy, with many familiar faces. He was her father, he was the lord who had beheaded the gleaner while Keira watched, he was the priest who had wed her to Roshannon, he was Terrak whom her father had wanted her to marry, and he was himself, a bottomless pit of craving and twisted understanding, who had never used the gift to soar in joy.

Yes, I can fight you, she thought. I will fight you.

She let images of Tanta, the steward's constable, and their archers waiting outside the camp flow into Roshannon's mind.

Steeling her will, Keira pictured herself as a coiled snake striking, then loosed herself. She cast off the dreamers by a sheer act of will, cast off Roshannon's consciousness, and plunged across the distance between the Red Man and Roshannon. She dove blindly into the other.

Staring at Roshannon in perplexity, the archpriest took a step backward.

Roshannon wet his lips with the tip of his tongue. "You felt it?" he said. "She is inside you now."

"She? How can that be? Women do not have this power," the

archpriest said, narrowing his eyes at Roshannon. "What other spirit possesses you?"

"None other now, for it's inside you."

Keira, having tasted the priest's spirit, slipped back into Roshannon, watching carefully through his eyes as the priest half tottered. So, she thought. It drains him, weakens him, as the dreamers said. He is not used to sharing the body.

"I am woman. I am here. Fight me, priest, if you are honorable," Keira said through Roshannon's lips. Through his eyes she watched an image of herself weave into being around the dust motes in a slanted ray of light.

"I will not match myself with any woman," the Red Man said, drawing himself up to his full height as he peered at the image shimmering in the air.

Keira laughed at the Red Man through Roshannon's lips.

"I am woman, why do you fear battling me? But I warn you, I have come to cast your soul into the void from which the Wheel is born. I am an honorable enemy. Are you?"

"Blasphemy," the priest said slowly.

"The truth is stranger than your doctrine has ever imagined," Roshannon said. "Alone you have been, tasting the witch gift yourself, because you are a witch, a half-souled one who has never joined with another. When she joins with you, you will know the fullness of your gift."

"Blasphemy. What demon are you, who speaks to me through a man's mouth and shows me the shape of a woman in the air?"

"I am both man and woman come for you, priest," Keira said through Roshannon's lips.

There is the embrace of the body, Keira thought, and stranger still, the embrace of spirit and will. The archpriest's spirit recoiled, tried evasion. Yet in the madly metaphoric spirit world in which they dueled, she merely had to think herself net, arrow, or hawk, to become the manifestation of those things, then pursue and catch him, and burrow deeply into him so that he could not throw her.

He was iron, embers, a wheel of willful fire, and she danced in and out of his consciousness, leading him, sidestepping, evading, becoming now his opposite, now his familiar.

The great, seductive danger of the duel was its intimacy. To battle him she had to know him, to know him she had to taste his essence, which meant sampling the depths of her own worst fears and loathings. To battle her, he reflected back at her own deepest agonies and despairs.

As she gained power, he gained it with her, twining himself about the fabric of her spirit. The rush of images assailed her, the sum of his life and experience, fascinating in itself, like shadow forms seen by a curious child peering down an endless well . . .

But always he was the Wheel turning; the Wheel mowing down time, seasons, flesh, and dreams; the Wheel spun from the void and returning to its depths.

They fought a soundless, wordless duel, drifting higher and higher above the tilt of the earth, reaching for the void and the end of light. They roamed so far there were no familiar landscapes, no blinking points of light below them to use as reference points. She had flown beyond her anchors, and he was still stronger, fortified by his belief in the inexorable turning of the Wheel. His terrible aloneness sucked strength from her will, reeling her in until she felt sudden panic. She understood: she could not win the spirit duel unless she fought it totally in the realm of spirit.

She was alone with her enemy.

In one desperate transformation, she became the path the Wheel traveled, and sent herself and the priest spiraling farther and farther from the territory of men into the void.

In their tent in the northern camp, the court dreamers stared unbelieving at each other. The twin dreamers' spirits floated in the archpriest's tent like chaff left hanging in the air after wheat is winnowed. Knowledge and dismay flowed between them, that Keira had tackled the archpriest herself, barring them from the duel.

Riva opened his mouth, slowly wet his lips with his tongue, a man forcing the actions of his body with great effort. "She is a fool, she will be lost in the void," he said hoarsely.

"If she is strong enough to thrust us off," Thaia croaked, "she stands a chance. There is still much work to do. Whatever happens, she has made our job easier." She floated downward, toward the man who lay on the pallet.

Riva squeezed his spirit into the archpriest.

* * *

Every hair on Roshannon's body stood upright, and the pain that had burned through his veins and faded while Keira looked through his eyes returned in full force. He screamed hoarsely, panicked and sick. Keira was gone, leaving behind an archpriest who was archpriest in body only. The brief contact with her had sharpened Roshannon's senses; the priest's body seemed gray and hollow—it was clear his spirit was elsewhere.

He stared at the archpriest, who looked at him in perplexity. "We must discuss our differences of philosophy at further length," Roshannon ventured.

The priest blinked, looking curiously apathetic, the shell of a man whose spirit is elsewhere, his face blunted like a fool's face, or the strangely vulnerable, unaware face of a dreamer.

"Philosophies," he said strangely.

"This bed is an uncomfortable one for a man to discuss philosophies from," Roshannon said. Stunned, he watched the priest bend and undo his bonds. He eased his legs off the pallet and stood, hobbling and wincing at each step. He took another look at the priest's eyes, realizing a different spirit animated them.

"Who the hell are you?" Roshannon asked.

"A friend, a dreamer," Riva whispered through the priest's lips.

A moment later, Thaia's spirit settled into Roshannon's body, ending his confusion and masking his pain. He yanked on his boots.

They trooped outside. "This prisoner and I must ride and talk," the archpriest told the guards outside. The guards looked no less surprised when the archpriest waved them aside with an imperious gesture, after picking four to accompany him. That unsettling blankness mantled his features, except for a gleam in his eyes. But the guards followed without a murmur of suspicion.

Roshannon thrust one booted foot in the stirrup and mounted, biting his lip to keep pain from overwhelming him. Roshannon expected the archpriest's spirit to return to his body at any time, crushing the escape plans. Yet he wondered if somehow the one occupying the Red Man's body could read Keira's fate. They rode outside the camp, to a hill that overlooked a small creek and offered a panoramic view of the many recent battlefields. Far in the west, the towers of Kum pricked the sky, glittering in the midday sun.

The archpriest halted, the guard drawing up around him as if they recognized the place. Roshannon felt as if his feet were seared fast to the bottoms of his boots, which seemed fused into the stirrups. Each step his horse took flooded his nerves with pain, wiping his brain of everything else. He did not dismount.

The Red Man continued a strange, metaphysical conversation Roshannon could never later recall. The sun beat down mercilessly. Suddenly a black-fletched arrow hissed into the throat of the gray-bearded guard, knocking him from his horse.

Roshannon, weaponless, kneed his horse into the archpriest's. Another man toppled from his mount with an arrow through his shoulder. A troop of pony archers, led by Keya, the steward's constable, Tanta, and Ni'An, broke from the cover of the woods and raced up the hilltop, three hunting cats running before them. Roshannon had never seen such a wondrous or welcome sight.

Keira floated over the landscape, her drifting spirit intertwined with the archpriest's. She saw the escort that ringed the Red Man and Roshannon crumple under a hail of arrows. With furious energy, the archpriest's spirit attempted to unravel from hers, rejoin his body far below, but she held him, with visions of the Wheel churning through her consciousness, and dragged him away.

She rose higher above the land, beyond the clouds, swimming an ocean of searing blue light. Cords of connection pulled at her, annoyances that bound her to things far below. Two annoying spirit presences brushed her spirit sides, tugged at her. But the old reality of flesh seemed dreams sloughed off, as a snake sheds a skin and grows another.

She eluded them, her head full of a notion to soar high enough to see how the world was set in the void, and the will that held the Wheel of creation together.

She fancied that vision; she soared, carrying the archpriest's furious, burning spirit with her, along the path that she had become.

Roshannon leaned on Ni'An, limping on his bandaged feet because putting his full weight on them still made him grind his teeth. The healers had bound his tortured, swollen feet in cloth, as boots would have been agony. Two camp healers and the dreamers stood guard over Keira, who had lain unmoving on the pallet for three days and three nights since the captured archpriest had been brought to the camp.

"She is in the daze, traveling in the void itself," Riva said. "Untrained, wild, she attempted too much. Her spirit struggled against us and cast us off. For some reason, she decided to fight the archpriest herself. Someone must stay with her and speak to her constantly, to draw her spirit back from the void. But I don't know if she will come back. Her spirit must choose."

Beren, the solemn-faced cook's boy, knelt by the pallet and laid his hand over her cold, unmoving one.

The shell of a man that was the archpriest stared at them all with the wide, innocent eyes of a child. He ate and drank, chewing and swallowing solemnly, focused totally on the action of eating and drinking. But he was a puppet without a master, the spirit gone from his flesh: He had lost his voice, his authority, the presence that had animated him and made him burn like candle flame among other men. The duel with Keira had stripped him of his humanity and of his evil, robbed him of speech, choice, and essence.

Roshannon thought at first the man might craftily hide behind this semblance of a daze, awaiting an opportunity to escape and reclaim his armies and his ambitions. He observed the Red Man whenever he took breaks from his constant vigilance over Keira, who did not wake. He wanted to hate the man who had tortured him. But the torturer and this wrecked shell were not the same creature at all. Whatever spark had made the archpriest himself, whatever had animated his hatred, driven him, fueled his awesome strength against the northlanders, had been blasted from him and scattered like ash on a wind.

By Keira, who did not wake.

Roshannon, fascinated, walked through the circle of guards and offered the Red Man food from his hand. A spark of comprehension lit the blank, staring eyes. Food, so basic to life, he understood. A glistening drop of saliva seeped from the corner of his mouth. He who had once been the archpriest took the bit of waybread dumbly and trustingly as an animal, his lips soft, warm, and wet against Roshannon's palm.

Roshannon's throat tightened. Despair and fury twisted in his guts. Revenge on a whole man was something he could stomach.

But this pathetic creature was no longer even a man. Roshannon watched him eat, mechanically, the jaw muscles obeying a greater imperative than any man's will, the simple will of all living things to survive.

"Do you know me?" Roshannon asked. The hollow man stared through his blank eyes, his lips twisting, his mouth working. A strangled, beastlike sound escaped his lips.

Roshannon turned on his heel, leaving the shell man to his keepers, the healers, and the picked guards who averted their eyes from their charge as much as possible.

The steward, who came to watch the Red Man every day, hailed Roshannon as he strode away.

"Why do you keep him alive like this?" Roshannon asked. "Is Keira Danio's spirit bound up in this creature now?"

"We cannot tell," the steward said. "They traveled far into the void, which takes its toll. If his spirit returns to his body, I doubt it would ever be the same. But I would like to talk with him, learn how he came into his power and began to use it. And learn how many other miratasu exist among the southlanders. If he never returns from the void, there is no chance to learn that."

"Unless Keira Danio regains herself, unharmed, and can tell the tale," Roshannon said.

The steward cleared his throat. "There is something you must know. She may never return or wake from the daze. She—"

But Roshannon cut short the steward's words by punching him in the face and knocking him down. Guards with drawn swords surrounded them immediately. The steward, propping himself up on his elbows, shook his head and gestured them away. He grinned at Roshannon, the blood dribbling from his nose and split lip somewhat spoiling the effect. Roshannon held a hand down for him, which the steward accepted.

"Did she know the danger?" Roshannon asked. "Was she even told?"

"The dreamers told her many times. She knew and accepted the risk."

"Will she be like this?" Roshannon demanded, indicating the archpriest, who now sat cross-legged among his keepers, running his fingers through the new grass like a child combing a doll's hair.

The steward pinched the bottom of his bloody nose with his

fingers. "No, probably just as if asleep. Our legends tell of Lir Twice-King, who lay in a mountain cave after the battle of Darenkoa, traveling in the daze a hundred years. Then he rose from his bed and resumed his life, becoming his own grandson's general and eventually king again, before he actually died.

"The gift is strange and seeks it own ways, follows it own purposes. It uses those of us who carry it as much as we use it. Mysteries do not offer simple answers. I am sorry." The steward closed his mouth on something he had been about to say and touched Roshannon's shoulder.

"She fought him because of love, Roshannon-ka."

Roshannon glanced once more at the strangely childlike figure of the archpriest. He walked away from the steward's tent feeling pity for the man Keira had destroyed. And a profound conviction that seeing what her talent had left of the Red Man would devastate her.

She lay as still as an effigy on the narrow camp bed.

Keira Danio, Roshannon said for the tenth time that day. His voice rasped hoarsely inside the tent. The healers had come each day, chasing him outside while they ministered to Keira. Perched now on a tripod leather stool beside the bed, he watched her, folding his fingers around hers, no longer flinching at how cold her hand felt. He sometimes lay beside her on the narrow bed to warm her body with his own. Once he fancied—but the lantern had been flickering—that her still fingers had moved, responding to his touch. Once in the light of the horn lantern, he swore her eyes fluttered beneath her eyelids, as if she watched dream things. When no one else was around, he spoke to her of sailing the necklace of islands westward into the hammered silver vastness of the ocean off Lian Calla, of sailing back the green line of islands into sight of the city walls and the harbor's arms; of battles among the infidels and recent battles.

Isharra came, and Xian Tanta, whose hunting cat slept beside Keira one night. One day Roshannon was explaining to her how he would teach her to sail a small boat along the shore. Someone coughed. Just inside the tent flap stood the boy Beren, solemn faced as a southern priest, yet silent as a witch. He frowned, turning as if to leave.

"Stay," Roshannon said.

The boy came closer, peering at Keira. "Why doesn't she wake up?"

"She is not asleep. Her spirit is not in her body. It is a different thing." Imagining it made his stomach queasy. "She pushed the archpriest's spirit beyond the edges of being, and her spirit hasn't found its way back yet."

"But the spirit only leaves the body after death." The boy held his hand above her nose and mouth. "Is she dying?"

"If her spirit does not return, she may die. So the healers say."

"Why do you stay by her?"

"She was my wife, once. A Sanctum priest married us. And she saved my life by battling the Red Man."

The boy's eyes widened. "She is very brave. When she killed the man who killed Hipolla, she looked so strange. She scared me. She seemed to go off behind her eyes somewhere, and didn't talk for almost a whole day. The fight with the Red Man must have been like that. But she will come back when she is ready."

Beren touched her cold hand. "I should hate her because she destroyed the archpriest," he said. "But I don't."

The void stretched forever, illuminated by the hard, perfect light of the stars.

Keira was alone with nothing but her enemy to define her. The great, grinding wheel that was the archpriest's spirit suddenly burst into flame, scorching the path that she had become. Too late she saw her mistake. Too late she sought to transmute her essence, to battle him further. But her spirit was locked, entwined with his, and ignited. Flames crackled wickedly, hissing a mocking catechism of destruction, of hatred and darkness and the ending of all things.

All is dross, and dross burns. Nothing survives the furnace which destroys and purifies, the fire whispered.

And she began burning with it, seduced by the logic of the flames' rapturous, insinuating voice, gloating and triumphant. She thought of death with acceptance. If she perished, at least she had taken her enemy beyond the reach of others he could harm.

But gold does not burn, she thought stubbornly. Nor does fire touch such things as love. Only hatred burns itself.

As the wheel of fire raged out of control, she gave herself to the great blaze, let it devour her. Greedily, eagerly, it consumed her and itself, convinced of its victory. Having nothing else on which to feed, it collapsed into drifts of ash and plumes of smoke. The winds of the void tore the bitter ash and smoke to nothingness.

But Keira's spirit floated free, the fine, feather ash that rises after a fire, wafted on its winds.

The taste of the archpriest's lonely, bitter spirit dropped away from her. She lost the memory of having lived in a human body. She was at last alone, in the mysterious eternity stranger even than dreams. She wandered, drifting on the ocean of the void, tasting the vast awarenesses of time, of space, of light.

An eye of light shone at her out of the darkness. In its streaming radiance she saw nine globes spinning about the eye in endless orbits. Intrigued, she darted closer, closer, until she rushed past worlds swaddled in vaporous clouds and rings of light, toward the great eye itself.

A tiny globe wrapped in clouds and cold blueness drew her attention. Curious, she wafted closer to examine the other colors. She had not found the Wheel, she remembered. Other memories began to tug at her. Like threads sewn through her, they pulled and twanged and demanded her attention.

Shapes and hues and presences spun through her awareness. She summoned the names that fitted with them: heat and cold, blue, sky, clouds, darting shapes—birds. The things she saw seemed familiar. She saw hills covered with blue trees. Their shapes haunted her. She saw a herd of wild horses running, and the dust cloud their hooves threw up tempted her closer.

She saw the tiny shapes of holds and farms spread across the land, and a flashing needle of a city on a rock. Kum, she thought. The funny name echoed through her awareness, like vibration building. She hung above the earth and watched people riding horses, and at last remembered that she had once worn flesh, and walked on the rocky ground, and leaned into the neck of a galloping mare, tasting the wind and the exhilaration of racing.

But she could barely remember who she had been, how she had fit into this strange reality. Voices, muffled but insistent, brushed her spirit, summoning her to some place she could not quite recall. She was curious about what the voices wanted of her.

Keira, they called, sending the absurd sound out into the void after her.

Images spun through her, a boy telling her she should wear a dress, a woman splashing her in a pool, a pair of eyes, one green, one gold, and a great wheel of jade and amber turning endlessly. She remembered she had once had hands and feet, flesh and skin that had covered her bones and spirit. And she remembered touch, and pain, and pleasure.

Keira. Keira Danio, the voices called.

They confused her, led her. They piqued her curiosity. She approached, closer and closer. Something in the voice was familiar. She recalled a spirit she had touched, and the face that belonged to that spirit.

But the voice had tricked her, snared her into an odd, small, cramped reality. This reality lay stiff as a log on something hard.

Keira, the voice said.

Who or what is this Keira-thing? she thought at the voice. Let me alone. Then she knew that Keira was herself. An annoying weight had settled on her legs and chest. She kicked at it. In the same instant her feet stung, and hot sparks shot through the long-unused muscles of her legs. She groaned and opened her eyes.

A boy slept in the corner by her pallet and a man sat on a folding stool nearby. He had a pleasant, dark face and stared sadly at the shadows on the tent wall. She stirred in the covers, peering at him a long moment.

He turned his face. Lantern light caught on the scar along his jaw as his eyes met hers.

"You," she said hoarsely. She remembered now.

She flexed her fingers, stiff and cold from disuse, and reached toward him.

❀ 20 ❀

Roshannon stood watching the high steward appraise the Red Man, that calm, deliberate examination of his fallen enemy. After Keira woke, the healers still visited the Red Man, poked and prodded him and spoke to him in low, gentle voices, stared into his blank eyes, shook their heads, conferred among themselves and went away. The northerners built a little pen for him, ringed round with guards so other soldiers and children could not taunt him. They guarded the shell man with the mixture of fear and slightly awed respect they would have granted the fierce spirit that once inhabited the now pliant, childlike husk of flesh.

Roshannon did not want Keira to see the ruin her talent had made of the archpriest. Ever since she woke she had refused to use her dream senses, recoiled from sharing his awareness. Not only her body but likely her mind had to heal.

He leaned on the fence, waiting.

The mute creature, still sparked by feeble curiosity, shambled over. Perhaps he felt some tug toward his fellows whose wills were still encased in their flesh. Or thought food was waiting there.

It was such a simple thing. It is mercy, and what Keira would want, Roshannon thought. He reached through the fence, intending to hook his sword arm around the archpriest's neck, ready to slit the man's throat to grant him release from his strange imprisonment.

But the man's head twisted so he could regard Roshannon from the sides of his eyes. In an instant, a vital spark returned to the lean, scarred body, the haunted eyes. The mouth twitched, the eyes reflected knowledge, depths of pain, aloneness, and bitter wisdom.

"Brother," the archpriest said softly, and smiling, died. Roshannon's arm slid along the man's shoulder, supporting him as he slumped against the fence. The man's body shuddered once,

300

then hung still. The dark, blank eyes focused on Roshannon and then on some point of nothingness.

Roshannon felt a strange comfort that this enemy died in his arms. Hoarsely, he called for the guards.

The steward never said anything to Roshannon about the arch-priest's death. The witches burned the Red Man's body on a great pyre while negotiations continued between north and south. It was the kind of funeral they gave their own honored ones.

After the archpriest's capture, the southern armies had lost their spirit. Fighting continued for weeks, but the election of a new archpriest occupied the southerners, and the Bala Kothi generals rode into the northern camp with truce banners, ready to make peace. The northerners granted Kum continued immunity and guaranteed safe passage of pilgrim merchants into the northern territories and back, for quotas of spidersilk, fur, and amber. But they took two thousand southern strategists, ka'in, and priests hostage and prepared to march them into the city, where the high steward said they would be educated in northern ways.

Cartheon's alliance with Lian Calla held, in spite of Roshannon bloodying Aramit Leyto's nose, which remained slightly crooked to the end of his days. "My blood sealed the alliance," he joked to Roshannon.

Both armies licked their wounds and rested before one moved south, the other north, marching their long lines of hostages back to Cartheon.

Around the campfires soldiers sang battle songs and love songs, and odes to Lady Death, giving the battle goddess her due. Keira mended rapidly and was pleasantly surprised that Roshannon adopted Beren Harth into his own clan with little prodding. She and Roshannon seldom saw each other. When they did meet, they treated each other with a formal stiffness, as if they had never met, both shy of each other, reluctant to stir the power that simmered between them. Slowly, Keira learned to use her stiffened and painful arms and legs again but kept her spirit walls intact, not once venturing inside Roshannon. Within several days of waking from the daze, she found herself bleeding and was relieved not to be pregnant. She practiced swordplay and archery with Isharra, Ni'An, and Xian Tanta, or worked among the healers.

A man wearing a muddy, bloodstained green tabard approached her one day.

"Keira Danio?" he said. "The steward wishes to see you alone."

She followed the courier, hastily combing her fingers through her hair.

The man grinned. "That will not matter to him."

The steward's tent looked like a strategist's, except for the dozen banners snapping on flagpoles before its entrance. Before the tent, a cook poked a brazier full of sea coals into life.

The courier gestured with his chin. "Go in, he expects you."

The southern woman swept toward the steward with the clean, sure power of an ocean wave gathering itself. He was exquisitely aware of his own will and hers circling, as she ducked inside the tent flap and straightened.

With a flick of his hand he dismissed the cook's helper, who had set out tea bowls.

"Greetings." The steward nodded to her and poured tea into the blackwood bowls. They were lacquered outside but gilded inside with gold leaf, which imparted a subtle flavor to the tea.

She sat opposite him. His dreamers said she had not used her gift since waking after the duel with the archpriest. But now he felt her psychic walls raised against him. In her soldier's clothes, with the light catching on her cropped hair, she looked more boyish than womanly. He could believe she had traveled five hundred miles alone from the heart of the southland, in man's clothes, and not been challenged until a scouting party on the edge of the Blue Forest caught her. When he tried to slip inside the mass of images that shimmered in her mind, a blankness closed over him, abrupt as a door slammed against an intruder. The same hardness of will that had sloughed off the dreamers and kept Roshannon-ka from tasting life through her eyes. He leaned back in his chair, stung and fascinated. She was less than half his age.

"It is good to see you in health again, Keira Danio."

"You flatter me, ka."

"You underestimate your importance, lady."

"My importance, ka? I am only myself, a sita's daughter from the southlands."

The steward laughed, studying her high cheekbones, the perfect round scar between her brows, a pockmark so like a Bala

Kothi rank mark, the features he had watched so many times while she wrestled the archpriest in the void, her body still as a carved statue in the dreamers' tent. No city lineage had those gray eyes. Gray eyes should not dream clear, the masters had said for generations. Her face resembled no council lords or their ladies; the dream masters and the spider masters had recorded all the lineages known to carry the gift.

"But what about the gold with the steward's seals, found sewn up in your cloak seams?" the steward asked.

"Ka. My mother got it from her mother. That is all I know. But I have a question for you." She went on as he nodded. "Your middle name, Li-Amaratsa, is one of the holy names of god, and yet you bear it as others do their ordinary names." She leaned forward. "Do you mean to mock southern doctrines?"

"Before the Sanctum priests twisted the name's meaning from its original intent, it meant One made in the image of god, One awakened, One in balance. In north and south, the original image of god was the being who is both man and woman. The priests came to see it differently, and to see the gift as abomination because it created equal unions of men and women."

Keira nodded. "Hipolla told me some of that story. Yet—"

"I answered, now I ask. About your mother," he said. "I can help you recall things if you let me." He laid his hands across the table.

"My mother, Rianna, was a merchant's only daughter and brought two servants with her as her dowry when she married my father."

"But she carried gold from a clan destroyed during the wars of Schism between north and south. In those times, witch lords were honored in one place, in others hung or burned, merely for using the gift or on suspicion of carrying its seeds. Gifted and ungifted turned on each other, brothers and sisters, parents and children betrayed each other, according to the way they saw the gift. Both sides used the talent badly. Linked couples were separated, one planted as a spy in rival households. Women were married to men they detested, and, once they were linked, used as those lords' spies. The most eminent philosophers in Cartheon argue still about how the gift should be used. Or if it should be used at all. To southerners, the gift is an evil twist of the spirit, a presumption of equality with the Wheel itself. True, it can be used to do evil. They forbade its use. They forbade intermarriage of gifted and ungifted, trying to reduce the spread of what they called a plague. And out of fear, they slaughtered the gifted. One of the first lineages the priests' armies destroyed was Lian Dar.

"Lian Dar's seal is on the gold your mother gave you, Keira Danio. If the blood of that lineage runs in you, we must honor you." He sipped tea. "You never saw your mother's mother? Not even in a dream?"

Keira stared into his golden eyes. "I dreamt of horses. Mother said grandmother had a way with horses. But I can't remember more."

"I can help you find the truth," the steward said. "Your dream self can see the past. Think of your mother, and give me your hand."

Keira looked down at her hands, then raised her eyes, focusing on the steward's golden eyes and fine-boned features. His newly crooked nose gave his face an ironic note. She wondered who had broken it. He offered her his hand. His spirit presence washed over her, and she knew him as the one who had touched her when she first floated over the city.

Roshannon was a river, a current flowing into oceans. But this man was the ocean itself. His will enfolded her, ready to surge into every crevice of mind and memory, not the feather touch of the court dreamers, but a frightening, exhilarating flood that would strip everything away.

"No," she said. She spun an image of foam on the curl of the wave, and let her dream body float free.

An image formed in her mind, of driftwood tossed and lifted, riding his will, and the wave could not crush her and the waters could not drown her. His will became an eddy, tugged at her, pulled her down. She spun the image in her mind, became a glistening, quivering bubble, and soared free, while the eddy, with no target, dissipated. His will became a river, running swiftly through mountains, netting the bubble in roaring falls, pulling her back into his presence. She became a fish, slick as silver with a flick of her tail, and the river carried her.

The river dried, dissipated into the air. She leaped free of the water, became a bird. As the water formed clouds too high for the bird to fly, she became a drop of water clinging to its underside. Lightning flashed, and rain sleeted down, drumming the ground.

The sound of rainfall melted into the sound of horses' hooves pounding.

"No," she said. "I thank you for your offer, but I would rather imagine my mother's and grandmother's lives than see them this way. I cannot join with anyone now."

The steward watched her a moment, then nodded, releasing her.

"More understanding between north and south would heal many wounds," he said slowly. "Your union with Roshannon-ka will be a salve, a first step."

"All southerners will see me as a traitor," Keira said.

"Some will. But others may see that southern ways drove you north, as well as your talent seeking its roots. Would you help us search out gifted ones in the borderlands and the south, to undertake a healing and reconciliation? My agents in Kum are posting notices that we welcome all those who dream."

"Ka. I can help with that work." Keira imagined other girls like herself, caught in the fever dreams and believing they were going mad.

She curled her fingers, smiling to herself at the daydream horses still racing in her head. The notion of breeding the mare and the highland pony crossed her mind, and she found herself imagining, with great interest, what the foal would look like.

The steward watched her. "Do you still fear what you are?"

"No. Of all wrongs I could do myself, fearing self-knowledge would be the worst."

"Self-knowledge is a hard road. But it is the beginning of power." He raised his tea bowl in a salute to her. "Lady Keira Lackland," he said. "I declare you your own lineage, for the service you have given the city of Cartheon and the northern army." He lifted a seal ring on a silver chain from his neck and placed it about hers. "This token will grant you entrance to the city at any time, for any reason. I hope you will come dwell among us, at least part of each year, and study with the dream masters and the healers."

Keira rose and bowed, looking into the steward's eyes that held all colors. They were intent on her, with purposes of their own.

"Propitious dreams, ka," she said.

"Propitious dreams, ka."

When Keira finally entered Cartheon, she wore out three pairs of boot soles exploring its streets with the inquisitive Beren in tow. One dusk she returned to the apartment she had been given. Located halfway up the steward's tower, its tall windows looked out on Cartheon's harbor and water gate.

The maidservant waiting in the rooms frowned at Keira's travel-stained soldier's clothes. "Quick, lady, get to the bathhouse in the courtyard below," she said. "You must go to the steward's hall tonight."

"Thank you," Keira said, meaning to dismiss her.

"Ka, let me take off your boots, your cloak."

Keira perched with her butt balanced on the window ledge, her legs stretched out so the woman could pull off her boots, but she kept her cloak on, dust, stains, and all. Kneeling, the maid removed Keira's boots in silence. Both her palms had been slashed to mark her as a bond servant, so wide scars showed against the pale skin. She rose, touched her forehead, and left with the boots.

The maid returned with the boots cleaned, oiled, and nearly unrecognizable, to accompany Keira to the bathhouse. The scars on Keira's back made her gasp, but she restrained her curiosity. Keira gave herself over to the luxury of the bath and the soothing attention of the other woman's hands.

The maid meant to dress her, too. After being so long without them, such attentions annoyed Keira. With a smile, the maid laid out woman's clothes, lavish and perfumed, on the bed. Keira fingered the richly embroidered cloth of the high, ornate collar and the slit skirts. She hesitated to put them on, yet was excited to see how she would look.

The maid coughed. "Your hair."

"It does not matter against the collar." Keira stripped and let herself be dressed and fussed over.

A manservant brought a mirror so she could see herself. The low-cut embroidered bodice, fastened with many hooks, exposed the tops of her breasts, but the skirt let her swing her legs easily. She strode back and forth before the mirror, fascinated by the spectacle of her bare flesh above the embroidered bodice.

The maid giggled and clasped her hands. "Lady! You must not walk like a soldier. But so." She minced across the room with short, swaying steps.

Keira could not see any advantage in walking that way. She touched her throat, thinking perhaps she could throw her cloak on last, to cover some flesh.

But the maid brought nothing to cover the bare spots. "A pity you have no jewels to wear at your throat." She bowed and nodded. "You are beautiful, ka. Remember not to walk like a soldier."

The steward's hall was a spectacle of sound and color, like ten of Kerlew Fair stuffed inside a vast building. Keira circled the edges of the crowd, seeking a quiet place to stand. One man carried a great lizard with scales like green armor. The creature had a blue crest and vibrant throat patches. It clung motionless to its owner's forearm; its blue-and-green tail hung between his fingers and trailed against his robe. The creature seldom moved, except to curl flies out of the air on its long, black tongue.

Keira began to feel at ease, as if she had dreamt a fantastic dream, and was walking through it now on a tour of inspection. But the dream was not her own.

"Keira Danio."

She turned. An austerely dressed Xian Tanta stepped from an archway. His mismatched eyes flicked over her in assessment.

"Ka." She nodded to him, the old ache for Hipolla stirring in her heart.

"Even I could not mistake you for anything but a woman now," he said. He drew a circle in her right hand and withdrew.

She looked after him in puzzlement. A red-gloved woman appraised her brazenly, and Keira stared back, greatly amused. Men and women's eyes flickered over her, measuring, judging, and weighing, until the steward's hall seemed one vast, strange marketplace.

She watched the lizard perched on its owner's forearm. The creature's tiny, green-scaled hand moved just a hair. Its throat patches quivered and it looked directly at her. Its eyelids folded shut over its yellow eyes.

Do such creatures dream? she wondered. And where are they from?

"That is a Bala Kothi dragon," a well-known voice at her shoulder said.

Roshannon wore finery, too, with the silver-and-pearl earring of the far-island clan dangling at his ear. His black eyes took in all of her. She felt herself flush, because of that bodice. The maid had snatched her old cloak off her shoulders as she went out the door.

"I am surprised you recognized me."

"Because you've changed disguises? But beneath those clothes you still walk like a boy. I knew you across the room."

Heralds knocked their green poles on the floor, summoning folk to table. She and Roshannon sat side by side, sharing tea bowls and beakers as tumblers and singers performed. But although the steward's hall was a feast for all the senses, Keira slipped outside to walk on the moonlit terraces.

Many had gathered outside to observe the night sky glittering with stars. Roshannon found Keira there, with Tanta and Isharra and his cousin. Ni'An held a spyglass out to her, tempting her to look through it. He helped her sight on the Red Wanderer, the sailor's guide.

"What do you see?" he asked.

"A globe with another before it, casting its shadow on the greater one."

"If you watched long enough," Ni'An said, "you would see the smaller move round the Wanderer. Because that world is round as a melon, and spins through the void, circling the sun, just as the earth and moon do."

Keira smiled mysteriously and traded glances with Roshannon. "Yes, I know. I saw that when I dreamt once. But what holds the world in the void? The Wheel itself spinning and holding the world on its path?"

"A will, a mystery," Ni'An said.

"But how do you know?" Keira demanded. "Have you dreamt it?"

She peered intently through the glass, then tilted her head backward to look at the stars, and their mystery mightier than the Wheel, the mystery of a thousand spheres traveling in the void, never touching, held to their paths by an immense will. Roshannon blinked, suddenly feeling dizzy. In that instant, he realized Keira had daydreamed herself one of those points of light spinning in the void. And meshed her awareness with his for the first time since she had regained consciousness in the healers' tent. A thin wire of connection grew between them, a rich, strange pleasure. He spread his legs wide, bracing himself, not trusting himself to take a step.

Keira handed Xian Tanta the glass and scratched his hunting cat between the ears. Her eyes locked on Roshannon's. Her lips parted as if she would laugh. A wave of dizzy exhilaration filled him as she imagined herself spinning faster and faster. He leaned back, nursing the moment of knowing and touching. It settled like warm tea in the belly.

A crowd of people, courtiers and silk workers and guardsmen, thronged onto the terrace to see the stars. Abruptly Keira lowered her glance, withdrew her mind. Roshannon looked down at his feet to regain his balance.

When he looked up she was gone.

She wandered the gardens and found a great circle of fruit trees. Gardeners had braided the tree branches together into a living tapestry perfumed with the scent of a dozen kinds of blossoms and ripening fruit. Just as Hipolla had said. She paced sunwise around the trees, brushing her fingers along their trunks. Their impossible glory transfixed her, reminding her of Hipolla's voice, describing wonders she could not bring herself to believe in: Of braided trees that bore a dozen different fruits. Of magic that men and women forged with their joined spirits. Of a world spirit that was both man and woman.

Tears slid down her cheeks, the tears she had stored away on the day of Hipolla's death and never been able to shed.

She heard a sound behind her.

Roshannon leaned against a huge gnarled pear tree nearby, his face shadowed.

She watched him, wary but glad he had followed her. Her senses opened, full of insistent, prickling life, like fingers too long cramped into fists, but at last allowed a luxurious stretch. Standing rooted to the spot, still she thought about running away.

Suddenly beside her, he touched her face, wiping her tears away with his fingertips. He brushed his wet fingertips across his lips, his eyes never leaving her face.

"Whatever makes you cry, Keira Danio, I would share it with you and halve the pain."

She couldn't speak.

"Besides the small matter of my life," he said, "I owe you favors for easing my pain in the archpriest's tent. I intend to repay my debts, lady."

He embraced her, and she was surprised how easily her arm fit around his waist, her hand just resting near the sword pommel balanced at his left hip.

"I cannot let you do that just yet. It—"

"Frightens you?" he asked. "You've well-nigh laughed in the devil's face, girl. Why fear me?"

"Not you. It, I mean. The magic."

"The more you use it the less you fear it. And this time there is no danger."

A reasonable answer, she thought. A wash of torchlight threw his face half in shadow, half in light. His fingers twined in hers, he led her through a gallery and up a stairs. Halfway up, he stopped.

She backed away from him, one step, to see him better. He saw into her, through her, as she saw into him. They were meshed together as a wedded couple was meant to be, wedded in spirit. For just a moment she wondered if her mother and father had ever been so joined.

Another twist of her mind showed her disaster. After the links of dream between them, if Roshannon turned on her, as her father had after her mother died, any death would be clean by comparison.

Damn him, he stirred her senses. She hardly trusted herself around him.

He grinned. "You are slow to make up your mind."

"Ka. When it is decided, it will be a long time so."

Ka, ka'innen. That was the rub. She wanted him, could feel herself lowering the shields that kept him from sharing her consciousness except during panic or peril when all barriers crumbled naturally and their awarenesses meshed. The wall between them was his lordly status, her stolid freehold roots. Yet the witches thought nothing of breaking such barriers. Isharra had pointed out to her the tall dream master who wore a fish-gutting knife through her sash to remind folk of her parentage, flaunting her origins like a perverse badge of honor. Keira imagined attacking the wall that lay between herself and Roshannon, dislodging its great stones one by one, rolling them over cliffs into a roaring sea.

He stopped, as if knowing she had reached some decision.

And he does, she thought, her heart beating fast. He knows *me*, sees *me*, he always has. And he waits for me to choose.

"What are you thinking?" he asked.

"I am tearing down walls."

"Is the job finished?"

"Oh, aye," she said, unable to suppress a grin.

"Hast dreamt well last night?"

She nodded. But the dreams that had shown him to her before had given her no help, no glimpse of the future.

"Do not share my bed if you do not trust me."

"That is good advice." She touched his face. "I've taken it and made my choice. I will go with you and be your wife, sit beside you with your clan."

"And do my bidding?"

"And sometimes do your bidding."

"Indeed. Your father was right about you."

"My father?"

"He praised you for only one virtue, that you bargain well. And I see he was right to do so."

They raced up the dim stairs, to his quarters. They burst through the door, startling the old manservant who dozed in the antechamber. He blinked at them. "Ka, shall I take off your boots?"

Laughing, Roshannon shook his head. He pressed a gold tor into the man's hand. "Go celebrate tonight. I will take off this lady's boots myself."

"Propitious dreams," the old one called as he backed out of the room.

Keira felt sudden panic as Roshannon turned to her. You want this, you chose this, the inner voice whispered.

She felt herself blush. This is no enemy I face here, she reminded herself. She ran a finger down the scar along his jaw, watching his eyes. Her senses were unraveling, her spirit gathering itself to enter his consciousness and revel in it, as she would let him partake of her awareness.

He stroked a finger down her neck, along the top of the bodice.

"Thou," he said to her, and "Thou," she said back to him.

They kissed shyly, as if they had never touched each other before. He stroked his hands up her sides, and his fingers stopped at the top of the bodice.

"How is this fast?"

"Little hooks, dozens of them, in loops."

He unhooked the first, second, third fastening, and kissed her neck, unhooked more, and kissed her throat, his hands busy. "Hmm. Maybe it is better if you wear boy's clothes," he whispered into the hollow of her shoulder.

She laughed at him and kissed him back.

About the Author

I grew up in rural York County, Pennsylvania, near the Susquehanna River. A 1977 visit to San Francisco left me with a serious crush on the city. I arrived at SFO the day after Halloween, 1979. A policeman at the airport who smiled at me was wearing (plastic?) vampire fangs, which I took as an appropriate sign. I've lived in San Francisco ever since, in a house that rode out both the 1906 and 1989 earthquakes. During the Loma Prieta quake, I dove under an oak table at the main branch of the public library.

DEL REY® ONLINE!

The Del Rey Internet Newsletter...

A monthly electronic publication, posted on the Internet, GEnie, CompuServe, BIX, various BBSs, and the Panix gopher (gopher.panix.com). It features hype-free descriptions of books that are new in the stores, a list of our upcoming books, special announcements, a signing/reading/convention-attendance schedule for Del Rey authors, "In Depth" essays in which professionals in the field (authors, artists, designers, sales people, etc.) talk about their jobs in science fiction, a question-and-answer section, behind-the-scenes looks at sf publishing, and more!

Internet information source!

A lot of Del Rey material is available to the Internet on our Web site and on a gopher server: all back issues and the current issue of the Del Rey Internet Newsletter, sample chapters of upcoming or current books (readable or downloadable for free), submission requirements, mail-order information, and much more. We will be adding more items of all sorts (mostly new DRINs and sample chapters) regularly. The Web site is http://www.randomhouse.com/delrey/ and the address of the gopher is gopher.panix.com

Why? We at Del Rey realize that the networks are the medium of the future. That's where you'll find us promoting our books, socializing with others in the sf field, and—most importantly—making contact and sharing information with sf readers.

Online editorial presence: Many of the Del Rey editors are online, on the Internet, GEnie, CompuServe, America Online, and Delphi. There is a Del Rey topic on GEnie and a Del Rey folder on America Online.

The official e-mail address for Del Rey Books is delrey@randomhouse.com (though it sometimes takes us a while to answer).